02·10·04

SURGEON'S APPRENTICE

Arthur Young

25p

LINDSAY PUBLICATIONS

First published in 1997 by
Lindsay Publications
Glasgow, G14 9NP

For M and M and H and A,
who all did it their own way so well

British Library Cataloguing-in-Publication Data
A Catalogue record for this book is available from the British Library

ISBN 1 898169 10 1

Cover photographs curtesy of
Great Glasgow Health Board Archives

The Publisher acknowledges subsidy from

THE SCOTTISH ARTS COUNCIL

towards the publication of this volume.

K1. 21. 2. 97

Printed and bound in Great Britain by Cromwell Press Limited

Contents

BOOK ONE

Chapter 1

I DON'T KNOW WHY THEY PICKED ON ME. There were umpteen other guys in the place. Later, Wilson told me it was because I looked as if I knew my way around. That was a laugh: me that had lit on the student scene all of twenty minutes before him.

I had just signed on at the University to become superdoc in five years time and taken a look at the opposition – all the other young, post-war hopefuls lined up to join the black-bag brigade. Then I was making tracks for the men's Union – the male students'club – a big, stone building at the bottom of University Avenue .

The parents stepped forward as I came up to them. He had on the dog-collar and black homburg of the professional Protestant, while she kept him company in a soprano-in-the-choir hat. Yet, there was a sheen about her fur coat and a cut to his Crombie that didn't match my notions of the average parish minister. Perhaps they'd been pinching pennies from the plate?

The boy held back, looking shy and awkward, and the mother spoke first.

"Where is the matriculation hall, please."

There were more notices showing the way than signs to Hampden on the day of the English game, but they just had to be twice times sure.

"Up those steps. Through the cloister. You can't miss it."

The boy smiled. He was half a head taller than me, with soft, blond good looks and an extra chin of puppy fat.

The father spoke. "My name is Wilson. This is my wife and my son Scoular. He attended Dalcudbright Academy."

That was a place among the buttercups of Galloway.

"Crown Street Grammar, myself."

This city establishment was renowned for its advanced methods of scholarship – the Bible at Assembly, endless hours of homework and masters who could wield a belt with ferocious dexterity. I could see the parents' satisfied look. I would have been well leathered into suitable presbyterian order.

I knew as much about psychology as you could pour in your ear, but it was obvious what they wanted – a mate for this loon in the big city. And here was I, fitting like a suit from Forsyth's.

Well, I had other ideas. This guy would be an outsize albatross, and all I wanted around my neck for the next five years was a medical fraternity tie and, on occasion, one Sadie Crossan after a torrid night at the tangos. But the grammar school had taught me social graces as well. I could wield a mannered brush off as well as any valet.

"You're starting in medicine?"

This time, they let him speak for himself.

"Yes. That's right."

"Me too. I'm Neil Aitken."

I stuck my hand out, all Young Men's Christian Association and manly. I ought not to catch anything too deadly at arm's length. But see fate? It's contagious stuff.

We had a little duologue that set the parents beaming. Just what they had hoped for, instant-mixed bosom buddy for their boy. It was time for Neillie to scarper: conscience clear, social niceties observed.

"You must excuse me, now. I've arranged to meet some friends. I'll look out for you."

I made like a dashing college chap but once out of sight I slowed to my usual bum's mooch. I met up with two of my school-mates, as planned. They were sprawled on the broad balustrade of the Union steps.

Kenny Gillespie and Sammy McFadden had been close friends since their days in primary school. I had been co-opted on to their board of management only in our last session, when it turned out we were the school's total entry in the Hippocratic hurdles. We had agreed to watch out for each other until we got to know the beasts in the undergraduate jungle.

I had been uncertain if my cash flow would stand the expense of the Union, but Harry Fleming, a former pupil with the sophistication that went with two years in the medics, had come back to school to wise us up.

"Take my word for it, boys. Join the Union. You can do fancy footwork at the Saturday hops for three bob. The grub is cheap. But the main thing is, it's where the lads go to spice the vinegar. Some men don't join, but they're odd. The work is bloody hard, and you need the company of other guys in the same boat."

Harry was so earnest, I had earmarked some of my post-office savings hoard for this extravagance. We became members of that workaday Bohemia and wandered around the big rooms, still handsome after the battering of generations of students. We glanced at strange London newspapers in the library, had buns and coffee in the smoke room, then gravitated to the great stone fireplace in the hall, where we watched the world come up the steps: a small, select world.

The University of Glasgow had few pretensions. Lip service was paid to the finer things of life, but dreaming spires and punts on the River Kelvin were as rare as six-metre yachts in the baby's bath.

Most students came from schools in the west of Scotland, a great fistful of academies and grammar schools scattered through the city and the county towns round about. Through the years the different coloured blazers and ties, the badges with the Latin mottoes, had become familiar. Most of the freshmen who came up those steps carried one of these distinctive codings, and amongst them were several guys that Kenny or Sammy or I had met before.

Finlay Hamilton, for instance, wore the chocolate and gold stripes of Glasgow High School. Over the years, he and Kenny had given one another a hard time on the rugby field, as they progressed through their rival schools. Then Sammy came across a guy he had known in the inter-schools debating scene, while I met a guy from Ayr Academy, whose sister had been the other end of a heavy necking session one holiday weekend in Lamlash.

You get the idea.

We found we each could hob-nob on such terms with half a dozen similar citizens, who in turn knew a few others. A spider web of relationships started up, and my project no longer seemed quite so daunting. These guys all seemed very much like myself.

When I was leaving for home, I noticed Wilson again. He was getting on to a number three tram with his parents. They were weighted down with textbooks and worried looks. I wondered when he would ever pry himself loose. But when I got back to my own family that night, cosy as a bramble patch, I found myself a touch jealous at the memory. Still, what the hell. Parents were Bostick people. You got stuck with them for life.

After that, I didn't see much of him. That was mostly chance. I didn't have to connive to avoid him. So I didn't feel too bad about what happened.

Chapter 2

I HAD SPENT MOST of the vacation working in a humping, dead-lifting, break-it-open-and-pilfer-it squad of casual labour at Buchanan Street goods station. For the two weeks before term, however, I was lucky enough to get a job working odd hours in a bar. This gave me time to get the ingrained grime out of my hands and to drop into the Union, where I kept up with the growing crowd of medics. Guys paired up, or formed little groups and trooped off to explore the campus, make notes of laboratory and lecture times and try to look liquor-wise and older than their years in the Kelvin bar.

Of course, not everyone came from the west of Scotland schoolboy establishment. There were teuchters from the Isles, Gaelic speaking to a chiel; black men; blokes from England; one refugee from the Dublin debt collectors; a smattering of ex-servicemen, older and more serious. But anyone who was aiming to wear a stethoscope was granted honorary membership of that lowland clan.

The men from Africa were renamed on the spot. I managed fine with McKinseboya and McM'bouto, but I had trouble with the phonetics of McNg. A couple of rejects from the English public school-Oxbridge axis, William Brown Jones and Robert Bracegirdle, were happily, if incomprehensibly to them, absorbed into this strange northern tribe as Wullie and Boab. One guy came from away east of Port Said. He had beautiful, doll's features. His eyes were Sam Browne bright in a yellow face, and he was all of five foot three in his high heels. His name was Tek Tok and he lived his Scottish days with us as Big Ben.

Wilson came into the Union only once that I saw. He shambled up the steps self-consciously, and looked around the place with sheepish curiosity.

"Who on earth is that gink?" asked someone.

"He's a medical?"

"Seems to be from the books he's carrying."

He had a personality like a de-Gaussing device, all attraction neutralized by his painful shyness. He slid a glance my way, but it was such a momentary, undemanding contact that I persuaded myself a nod was all it was worth. He dropped his eyes, then slunk back down the steps. Despite myself, I felt sorry for the poor sod. Next time I would do better by him.

But at the Dean's pep talk he sealed himself in derision, and I had neither enough interest in him, nor enough of the full cream stuff of human kindness in me, to brave the ridicule that washed over him in the following weeks.

On the Friday before term started, I filed into the steep, serried seats of a lecture hall, along with a hundred other guys. Some thirty women were in the front two rows. It was our first glimpse of our medical co-eds and there was a buzz of interest over the blue-stocking talent.

Places had been allocated in alphabetical order, and I squeezed past an Aaronson to sit between an Abercrombie and an Alexander. We hadn't spoken before, but knew each other's faces by then.

"Hi. I'm Neil Aitken."

"Hi. I'm Fraser – Drew – Henry – "

We all spoke at the same time, and laughed at the confusion.

Fraser Abercrombie was a dapper dandy from Allan Glen's School. He plunged into his problem at once.

"I can't get my family to be serious. You guys must be honest. D'you think this looks all right?"

All over the shop, boys were adding trimmings to help the student image: curly stemmed pipes, soft hats. Abercrombie's cast to the grown up state was a Cesar Romero moustache.

Drew Alexander, an east coaster from Buchan, slewed round and gave the problem his earnest attention.

"Great. Needs another week, maybe. Whajasay, Henry?"

Henry Aaronson was a slight, shy boy, who wore his Jewishness at low key.

"Suave," he said with envy. "I could never manage that. You look at least twenty-five."

The moustache set off Fraser's swarthy, good looks. I nodded in agreement.

"Gee, I'll love you guys for life."

At that, the big bell above us bonged three. A porter closed the door. On the third stroke, Sir John Thompson, Professor of Medicine, and Dean of the Faculty, swept through the lecturers' door in the other corner and on to the podium. Punctuality was a fetish with him.

The gold tasselled mortar board and the gold-braided gown were impressive enough, but Jakey Thompson's personality commanded the respect of a Maxim gun loaded and cocked.

"Ladies and gentlemen. Thank you for giving up your valuable spare time to attend today."

Most of the students around me had taken a prolonged holiday in the three month break since the end of school, and this remark earned a titter from them. But with my recent memories of the greasy, sweaty, miserable work in the goods yard, I reserved my hilarity.

His face, lifted to us, was urbane, but the sense of power was immense. "What you will hear today appears in no syllabus. No examination will be set on its content. You may even consider it a bore." He smiled in bleak understanding. "Young people never want advice. Nonethelesss, I am going to give you some. If even a few of you take my words to heart, I shall consider the time well spent."

The quadrangle door opened. Two late-comers stood, startled and flustered by the prompt start. They had expected a few moments' grace. They crept to their seats. The Dean continued without pause, but he wasn't pleased. The porter eased home the bolt to prevent further interruption.

"First, let me congratulate you on getting here. We accept only the cream. This leads, I find, to certain – ah – differences with my colleagues in other faculties. But you will have to learn to live with your undoubted superiority."

This was bull-shit of the first order and we all knew it, but it was nourishing stuff to feed our medical roots.

"You will find a great difference between this establishment and school." Someone tried the bolted door. The big, iron handle squeaked up and down.

"There, you had teachers to supervise your work. Here you will be quite on your own."

Faced with the locked door, most people would have accepted that and left. This idiot clumped along the echoing passage that led behind the auditorium to the lecturers' door.

"Some of you will find the adjustment very difficult."

The handle clanked down and, before the porter could reach it, the door swung open with a creak that would have graced a Boris Karloff movie.

Wilson stood in the doorway.

For a second there was a disbelieving silence, then the Dean's voice was drowned in a wave of whistles and stamping feet. Not that he paused. If we didn't want to listen, his words were our lost pearls.

Wilson flushed to the neck, the cheeks, the ears. The porter put his finger to his lips and pointed to the front row of women. Wilson tiptoed to it, half-crouched and squashed in at the end. The noise settled and Sir John Thompson gave him the benefit of a baleful patrician stare. Then we caught up with his words.

"What makes a doctor? I have to tell you, I do not find that an easy question to answer."

There was a mutter of surprise.

"You all went through a personal interview which, although I hope you found it courteous, was also as searching as we could make it. We were looking for something extra. Something that might loosely be called the right character, for, make no mistake, it takes more than book learning."

There was a mutter of discontent; a shuffle of uneasiness. This was not the message these young stars had come to hear. But the thin-boned face had the taut, gaunt look of experience that would not be gainsaid. An unwilling silence of acceptance fell.

"Despite our care, we shall have failed some of you. It is a matter of regret, but of statistical fact, that a number of you will not complete the course. And not all of you who qualify will go on with your career. Somewhere between one sixth and one fifth of you will never practise medicine."

There was a gasp of shock; of disbelief. This old crow was having us on? But there was no vestige of humour in that face.

"Some of you will fall out because of the accidents of life – fate if you will – but by far the biggest number will be for reasons that are difficult to define, except to say they did not have it in them from the start."

Failure was not on my schedule, but I had a sudden sensation of being cold. I eyed the students around me furtively. It might well be him, or her, but surely never me.

"If, during your undergraduate career you find yourself struggling, seek help from someone quickly. Your tutor. Myself. My door will always be open. Or if you see a fellow student in trouble, do not hesitate to extend a helping hand. You may save a colleague."

Then he changed tempo. Having posted this startling warning, he went from the high drama to the circus of student life.

"I shall dwell no longer on these things. Today is an auspicious start in what is the most satisfying career open to any man or woman. It is a long course. Five years of arduous study. But medicine is not all about books and work. It is about life. You must learn to live it in a full and rounded way."

I nodded to myself. That was the style I was aiming at.

"Finally, while I do not have the requisite experience to speak for the ladies, for you gentlemen, I cannot overstate the value of a good wife."

He gave the phrase all the chauvinist emphasis of an Old Testament patriarch. There were intimations of meekness and submission and golden dowries in his words. "A suitable partner and a sound domestic background can be of inestimable value."

Suitable, I noted. Not a word about love. From his tone, I took it he meant someone who kept her knickers on at parties. And sound. If becoming a doctor was as difficult as he said, perhaps she should also have a father with a big bank balance.

Then we were at the nuts and bolts of starting a career on Monday.

"Later, you will be left to make such arrangements for yourselves, but until you get to know one another, lecture seats and laboratory benches have been allocated in alphabetical order."

So I was joined and happily so, to Abercrombie, Alexander and Aaronson: and distanced from Wilson by most of the alphabet and, even more, the Dean's ironic revenge.

"Perhaps you, sir, – " he pointed at his hapless victim " – will share a bench with some of the ladies. You may learn some of the gentler virtues, as well as that of punctuality."

There was a yell of derision and delight and, as I left the lecture room, safe in my all male alliteracy, I shook my head. Of all the guys who might end up as one of the Dean's victims, Wilson seemed high on the list.

Chapter 3

THOSE FIRST TWO TERMS WENT PAST like the Minute Waltz.

By day, I made stinks and learned about the nervous system of the frog. In the evenings, I revised the day's work, with a two hour break on Tuesdays and Thursdays, when I went for a few rounds with the railwaymen at the LNER boxing club. Friday nights and Saturday mornings, I pulled pints in Jimmy Docherty's bar and Saturday nights I went dancing with Sadie Crossan.

At the end of the second term I sat my degree examinations and the following day I saw 'p' as in pass after my name in both physics and zoology. I grunted with relief. The Dean's warning still glowed red in my memory.

There was a good natured scuffle in the crowd: laughter, and a bit of the physicals. I saw Kenny and Sammy looking happy, then looked for my chums in lower case. Win, lose, or draw, we had agreed on a beery celebration. When I caught sight of them, all thumbs were up. We linked arms to march on the Kelvin bar, but since Henry then begged off for family reasons, we marched him to a tram instead.

"Penny half for the wee fella?" we urged the clippie, as we lifted him bodily aboard, but she belled her driver away from such nonsense.

Abercrombie was spending some of the holiday with Alexander and the pair of them dived into the Union locker room to get their gear. I waited outside on the steps and was taking an abstracted view of the passing show, when I noticed Wilson walking past. He was on his own and he was blubbing: slow tears running down his face.

I was appalled. If his compeers caught sight of him, they would roast him. I nipped down the steps and grabbed his arm.

"Wilson. For the Lord's sake. What's the matter?"

"I've failed my physics."

"Failed – Well, that's hard luck, but it isn't the end of the world. You'll get it in September."

The University allowed a second attempt then.

"I can't. I'll just never do it."

Off shoulder, right, I could see a pile of guys coming down the hill.

"C'mon, Wilson, don't let them see you. Of course you'll manage it."

I whipped out a hankie.

"Pretend you've got something in your eye."

I urged him up the steps.

"But I'm not a member."

"Be my guest."

I hustled him to the basement washroom, past Fraser and Drew.

"Something in his eye," I said cheerily. "Catch up with you in a minute."

The performance wouldn't have won an audition for Hamlet, but it did for that medical matinee. I mopped the tears from his face and he let me, like a wean with a skinned knee. Then I steered him into a quiet corner and asked what the hell it was all about.

It was an unfortunate story, but not unique. Two other men in the year had found themselves in the same boat. It was still possible to enter medical school with a classical background only: Latin and Greek the main highers; no sciences at all on the board. The old idea that a grounding in Ovid and Homer would fit a boy for any University course died hard. But it was – and disastrously for Wilson – an outdated concept.

"I've found the physics and chemistry quite over my head. They go so fast. And it isn't like school. You can't stop them to ask questions."

The lecturers did rattle on, indifferent to individual problems. The Dean's first words had come all too true for Wilson.

The two other guys from classics schools had been in the same sad state but their problems had been quickly understood and they got support on all sides. Every time they sat down for a coffee or a beer, they were made to reel off formulae and equations, until they knew them by heart. I had noticed passes at their names.

But this poor gink had been left to a Coventry of his own making by day and to groan into his pillow alone at night.

"What will I tell my parents?"

My beer-mug hand was twitching but, hell, I couldn't just leave him. "Nuffin," I said with conviction. "Keep your face shut. They won't necessarily find out. Come and have a drink and we'll sort something out."

His face was a mobile of changing emotion: uncertainty, surprise and, at last, hope.

"D'you think we could?"

I heard the weasel pronoun. We, indeed. And who had said it? Lord. What had I let myself in for?

"Sure. Sure. Come to the bar."

"But I don't drink."

I sighed. This was going to be worse than I had imagined.

By the time we reached the snug, the red in Wilson's eyes would have passed for a mild cold and the guys were on a high that had little to do with alcohol and a lot to do with percentage marks.

"New man needing beer," I called.

There was a moment's hiatus, the merest blip in the boozy brio of a dozen assorted medical gents. But not a black ball was produced, even if he was a stumer, not that hilarious morning.

"Great. Get him fell into proper drinking order."

I sat him down beside Mickey Mulligan, our lapsed Catholic from Dublin and went to fetch a round with my hard saved silver: pints of Younger's heavy, a thin reeking, bile of a beer that knowing men in boiler suits downed in life-giving quantities, with quarter gill chasers of whisky. We managed two rounds of this stern indoctrination to Glasgow manhood, before city by-laws broke up the party.

Wilson and I ambled back to the Union and I got his story in mildly squiffed, uninhibited detail. He was an only and late child. His father had a country parish. His mother had been a research fellow in biology but her talents had been diverted to umpiring the Women's Guild. He had his parents' bent for bookish ways.

When he decided to become a doctor, the psi's built up like my Uncle Willie Reid's coal train taking the long climb out of Cowlairs. The whole aim and purpose of this small group became centred on him getting a place at University.

"They both coached me. They'll be so disappointed. That's why –

how –" He broke off, embarrassed by the memory of his tears. "D'you really think I could get off with not telling them?"

"What newspaper do they read?"

"*The Scotsman.*"

That genteel organ of the Scottish gentry was Edinburgh oriented. It wouldn't carry the Glasgow passes.

"You assure them you've passed. Mug up your physics over the summer. Then take the resit in September."

He had never contemplated such enormity.

"You're going home now, are you?"

Yes. There's a train at tea-time."

"C'mon, then. We'll get your stuff, then I'll take you to the station." The look he gave me was straight out of the hero-worshippers' bible.

He roomed with a couple of spinster ladies. The floor was laid in wax-cloth, rag rugs and the smell of floor polish. There was a sampler over his bed exhorting the Lord to have mercy on him, a draught under the door that would have refrigerated the Paisley ice-rink and a folded newspaper inside the front door for his shoes.

"God Almighty," I said, as we escaped with his bags. "You can't possibly go on staying there. Can't you get into one of the halls of residence?"

"I left it too late. Then my father did wonder about a flat, but until I found my way around, he thought this better."

"A flat of your own?"

I couldn't help my surprise. Country ministers were notoriously lean in the stipend.

"Yes," he went on ingenuously. "My father has some capital, but he doesn't want to use it. Not until he comes into Grandpa's estate."

I gazed at him. The middle classes were showing their paces. This explained the fur coat and the Crombie.

A couple of ideas began to form. The first, sparked off by a memory of the Dean's address, was as unwelcome as a nightmare, but with the same compulsive, illogical certainty. "How'd you like to dig with me next term? You'd have to share a bed. But I could help you with your chemistry. Make sure you get that."

He turned to me like I was the Holy Ghost in flannels.

"Would you?" he breathed. "That would be marvellous. My folks would be so pleased. They've asked me once or twice about you."

"Fine," I said, resigned to what my own big feet had led me into. "You can drop me a line."

I gave him my address, put him in a compartment and waved him goodbye. I was walking past the Shell, doing George Raft's 'Scarface' trick with my last shilling, when the second idea firmed into definite thought.

My Granny Aitken always held that if you stuck around money, some might rub off on you.

Chapter 4

I CAUGHT A TRAM TO FAIFLEY, back to my own brand of parental relationship. This was as close knit as an unravelled jersey: had been so since the accident that left my old man like an oversize Pinocchio with the leg strings cut. The event had pulled the pins out of the family knitting pattern and the new design hadn't shaped up too well.

Jock was still in bed. He usually stayed there until Maisie – big Maisie, my mother – got home from her work in Bilsland's bakery. Normally her Saturdays were free but she had taken on extra shifts during the hot cross bun season. She wouldn't be home until six – and that was a help.

You might have thought that pity or mercy or compassion would be the emotions commanded by Jock's predicament. But the tigers the three of us got to ride in our own ways were guilt and frustration, with Maisie astride the biggest jungle cat. Her emotions, uneven and jagged at the best of times, became seismic. Helpless to help her man or, perhaps most of all, herself, she could rip and gouge without thought. I understood more by then, but it had hurt when I was younger.

In pairs we managed. Jock and I had a close, male companionship when she wasn't there. Then, Jock and she had been able to add a dimension, a sufferance, to the usual accommodations of marriage, to cope with his emasculation. And Maisie and I had a stand off truce. She was not for investing her emotions in any more men.

Yet, she had supported me with a loyalty that humbled me.

When I came back from school with the headmaster's note that I try for a bursary, followed by University, she only said, "We'll manage," and buttered another scone. With no more agonizing than her next floury bite, she committed herself to me for years of going without an extra wage in the house; of supporting two men, both entirely dependent on her.

She had never made one word of complaint and my fealty to her could be no less.

Yet, for some reason, when the three of us were together for more than a meal-time, the atmosphere became as touchy as a four-second fuse.

"I managed a pass," I announced and got the man's hug I craved, leaning in over the wall bed. We blethered for a while, then I fixed him a cup of tea.

"You'll tell her the news?" I said. Maisie wasn't expected for an hour yet. "I'll see her again. Granny Aitken will have my tea ready."

"Aye." Meals had always been to the minute in his mother's house. I emptied his urine bottle and left.

My grandmother's house had the same accommodation – two rooms and scullery, with a quick dash to a mid-stair cludge when required – although the luxury of head-high, art-nouveau, magenta-and-cream tiles in her close gave it the ineffable, added *ton* of Partick.

When I stayed on at school, instead of going to work at fourteen, I soon found that my books and studies assumed a dimension that didn't fit with my old man's wheelchair and the steel gantry and chain mounted over his bed. Since all the requirements of my grandmother's widowed life were housed in her kitchen – piano, sewing machine and all – I started going to her other room to do my homework. Gradually, I oozed all my stuff there, spread myself in comfort, and, eventually, stayed to sleep.

I never had a row with my folks. In fact, no-one said a word. But the more it went on, the more it suited all round. My Granny Aitken had company and big Maisie moved into her own front room, with a scatter of clothes any old where, and a slitter of toiletries on the mantelpiece.

Jock was the only one who lost out: no woman in his bed – a subject I found too painful to contemplate.

That night, when I went in, I gave the old lady a cheery kiss.

"Ye passed then?"

It was no question: a mere statement of the necessary. If Wee Neillie wanted to be a doc, he had best get on with it.

"By the way," I said, as I slavered my way through the ham and egg tea she had for me. "Would you mind another lodger? A student like me. He could share the room and bed. It would only be for three months. He's a well behaved lad. Quiet."

"No' like you, then."

Her tone told me that Wilson had a Partick address if he wanted.

During that Easter vacation, I replenished my penny bank by working extra hours at the pub and Wilson wrote to accept the offer of digs. I met him off a Galloway train the morning term started and by ten o'clock we had taken the first breaths of the pervasive formalin that was to impregnate our clothes and hair for the next fifteen months.

Now that the alphabetical regimentation of the first two terms was over, the tiers of seats held a jumble of gossiping groups with all the rationality of a Lexicon pack. I felt Wilson check beside me and guessed his dismay as memories of his previous loneliness hit him. I hoped the A-squad would come through with support for this little boy lost. I spotted them, and led Wilson up the steep aisle.

"Hi, Drew. Hi, Fraser. Wilson is staying with me for this term. His digs were rotten."

Well, he had dreed his dree of derision among the women and had showed willing, if unpractised, at the session in the Kelvin bar. They nodded affably.

"Where's Henry?" I asked.

"Didn't you hear?" asked Drew. "Henry's in hospital."

"What."

"Yeah. Poor little bugger's got rheumatic fever. Seems he'll be off for six months or a year."

"God. I am sorry. Where is he?"

"The Royal Infirmary. We must go and see him soon."

I thought of the bright, inquisitive, brown eyes. Henry would be reluctant to leave the feast of life, even for a few months.

Alexander looked at Wilson, then at me.

"We'll need a fourth for our anatomy group."

"Yeah. Want to join us?" Abercrombie asked Wilson.

I almost sighed out loud. Good for the lads.

"Oh, yes. Thank you. Thank you all."

It had been a long time coming, but now he could tell his folks he had two more chums from a single blow of fate.

At that moment the Professor of Anatomy walked in. Adam Henderson was all of five foot eight and weighed thirty-five pounds to the foot. He stood very firm on square-toed black shoes. He had short black hair and a black, toothbrush moustache. He got right to it.

"Good morning. It will be self evident that the study of anatomy is the study of the mechanism in which the whole activity of medicine is practised. You must know your way around the machine. Be able to take it to bits and put it back again."

The voice coming from the barrel chest was gargled through a drain-pipe throat.

"The word mechanism is simplistic in the extreme. The human body is a wonderful, subtle creation. The acme, so far, of evolution. I know of no more fascinating study. Yet, here I must issue a word of warning. The subject is huge and complex. You will spend no less than four terms in its study. There is no easy way to do this. You must work steadily. And revise. And revise. And revise. With patience and application, it can be mastered."

Drew Alexander looked at me and blew out his cheeks.

"One last word. For those of you who persevere, who seek deeply enough, you will find this great subject has a pattern, almost a logic, of its own. If you find that key, your studies will be enriched beyond measure. Now, as an example of pattern, let me draw your attention to the beautiful symmetry displayed here." He turned to a whitened, demonstration skeleton, grinning at us in derision.

Then we were off, pens scribbling, minds stretching at the impact of the strange. For an hour we were in pell-mell pursuit of this vast, new subject. Then, with the same deceleration as a fairground ride, we were back on earth. We were all shook up and jangled but, by God, we were exhilarated.

And there was more to come.

"You may break for fifteen minutes before your practical dissection starts. Give your names to the demonstrators who will allocate you tables."

Chapter 5

THE THOUGHT OF STICKING EXPLORATORY HANDS into a corpse had been the subject of unspoken speculation. No matter how brash the student, the contemplation of this event brought the fear of ignominy. Suppose a guy was sick, or fainted?

So we were all surprised to find the body hall a vast, airy room, full of cheer and chatter and life, despite the rows of waxy corpses. Any gloom of morbid preoccupation was dispelled by the cones of yellow light from the big lamps set over the dissecting tables.

The second year men already working there, comfortable in stained coats, gave us the slow foot stamp that mocked our pristine whiteness. We stood beside our victim, not sure how to start.

"You don't need the blade of your knife too much," explained Geoff Watts, one of the seniors. "Once you have the skin opened up, you'll find blunt dissection with the handle more useful."

We tossed for the first cut of a thousand learnings. Abercrombie won. We had been awarded a leg to work on and he took his knife down the pallid, orange-peel skin. For an hour we all took a turn at stripping off this covering; at poking inexpertly in strange structures, trying to match them to the diagrams in the manual. Despite the interest and the novelty, however, I felt uneasy and was aware of a strange chill of incomprehension.

I dismissed this as vapourings, not worth serious consideration. Then, initiation over; now also casual in our oily stains, we washed the grease from our hands and poured back into the ordinary world.

"C'mon, Neil," ordered Drew. "Pints on me at the Kelvin bar."

"Just what I need. But I have to meet my big brother in the Union. I'll be along as soon as I can."

At the beginning of term, all freshmen had been teamed up with a fourth year student. He was supposed to act as nanny and general nose-wiper. My minder was Malcolm Ritchie, whose advice had been simple.

"What the hell can I tell you? You look sensible enough. Go stew in your own juice. It's the only way to learn. Here's my phone number. Call me if you land in jail."

I appreciated his genuine, if laconic, interest, and had returned the compliment by not bothering him at all. A few days before, however, he had left a note for me on the Union message board.

"Saw your name on the pass list. Well done. Time to have a yarn now. Coffee and buns on me."

I left the others and went to find Malcolm.

He was waiting for me.

" 'Lo, Neil. First day on the bodies,eh? Never quite the same as the common herd after that."

He waved a ten-bob note at me and asked me to get us a tray of eats. When I got back, he was giving the biggest yawn I had ever seen.

"Doing a student residency in Robroyston. Been up most of the night," he explained. " Worth a guinea a box for the experience, but murder on the sleep."

Robroyston was one of the big Glasgow Corporation sanitaria that ringed the city, built to contain the constant cull of tuberculosis cases. I was impressed. As a sub-doc, first-line stand-in, he would be taking most responsibilities short of signing death-certificates.

"That must be great. Sometimes I wonder if I'll ever get to see a patient."

So far, we had been confined to dusty lecture rooms and stinky laboratories in the old Victorian campus.

"It can feel like that, I remember well. And that's what I want to talk to you about. Now, listen."

His attitude was brisk and purposeful, quite unlike the last time.

"As you know, you don't officially start clinical work until third year. When that time comes, there's always a scramble to get into the best clinics. You can easily be left out. What you should do is find your way about beforehand. Go visit these places. Offer to do the scudgy work. Wheel trolleys. Shave the men's balls pre-op. Do some clerking. That kind of help is always needed. Give the ward sister sweeties. Get your face known to the consultants. Then when it comes to taking names officially, you'll have a head start. Here's a note of the places I found best."

He handed me a list of names: the medical staffs and their foibles; the sisters and their fancies. It was obvious he had taken a lot of pains with this.

"Malcolm, this is great. I do appreciate the trouble you've taken. I'll make full use of it."

He seemed gratified.

"Good. Now, any other worries?"

I remembered Adam Henderson's warning and the little quiver of unease I had felt.

"Um. This business of anatomy? Is it as hard going as the prof made out."

"Too true. It's a slog, all right. Not that it's abstruse. Everything is there in front of you. It's more a matter of memory. But people constantly underestimate the sheer volume of facts to be mastered. Tell me, does the Dean still give his gloom and doom talk?"

"Yes," I laughed. "Quite startling."

"But all too true," warned Malcolm, with the certainty of one who had lived through it. "Second M.B. is where the biggest number fail. Anatomy is a real trap for the losers."

This time I couldn't shrug off the tremor. It was of fear.

"Enough about me. How is your work coming on with the finals?"

Malcolm raised his arms in supplication.

"Oh, I'm working well. But everyone needs a bit of luck."

He got up to go. I pumped his hand, slapped his shoulder and got a buzz from his advanced state of grace.

The degree examination in anatomy was fifteen months away, however, so Wilson and I put that subject on a steady back burner and concentrated on chemistry and botany. I weaned Wilson's mind away from a background of Latin vocatives and into the ways of chemical valencies, while he kept me right with his mother's notes on dicotyledons. We must have done something right, for at the beginning of June we climbed the hill to the faculty notice board and saw our names on the pass list. Wilson was ecstatic.

"I've passed. I've passed. Oh, what about you?" he added in a guilty afterthought.

I forgave him his lapse. I couldn't be miffed with anyone that morning.

Scottish drinking laws had no sense of occasion, and there was still an hour until opening time. The morning was already hot. Opposite the main door, a grassy bank overlooked the Kelvin river and its park. We spread ourselves in bliss and, as I shut my eyes against the sun, I realized that for the first time in my life I felt utterly weary. Not tired in the physical sense: more an exhaustion of the will. I had been indoors too much: had the head down too long. The scaling of the middle-class heights had been more taxing than I had expected.

Wilson was stretched out beside me. He half turned.

"I thought I might take a summer job. Something to fill in the time, you know."

I had a wry grin to myself. I would need a summer job too, but there was nothing vocational about my needs. My cash box had an empty rattle.

"I thought of farm work. There's a farm near my home. I help there sometimes. At the hay. Milking. That sort of thing. It's quite fun."

"A farm?"

His words chimed a chord with the moment, the hot sun beating down on my face, the scent of the grass.

"Y'know, young Wilson, I think we'll make something of you yet. That's not a bad idea."

"You'll come?"

"Yeah. It's just what I need."

Down at the student work bureau, we found a job on a farm near Edinburgh.

"Two students needed to help with the harvest. Four weeks. Start at the beginning of August."

Wilson's folks wanted him home for a while, while I had trysted extra hours to Jimmy Docherty in July, so his men could get holidays.

It all fitted like an omen and I should have known. But the fey bit of me that I got from my Granny Aitken had gone for a stroll just then.

We shook hands on it, hilarious at the thought of our yokel idyll. He gave me another of those looks that bothered me, all gratitude and trust. Then we marched on the Kelvin bar and drowned all such noble notions in a line of McEwan's export ales with golden chasers.

Chapter 6

THAT JULY I HUMPED BEER CRATES, rinsed whisky glasses and emptied out fag ends. But I also put Malcolm Ritchie's notes to work. He had a good word for the Northern General, a battle-scarred hospital set amongst the tenements of Garscube.

"Great place to learn casualty work. Friday receiving. Always looking for an extra pair of hands, especially after the pubs empty."

So, after the bar was shut and cleaned one Friday, I took a late tram across town to this great, grimy Victorian edifice. The casualty department was in a single storey block known as the Gatehouse. It fronted on Garscube Road, a busy, canyonway of tenements that led to the posh, northern suburbs. It was separated from the main building by a car park and connected to it by a series of subterranean passageways. I found the houseman and introduced myself. This superior being, in a white, bum-freezer jacket, seemed pleased to see me.

"Hi. I'm Willie Roberts. First year, eh? You're keen. Still, that's the way to learn. D'you know how this organization works?"

"No."

"Right. The chief is a man called McKenzie. Boss McKenzie. And a right bad-tempered bastard he is. You want to keep out of his way. There are four subs. Baillie, Richards, McFarlane and Mair. The only one you'll see here is Bobby Mair. He's the Gate surgeon. If you're not cack-handed, he'll let you try things after you've watched for a bit. All casualty and emergency stuff comes through here for assessment. We either deal with it on the spot, admit it to the casualty ward for twenty-four hours, or admit it to the main wards. Now, hang your jacket over there."

Without more ceremony, I was given a wraparound gown and admitted to the business. Any qualms I might have had about my inexperience were soon dispelled by the bright, brisk nurses; their constant laughter no matter the disaster they were asked to deal with; and the precarious frivolity of their lace caps. They soon showed me what was needed: roll your sleeves up, use your loaf and get stuck in.

I helped the porters with the labelling and the stretchering and holding down drunks and watched, awed and envious, when Willie disappeared into one of the examination rooms with the Gate surgeon, to ponder over the more serious cases.

Still, I was happy. Malcolm's advice had been excellent.

A lull occurred. I was lining up a few phone numbers from the lace-caps for future use, when Willie stuck his head round the door.

"Come and see something odd."

I followed him to one of the examination rooms.

"This is Aitken, sir."

Bobby Mair had mended propeller-sliced aircraftmen and shrapnel sieved aviators for some years in the RAF. He was now trying to re-establish his civilian career from this middle grade post. He nodded at me.

"Starting early, I hear?"

"Wanted to see what goes on, sir. I'm green as grass."

"H'm. What do you think of this then?"

I looked at the table. A workman with the stubbly face of a twelve hour day – a shift plus overtime – lay on the table. The out-patient sister had just flayed one leg of his dungarees with a pair of plaster shears. I saw that the thigh was transfixed by a length of galvanized wire, from the groin to just above the knee. It was my first experience of the utter vagary of industrial wounds.

"How on earth did that happen?"

"It seems he was loading coils of the stuff onto a train. A rush job. Piecework. They had to get on with it. The coils were three feet wide, and the size of cartwheels. They found it faster to freewheel the things down a wooden ramp, than use the crane."

"We shouldn'y have been doing it, but it was rare fun," the man said sheepishly.

"Some fun," said Willie. But the gibe was compassionate.

Bobby Mair went on.

"Anyhow, one end whipped loose and skewered him like a big, curved needle, as you see. Now, do we admit him, or deal with him in the casualty ward?"

Beds were precious and full admission a more time-consuming procedure. I kept mum, ignorant of such things, but Willie tried his not-quite-one-year-qualified best.

"There's not much bleeding. And no obvious bone or nerve injury. He's not in shock. The main problem will be bacterial contamination."

He looked to see Bobby Mair's reaction. It was good. The surgeon nodded. Encouraged, Willie soldiered on.

"We might get off with it if we tease out the wire and try to feed a gum elastic catheter through the track behind it. Cut windows in the catheter, and irrigate the wound with Eusol."

"What's Eusol?" I asked blankly.

"Edinburgh University solution. Hypochlorite. Great stuff for cleaning out dirty wounds. Anything else?"

"Anti-tetanus injection?"

"An absolute must. Anything else?"

"Penicillin?" tried Willie.

"Right again. The wonder drug."

He swivelled round to look at the patient.

"We'll keep you for a night in the casualty ward. If all goes well, you can go home then and attend for daily dressings. All right with you?"

"Yes, doctor. I don't want to be off my work any longer than I can help."

The welfare state was still a light on the horizon. In his world, he had to be able to make money again as soon as possible.

"When did you eat last?"

"Four o'clock. But it was just a cup of tea."

I knew the syndrome well. Men who do hard physical work for a living don't eat much until the day is over.

"Almost seven hours. Stomach should be empty. And he won't need a deep anaesthetic. Right. Give him a pre-med. Get him prepped. Fix a catheter. You gas," he said to Willie.

"And you," he looked at me. " I could do with an extra pair of hands. Say half an hour."

The out-patient theatre was a red-rubber apron and pair of latex gloves place, where the niceties of asepsis came second to ad hoc disinfection of wounds contaminated by grease or boiler dust or horse dung.

Willie got busy with the sleepy fumes and Bobby Mair concentrated on the surgical problem. He caught the wire with a big pair of pressure forceps, and started to wriggle it out slowly.

"Feed the catheter behind it, Aitken. Use your fingers like eyes. Don't use too much force, but keep up to the end of the wire or the track will close up."

I felt the small of my back prick with sweat, as I wrestled with the finger-light task.

"That's fine," said Bobby with satisfaction and pulled the wire clear.

But he spoke half an inch too soon.

As the end of the wire cleared the top end of the wound, a thick, pulsing pillar of red mounted three feet into the air and sprayed everything in sight, like an uncapped gusher.

"God damn and blast," swore Bobby in vexation. "He's got a perforated femoral artery. Sister. Get a major pack open."

I noticed she was ahead of him.

"You!" he barked at me. "Hold this swab over the wound. Press hard."

I put both thumbs onto a gauze pack, and squeezed for dear life until Bobby slid a rubber tourniquet under the thigh and twisted it tight. He hauled on a sterile gown and changed gloves with a zip and snap of rubber.

"You change too," he ordered.

He cut down on the artery and exposed a half inch, longitudinal, ragged hole where, in its to and fro passage, the wire had abraded the vessel wall. Then I had some brusque, profane surgical tuition, as he clamped, then tied off, the big vessel on either side of the perforation.

"Hold the bloody thing steady. You're waving it about like a tree in a gale."

"Cut the suture, man. Cut cleanly. Don't saw at it."

"Watch how I do these ties. A reef knot with an extra turn. Not a granny."

It was my first introduction to the monosyllabic litany of surgery: clamp, hold, tie, cut. And in that workaday, blood-spattered room, I knew I had heard a siren song.

Later, they asked me to have supper with them in the night mess.

"You seem to have a reasonable pair of hands," said Bobby. "You'll find plenty to do here, if you really want."

The offhand compliment sent me home on a two o'clock tram, on the most beautiful night I had ever seen.

BOOK TWO

Chapter 1

FOR THE REST OF THAT JULY, I got a real adrenalin kick from my Friday visits to the Northern General. I was almost sorry to leave to go to my farm job but I had taken Malcolm's health warning to heart. I set off for Queen Street station with a pair of black, Dunlop, work wellies strung around my neck; carrying a fibre suitcase held together by a belt and wheeling a Sorearse and Rustwheel bicycle: an iron-framed, black-enamelled behemoth I had borrowed. Since the farm was knee deep in countryside, Wilson and I had agreed to take bikes. We planned to swan around the country byways of an evening, sup at a malted hop-shake here and there and treat the country maidens to a spot of student badinage.

I found Wilson beside a shiny, three-speed Raleigh. He watched my arrival with a condescending grin that I offered to remove with the back of my hand. We sashayed a wobbly path through the crowd to the ticket barrier. As we did so, a harassed woman got in the queue behind us. She was carrying a bulky, cardboard box. Her back was arched against the strain: the thin neck muscles corded.

I didn't have a free hand but I nodded at the seat of my bike.

"Rest it on this, if you like."

She wore a camel coat, with a tie belt tugged tight on a gaunt frame; a tan coloured slouch felt hat with the brim pulled down. From under this, she gave me a startled look. My gesture hardly warranted the rose from her hair, but I thought I was worth more than the unsmiling "Thank you," she muttered. Maybe she had been warned against encouraging strange men.

She held the box on the seat as I trundled the bike along the platform.

"I should have called a porter, but I couldn't see one."

It was a struggle, but she was trying to be polite.

"I'll wear my railway hat next time."

The smile wouldn't have made a toothpaste ad, but it was an improvement.

At the guard's van I left Wilson to supervise the loading of our stuff and hefted the woman's box onto my shoulder. Even I grunted.

"Jeeze. The family silver?"

That won another faint smile. I'd wear her down to a laugh if she wasn't careful.

"Where'd you like to sit?"

"This would do nicely." An empty, non-smoking compartment.

I opened the carriage door for her, climbed up behind and swung the box onto a rack. "There you go." Muscles was my middle name.

"You've been very kind."

Was there a hint of dubiety in her tone? Was kindness everything? She fumbled with the clasp of her bag.

Fine bone lines; a long, delicate upper lip; wide-spaced eyes carried the potential of loveliness. But some hurt had cast the features in a mould of permanent bitterness; the mouth in a thin line that showed why smiles were difficult.

I put my hand up to stop her.

"No. No."

I was more brusque than I intended.

"My pleasure," I added more equably, and left her.

Our stop was at Dalmeny, the southern station of the Forth bridge. I was helping Wilson unload our gear when I noticed her leave the station with a porter, the box loaded on a hand-cart. I wondered what could have caused such a sad, heart-burnt face.

Wilson and I set off along the narrow, leafy road. At first I was wary of all this raw countryside. The place was full of strange greenery that threatened my city certainties. I eyed the long grasses, the summer flowers, the airborne seeds; sniffed the air, which was full of heavy scents.

Wilson was in raptures from the start.

"Isn't the meadow-sweet lovely? And the fields. Look at the different shades of gold."

Acres of ripened crops spread around us in a big mosaic. His musing tone became more questioning.

"You know, there's much more grain here than in the west. I haven't seen a dairy farm so far."

In my ignorance this meant nothing to me. A farm was a farm was a bunch of fields. I dismissed his words as mere pedantry – until next morning.

Eventually, we came to our lodgings for the next four weeks. A group of three farm steadings stood in the angle of a Y junction, making a scatter of stone built barns, bothies, and cottages. One big farmhouse faced the road. From the open kitchen window, a woman waved at us.

"Are you the student laddies?"

We nodded and she came out to meet us. She was a real armful of

farm-wife: big-breasted, broad-beamed; really pretty, with a blooming skin, pansy brown eyes and a make up of flour dabs on her nose
and forehead.

"I'm Agnes Greig. I'll show you where you've to bide."

She led us to the end cottage of a farm row: stone-flagged floors, a
cold tap in a lean-to scullery and a pail and scrubbbed seat privy out
back. The two roomed bothy had, in the kitchen, a range; country
joinered table and stools and two old high-backed chairs in honest-
to-God, prickle-the-back-of-your-legs horse-hair. Four truckle beds
made the bedroom into a dormitory for casual labour.

"You'll meet the owner only whiles. He's a Major Armstrong. A toff.
He stays in the big house behind the trees. You'll get your orders from
my man, Sandy. He's the grieve. You'll get coals and sticks in a shed
out back, but you winna light the fire afore lousin' time."

Country words spiced her speech: archaisms that sang an old tune,
even to my city ears.

"You get breakfast and dinner in the fields. I'll give you your
evening meal on work days. Saturdays and Sundays, you fend for
yoursel's. Tea tonight is at half past five. Come to the kitchen door,
and bring your ration books."

She left us to our unpacking. Wilson set out his physics notes on the
table.

"I'll have to work nights for my resits," he apologized.

"And the rest," I disabused him. "You get me to answer to all your
waking hours, and your bum kicked for every mistake."

"That's great of you. Really great," he said, all pink with gratitude.

As ordered, we appeared in the Greigs' kitchen at meal time. It was
a big square room. In the middle was a big, square table. At it sat a
couple of children and two big, square men. The men eyed us with
jovial contempt, and the children found us a giggle. I felt like a fair-
ground geek.

There were nodded introductions and Agnes said, "Rab, come and
give me a hand."

Obedient as a collie, the elder son went to the Aga and held up a
couple of dixies, which his mother filled: one with cottage pie and
cabbage, the other with stewed rhubarb. While this was going on, the
grieve told us what would be expected of us in the next few weeks.

He was sandy by nature, as well as by name. Age had turned a yellow mane into a gold and salt frieze around his scalp; freckles, big as
sultanas splotched his skin and the backs of his arms and the broad,
brown hands were covered with golden down.

"We start the hairst tomorrow. We're a mite short-handed, so ye'll hae tae muck in. Hard."

The men grinned at us again and the two children, long time afterthoughts to Rab, giggled even more. Even the pansy eyes, glancing up from the steaming pans, were mocking. Then the girl could contain herself no longer. She burst out.

"Students. They sometimes dinna stick it. They run awa' hame, beat."

That rolled them in the aisles. Students were the biggest laugh since Danny Kaye. I looked at Wilson, suddenly unsure of what he had got me into. Still, I had hodded bricks and wielded a pick at holiday jobs ever since I was able. Farm work couldn't be that different?

"I'll hae ye up at six on the dot," warned Sandy as we left with the food. " Work at seven."

We reduced the food to crumbs and shreds, I coached Wilson for a couple of hours, then we fell into bed to make what we could of strange country dreams.

Chapter 2

As promised, Sandy rousted us from our iron beds next morning.

"Rise and shine, ma wee laddies. Come away, noo. C'way. You're working for your siller' noo. No' loafing at your college. Be at the Coalheugh yard at quarter to seven."

He clanged a dixie of tea on the range to take the shock from our cock-crow awakening. We drank the tea, splashed our hands and faces in cold water from the scullery tap and went to find out why we were so funny.

The three farms clustered together at the road junction – Preston's Mains, Preston's Neuk and Coalheugh – all belonged to this Major Armstrong. We met up with the work gang and Whynie Deuchars, an older farm hand, explained.

"Places like this were ca'ed fairm toons in the old days. It might take twenty men to run a big one. When you added in the wives and bairns, they were like wee villages. They were like that for generations. Right up to the war."

But the expediencies of economics and war-time labour, had led to the three farms being worked as one unit. The permanent work force had been greatly cut from those hey-day times, and was supplemented at harvest time by a rag-bag of casual labour. That morning, there were farm wives and their weans; ratings from Queensferry and landgirls from the hostel at Dykeliston; an off duty polis and a bus driver; even a bookie's runner.

There was an air of expectation about this motley gang, which increased as a couple of Oliver tractors rolled into the yard: massive; panting paraffin fumes. They were driven by a lean, thin-lipped pair I guessed to be father and son. From the other end of the yard appeared the rest of the locomotive power: three pairs of Clydesdale horses. They had creamy manes and spats. Their harnesses glittered. They looked infinitely patient and utterly noble. There was a little "Aw" of admiration. They were led by two older men and Rab, all big-shouldered from wrestling ploughs.

Reaper binders were rolled out and hitched up, while Sandy Greig moved about, giving orders.

"You," he said to Wilson and me. "You work with this lot."

I nodded sleepily at another four of the casual gang, and the whole caravan moved out of the yard. We arrived at adjacent fields of grain. Someone with a scythe had already cut swathes away from the hedges, to give the reapers room. The six of us filed into the first field, behind the tractor, and we were off on our summer lark.

Before that, I had had a vague idea of countrymanship, endorsed by Wilson's experience on a dairy farm. You leant on a gate and contemplated cows and chewed straw.

Well, there were gates all right, umpteen of them: but I passed them at a brisk trot. There were cows, too, but only a couple: cream and brown Ayrshire ladies, milked hurriedly to supply the farm families. I got the straw bit right, though.

The three farms grew nine hundred acres of the stuff: oats, oats and more oats, with a wee puckle of wheat thrown in for variety. Since it was cut by reaper binders, every last stalk had to be stooked, carted and stacked by hand: and all in the precious sunshine hours our Scotch mist climate allowed.

I was introduced to a whole new ethic of hard graft and Wilson to a world he had never dreamed of. His notions of country idylls went right out of the window.

We followed on behind the tractors, gathering up sheaves and forming them into A-shaped stooks of eight or ten. The morning was fresh and cool, the stalks tickled and the grain smelt sweet.

But the tractors drew inexorably ahead and spat out sheaves with mechanical implacability. What started as an amble increased to a brisk walk and ended up a jog-trot to keep up with the wretched green machines. We poured sweat, while our backs grew knuckles, then whole fists of lumbar pain.

After two hours, there was a halt for tea and soda scones and a review by Sandy.

"Aye. You're a wee sint ahint, lads. Mind, you dinna get your money till a' they cut sheaves are stooked."

He winked at us in high good humour.

The rest of the week was like that. We worked from frost rime to sundown. We worked through showers and despite heat. If the rain came hard, we found students were special. While the casual day labour was sent home and the farm staff went about inside jobs, we were handed three foot billy knives and set to trim the miles of hawthorn hedges that edged the fields. Then we worked into the next night's gloaming to catch up with the stooking.

Our palms were stripped bloody, then grew blisters on the raw bits. Our fingers were pincushions of thistle prickles and felt the size of bananas. At lousing time, we walked with the bent, stiff backs of old men. At night, there were no visits to the pub and we died small black deaths by half past nine.

Being students would have made us butt enough, but Wilson was something extra. Despite his size, his innate softness destroyed him. In the mornings, his eyes stayed gummy with sleep. For the first couple of hours he worked like Coppelia's brother. During breaks he wanted to snatch a shut-eye anywhere: a barn floor, beside a hedge, under a trailer. But I wouldn't allow that. I gave him a boot in the arse and insisted he crammed another wodge of physics down his craw.

"Whass Ohm's law? Whass an induction coil? Whaja know about field forces?"

"Aw, leave me alone. I'll never pass. I should've stayed home."

But I only booted him again.

Our country cousins didn't know what this was about, but it added to the lore of student queerness. They razzed us all the time, but it was good natured. The exception was the Watsons, father and son, who drove the tractors.

They nailed Wilson as a soft touch with manners to offend them. Anytime he got in their road and often when he didn't, they gave him stick in sour, bilious sarcasm. Wilson's only answer was to blush and keep his mouth shut. I thought that was sound policy.

The father was a thin, ratty-faced man, with the sleekit leer of a clype. The son was a wild, noisy guy, who wore his bunnet on the side of his head. He was forever rummling up the farm lassies with squeezes and feels and Kamasutra promises that made them shriek in delicious apprehension. He handled his tractor like a dodgem car. He was a hasher, careless and clumsy; crunching gears and taking lumps out of gateposts when the grieve wasn't around.

But what really made me blink was his invective. I was raised on four-letter words in the back-courts of Faifley, but this guy brought something new to them. They spittled out in venom at anyone or anything that got in his way.

I marked him out as a right bad bastard and kept well clear of him.

When the first weekend came round, I allowed no let up on Wilson's work. On the Saturday, after lunch, I laid down the law to him.

"Right, young doctor, we have been all through the subject of electricity. There's a sheaf of past papers. Get on with it."

"What are you going to do," he asked wistfully.

"I am going to have an hour or two in my scratcher," I promised him.

I laid myself blissfully on my bed in my dungarees and dirt, while he unscrewed his pen and groaned. "Life can't possibly get any worse."

He should have kept his mouth shut

Chapter 3

AT TEATIME, WILSON FRIED US KIPPERS from Cramond, while I marked his papers. "Straight seventies," I announced.

We whooped, and later I took Wilson off to the village to clink glasses. The only pub was an unlovely boozer in the old, hard mould: spittoons and sawdust and the segregation of strangers. Anyone from out of the district was stared into a corner, away from the fire and gossip. Some of the farm people were there, and we exchanged wary nods. No exception was made for us, however and we sat in our own company.

"My turn for the first round, Neil."

Wilson was as excited as a bairn getting a present from Santa. He marched to the bar and ordered up as to the manner born.

"Two halfs 'n' halfs, please."

The barman set up the drinks. Eager to crow about his success, Wilson grabbed one of the whiskies, toasted me, and put it down in a oner. His mouth puckered, his eyes watered, but, by God, the kid was learning. He threw his arms wide, lampooning his own bravado – and knocked the brimming, pint glass that a guy at the bar was just lipping. A great dollop of beer sloshed over the rim and down the guy's front.

It was a Wilson boner of vintage quality and consternation was written all over his big, sonsy face.

"Ya stupit student bastard."

The place was suddenly and warily silent. The venom was replete with physical threat.

The wet victim was young Watson. He stood with his father at the bar.

"Ya fuckin' la-de-dah ijit. Whit ye gonny dae aboot this fuckin' mess."

Wilson tensed into immobility, but I knew it wasn't fear that froze him. He didn't have the nous to scent the danger. He was embarrassed clean out of his wits by the knowledge that he had done it yet again.

I made up for him. Young Watson's voice scared the shit out of me. I had seen too many tanked up men in Jimmy Docherty's bar to be in any doubt. This guy was at the fumy level that only fight will sublimate.

Wilson tried to apologize.

"I'm sorry. Please let me buy you another drink."

As young Watson took the measure of his victim, his mouth eased into a thin grin.

"Too bluiddy true, ye will."

Wilson turned to the barman.

"Another pint here, please. Uh. Two –"

He included the older Watson to show well-meaning: smiled in a bright, foolish way. It was the wrong body language. Young Watson nodded at the drinks being set up.

"Mebbe a wee whisky when ye're at it, eh."

The truth of his situation dawned on Wilson. He swallowed.

"Yes. Of course. And two whiskies."

Young Watson's smile became beatific in its malice.

"We'll huv big wans. An' whit aboot this mess?"

"Of course. My fault. If you get it cleaned, I'll pay for it."

"Suppose you pay for it noo?"

The blood rose in Wilson's face then: the slow surge of shame as he realized the extent of his humiliation.

"All right."

Anything to get out of this awful mess.

He pulled out his brown pay envelope, emptied it into his hand: three pound notes and some silver. Everyone knew Pullar's would clean a mink coat for no more than a couple of bob. He picked out two half crowns and offered them to young Watson, a beseeching bribe to end the scene.

Young Watson's smile increased to a disbelieving laugh. He ignored the silver, and plucked one of the pound notes from Wilson's other hand.

"That should aboot pey for it."

Wilson's face was a hot hurting red by that time. At Watson's words, I could almost feel his relief.

But the goad wanted yet another prick of blood. Young Watson fished a khaki kerchief from his pocket.

"Noo, wipe it up."

Wilson couldn't believe his torment wasn't over. But enough was enough.

I got to my feet with a great scraping of chair and table. Young Watson's eyes swivelled to me, the smile suddenly gone. I plastered an inane grin on my face, and went over to the bar, all stupid.

"C'mon, you pair. A fella could die of thirst in this place."

I barged between them, ready to duck and run. But the bubble of tension burst. There was a barful of sniggers at Wilson's humiliation. Young Watson looked around, and realizing the extent of his triumph, he shrugged us off in derision.

"Saft bluiddy students."

Wilson and I sat it out for a couple of rounds to keep some face, then walked home. Wilson didn't say a word. It was a side of life he had never imagined. The explosive reality of the situation had shocked him.

"I didn't expect it, you see," he explained as much to himself as to me.

"I know," I tried to reassure him. "But you did the right thing, keeping it calm."

"You think so?" He was still crestfallen.

"I'm sure so," I laughed. "I'd have run for my bloody life. You'll know better next time. Anyhow, tomorrow's the Sabbath. We'll get a long lie."

But that wasn't the country way of things. We had been deep in that old cloud nine for sixty extra minutes, when Sandy came in, clattering a tea pail.

"C'way, noo. Seven o'clock. It's to be fine the day. The Major wants some extra hours. Time and a half for ye lads. Is that no' worth it."

We should have had double time for making him laugh so much.

By the end of the following week, the main burst of oats had been cut and the work seemed easier. One pouring wet morning, Wilson and I were sent to lift fallen stooks. We were wrestling the soaking sheaves upright, when he burst out with the 'Ball of Kirriemuir' in all its bawdy invention.

I paused in the downpour to marvel, but when I thought about it, it was the perfect answer to the whole sodden morning. I joined in, and we gave the rain-scoured fields a bravura performance of the whole twenty-seven verses. When we stopped for breath, I said, "We're either bloody mad. Or enjoying this. Or both."

We yelled for the sheer joy of being alive and belted into one another with dripping sheaves of straw, getting grain ears and chaff and big, icy pearls of water in our hair, up our noses and down our necks. We ended up flat on our backs, faces up to the rain and unable to move for racking, soundless laughter.

Wee Sandy Greig brought sanity, along with a field breakfast of scones and tea. We wrapped a green tarpaulin around our shoulders and sat in the lee of a tree.

"What brought on that spasm of sol-fa?" I asked.

"I suddenly feel confident about my exams. I think it's going to come all right."

From that time, too, I came to see that Wilson and I were part of a way of life that had gone on for centuries. As the fields were cleared, as the great, mellow stacks rose in the yard, I was aware of a pattern of shorn fields stretching away in all directions: as far as Berwick, as Europe, as all the continents of the earth. For the first time in my pavement-girt life, I had an inkling of the great cycle of death and rebirth that gives meaning to our lonely, lovely planet.

When we came to the last field, I stuck my pitch-fork in the ground and looked around in real satisfaction. Sandy was passing.

"Y'know, I'm glad I've done this."

He gave a growl of laughter.

"Ye micht no' be sae keen, laddie, if you'd had tae spend a life at it."

He remembered the days of six-month hirings: men in fee for a leaking roof; tatties and a jug of milk a day and a meagre handful of silver at the end. He paused, then nodded.

"But I ken what you mean. You should look weel on it. You'll no' see the like again on this fairm."

"Why?" I was surprised.

"The Major is set tae gie up the horses. He's tae buy a couple o' they new, light-weight tractors in their place, and a combine harvester. And an engineer's been spoken tae build a silo in the stack-yard."

I had a spooky time-slip and had a vision of the generations of stooping, bending, heaving figures who had wrought so hard to get the harvest in; to stand off the winter in the days you couldn't get a can of Spam at the corner store. I felt a moment of regret, but then Sandy chased the ghosties.

"You and your freen'. You'll be wanting away back to your picture-houses an' dance halls, eh?"

"You bet your life."

The charms of the country were all very well, but I was starved of the smells of smoke and soot. And girls, those things that were made to love and kiss. All thoughts of them had been buried deep in weary, aching celibacy, but now I was bulging at the seams, like a paid up member of the Charles Atlas club and raring to get back to Sadie Crossan.

"Aye. Weel, you've worked no' bad. Best student we've had yet."

His modified praise left room for improvement.

"Noo, I've seen you gie Agnes a haun' aboot the kitchen. You could help her again, if ye've a mind."

Agnes's cooking was a treat. I tried to show appreciation by shining up the dixies and drying her dishes, while Wilson was busy with his books.

"Glad to. Anything."

"Weel, the Boss likes to celebrate the last raik coming in. There's tea and food and a dram. And there's a competition to see who can toss a sheaf the highest. There's a pound or two in it for the winner."

"Like a harvest thanksgiving? Sounds fun. What can I do?"

"Aye. They ca' it a kirn. The wife has the arranging o' it, but she needs help. You can louse now, and meet her in the stackyard. Get your freen tae help. And you'll hae a shottie at the competition yoursel'."

It was no question, more a good-natured order.

"Me? I wouldn't stand a chance. Your Rab or young Watson will win."

They were both casual masters of the pitch-fork art; the final wrist flick that sends a sheaf an extra foot in the air.

"Maybe. But I've had my eye on you. You've found the knack of a fork. Even more, you're a bugger to be beat."

I agreed with good grace. I might as well. There was no arguing with this guy.

Chapter 4

I GOT HOLD OF WILSON AND WE WENT TO start in the loaves and fishes business. To Agnes's orders, I set up a paraffin stove with ovens and burners, well clear of the ricks; laid out trestle tables; lugged baskets of crockery, crates of beer and lemonade, and slopping full five-gallon tea-urns, while Wilson prettied up the tables with some coloured crepe paper he scrounged, and some old milk bottles filled with the last of the summer flowers.

The Co-operative bakery van arrived with the haute cuisine. A back-hander had soothed away the strictures of rationing. There were bridies and sausage rolls; fern cakes and paradise slices: Escoffier with dividends. The farm wives pitched in with sandwiches and pancakes, and Sandy Greig appeared with a couple of stone jars of whisky to top it all.

He looked around in satisfaction.

"I hear them comin' in noo."

The carts began to rumble in, and the final sheaves were tossed up to Whynie Deuchars. He was centre stage as he finished the last stack: round and round on his knees, placing the sheaves with fast, unflustered care. He pulled the final sheaves into a cone shaped head, needing only a thatch of more durable wheat straw to shed the rain.

His present pre-occupation was to top-out, climb down, and sink the first official drink of the afternoon: a man-sized quaich of a dram from the Major's own hand.

The owner and his wife and family arrived on the scene, just as Whynie climbed down from twenty feet of corn stack. I stood among the forelock touchers, and gazed at my betters.

The dame of the house led the way, a heavily bosomed, heavily jowelled woman, with a frank moustache and a frown of permanent displeasure. The Major came immediately after, a spare, sparse-haired man of fifty, all military experience of handling men helpless in face of this overpowering ogress.

The youngsters came last: three of them. I had only caught glimpses of them as they cycled along the tree-lined, private drive, but the gossip of the fields had filled in the genealogy.

The son, a year younger than Wilson and me, had just finished his schooling at Glenalmond, and was bound for the disciplines of Sandhurst. The daughter, home from a Harrogate boarding school for young ladies, turned out to be the girl of the celebration. Two years younger than her brother, the coincidence of their Christmas births had led to the conceit of calling them Noel and Noelle.

She wore a limp, white hat that fell over her face in folds, so you couldn't see much of her, but from my place among the sweaty, I caught a glimpse of blue eyes that weren't missing a trick. Sandy lifted her up on a cart so she could see better: and she proclaimed.

"See. I'm queen of the harvest."

Her gargoyle mother gave an indulgent nod, Whynie downed his dram and the Major made a speech of thanks. Then Angus Martin took up his fiddle, the vittles came on offer and the whisky started to flow. Sandy set up a makeshift office in the barn and the Major produced his ledgers and some canvas bags of cash. The good feelings that go with well earned pay in the pocket and some free drams in the blood, began to swell like a loaf in the oven.

There was a lot of joshing and the usual, earthy farm banter took on a promissory tone as the young blades chased the girls and rolled them in the sweet straw. The atmosphere became frankly sexual, enveloping Noelle on the cart. She danced about in a sympathy I don't think she understood and her face took on a funny, glittery look. Then, when her father closed his account books, she shrieked.

"I command the tournament to proceed."

Queen indeed.

An arena was cleared, a rope put up, and every man in the stackyard had a go. As I well knew, young Watson and Rab set the pace. The casual day workers were soon knocked out. Then McIntyre, Fergusson, Yuille, all older farm hands, failed. Then the grieve himself fell out.

"Too bluiddy auld and stooky," he laughed.

Wilson surprised everyone to start with. He always was an awkward mover, jerky and graceless, but to begin with, his new grown muscles gave him strength to overcome his awkwardness. As the competition went on, however, his efforts became less co-ordinated. At his ignominious last throw, he put every ounce of fresh won beef into the effort. But he spun around too soon. The sheaf came off the fork in the low trajectory of a shell. It hurtled over the jollified crowd and caught little Queenie of the harvest cart, smack in the face. It sent her white hat flying, burst around her in a shower of straw, and dumped her hard on her fanny.

Wilson and I had been a joke-a-minute, double act since we arrived, but then he took star billing on his own. His farm-yard fans howled in delight.

"Oh, Lord," he muttered. "Trust me."

He raised his eyebrows and grinned with hard won insight.

"I'd better go over and apologize."

In turn, the others failed, until three of us were left: Rab, young Watson, and to my genuine surprise, myself. Rab winked at me.

"By God, I can see why faither warned me about you." Then he grinned with the certainty of strengths not yet drawn on.

I glanced at young Watson. His lean face was in tight control, but the look in his eyes was feral. Whatever the joke between Rab and me, he sure as hell wasn't sharing it.

Then I was spent, my urban antecedents found wanting.

The rope went up another inch, then another. But at that height neither Rab nor young Watson could beat it. A draw seemed fair. There was a cheer, and a great mill of contestants, shaking hands, exchanging swigs from flat, brown half bottles.

Rab hit me a great country wallop on the shoulder.

"Well done."

I half turned to the man beside me, to include him in the camaraderie. It was young Watson. But he was nobody's comrade at that moment, especially not mine. He looked at Rab, then switched his eyes to me with all the regard of a dock-eared cat sizing up a mousy mouthful.

"The Greigs' wee pal, eh."

The thing was over in a second, unnoticed in the throng, but I knew I had been staked out like a butterfly in young Watson's specimen box of things to dislike. Then the three of us were urged over to where the Major was standing. The other pair had some encouraging words from him, and a fiver apiece from one of the canvas bags. Then he turned to me.

"You're Aitken. Greig has told me about you."

What he heard couldn't have been too bad, for he slipped three quid into my hand.

The crowd was breaking up then, and I went to get Wilson. We had planned to pack, bike into the village for a quick last look at the bright lights – all four lamp posts – then off on the ten o'clock train next morning.

See best laid plans?

Having helped clean the straw off the Queen of the occasion, Wilson was standing in the family group answering Mama's in depth appraisal of his social situation. At the end she gave a sniff that indicated faint approval of the cloth, and none at all of the income prospects of a parish minister. She didn't know about his grandpa.

She turned to her husband then. "I think that will do now, William," she commanded.

"Very well." He spoke without any inflection in his tone. He had given up arguing years ago. Then the son muttered something in his ear.

"Perhaps the young people might stay out for a bit? If they were back by seven for dinner?"

"Oh, yes, Mummy. Please." Noelle was all over her mother: hanging on her arm; making a pretty, pouting moue.

"We'll see they come to no harm."

I looked at Wilson in surprise. For once there was assurance in his voice. Then I recognized the manse training: used to helping at the Sunday School parties and softening up the matrons of the Womens' Guild.

The Major seized on this.

"Yes. Noel and these young men will see she's looked after."

Mama still fretted like a swan with a cygnet.

"Connie will be there, too."

The third youngster: the ugly duckling: the one who didn't fit: a Cinderella creature. I had heard she was a younger, orphaned niece; only child of the Major's sister and unpaid skivvy to the whim of Ma Dreadful. While Noelle had a Dresden china prettiness, Connie had an aura of indistinction: mid-brown hair, sullen, unremarkable features; make-do clothes. But on this ocasion she might have her uses: a further chaperone, another layer of protection for her darling.

"Don't worry, Mrs Armstrong." It was Wilson again, treading fearlessly where strong men quailed. "We'll have them all back in good time."

Sandy was standing near. In a pleased voice he muttered, "Company for the youngsters. That's good. The mother's that feart they get their haunds dirty."

Then he left with the Major and his monstrous missus.

I wondered what the five of us would do, but I needn't have worried. The minute the mother was out of sight, Noelle made a dead set at Wilson. She had the looks of a winsome elf but she had all the instincts of the Baba Yaga who ate young Russian men for tiffin. Primed by the atmosphere in the stockyard, her face glittered as she looked up at him.

"Ooh, I've never seen anyone take on Mummy like that before, have you, Noel?"

"You've made him blush," said the brother in disbelief.

Muted under his golden, weeks-in-the-open tan, the flush gave Wilson's complexion a dusky, attractive tinge. Noelle gazed up at him.

"Coo. I have too. D'you think he's gone sweet on me, Connie?"

But the cousin knew the trouble these pretty ways caused.

"Leave it off, Noelle."

"Not likely." She gazed at Wilson, interested in the reaction she had produced. "Tell you what, Noel. You can go visit Sheila Fullarton. While we –" The glitter became almost pyrotechnic " – get to know one another."

"That's not what mother meant," objected Noel. "Besides, what about Connie?"

The cousin stood slightly apart, embarrassed at being brought to notice.

So far I hadn't said a word but at that I looked at the girl and chipped in.

"We'll be all right, won't we? You can give me a hand if you like."

I gestured at the tables. I had offered to clear them up as a final gesture to Agnes.

The thought of having a definite place in the scheme of things cheered the girl up. Her sullen face loosened. A change of kitchen would at least be something different.

Noel loped off. Noelle took Wilson's hand, and they swung off in a parody of a pastoral romp. He went with all the volition of a hypnotic subject.

I didn't push conversation with Connie, but treated her with mild courtesy. By the time the others returned, I thought her ego seemed in better shape.

Noel looked pleased with himself, and it was clear he had been involved in a necking match. I suggested he got the rest of the lipstick off his chops before Mama caught sight of him. When the other pair appeared, Wilson had the slightly stupid look of someone whose emotions have just been mugged. Then, when we said good-night, the rest of us were given a re-run of the proto-sexual encounter he had just survived: an inexpert, salivating, half-nelson and mouth-lock from Noelle, that rocked him on his feet. She backed away from him, the glitter on her face fired into a glaze that would have decorated bone china.

And Connie? That left her looking at the ground: unkissed, ignored again. Hell, I couldn't have that.

"Can't leave us out, can they?" I asked, and reached for her hand. I gave her every chance to draw back if she wanted, but she closed her eyes and stepped forward resolutely.

As Prince Charming, I didn't rate high. Such a gentle kiss. So undemanding it wouldn't have made Sleeping Beauty stir in her sleep. But perhaps it might awaken some healing self-regard in this waif.

The hazel eyes flew open at me, startled. Then the three youngsters ran off across the yard. Wilson and I watched them out of sight.

"That was absolutely wonderful," said Wilson in the purple prose of his sudden, new love.

I shook my head in envy. Love was not for the likes of me. My pericardium had to stay intact for the next five years at least.

As we ate supper, I read him a lecture on the ways of young ladies with an army of hormones running riot in their circulations.

"That Noelle. She's big trouble for the jock-straps, believe me."

I might as well have talked in Sanskrit, for all the attention he paid. Well, we would be back to home and medicine next day. That should give him time to cool his ardour and unscramble his wits.

See unscrambling wits? It's easier with eggs.

Chapter 5

WE STEAMED BACK TO QUEEN STREET, where I bade Wilson goodbye and good luck with his coming resit. Then I walked out into the big, smoke-blackened, Victorian city that paced my pulse.

I had forgotten what an engine the place was: a ding-a-ling fire-bell to flush any remaining rustications the hell out of my system: cars, buses, the huge, slab-sided tram cars: bells, horns, hooters: pneumatic drills and iron, dray-horse shoes: the scuff and shuffle of a million feet: and above all, the beehive buzz of the people as they blethered, gossiped, laid forth, laughed, swore and grieved about life in its great, cobbled, steel-railed streets.

I had saved my sweetie coupons for the month and persuaded a chocolate shop chit to fish under the counter and slip me some of that still rare confection, for my Granny Aitken and Maisie. I also dropped in on Jimmy Docherty, and bit his ear for a bottle of equally scarce, decent whisky for Jock.

I was well satisfied with my reception in both houses. The admiration of my tan; the wonder at how big I seemed, pleased the little boy in me. But I also knew a great dismay.

After the sweep and space of the fields; after the careless mess of two young men fending for themselves, these houses I had loved so much were no longer couthy and cosy, but small and irritatingly poky. I felt so disloyal. Besides, what could I do about it?

Later in the week, I saw Wilson's name in the *Glasgow Herald*. His resit was in the bag. More, I had an ecstatic letter from him, arranging for us to meet. The big, splurged writing ended cryptically.

"The biggest news is not my pass. I have a real surprise for you."

Wondering, I went to the Union to catch up with him and the rest of the guys. That was a joyous affair: Wilson, Drew, Fraser, Miffy Allan, Des Craig. The roll of friends grew. We swapped stories of holidays; held post-mortems on who had flunked. The Dean's prediction was being proved, slow but sure: enough to give anyone a spasm of the wind up vertical if they thought about it too much.

After matriculating, we went back through the cloister. It was full of stalls, where the various student societies set out their wares. Wilson stopped at the swimming club, the Dolphins.

"We need a good breast stroke," said the committee man.

"Naah," Wilson shook his head. "Freestyle."

"You'd need to be very fast," said the guy discouragingly. "Lots of good speed men about."

"Oh, I'm fast all right. I can clock sixty for the hundred. I'm sure I can go better, but I've never trained seriously."

I wasn't sure what all that meant, but I looked at Wilson with a new respect. The lad was coming out of his shell.

"If that's true, I'm very glad to meet you," the Dolphin man said, suddenly impressed. "I'm Matt Davis. Fill in this form and meet us at the Western Baths. Monday at seven."

We went down the steps into the sunlight.

"This is where we first met," he said. "Lucky for me."

"Gahn," I scoffed.

"No. I know what I'm saying. But perhaps I can pay you back now."

"I don't – "

He waved my mouth shut, and led the way to the Kelvin bar. He set beer in front of us, and told me his news.

"My grandfather died last week. I'm sorry about that. He was a nice old man and very good to me. But it means my father will come into the money now. We'll be quite well off."

The qualification had a comforting nonchalance.

"One benefit is that I am definitely to have rooms of my own from now on. My dad realizes how unsuitable the last place was. But he'd like if I would share it with someone. I – we – wondered if you would be interested. You wouldn't have to worry about the rent. Only share the heating and the food. What d'you say?"

What do you say to a miracle? My problems of living space answered at a stroke. God could expect me back on my knees that night for the first time in years.

"That would be great. Marvellous. I'd like nothing better. Uh. I'll write and thank them."

"No need. They've left it to me – us – to find a place. They'll come up to town on Friday to vet it. You'll meet them then."

We picked up a noon edition of the *Evening Citizen*, circled some possibilities in the 'Lets' columns, then climbed the steep slopes of Hillhead. We inspected apartments fly-blown and meagre; frowsted and roomy. We met landladies who allowed baths on Tuesdays and positively no girls or cooking. In the end, however, we came to a top-floor, top-of-the-hill, service flat with few restrictions.

Wilson's aesthetics were engaged the moment he stepped in the door. The flat had been formed from a bedroom and dressing room of the original house. It had superb, Italianate plaster-work, windows that would have graced an orangery, and a view to the Finnieston crane. These grand features quite overcame the grubby paintwork and the seedy, run-down furniture.

While he gazed at the view, I went to look at the bath and the cooker on the landing which we would share with the room opposite. 'Miss M. Taylor' was printed on a card pinned to the door. The statement gave no hints and I wondered what kind of woman would live in such shabby splendour? Was she one of the old brigade? Or a Mimi type seamstress alongside whom I could boil eggs of a morning, in comfortable deshabille? But the truth was much more prosaic.

"Who's Miss Taylor?" I asked the landlord.

"She's another medical student like yourselves. A bit older though."

"I bet that's Minnie Taylor," I guessed.

This was a Jenny Wren of a lass, maybe ten years older than us, with a perpetual worried look.

"Of course," agreed Wilson. "That's just who it will be. All medics together. Good."

My Granny Aitken took the news with equanimity, as if she had been expecting it. Later, I went to see Jock and Maisie. He was up and dressed and in his wheel-chair, on one side of the range fire. Maisie was in her mother's old American rocker across from him.

"I've got a chance to move in with Wilson. He's got a place of his own."

They were happy for me.

I looked around the room: a living room in truth. This was my background, whatever became of me; the whole world I could circumnavigate in twenty seconds flat; the parents I loved, with all the inadmissible, lumpy emotion of a new recruit to the adult ranks.

I had a sudden sense of sadness and loss. This would never be my home again.

When Wilson's parents came to vet the digs, they looked around uncertainly. His mother resolutely paid no further attention to the grubbiness, as she helped Wilson unpack the woolly pullovers she had knitted for him and stacked the cupboard with jars of home-made marmalade and jam. His father looked around more carefully. He couldn't miss the fag burns on the mantelpiece, the sagging couch, the mouse droppings behind the curtains.

"This is what you want? You'll be all right here?" He was making it clear he would take my word for it. "We're so glad you can stay with him. You will let us know if he gets in – if he has any –"

He let his formless worries fade into inarticulation.

"We'll be just fine," I assured him, accentuating the pronoun. He could depend on me being around to keep an eye on things.

Any doubts he had were further allayed by the appearance of Minnie Taylor, a plain-Jane little dame in flat shoes and a tammy. Although we knew one another by sight, because of the size of the class neither Wilson nor I had spoken to her before. After introductions all round, Minnie said, "I heard you were coming, boys. It will be nice to have you as neighbours. I find myself a bit on my own, here. Knock when you've finished settling in. I'll give you some tea."

"What a pleasant girl," said Wilson's mum, when Minnie left. "I'm sure if she stays here, it must be quite suitable."

The reverend agreed with obvious relief. He was glad to have the decision endorsed so easily. It was even faster than prayer.

Later we crossed the landing to Minnie's nest of no-nonsense comfort. A battered easy chair on one side of the fire had been smartened up by the Cameron tartan travel rug thrown over it. A severe study table, set with neatly stacked books and pencils in a mug, was placed in the window. On the blotter lay the text she was currently reading: a plain-covered, gilt-edged, well-used Bible. Her respectability was further enhanced by the tight braid in which she wore her fine hair, and by the selection of home baking she produced from tins.

Minnie had had a true calling. At the age of thirty, after years of faithful service, from office lass to secretary, with an elderly bachelor solicitor in Peebles, she had been awarded an unexpected, golden goodbye when he shut up shop.

"I'm quite alone in the world, so I sat down and thought about what I should do with the rest of my life. I prayed, of course, and – well – I'm going to be a medical missionary. I had to go back to school. Night classes. I wasn't sure if I could do it. I had to work so hard to catch up. And I've just had two resits. But I passed and I'm still here." She declaimed all of this in a rush, with a mixture of pride in, and defiance at, such an unlikely background.

Her visitors were all impressed: Wilson's parents because of her sober, try and try again, Christian example; Wilson because he had just been through the same trauma of first time failure; and I because of the effort this must have taken.

There were a few other mature students in the year: a pharmaceutical chemist, an airline pilot and some ex-servicemen. No matter the variation in background, they had all been at the sharp end of responsibility, with their wits honed on the steely exchanges of life. A change of discipline, while difficult, could depend on a mind broadened by all kinds of practical experience.

Minnie's leap back into the learning stream, after so many years in her cosy backwater, was of another order. To her it must have seemed, must still be, a great, whitewater torrent. No wonder the serenity her faith strove towards was underlaid by a slight edginess, and belied by a constant, if tiny, frown of worrry.

I looked at her with real respect.

When Wilson's parents left, they insisted that we should not see them out. Not a drop of Minnie's good influence should be lost. The three of us chatted on for a bit, then it was time for me to start earning my couchette.

"C'mon, young doctor. We've still some things to get in order."

Minnie nodded approvingly, and I headed us back to our books and medicine.

BOOK THREE

Chapter 1

IT WAS THE PRESCRIPTION AS BEFORE: lectures, dissections, laboratories, tutorials. In our first evenings together, Wilson and I mugged up fine print and chanted bawdy, rhyming jingles at one another to irrigate the arid acres of anatomy.

> "The lingual nerve,
> it took a swerve
> across the hyoglossus.
> Said Wharton's duct,
> 'Well, I'll be fucked,
> the bastard's double crossed us."

But differences soon appeared.

Wilson became enthusiastic about the Dolphins and began to bring his guys home to dry their Jantzens. I was made welcome enough in this splashy company but I never felt entirely at home.

He soon established a howff that would have gladdened the heart of Rabbie Burns himself. The place reeked of Balkan Sobranie and McEwan's Export ale. Guys dropped in for coffee or to toast cheese or just for a heat. We could have started a hotel with the numbers who wanted to stay the night. Buoyed by his grandpa's legacy, Wilson never gave it a thought, but expenses became more than I had bargained for. I had to work some extra hours for Jimmy Docherty to stay solvent.

But there was more. While Wilson's confidence grew like a sunflower with its very own sunbeam, mine was wilting at the edges. And the cause of my distemper was anatomy: the study of the parts of man.

I managed well enough with physiology, the other degree subject of that year. The chemistry of neural transmitters, of muscle metabolism, of protein synthesis; the physics of permeable selectivity, of partial gas-pressures were trained around the scaffolding of past work. I could tease order and reason into these new concepts.

Not so with anatomy. It stayed a monstrous grind of memory.

Now, besides the daily, regional dissections, we were immersed in systematic studies. We pored over the tracts of the central nervous system. We peered down microscopes at the cellular architecture of the ductless glands. We crammed the intricacies of brain, of liver, of kidney; the details of the genito-urinary, gut and cardio-vascular symptoms into our memories.

Wilson and I fed each other question and answer over the corn-flakes in the morning and washing our smalls at night. All over the flat were plastered diagrams and memory aids to be studied while shaving, dressing and facing both ways in the loo. I stuffed my mind with these sawdust facts, but no matter how I tried, they would assume no cohesive shape. They simply spilled out of the holes in my boots.

The newborn Wilson was pleased with a modest pass.

"Now, Sir Neil. I have passed this week's spot exam by a whole one per-cent. To celebrate, I'm off to a dance at Whitecraigs' tennis club with some of the Dolphins."

Dancing was he? There was a turn-around. I had put away my slippy dance shoes and watched Sadie Crossan waltz away into the moonlight with some other guy, to give more time to my books. I gave him a sour look. And when, the very next week, I ploughed a spot exam on the sympathetic nerve supply of the head, the early tremor of uncertainty had grown to a shivering panic. If I was struggling this bad so early in the session, God help me in the June professionals.

I gave up all Wilson's matey evenings and went next door to work with Minnie.

"Neil. I do feel for you. The work is a constant worry to me." Minnie's sober ways were constantly embellished by the unconscious tricks of anxiety: nibbling her lower lip; fiddling with her mother's wedding ring, which she kept on a chain round her neck. "But, if I can do it, so can you."

I tried to smile confidently, but such crinkles as I could screw up had a tight feel. It would be the come-uppance of all time if I went to the junk-yard of scrapped students: me that had no room for failure.

Then a friendly tutor had a word in my ear. It was the last week in November. He was doing an intensive tutorial on the brachial plexus, a convoluted network of nerves that courses through the neck to feed the arm and hand, when I fell asleep. I wakened with a bang of wood-en seats as the lecture finished and the other students got up to leave. There were only a dozen of us in a small room, so I couldn't miss his eye as I jerked awake.

"Was I that boring?" he grinned faintly at me, as I trailed out last.

"No. No. God, I am sorry." He was a nice guy, easy to talk to. The last thing I wanted was to offend him. "I'm finding it hard going."

"H'm. Working long hours?"

"Yeah. I simply can't get it to make sense. I need something to hang it all on."

He nodded in sympathy . He knew.

"Function is the best bet. Figure out what a structure does? Why it's where it is? Then add the nerve and blood supplies. But you're looking a bit frayed to me." Any farm tan had long since disappeared. "Haven't you got an auntie in Dunoon? A weekend at the sea?"

I shook my head. All my relations got home-sick on a day trip to Rouken Glen Park.

"Well, take it easy. You don't want to end up in Mearnskirk."

He was reminding me the medical faculty paid an annual forfeit of illness to the city hospitals, brought on by chronic strain and lack of sleep and fresh air.

It was all good advice, and later that day I again pulled on waxy tendons, making dead bones move. I could see what I was doing; knew what the tutor was getting at, but the idea of function wouldn't come to life. And as for a health giving break, how the hell was I ever going to manage that?

See conundrums? Answers come when you least expect them.

A couple of days later, on a visit to Jock and Maisie, I found a letter waiting. The writing was strange, so I slit open the envelope and had a look at the signature first: Alexr Greig. For a second it didn't click, then, "It's from Sandy Greig. At the farm. What can he want?"

They had found a wallet stuffed with fivers and was it mine? But nothing so dramatic.

He hoped I was doing well in my studies, and there was a matter which might be to mutual advantage, for discussion of which he sent invitation. I could spend the night in the bothy, if wished. It would be convenient to bring my friend, as the matter might touch on him. Could I please advise arrival time Saturday, if suitable, to tea. Yours truly.

A genuine sincerity shone through the stilted phrases.

All thoughts of the farm had been wiped out; buried under my mountain of worry. But I had a sudden memory of peace of mind; of wind-blow and plant-form; grasses, grain stalks, green-sheathed hedges. My sense of smell, filled with formalin reek and beer fumes from Jimmy Dochery's bar, suddenly craved a sweeter perfume.

"They want Wilson and me to go for a night next week-end. Something they want to talk about. But I've no idea what."

Later that night, when I told Wilson I was taken aback by his furious flush; and I had seen the same, slightly foolish grin on his face not long before.

"I've had letters too."

"From the farm?" I was surprised.

"Well – yes. In a way. From Noelle, actually."

I remembered the wet-mouthed ferocity, but that alone hadn't caused the love light in his eyes. It must have been some correspondence.

"You'll be coming with me, then?"

"You bet. I was trying to work out some way of meeting her over the Christmas vac. This may help."

When he had gone, I took good care to rifle his stuff; see how hard this breeze of romance was blowing.

There were two letters amongst his shirts, all in swirly, violet ink. The first one went on about how handsome he was and how big. She only came up to his heart. And a medical student. The girls in the dorm couldn't believe her luck. She simply had to have a photograph. She'd simply die if she didn't hear from him. It was lummox lure of the first order and he must have swallowed it whole. I could guess what he had written from her reply. She'd adore to be his girl. She would be seventeen soon, and would show him she wasn't too young. His photograph was marvellous and the girls in the dorm were all mad jealous. They simply must meet over Christmas. She'd simply die if he didn't manage it.

No wonder he was all lit up.

Since we didn't have bikes or luggage, this time we went by bus: a local service that dropped us at the village cross-roads. We left the city in a drizzle of wet, sleety snow that burst on the window in wet splotches. Past Bathgate, the sleet went off. By the time we reached our stop, a crescent moon glittered low in the early darkling, and a few brilliant stars were out. We were glad to get out of our cramped, chilled inactivity, and set out at light infantry pace for the farm.

This was a different countryside from the one we had known in the summer. Then, it had been wet often, but dried out in a day or so by the sun and wind. Now it was soaked to the heart; sour; cowed. The trees in the moonlight had the stark quality of a steel etching; the gateways to the fields had been gouged by cart-wheels into wet, puddling quagmires; and the roads had been slaistered by a thin sheen of fast freezing mud. I could imagine the bleak inimicality of an ice age. I shivered, not only with cold.

As we came up to the group of steadings, squat and four-square after the batterings of a hundred such winters, I was glad to see the yellow lights, and inside, to be welcomed back to the human race.

Maisie had scrounged a box of biscuits from her bakery, to grace the Greig board; I had raided the bus-station kiosk for comics; and Wilson had come good with a pot of his mum's marmalade. We swapped these for handshakes to crack a walnut, squeals from the bairns and a kiss from pansy eyes herself.

"I want you tae meet Matt Findlay," Sandy nodded at another man sitting at the fire.

From the first, I felt I had known Matt for ever. He was a grey-haired man: not big, but strong and compact looking; easy to smile. He had a sense of calm, of competence. I came to think of him as indestructible.

"These are the lads I was telling you about, Matt."

Then, for the first time, we got to sit at the big, square table, among the big, square men. The chat was mainly about farm matters and, as Matt talked, the grieve showed an oncoming he rarely allowed other men. Not that Sandy was the autocrat of the harvest field: he used his authority lightly. But he was the grieve all right and nobody argued with him. Now, I noticed, he gave full weight and consideration to this man's remarks.

After the meal, Sandy produced a dram and got down to cases.

"You'll mebbe mind I was saying there would be changes on the fairm? Weel, they've cam' aboot sooner than I thocht. The horses are a' awa, noo."

There was a brief silence, a moment's mourning for the passing of an age. Even I, who couldn't tell the rear end of a horse from the back of a bus, felt it. The presence of that four-footed power-house was everywhere. The whole place had been built around them: stables, tack-rooms, cobbled causeways.

"More men hae quit than the Major bargained for, but he doesna' want tae fill these jobs full time again. Yet, he needs men tae work Saturdays and the Sabbath. And then there's a' they holidays men want noo. He wants tae find casual labour instead. That's mebbe where you could come in." He looked at me speculatively. "You're a canny lad, and I ken you need a job on the side. It would fit weel if you were free at weekends. You'll mind what I tell't ye aboot the new tractors? Richt handy they've turned oot. Work a' day and nicht. Turn like a peerie. And a power-shaft forbye. Matt, here, has been engaged tae supervise and service the machines. He'll say who's tae drive. We need tae mak the drivers mair accountable."

The Watsons' hash-bash driving must have taken its toll.

"Matt will teach you tae drive and maintain the tractors, for when he's no' here. In the winter months, you'll be expected to fill in for the Watsons at the reeds. If Matt and the Watsons are away thegither, you –" he swivelled round to Wilson "– could help out –" his tone went a touch dry "– And I hear there's mebbe other reasons you want tae come aboot here."

Trust the country mafia to sniff out a romance.

Wilson looked happily guilty, and I just looked happy. This remarkable twist of fate meant he'd be near his half-pint amour, and I'd get out of Jimmy Docherty's fug at weekends. We made arrangements to keeep our working gear at the bothy and bikes at Dalmeny station.

"Fine then. Matt will show you the ropes the morn's morn."

Chapter 2

IN THE MORNING WE HAD A MUSTY-SWEET, winter stoutener: a plate of slow-brewed porridge from Matt's haybox. Over it, he explained our tasks.

"There's corn to lift from the stackyard. Swedes to cart from the big shed. The cattle to be watered and fed. The reeds to be mucked out. The Watsons will be there now. We'll go and catch them."

In the autumn, several hundred cattle were brought from Ireland. These were fattened through the winter, ready for slaughter in the spring. The youngest were housed in reeds: big, open quadrangles, backing on a byre or a barn for shelter. They were railed off by fences of wooden posts and spars. At the back were low, sloping roofs of corrugated iron, under which were racks for hay; troughs for cake and water.

For all I didn't like the Watsons I had to admit they won respect as stockmen. Their experience was deep and widecast and for that they were forgiven a lot. When we arrived, they were already at work.

In the dark winter morning, bare, electric jury lights swung in the wind. It was sleeting again, and the cattle, meek and yielding from being castrated and polled, huddled into the shelters at the back. Their snorting breaths; the carpet of straw, soaked by splashing streams of piddle and gouts of puddling ordure, steamed into the blackness above.

Working against the lurid light; in and out of the coiling reek, the Watsons swore, shouted, punched and prodded at the beasts to move them. The tines of their six-pronged graips gleamed steel-bright in the harsh light, a new design of devil's fork straight from the pits of hell. When they saw us, they stopped and leaned on the graips.

"This is the pair o' lads that's to spell you. You'll mebbe mind them from the summer?"

They hadn't forgotten. "The Greigs wee pals again, eh?"

If Matt felt surprise, he kept it to himself. "You can show them what to do. I'll away for the tractor and trailer."

With thin, bad grace, the Watsons started our instruction: one line, scant information on how much straw to spread; how much feed to give; how to spot the runny nose of pneumonia, the staggering gait of mineral salt deficiency, the thin scour of enteritis. Then they threw the graips at us.

"Aye. Let's see you get some shite on they fancy claes."

We had on street rain-coats, and gum-boots borrowed from the Greigs, no way dressed for this kind of work.

"The hell with them," Wilson muttered. He grabbed a fork and started to fork the steaming litter. I could do no less and joined him. It was only then I noticed their grins of triumph. They had hooked our pride with an expert, barbed cast.

The effort of keeping our coats from being soiled made our movements twee and finicky. The Watsons loved it. They enjoyed their glorious moment, then stalked off.

"Might as weel leave ye to it, seein' you're that bluiddy smart."

Matt was soon back with one of the new tractors and a low sided trailer. "Are that pair away already? They shouldna' be. And you'll get in such a mess."

"Initiation for the new boys," I explained.

"Aye," he agreed. He knew their style. "There's some clean sacks in that shed."

We cobbled together aprons and leggings, and Matt helped us finish the job. His slow, regular rhythm of work contrasted with the snatch and grab of the Watsons.

The load had then to go to the midden, where it would lie and rot until spring. Matt let us drive in turn, showing us how to back the trailer, wrong way first to stop it jack-knifing; how to gentle the new horses teamed under the bonnet; how to stroke the fierce clutch. At mid-day, we washed away as much of the dung smell as we could and Agnes fed us again.

"The lads did fine, Sandy," said Matt, and we were hired.

"When could you start?" Sandy asked.

"I work in a bar. I'd need to give some notice. Say over the Christmas vacation, and weekends after that."

"Right. I'll work out a schedule for you."

Wilson and I set out to catch our bus back to town. On the walk, I said, "I've not seen anything of the Major or his family. Is your young lady still at school?"

"Yes. Not home until the hols. That won't be long now." Hoisted into the sky, his face would have given off moon-beams. "But, the cousin, Connie, I hear she's about. So Mrs Greig said. She's at a local school."

I nodded. No point in cashing the family bearer bonds to educate her. Besides, this way she would be at the gorgon's beck and call.

At that, the family car, a sedate, pre-war Daimler, passed us heading for home. The Major peered at us, suspiciously at first – the land owning classes don't take to strangers – then with a half acknowledgement. The Harridan beside him ignored us. Connie sat in the back. She stared at us, at first without recognition: expressionless, walled into a bleak and private misery.

I glanced back at the car. It had dawned on her who we were. She was looking out of the rear window with the glimmerings of a smile and wagged four fingers at us. Small gestures, not looking for much of a reply: taking nothing for granted.

That was no way to play the peever beds. I waved back, a great, windmill salute that at least one person on this earth was glad to see her.

The interlude took my mind off things for a brief and blessed spell, but back at el rancho medico my war of attrition with Cunningham's Manuals of Practical Anatomy showed no sign of a victorious conclusion, and the term came to an ignominious end. I felt this worse, because the rest of my brothers in body lore were pulling ahead of me. As the rows of bodies yielded their bones to the scalpels and forceps; disintegrated into shreds of flesh in the bins, there was a cheery confidence around the table. Their pass marks improved as mine worsened.

On the last Friday of term, Wilson added to my gloom.

"There's a hop at the Union tonight. The Dolphins are making up a party. You'll come, Neil?" he asked. "You're getting to be a bit of a dog, these days."

It wasn't that he wished me bad, but he was quite enjoying our role reversal.

"I'll see. You go ahead. I'll maybe join you."

In fact I went to Minnie's room to visit. They would never miss me. She gave me tea and symphonies on a windy-up gramophone, much more to my mood. I looked around at the sparse array of Christmas cards; the tree-branch dusted with sparkle and hung with a few frugal baubles.

She lifted the needle from the groove. "Things any better, Neil?"

I shook my head.

"You've got a block. That's what it is. Chuck it for the holidays. Don't look at a book."

She was spouting treason. I had planned a murderous assault on the wretched subject for all my nights at the farm. Yet I found her confident diagnosis attractive. I was sick of the whole thing, and I had nothing to lose.

"You think so? Y'know, Minnie, I believe I'll do just that."

At the door, she stood on tiptoe to kiss away my worries, and went back to her lonely Christmas.

Back at our place, I found Wilson asleep on the couch, snoring off too much beer. The place was littered with bottles and fag-ends. I threw a quilt over him; cleared up around him. I gathered my notes, dissection plates and textbooks; put them in a pile. Then I pitched the whole lot in a corner. Wouldn't it be just hilarious if Minnie's unlikely prescription worked; if this visit to the farm broke the stranglehold the wretched subject had on me?

Chapter 3

THE SCHEDULE SANDY ARRANGED FOR ME was full of gainful opportunity. "I can find work for you every day, but in particular I need help on Christmas and Boxing Days, as well as New Year's Day. Some of it would be double time."

Carol singing didn't have a look in.

Winter in these parts is often paradoxical, the worst cold coming only after the mornings are lightening into spring. But that year, the winter had started early. The ground was already frozen fast, the lea happed deep in snow. For the first days of the holiday, however, there was a slight break in the weather. The sun, in its low arc, came out. The day temperatures broke above freezing. There was a Christmas card look about the place.

By day, Matt and I worked about the steading in quiet companionship. At night, we sat on either side of the kitchen table. He played endless games of patience, while I looked into the fire and waited for Minnie's cure to work.

I came across the Armstrong youngsters and Connie, making a snowman one day. Noelle made a feast of asking if her swain was indeed coming and showed the gallery how gratified she was by my reassurance. But there was nothing calculated in the glittery look that suffused her sharp little face again. That was spilling out of the gonads and I hoped he had an instruction book on how to handle that rush of female humours.

The clear spell didn't last and the day Wilson arrived, the small window in the weather was curtained over by massing snow clouds.

"You'd better get as much kail cut and under cover as ye can manage," Matt said.

So, without time to find his girl, Wilson was right into it. On the third journey, however, he was standing behind me on the gear casing, when he pounded my shoulder.

"There they are. On the duck pond. Go round that way."

The three of them were playing ice-hockey with a tin can and walking sticks. When Noelle caught sight of Wilson, she up-ended her brother to stop the game, and ran on her skate toes to get at her Lochinvar.

"Hi, kid," I said to Connie. "Had a good Christmas?"

Three months had made a big difference to her. The woman's face arising out of the splodge of girlhood was good: broad, brown, and peasanty, but with an unequivocal femininity I liked.

"Not bad," she said.

Not good, either I guessed. Santa had brought modified cheer.

I looked over at Noel to say hello. He was still sitting on the ice.

"You'll get frostbite of the bum if you don't get up."

"I can't. I think it's broken. My leg, I mean. I heard it crack when I went down. Now it won't take my weight."

He tried to grin at me, his Sandhurst conditioning not allowing him to fuss, but from the tight lines on his face, I guessed he was in bad pain. I prised Wilson off Noelle and got him to support the boy, while I had a look at the injury. The lower leg was already badly swollen at mid-point.

"Hang on tight," I said and, grasping above and below the swelling, made miniscule contra-rotations with my hands. My time in the Northern General had taught me the unmistakable feel of crepitation, as the jagged bone-ends grated on one another. Despite my care, he gasped and went white.

"It's broken all right," I said to Wilson.

"You sure?" he said. He seemed surprised.

"Oh, Noel. I'm so, so sorry."

Noelle knelt beside her brother, but beseeched the rest of us with eyes that made sure we saw her contrition. I persuaded her out of her act and into her shoes.

"He'll need an ambulance. Why don't you girls go on ahead and arrange that."

I borrowed the girls' woolly scarves, broke a couple of the walking sticks in half, and got Wilson to help me splint the leg. Then we lifted the boy to the trailer and wedged him amongst the kail. I drove to the back door, while Wilson held the boy steady. The Major and his dreadnought came out to meet us, but she was in command, as usual.

"Bring him in heah."

The house was a solid Edwardian Villa, with sub-baronial pretensions, and a warren of stone-floored utility rooms to the back. 'Heah' turned out to be one of these that had been converted into an office, where the Major interviewed grain merchants and gave Sandy Greig his orders. Noelle made a big production out of seeing we all got hot sweet tea but I noticed it was Connie who manned the kettle and tea-caddy and set out the cups.

The next commotion was Noelle insisting she went to hospital with the patient.

"Scoular and me, Mummy, we'll go with him. Make sure he's all right." She made it sound like a life-saving dash.

Without thinking, I had asked for pen and paper and scribbled a note of the findings. Of course, I always did this to someone's dictation in the Northern General, but it seemed reasonable to do it myself, in the circumstances. Now, I handed the note to Noelle.

"Give this to the porter at the hospital. It may save you a wait."

She looked at Wilson doubtfully, but he was helping with the stretcher. So, she tucked it in a pocket, then disappeared into the ambulance on her errand of mercy, while I went back to cutting kail.

I was uncoupling the tractor for the night, when the ambulance came back. Wilson appeared at my shoulder in a few minutes.

"How's the patient?" I asked.

"That's what I came to tell you," he said. "His leg was broken, as you thought."

I shrugged noncommitally.

"Anyhow, the doctor commented on the splint and your note. Said it was very professional. Noelle is impressed, Noel and his parents are grateful, and I'm curious. I noticed you were quite positive about the diagnosis."

"It isn't difficult. Once you've felt crepitation, you never forget it. You should come to those sessions at the Northern General with me. They're full of that kind of stuff."

"Maybe I will. Anyhow they want you – us – to come over to-morrow night."

"Come over?" I eyed him uneasily. "What for?"

"So they can say 'thank-you'. As well, we can play Monopoly and have cocoa and biscuits."

On second thoughts, this was Minnie's prescription to the letter: anything but those bloody books.

Next evening, we spruced ourselves up after tea and left Matt in his slippers and braces. He wore a pair of thin-shanked, steel spectacles down his nose; a hussif with needles and thread open on the table. He was darning a hole in a sock. As I shut the door I looked back on him, composed in his self sufficiency; knowing he had done a day's work well, and better than most. I hoped doctoring would bring me such satisfaction, if I ever made the grade.

When we got to the house, Connie let us in. The family party was in a room that would have won prizes as a funeral parlour: dark green curtains, a dusty rubber plant and a feeble fire that gave off tired smoke. Some tinsel and a few seasonal baubles only pointed up the gloom. The Major and his Sybil were on either side of the hearth. He sat under a dim lamp, reading the *Daily Telegraph*, while she listened to a wireless beside her left hand. She was a twiddler of the worst order, and treated us to a constant orchestration of atmospherics all night.

She stopped long enough to give me a grilling that would have awed Scarpia. Within five minutes it was clear she didn't know what the medical profession was coming to, allowing people like me in. I was dismissed to join the young people in the corner. Wilson and Noelle were setting out a Monopoly board. Noel was lording it, with his clubbed foot on a stool and Sheila Fullarton, a pretty red-head, giving him the amused sympathy such accidents seem to cause. He stuck his hand out at me.

"Hi. Thanks for what you did."

Sheila had a run of luck and, by half-past nine, had enough hotels on the board to scupper everyone. Noelle pouted and declared she'd had enough. Connie and I were sorting the money and property cards into order, listening to the low mutterings of the love-inclined, when I heard Wilson's voice go up a couple of keys in excitement.

"You mean you might not be going to Edinburgh?"

"There's a good chance. I've been working on Mummy to let me go to Glasgow instead. Wouldn't that be super. We could see each other every day."

Noelle had artistic leanings, and plans had been made for her to go to the Edinburgh College of Art. I wondered if even Noelle's wiles would be enough to divert such a long set plan. But I reckoned without the *force majeure* of money.

Then it was time to feed this Hecate of the air-waves. All other activities took second place.

"Connie, wheah is the suppah?"

The girl stood up at once. No one made a move to help. Her fortune cookie said she was always going to be a loser in this house.

"C'mon. I'll help you," I said.

We went through to a scullery like something out of the Snow Queen's kingdom: frost flowers on the windows; grow your own chilblains while you peeled the potatoes.

"Would you like to light that?"

She looked with loathing at an elderly Main gas cooker.

"Sure."

It was very coy about catching alight, then it went off like a small grenade.

"Lose your eyebrows there."

"Oh, I have. I have."

She was too young for that kind of bitterness. I tried to lighten the conversation.

"So, what are your plans for the big world?"

"Another year at school. Then I've to go to secretarial college."

She said it as in prison sentence.

"You don't sound too enthusiastic?"

"Ugh."

So much disgust and frustration in one small syllable.

"What do you really want to do?"

"I want to go to the RSAMD."

Everyone in Glasgow knew the Royal Scottish Academy of Music and Drama in Exchange Square. I was astounded. I would have thought of her tramping grapes; kneading bread; churning butter.

"You mean wigs and greasepaint?"

"Oh, yes."

There was a real stamp of desire in her tone.

Perhaps you didn't need long blonde hair and a swimming costume figure? Perhaps there were parts for girls with peasant looks? And the face that was emerging from the sulks of her unhappy years was going to be the stronger for that experience.

"Well, why don't you?"

"How can I?" she said crossly. I shouldn't tease about something so important.

"I'm serious."

"What – ? How – ?"

"Listen. College isn't like school. You don't have teachers marking a register and sending reports home if you play hooky. It's all up to the student. So, you set out in the morning as if you're going to secretarial college, but, surprise, surprise, turn left instead of right and you end up in drama school. Who's to tell."

"That isn't possible."

"Believe me, it's perfectly possible."

I looked at last year's blue dress – wrong colour for her vixen looks; ludicrously tight on her solid frame – and warmed to my theme.

"Listen, kid. People like us. We have to take chances. What've you got to lose? So auntie finds out and you get hell for a week. What's different? It wouldn't be easy, but you've got – what? – eighteen months to scheme and plan. Lay a false trail. Agree to go along with the shorthand and typing. Make sure you're seen reading the syllabus. Get yourself a typewriter, even. No harm in teaching yourself to type. But you keep another file on drama school under your bed. When the time comes, you apply for that. Give my address for correspondence. Real cloak and dagger."

"You would help me?"

What I could do for her was no more than hold her coat as she spat in the eye of fate, but the thought of someone in your corner to hold the towel and tell you why your head is ringing like a bell, is always a comfort.

"Sure. I'm going to be about the farm at weekends for the foreseeable future. Tell me if and when you make up your mind. We'll lay plans."

I carried in the tray for her and held it while she served the mugs of cocoa and the crumbly biscuits. I noticed she looked at the family as if she had never seen them before.

In our absence, Wilson had been summoned to sit beside Mama

again. The possibilities of Noelle's change to the Glasgow School of Art were being assessed in further, minute consideration of Wilson's social eligibility. Until then, he had been diffident about proclaiming his grandfather's loot, but profits will out and in his disingenuous prattle, he let fall a nugget of hard news even I hadn't heard.

"My dad's going to take delivery of a new car next week. I can't wait to see it."

To get a post-war set of wheels you had to sell your sister, or have a warrant from the king himself. Since Wilson was an only child, it could only mean that Wilson's dad had juice away beyond the average country minister. Mama lit on this like a butterfly on a buddleia.

"A car?"

"Yes. A jolly nice one, too. A Lea Francis."

This small volume, expensive marque was out of the same sort of stable as the Daimler: no flivvers in that company.

I caught a look that flashed between Mama and her daughter. It came from different poles of the female spectrum: the maid and the matriarch. But no matter the viewpoint, from that moment the ends became identical. There was no doubt that Noelle would go to Glasgow School of Art and a suitable match, by the Dean's definition, came a step nearer.

Chapter 4

WILSON LEFT EARLY, TO SPEND A FEW MORE DAYS AT HOME.

"My mum. She likes to fuss over me a bit," he explained, half-apologetic, half-resigned.

"You should be so lucky. She's a lovely lady," I said, half-rueful, half-envious.

Such half-truths encompassed a whole handbook on parental affection, and he nodded at our understanding.

"You're not working over the holiday?"

"No. I thought I'd give it a rest."

I didn't go into Minnie's part in this decision.

And, right enough, her prescription seemed to be doing something. Working about the farm soothed my feelings of panic. Being caught up in a much bigger scheme of things brought a sense of proportion, though I wasn't sure where it was all leading. Then, one dinner time, I had what was no less than a vision.

Matt and I were walking behind the Coalheugh barn. The wind had blown most of the snow off the grass, which stood brown and tufted. In a quiet voice he said, "Slow your pace a wee. Keeep talking to yourself out loud. Walk straight for the gate."

Wondering, I recited 'Wee Willie Winkie' and watched Matt as he stepped aside. He kept a parallel line, three feet away from me, walking quietly, his eyes fixed on something ahead. Then he made a flying leap that landed him belly flat, and with a rabbit by the ears.

I would have passed unseeing, but Matt's wise eye had spotted it in the camouflaging grass, where it had been lured by a blink of winter sun. There, scared by my noisier progress, it had frozen into an easy prey for Matt's country cunning. He held it up by the back feet and knocked it dead with a skelp across the back of the neck.

"A tasty supper for us, lad."

Then came the start of my lesson. He opened up a jack-knife and slit the belly. The guts spilled out. He cut the bowel loose and emptied it into the hedge. Then he lopped off the feet and head; separated the fur at the edge of the belly gash and stripped it off.

He held the carcass in his hand.

"See the big haunch muscles that made him jump and jouk."

He had done this countless times, but the sight still made him marvel.

"My, but here I'm telling you."

He laughed at his presumption.

But he was telling me: something I hadn't been able to see before.

The muscle coverings still glistened and shone with the immediacy of life; still quivered and leapt to the touch of Matt's knife point. In the depths of my imagination, a cold engine fired and function came alive for me in the corpse of a jinking rabbit.

It wasn't that the big muscle masses simply levered the body into the air. This was what gave him his characteristic, dodging run; kept him alive; gave him an even break against old Rufus Fox. The arrangement of muscles that made his ears flatten, his whiskers twitch, his white scut flash; the whole apparatus was an expression of his very rabbitness.

That night, the stew was excellent, and my new perception dazed me. I couldn't wait to get back to the anatomy lab to see if this new concept brought on by old Brer Barebones on my plate would come good for humans.

It did. From my first day back at the dissection tables, anatomy began to work for me. Of course, I had to go back to the beginning, to rejig all the plodding, badly understood work and still keep up with the new stuff. I was never a brain-box; always had to work hard for passes, but I had never worked like that. I began to get headaches and my right eye developed a tic when I was tired.

The whole class was caught up in trying to master the huge subject. There was a thoughtful, more serious air under the student junketings, as everyone realized what they had taken on. It was more than a test of learning. Like running a marathon, it needed pace, judgement and effort beyond imagination. And, as the Dean and Malcolm Ritchie had foretold, some students began to give up the ghost.

Dessie Morris, for instance, began to drink too much. He would turn up for the afternoon classes half-stewed. He would slip out for a pee and not come back. Walter Menzies found that bridge – of all things – was the diet his nimble mind craved. There was a big school in the Union and he began to spend most of his time there. Annie Syme burst into tears one day. She left the lecture in obvious distress. She came back a week later to say good-bye.

"The Dean was so kind. But I realize this is not for me. Never was. Thank God it's over."

A camaraderie of common cause grew up amongst the survivors. Outside the classrooms, friendships flourished. There was a borrowing of half-crowns, bets on the Rangers' game and discussion of whether you should do it with girls.

Billy Anderson had announced himself an accomplished seducer and he summed up the subject one lunch time. " 'F she's been there before, why not you as well? But, if she hasn't, s'not done. And you definitely don't screw the girl you're going to marry."

My background, my upbringing set me apart. I was used to girls who were harder in the tits; equally thrusting; keen to nail a man as soon as they could, any way they could. I thought Anderson was a dreary lecher but from all the nods and head wagging, I could see that his ad hoc exposition of '47 morality had the stamp of middle-class approval; and Wilson looked as if he had seen a great truth. Well, that might suit his romantic notions but what about Noelle when she got that glittery look?

I was well content in that fraternity, satisfied with my Friday nights at the Northern General and truly happy when I took a milk train to the farm on a Saturday morning.

That winter was notorious. It rolled in from the east in great drifts of snow that paralysed the country. The papers were full of it: abandoned lorries, stranded trains, villages out of food. It reduced the farm to a state of siege. Deep frosts set in, tightening the investment. It was a constant fight to keep things going. Matt and I tholed snow-burn. Our skins stuck to frozen metal. We wrought in winds that stalled the very will to live. And when I fell into bed at night exhausted, I listened to the winter wolf snicker and howl at the door. Once again I shivered. In my citified ignorance, I had thought this beast long caged by civilization.

But once again in my life, I was glad I had known this experience; lived this struggle at first hand.

It was May before the last, hard-packed snows disappeared completely, and the long, pounding grind of second year began to come to an end point. The second degree examinations loomed.

At the beginning of June, exam fever broke out. It was a bit like mumps, spreading sporadically, people getting the bug here and there: black-eyed, jittery, talking too much or not at all. Wilson got a mild dose.

"I'm going to stay at the flat and work weekends. Want to stay and work with me?"

Wilson had given up all pretence of wanting to work at the farm during the cold weather and, since Noelle wasn't there either, he usually went home at weekends.

"No. Thanks, but I don't want to change my routine. I'll go to Preston's Mains as usual."

He nodded equably at my superstition. Lucky charms and four leaf clovers were all the rage.

On the Sunday morning before the exam, Matt and I were finishing breakfast, when Sandy came in. He was red in the face.

"The march fence between us and Littlehaugh is doon. There's some o' their stirks got intae the top wheat field. Awa an' get them the hell oot o' there before they get the bloat, then mend the bluiddy thing."

March fences were the stuff of feuds and blood letting. Boundaries set centuries before, they were more sacrosanct to an owner than his wife's virtue. A ruined field of grain or a neighbour presenting a vet's bill would be irredemable shame in the grieves' brotherhood.

We took a trailer loaded with fencing gear and shooed the beasts back to their side of the law, then we had a go at the fence. We dug a hole and wrestled a new corner post into place. Then Matt paced out the positions for four stobs to carry new wire. These posts were four inches square, and sharpened at one end, ready to be battered into the ground.

"Damn it all t'hell," swore Matt. "In a' the hurry, I forgot to bring a stand."

By Farmer Sod's law, we were in the field farthest from the farm.

"There's an empty oil drum in the trailer," I said. "Would that do?"

Matt was irritated by his own carelessness. "We'll juist bluiddy well make it do."

It was the shoogliest work platform you ever saw: an invitation to a Buster Keaton disaster. As the heavier man, I got to hold on for ballast, while Matt climbed up to whack the stobs home. I squinted up at him as he worked.

He stood on the two, narrow platforms of his steel-studded work boots, skiting about, laughing and swearing, making impossible calculations and allowances as he whirled the flat-headed, seven-pound, iron mel through the air – and smacked the stob-end clean on target every time.

Suddenly I saw it: Adam Henderson's logic. All the individual lessons of function of the past months came together in the only way they could.

There had been dinosaurs and diatoms, fur and feathers, animals that burrowed, some that bounded. But of all the blueprints of nerve and muscle, bone and sinew, brains and blood, this was the one that stirred the gravy.

All around us were the roads and railways; the boats and bridges; the steeples and slate roofs he had built.

This was the house that only Jack could build: Jack Human.

"Time for a spell," said Matt, when he was satisfied with the work. "Fetch ower the flasks and the pieces."

We sat by the mended fence to drink our tea and eat our scones. We listened to the kirk bells of that calm summer morning. We talked little. Sometimes I opened and shut my hand, watching the movements from a new plane of understanding.

"You're looking pleased with yourself," said Matt.

"So I am, Matt. So I am."

Later, I told Sandy about my examinations.

"I won't manage to be here next weekend because of them."

"Aye," he said in understanding. " But I can depend on you for the rest o' the summer? I need tae mak' up rotas."

"Try and keep me away."

When the exams did come, the physiology paper and practical felt good and, when at the end of the viva, the examiners gave me a friendly nod, I thought I was home.

But anatomy was different.

I wrote the paper in a haze. When I came out of the hall, I found I was shaking slightly and I couldn't remember a word I had written. At the spot exam, dissected specimens were laid out and candidates had to identify structures indicated by markers. I suddenly found myself rattling off nerves, blood vessels, ligaments as if I had seen and memorized them in a dream the night before. And when the viva came, the prof and the external examiner were kind for the first moments.

"We want you to be at ease. You have passed well, so far. You should know that this viva is for honours."

Then they took me to the cleaners: cool, polite, and totally unhelpful.

Afterwards, I went to the wash-room and sluiced my face and hands with Loch Katrine's best, cold and slightly shocking, even in midsummer. My friendly tutor was there before me, having a pee. He had been setting slides and fetching specimens during the viva.

"It sounded as if you knew your stuff, but I can't tell if you gained distinction. They mull it over at lunch. Depends how much port they drink."

He winked at me for luck but I felt in my bones I needed neither port nor luck. That skinny bunny had done something important for me.

The results went up the following day. Wilson and I joined the usual ruckus at the notice board. Taller, he craned over the crowd and picked out his name.

"I made it. I made it." He was ecstatic. "Isn't that marvellous. Noelle will be pleased. And my parents. Wait. I'll see if I can spot your results."

But Drew Alexander was there before him. "Aitken. Neil Aitken. He's got honours in anatomy. Where is the swotty bugger. Rag the bum."

I pretended modest surprise as my shirt was pulled out, my shoe-laces kidnapped, and I was led by a haltering tie to the Kelvin bar, where I paid a handsome ransom of export ale for my release.

Next morning, Wilson and I shared a happy, if mildly nauseating breakfast. Noelle did not break up from school for a few weeks and he was going to spend a holiday with his parents.

"See you at the farm in August."

"Just think. Next year we get to see real, live patients."

It wasn't until that moment our passes really sank in. We had cleared the big hurdle.

Chapter 5

I WAS KEEN TO SPEND AS MUCH TIME as possible at the Northern General and, when fixing my hours for the summer, I asked Sandy a favour.

"There's a clinic I would like to attend on Fridays. If I could arrange my day off to suit that, it would mean a lot to me."

Sandy was agreeable, so on those mornings I combed the hayseed out of my hair, and went on the earliest train to make a further investment in a surgical career. I had been there two weeks when it paid a dividend that beat the hell out of anything in my Granny Aitken's Co-operative pass-book.

There were two residents to each surgical firm. On receiving days, one manned the wards, the other the Gate. They did a six month stint, swapping posts at the halfway stage. They occupied a suite of lofty, dingy, beige-distempered boxes – bed, bath, and sitting rooms of unsurpassing gloom – at the hub of a four ward complex: central and handy for a night nurse with worries about the fractured femur in bed seven, who had developed a temperature; or the gall-bladder in bed nine, whose drip had stopped. I got to this palatial slum about eight in the morning, and put on the honorary bum-freezer Bobby Mair had awarded me.

"If you're this keen, you might as well get your food free."

I bolted my hospital breakfast, anonymous in a horde of sleepy arse-alikes, then beat it for the more sustaining surgical fare to be found at the Gate.

Not that I was the boy wonder, nor did I kid myself. All day I got gravel scrapes to scrub and dress; minor lacerations to sew; skelfs to remove; exquisitely tender, blood-bulged nails to pierce; boils and carbuncles to incise and pack; water-filled knees, and blue-black, sprained ankles to bandage.

The major traumas; the acute abdomens; the shocked, stricken harvest of surgical emergency, went into the examination rooms to be assessed by Bobby Mair and the Gate resident. I knew such things were above my head and beavered away at my tyro tasks, with only the odd, wistful look in that direction.

One day I must have been showing my thwarted aspirations, for Bobby took me aside and gave me a word of advice.

"You have to know something about pathology, before the major stuff will mean much to you. Content yourself here for a while. This is all good surgeon's apprentice material."

Surgeon's apprentice: the phrase attracted me. It had a comfortable ring to it. Could it be a warranty of things to come?

"A lot of students never learn to sew a wound neatly. They leave scars that wrinkle and pucker. Some wee lassie who comes off her bike on her face in Ardnamurchan may be glad of the techniques you're acquiring here."

That settled me to my handicraft.

But I found the Gate had more to teach me than mattress sutures.

Writing up notes at the wall desk; shuffling the porters' labels into some kind of priority, I learned from the faces of the slow moving legions; the punters who sat on the hard benches and tholed, shuffling along the wooden seats as places fell vacant, waiting for whatever relief this rackety, fearful place could bring.

I had lived amongst them since my birth. I could recite in detail the circumstances and life styles implicit in the oily dungarees, the bowler hats and business suits; the fur coats, the floral pattern pinnies. I thought there was nothing about them I didn't know.

Yet, as I watched the hope and despair; the courage and abject terror; the faith and disbelief; the grief and laughter, I realized how little I really did know of them; of the huge caverns of the human psyche. I felt daunted, dwarfed, and painfully immature. I schooled myself to yet more patience and set myself to learn these new lessons.

Then, at the end of the month, I had a lesson that was to change my life.

The houseman on the Gate at that time was a guy called Hammy Skinner. He was a shy, fusionless bloke, who was as handless as a convicted Muslim thief. It made his day if he could get the top off his breakfast egg.

He was a book man through and through, but since the tome that would cover every manifestation of malign fate that spewed into the Gate, never would, never could, be written, Hammy was often lost.

He was perfectly frank about it.

"I'm not keen on this. I'm aiming to get D.Hamilton Skinner, consulting psychiatrist, on a brass plate on a house in Park Circus. I won't have much call for this sort of stuff." He waved at the benches outside. "But it will look good on the *curriculum vitae*."

He gloved his hands against the pestilences crawling in foul, green pus and the sticky reality of spilled blood, without enthusiasm. So, with his unspoken consent, and Bobby Mair's tacit connivance, I got my hands on things I maybe shouldn't.

The receiving firm signed off at midnight, but every case that had been logged in the book until then was their responsibility. The Gate staff had to clear their feet of minor cases and the ward theatres had to work through whatever load of surgical emergencies had been admitted.

As a routine, Bobby Mair checked that the dregs of the minor stuff could be handled by Hammy or myself, then he went over to the wards to take his place on one of the operating teams.

One night the place was stuffed with acute emergencies. At midnight, Bobby had a panic phone call from the main building.

"They need everyone who can stand on his feet. I'll leave the pair of you to finish up."

He squinted at the benches outside. Two patients were left to us: both men. Each was handcuffed to a polis. One had the tribal markings of a Rangers' fan: blue woollen scarf, and blue, knitted bunnet with a toorie. The other had a red muffler around the lower half of his face, team colours I didn't recognize.

The handcuffed pair were from the Black Maria special, a recurring phenomenon of Friday night pathology. At quarter to midnight, a dark blue van with grilled windows arrived in the yard. An assortment of villains and vagabonds was yanked into the receiving hall by constables not given to argument. Many of the prisoners were marked by one, even two, lacerations on the top of the skull. These were characteristic and uniform: one to two inches long, with a narrow band of contusion on either side of the wound.

"Prisoner fell while trying to escape, doctor. Banged his head on the wall."

Never a felon uttered a word of protest, nor was the term 'civil liberty' ever mentioned. It was accepted on both sides of the law, that a beech-wood baton applied to the skull with the practised precision that stopped just short of fracturing it, was the simplest way to quell the tide of fighting and sheer bloody murder that spilled out of the Glasgow pubs on a Friday night.

Bobby Mair crooked a finger to summon the Rangers' supporter. Under the tooried hat he found just such a judicial laceration.

"You'll manage that," he said to me.

Then he summoned the guy with the red muffler: except, when he came close, you could see from the tasselled fringe it had once been white. The rest was a sopping mat of blood.

I peeled off the ad hoc dressing. The cheek gaped in a wide, secondary smile reaching from the outer angle of his eye to the bone under his chin.

"A blade," was all he said.

The open razor, that weapon of coldest steel and nerve had gone out of fashion during the war, but the odd expert still sprouted one from a waistcoat pocket. This guy had been playing against the Sheffield Shavers.

Hammy Skinner said, "Aw, Christ," in *sotto voce* nausea and looked away.

Bobby assessed the wound.

"What do you think?" he asked us.

Hammy was too busy licking his lips.

"Clean cut," I tried. "No major structures involved. Needs time and patience."

Bobby looked at Hammy's white face and shook his head.

"Think you can deal with this, Skinner? Use a local."

Hammy looked miserable.

"Come over as soon as you've finished. They need every pair of hands."

He disappeared to the wards and I renovated the skull of the jughead in the treatment room, while the polis had a fly cup with the porters. Then I went to see how Hammy was doing.

He wasn't. He went down with a pole-axing migraine just as I went in the door of the OP theatre.

Lack of food and sleep; doing something he hated; the bright lamp and the glittering steel instruments, all combined to leave him sick and half sighted. He had done only the first few sutures, but had to stop, snatch at his mask and rush to vomit in the slunge. When he came back, he muttered, "I'll need to lie down. Can you go on with this?"

"Sure. You look hellish."

He face had turned a greeny yellow.

"The other doctor's unwell," I explained as I took over.

The hard man displayed a sardonic lack of reaction to my implied elevation into the graduate ranks, but at least he didn't scarper, trailing bloody sheets like some wised up victim of Sweeney Todd.

The pert lace-cap, already scrubbed, winked at me as I did my time with a hard brush and carbolic soap. I pulled on gloves, snapping them taut, then hooked a stool under me with my foot, and settled to the rest of the cheek wound. I was in my element.

When the last suture was in, I mopped the wound dry of blood, and allowed myself a brief satisfaction. His scar would be as clean and taut and noble as that of any duelling Von with a sabre and a buttoned, student cap.

"That's it," I said, and started to help nurse with the dressing.

"Will you put a bandage on this, too?"

The hard man talked little: the way of his kind. He held up his right hand. The palmar surface of the fingers had been slashed open across the second joint.

"Next stroke," he explained. He had caught at the razor to save his face from further damage. "It doesn'y seem bad. The bleeding has a' stopped."

His creed had let him make little of it.

"It may take more than a bandage. Can you clench your fingers?"

The top joints were adrift and powerless to shut. I poked into the wounds with a pair of fine forceps. The four wounds were identical. The flexor tendons had been severed. Unless the cut ends were apposed and sutured carefully, the hand would be left useless. He wouldn't be able to pick a daisy, let alone wield a weapon.

"Why didn't you mention this before?"

"It didn'y seem much."

Shock often does that, the body opiates dulling pain and true realization. "This will have to be mended. See how your fingers aren't working."

For the first time he seemed alarmed. "Can you fix that?"

He looked at me. Fine he knew my student status. And I, too, had a problem.

As a tool, the hand is unsurpassed anywhere in nature or the mechanical sciences. It is a complex mechanism that can be co-ordinated to do a million tasks in milliseconds. Hand surgery was a specialty in its own right, and I had no wish to overstep my privilege. Yet, with the wards under siege, and Hammy out of the game, it would be a hassle if I had to fetch Bobby Mair back.

I probed into the wounds again. The structures had been cut through with the precision of best cutler's steel. The ends were lying close; easily identified. There was no obvious damage to the nerves or vessels, which run up the sides of the fingers. This was a straightforward problem in applied anatomy. With my recent exam success still burning bright, I decided.

"Sure. It will take a little time, though."

It was my turn to wink at the lace cap to keep my spirits up.

"Re-set for this, will you? I'll do it under a block."

She positively beamed her encouragement and I had hopes for our future relationship as I changed my gown and gloves.

I was deep in this finicky job when the door battered open. A voice, harsh with temper, cut across my concentration.

"Skinner. Are you going to be all bloody night here? If I phone for you to come to my wards –" The possessive had all the imperiousness of a Roman emperor "– I expect you to get a bloody move on."

I looked around. It could only be Boss McKenzie.

Chapter 6

THE FIGURE IN THE DOORWAY was an original, ethnic, bony, ginger-haired, blue-eyed Scot: a comic character right off a seaside post-card. But the kilt and the moth filled sporran had been replaced by a dark blue suit with chalk stripes that would have made a primary school teacher stamp her feet in envy; and the boots and white gaiters by a pair of shoes that glittered to satisfy an adjutant in the Guards.

He penetrated the anonymity of my cap and mask disguise.

"Who the hell are you? And what's this? Where's the laceration of cheek?"

I could see why his temper was a legend.

"Name's Aitken, sir. I'm a senior student. The patient didn't mention this wound to Mr Mair. But, when I had a look at it, I thought I could do it. And since everyone was so busy – "

My excuse tailed off, feeble even to me. Truth was, I had wanted my hands on it; craved that psyched up feeling.

The blue, northern eyes glared at me. "Have the tendons gone?"

"Yes."

"Then you're away out of your league, sonny."

So I was. And I knew it. And I was a black, Celtic incomer to boot. But the dismissive contempt stung. Bugger him.

"I was only trying to help. When I got down to it, it seemed simple enough."

My voice had an edge to it I couldn't help. I was on the point of stripping off my gloves and throwing them in the pail, when he said, "Show me."

I was on the third finger by then. I demonstrated the anchoring sutures, ready to be drawn tight. It looked all right to me: really neat, in fact.

"Hmph. Where is Skinner, anyhow?"

"He had to lie down. He took a bad migraine."

"You'd better get on with it then. But when you've finished, come across to my room. I want to know more about this."

He whirled on his heel, the exaggerated bully-boy swagger emphasizing the trouble I was in.

The hard man on the table screwed his head around.

"Good for you, son." I had one vote of confidence. "You've got tae stand up tae fellas like that. 'S the only thing they respect." He spoke from a world where respect was valued above gold: earned in blood, if need be. Mine was going to be all over the floor from the sound of things. "Besides, he hasn'y took you aff the case."

That hadn't struck me. I brightened until I walked over to the main building and went up in the big, bed-scarred hoist. By the time I got to fifth floor I wasn't feeling at all perky.

I caught at a lace-cap as she whisked by on blurred feet. They weren't allowed to run, so they had developed this hovercraft motion.

"Where will I find the chief's room?"

She pointed to a door, and gave me a warning.

"You knock. And then you wait until you're told to come in."

"Thanks."

Any words of advice to the worried were welcome that early morning.

I went to the door and knocked: three chaps on the door of my medical future. At one in the morning there was laughter and chat going on behind the door. Had no one heard? Should I knock again? Try the door? But the lace cap had been clear. I waited and felt my nerves begin to fry gently. This was a chief who knew how to cut a guy down to size.

In time; in his own good time, came the unmistakable, high, highland phonemes.

"Come in."

I walked in on Boss McKenzie holding a tea-court, with all the patronage of a Lancastrian baron. He was wearing the robes that showed him in all his power: surgical whites splashed with red roses of blood.

A few chairs were ringed around the room, all taken by men in similar operating ducks or white coats. Apart from Bobby Mair, I knew none of them. I stood ready to take my licks, while they waited to hear his pleasure with me.

That was easy. He ignored me.

I found I was in on a council of surgery: who was to do what with the remainder of the huge surgical overload that had landed on the firm in the past twenty-four hours. Standing in front of Boss was Hugh Gillies, the ward resident, whom I had already met in the breakfast queue. He scribbled names on an operating list, as Boss doled out the cases according to his staff's experience and his own caprice.

"Richards. And you, Baillie. You can tidy up what's left. Better if you do the perforation, Baillie. You take on the obstruction, Richards. And Mair, why'd you leave this boy without supervision?"

The question was slipped in; bland as a bonbon laced with belladonna. The room stilled, waiting to see how Bobby Mair would bite on it.

"Just following your own example with me, sir. You always gave me lots of responsibility. Said it was good for me."

Boss beamed with satisfaction. If he had said that, it must be right.

"So I did. So I did."

The collective sigh was audible, though whether it was of relief or disappointment was difficult to tell.

The old bugger never looked at me yet, and I didn't know whether to stay or run. Then a guy with chubby cheeks and hair growing thin on top moved his backside half off his chair, and patted the vacant bit.

"Come and park your bum here. I've got it nice and warm."

He had the wet, hoasty chuckle of a forty a day man. I recognized the behaviour: near the line; not afraid to break ranks. This was a court jester. Still, such characters made powerful friends. I sat beside him gladly.

"Got to stand up to this old tyrant," he muttered in my ear. "Most of this lot shit their breeks if he looks at them sideywise. Mind –" he chuckled again, his fag-raped voice hoarse and confident – "Don't be as cheeky as me. I get off with murder because I'm only passing through. And he knows it. I'm waiting until I can get a registrar's job in neurosurgery."

Neurosurgery and baiting Boss McKenzie? This was some guy.

A ward sister came in without a knock, and with the fanciest lace cap you ever did see: tied up one side of her cheek and neck with a big, white bow.

"Is she special that she doesn't need to knock and wait?"

"You're tootin', boy. Queen Bee. Boss hand picks his sisters. Some for the nursing. Some for the nookie."

He gave me a leery wink.

"Her?"

"Nursing. Top of the tree. Creme de la Nightingale."

Under the lace cap, a stern face was lecturing Boss.

"The man is in great pain, sir. I really do want someone to come and see him now."

Boss mimed amused alarm.

"I'm getting into hot water here. One of you had better go with sister and put a suprapubic drain into that man with the acute retention. You, Minty. Take that young fella and show him how to do it."

My friend chucked in his cap and bells, and took on to be a doctor for a while.

"That's us. Out you go."

I scrambled to my feet and raced to get the door open for the sister. No one had said I shouldn't kow-tow to her. Outside the door I said, "I'm Neil Aitken."

"Hi. Minto Millar. Minty to my friends. This is Sister Dorothy McWilliam. But I remember her when she was a probationer."

He stole his arms around her waist, and his tobacco-roughened chuckle echoed in the big, booming stairwell.

"Mr Millar. This young man will be getting the wrong idea. He must remember my word is law in the ward."

Whatever had gone on between them in their younger days, over her head Minty now nodded a solemn amen to that.

She went ahead into the ward, and led us to a patient hidden behind screens. He was an old guy: bald, with long wisps of parietal hair plastered over his pate. He was panting busily: giving himself something to think about besides his pain.

The sister pulled down the bedclothes: uncovered his belly, taut, and distended in the lower half.

"You take his story," Minty said. It's one you should get used to. You'll hear it a lot."

I listened to the bane of ageing man: the great prostate story. The slowing of proud waters; the imperfect piddling; the dribbling; and then the night of the can't pee no-how.

"Palpate here. Percuss there. Big bass drum here. Bag of water there. Now, I'll show you what to do. Doesn't matter what kind of a doctor you turn out to be, this is one thing you should learn. You might be glad of it in a snowstorm one night, if you can't get a case like this into hospital."

He turned to a basin: scrubbed his hands: nodded at a trolley already set.

"We do it with that."

"God. What's it called."

"Trocar and cannula. Cruel looking bloody thing, isn't it." A thin metal tube was skewered through by a tight fittting punch. This protruded from the bottom of the tube about half an inch, and ended in a sharp, three-edged, dagger point. "You do it fast. Inject the skin with a little local, just above the pubic bone. Little incision, just so." He sliced the skin for a neat inch, then positioned the dagger in the wound. "The relief is so great, they forgive you on the spot. That's the theory, anyhow."

He grinned at the man, and rammed the dagger home: through abdominal muscle; through bladder wall. The old man gave an almighty yell of surprise and pain. Then Minty pulled the trocar clear, threaded a catheter through the cannula, and let off a fountain of glittering relief.

As predicted, the old man sighed in forgiving ecstasy, and Minty said, "Tinkle. Tinkle," with a laugh.

I toured around at Minty's heels for an hour, getting the feel of what had been going on in the wards, and a first look at the practised shambles of the big, two-table theatre that had been on the go for twenty-six hours. Afterwards, I had a doze on a couple of chairs in the residents' lounge, and finished my sleep on a milk train to the farm.

I yawned my way contentedly through the day's work. I had found my niche all right.

BOOK FOUR

Chapter 1

THAT AUGUST, THE HARVEST WAS DIFFERENT.

The new combine harvesters delivered a spew of grain from a spout at the side, and dumped out a ready-bound straw bale every few yards. Tractors raced to the new storage silo, big as an air-ship on its nose, and left trailer loads of grain. My job was to shovel the hard golden fruit in front of the vacuum hose. It was all impressively efficient, but I missed the mellow smell of the stacks, and their massive comfort against the coming winter.

Wilson had come back from his holiday in a glow of south-coast suntan, and he helped me sometimes, but there were even more differences in our situation.

He had never needed the work, even for pin-money, but he was now appreciating the real meaning of his grandfather's hereditables. There was a careless assumption of lots more where that came from. Where, before, he had always shown an ingenuous generosity, there was now the faintest whiff of condescension.

As Mother Armstrong contemplated the synergy of assets, he was accepted into the household with an archness which was the nearest she could come to grace, while the Major modified his usual brusque tone when talking to him.

He still stayed at the bothy and Sandy found occasional work for him but the pretence grew thin. By day, the favoured couple cycled abroad or took bus trips to Edinburgh, although come the gloaming, Noelle's mama grew restive. That was the time when youth was tempted, and innocent girls lost their maidenhood. It rationalized her anxieties on this score if they had company in the evenings.

"If you and Connie will come too. Make up a foursome. It will keep Noelle's mother happy."

"The things I do for you."

He gave me a look of mild calculation, then nodded. I wouldn't let him down. After all, he paid the rent.

So sometimes Connie gave up her apron, I climbed out of my dungarees and we acted out a foursome farce for the Great Horned Mama: a bike run, or a visit to the tin roofed cinema in Dykeliston. One sunny evening, a blow out in Connie's front tyre left us stranded, while the other pair bowled off.

"Thank the Lord," said Connie. "Any more of that lovey-dovey stuff, and I'll fwow up."

"Mustn't mock the higher romantics," I reproved. "C'mon. I'll spoil you."

We dumped her bike, sat her on the bar of mine, and wobbled off to South Queensferry, where I plied her with Barr's Iron Brew and ice-cream with red stuff on it. Under the influence of such addictive substances, our camaraderie grew: chums in adversity, rubbing along on hand-outs and such wits as we had.

Or so I thought.

We wandered down to the Forth shore, where she sat beside me as I lay on my back and watched the trains that rumbled over the famous, red, latticed bridge.

"Now that Noelle isn't here, tell me if you've had any more thoughts about drama school?"

"Ooh, yes. I've got it all worked out."

Six months after adding the yeast of rebellion, I had brewed a ferment of mutiny. I laughed.

"Good. Tell me all about it."

"The big problem was to get my fees paid. I might have slipped a cheque past Uncle William, but never her. But one day they were talking over Noelle's plans for art school, and Aunt Winnie said she should have a bank account of her own. Learn to handle her own money."

She laughed delightedly as she re-ran her stroke of luck.

"Then Uncle William said I should do the same when I went to college. Have a quarterly allowance and look after my own fees and expenses. The whole thing just fell in my lap. Oh, I'm so glad I listened to your advice."

"I give it free to friends."

"Uncle William is kind in his way, but I can't turn to him. I often used to wish there was someone older I could turn to. And then you turned up."

A knight in shining armour? There was a new idea.

Her laugh suggested my breast-plate needed a brisk rub with metal polish. Still, a slightly rusty knight might have his uses.

"It will be nice to have you around until I'm twenty-one."

"What happens then?"

"That's when I come into my own money. I'll be able to do what I like."

A coal train from Fife was passing overhead: twenty carriages of black diamonds for the fire-places of Edinburgh. I counted every last one before I spoke again.

"Will that be nice for you?"

"I'll love it. Oh, I suppose Aunt Winnie does it for the best."

Grudging admission that the shakedown clothes, the local school, were good guardian precepts. Keep the capital intact. Don't encourage spendthrift ideas.

"But Noelle gets so much. Oh, I'll shop and shop. Buy and buy."

"You won't be long in gettting through it at that rate."

"No. There's plenty. I'm not sure how much. But enough to give me an income."

She displayed the same casual acceptance as Wilson had shown. I thought I really must get someone to leave me a bundle. It did such wonders for the future. Still, as there was no one on the family tree liable to leave more than the money for a plate of ham after the funeral, perhaps I should consider an alternative? Why the hell should Wilson be the only one to take the Dean's advice?

But suppose I didn't want a schoolgirl around my neck; not even one with expectations; not yet? Suppose I just wanted to keep her on ice, in case I ever needed that gilt edged commodity, a suitable wife?

A kid like her with few friends, her nightmare auntie, her indifferent cousins, she'd be a pushover for anyone with a kind word to say. From her own account, I was already on the way to being a knight errant of sorts. If I wanted to cultivate the role, she wouldn't know gratitude from love-in-a mist. And if, in the end, I did the noble thing, and rode off into the sunset, waving a selfless goodbye, there would be no harm done, and not a dry eye in the house.

I bought Connie more fizzy drinks, to celebrate my new role, then stood on the pedals of my bike to get us up the braes on our way home.

"I'm going to burp," she announced. "S'all your fault."

"I'm long suffering," I panted, my nose buried in her hair.

All knights, especially those with utility markings, suffered gladly in a good cause.

Although there were only quarter of the hands to get the work done, the harvest was finished a week early.

"What do we do now?" I asked Sandy.

"Ye'll can help at the tatties."

A parcel of land had been won back from the army at Easter. The crop of Nissen huts and gun emplacements, planted to protect the bridge, had been replaced with maincrop potatoes. The remark was bland, but his wink worried me. Matt also seemed amused.

"Too big a job for casual labour alone," Sandy explained further. "The howkers have been engaged. They'll be here in a couple o' days."

It happened that I was in the yard talking to Wilson and the two girls when the gang arrived, so we had a ring-side view. They came in a livestock lorry: thirty of them: mostly girls, with a few younger brothers for leavening. When the tailgate was let down, they rampaged into the yard, wild as a herd of mountain fillies. They were raven-haired and red-cheeked. They had coarse black stockings rolled above the knee, and chubby thighs, bare to the leer. They had wicked, laughing eyes with one thing in view: men.

They noticed Wilson right off: his height, his blond hair, his soft good looks. They made a set at him, screaming, swooning at his feet. Bobby soxerie was universal.

Word spread fast, and the yard filled with people come to see the show. Young Watson wandered up beside me. He nodded at Wilson in knowing sarcasm.

"He'll no' have come across the likes o' they before?"

"I doubt it. Nor have I."

"If that lot get the haud o' his prick, they'll leave it like an empty sausage skin. An' look. See the Noelle wan. She's no' sure what's goin' on either. She's wonderin' what she's been missin'."

His voice took on a speculative tone, and he looked at Noelle with a new attention.

Nymphet hands were goosing Wilson's crotch; plucking at his belt. Noelle's eyes were indeed wide. This was sex as she had never imagined it: hot, raw and lusty. The glittery look came over her face again. Just then, the agent and his daughter arrived in a war surplus Jeep, trailing a caravan. The howkers were called off and into some kind of order.

The daughter was a frank, vivacious girl, with a bust fit to bust, and knowing damn fine what she had on offer. She shooed the girls ahead of her, up the wooden steps to the barn loft.

"Will some of you men lend a hand?" she asked.

Young Watson snorted. He'd do not a damn thing he wasn't paid for. But Rab stepped forward, and I went to join him. We helped unload thirty immigrant trunks, and thirty folding beds. As we worked, the glances between Rab and the girl became obvious, and their hands touched too much to be sheer accident.

Despite their wildness, the girls soon had the loft in order: blankets and pillows stacked on the beds, army style; a trunk at the foot of each bed. I had expected the rank smell of the previous month's sweaty work and few baths. There was, instead, a scent of fresh straw, of soap, of hair, of young bodies, as attractive as any boudoir.

When Rab and I left, they were setting out combs and mirrors, crosses and rosaries: used to making a home under any old roof, a folk memory from the days of famine; of the trip to the Americas.

We started on the tatties next day. The girls dodged along the rows, behind the digger, as it undermined the clutches of potatoes. They bobbed and weaved, trunks horizontal to the ground, knees in a crouch, grabbing up the tubers in double handfuls and chucking them into wire baskets.

At the field-head, Whynie Deuchars and I bagged the potatoes at two hundred and twenty-four pounds dead-weight, then hefted them into contractors' lorries. It was the heaviest work I had ever done. I tore a nail out on the coarse sacking, and managed not to rupture myself.

The Watsons drove the tractors and they surpassed themselves with their invective. The Greigs in particular came in for abuse, the affair between Rab and the Irish girl, Siobahn, apparently the touch-paper.

"Imagine. Gaun' wi' a fuckin' pape."

In that strong, presbyterian countryside, a morning's horse ride to hear John Knox, it wasn't hard to scratch the covering from a bigot. And the brighter the affair burned, the more would young Watson have had them tied to the stake for heresy.

It was obvious that their love making was climactic: hectic faces, bruised lips, bitten necks. And that was what you could see. If it had simply been physical, I don't think it would have affected young Watson so much. He was in his element at the wholesome, wholesale houghmagandie on offer on all sides. Every guy in the district who had the notion and a john that would stand without a splint, gathered in the road junction to meet the girls when, washed and fed, freed from their murderous job, they poured out of the barn to click with whatever man they could.

I suspected what upset young Watson, was the happy exchange of looks between the couple; the frank avowal of love. I thought he was jealous.

Chapter 2

BY THE TIME I GOT BACK TO TOWN IN September, I had been out of circulation for three whole months. My Friday trips to the Northern General and the occasional brief visit to my folks, had been done at a blinkered canter, with no time for dawdling. So for a day or two, I breezed about the city, catching up on the social scene.

Noelle came up to town one day, with Connie for company. Wilson and I met them at the station, but at once he took his girl off: squire her about the shops; choose paints and brushes for her course; dream-plan their future dining-room from the window displays of the furniture shops.

Left to our own nefarious devices, I took Connie to visit the Athenaeum, the *bijou* theatre attached to the drama academy, and helped her spy out the land for her next year's campaign of deception. Then I took her to Copeland's where my mother's sister, my Aunt Effie, ran the lingerie department. Decent soul that she was, she stood the round-eyed kid a pair of filmy nylons.

"I'll keep them for special," she breathed. "Noelle pinches all my nice things, but I've got a place I can hide these."

Effie gave me a look that wondered where the hell I had dug up such a waif, and made it two pairs. Then she promoted the pair of us to a cost-price, slap-up lunch, courtesy of a mate of hers who ran the restaurant.

On the tram back to the station, I realized Connie had gone quiet.

"You all right?" I asked.

"Yes. It's just – I've had a great day. I'm so happy."

The vixen eyes were wide and vulnerable. I was notching up knightly points despite myself.

A couple of days later it was time to matriculate and I went to the Union. This time the greetings were hilarious, rude, familiar: the friendships strong. The September resits were over: the results known. Anatomy had claimed its victims. The flunks had been sent down: gone for good. The Dean's prediction was still being fulfilled. It made for sober gossip. Drew Alexander said, "D'you realize the number of people who've failed the course so far? And if you add in Jimmy Turner –"

Turner had fallen from a train: no glamorous Cock of the North, panting its way to London, but a piddling local on the Cathcart circle. It had severed his legs mid-thigh, just as effectively. He died of shock and haemorrhage.

"– and Robert McIntosh – "

McIntosh had perforated a duodenal ulcer while on holiday in South Uist. It had been a pinhole thing, causing minimal symptoms and a reluctance to call the doctor from twenty miles away. When he did get to hospital on a gale battered fishing boat, all the delays added up to a fatal procrastination. Peritonitis is even handed. It kills anyone who ignores it.

"– and Morris and Menzies and Annie Syme, it comes to twenty six."

We looked at each other in relief that we were still there. In celebration we flocked off to the surgical supply shop to kit ourselves out with tendon hammers and instruments to see in ears and eyes and stethoscopes. We let the white ear-pieces peep coyly from a pocket – let the common herd see and wonder – as we went on to choose textbooks for the year's degree subjects: pathology and materia medica. Then it was back to the Union for the big subject of debate: which clinics to attend?

Until then the Gilmorehill campus had contained us, but now we would spend little time there. The wards and out-patient departments of the city hospitals would be our main classrooms. Most people opted for the better known hospitals, but more than happy with my own experience at the Northern General and backed up by Malcolm Ritchie's notes, I persuaded Wilson and my A buddies to come out to the sticks with me. Minnie had also said she would join us, and, since junior clinics were in sixes, I preached for a convert to make up the numbers.

"What's so special about that old dump?" asked someone.

"The very fact that it is just that and hasn't got post-graduates and research fellows crawling all over it. By the time patients have had all those guys sticking fingers up their bums and taking off blood, they ain't going to be too enthusiastic over six junior students doing the same thing all over again."

"I'd like to join you."

Luke Kinseboya spoke in a polite Paul Robeson base.

"Only if you tell us how you knit your hair."

Luke's face had been slashed in boyhood, in accordance with some tribal custom. The wide cicatrice mocked our porridge and sporran couthiness. He fingered the marking and grinned at me.

"Sure. Just as soon as you've passed the initiation rites, you get the pattern."

On the first morning of term, the six of us met outside Cranston's tea-room and picture-house, and bought three-ha'penny rides to Maryhill. The other five looked dubious at the first sight of the big, grimy, Victorian pile, but I rallied the fainthearts. We had booked in at the medical clinic of Tommy Forrest, and I impressed the others with my intimate knowledge of dungeon shortcuts and twisty back stairs.

We found the teaching side room full of the latest aids to medical education: a blackboard on the wall and an array of wooden desks and chairs right out of Dotheboy's Hall.

"Haw, find seats, will you."

Tommy Forrest had come in the door behind us. He was a little guy with straight, fair hair, and an off-centre parting.

"Haw, all bright and shiny new, eh?" He let our sheepishness browse for a moment. "Nemmind, we're going to change all that. Now, let me remind you that the heart is a pump. First we're going to talk about one of the things that can make it go wrong, and what happens because of that. Then we shall go into the ward, and examine one that is in trouble."

He told us about mitral stenosis, a slow, progressive, intractable scarring of one of the heart valves, caused by rheumatic fever. Then he led us into the female ward. There were screens around a patient. We slipped behind them and ranged about a grey-haired woman propped up in bed. She was emaciated. There were patches of blue tinged blood vessels high on her cheeks. She breathed in great gasps that were hungry for life. Her thin body was shaken by the desperate pulsations of her failing heart.

"These young doctors have come to examine you, Mrs Boyd. They'll be very gentle and their hands will be nice and warm."

We sidled to the nearest radiator feeling foolish, but the irony had done its work.

"Put your hand here –"

We felt the slap of the heart against the inside of the chest, as it strained in pulsatile effort to overcome the obstruction.

"Listen there –"

We heard the harsh rasp of blood being forced through the thick, distorted valve flaps.

"Now, listen here–"

We heard the crackling sound of tiny air bubbles bursting through the fluids that were being dammed back in the lungs and drowning her.

Back in the side room, he explained the signifiance of these queer phenomena.

"She's dying, of course," he said breezily. "A week or two at most."

He went on to consider causes, prognosis, treatment. But I couldn't get my mind off the woman dying in public; patiently exhibiting herself so that I – we all – could use these signs and symptoms to fashion our new careers. The others, too, began to show signs of shock at this abrupt, workaday introduction to death at close quarters. They became restive, yawned, looked out of the window. Tommy Forrest nodded knowingly.

"Haw, you look as if you've had enough for a first morning. Coffee time, I think."

Ahead of students from the other clinics, we made a relieved rush to Pacitti's cafe. Right opposite the hospital, it was used to this sort of student invasion, and served gallons of coffee to short order. Minnie turned to me.

"You were so right, Neil. Six of us were more than enough to be pestering that poor woman. It was hard to see her so, and know nothing could be done."

Minnie had had a hard time over the summer. For all the encouragement she had spared for me, she had failed anatomy in June. She had spent the whole summer in her frowsy room, going over and over the coloured diagrams. Although she had passed at the second sitting a few weeks before, the constant fear of failure had taken it out of her, and the little nervous habits were more pronounced now.

It was clear she felt for the woman even more than I: the intrusion, the indignity, the objective contemplation of imminent death. But coffee and doughnuts proved good antidotes for such intimations of mortality. The blue shadows under her eyes seemed to lessen.

But it wasn't to last.

The second class of the morning was in a small auditorium in the hospital basement. Some forty of us clattered up the steps and sprawled at ease until the lecturer came in. Anything more like an absent minded professor you never did see: come to Jesus sandals, thinning hair cascading down to his collar, thick spectacle lenses mounted in a gold wire frame.

" So far in your careers," Salmond Aitchison began, "you have built up a knowledge of the body, and how it works in health. Now you must learn the workings of the men of death."

That subject again. It was the first intimation that from now on death would be with us after coffee breaks as well as before –and during lunch, and sleep, and cleaning our teeth, and making love, and mowing the lawn – and we'd better get used to its insistence.

"I hope to show you that in the very ways of death, there is a sombre beauty –"

Beauty on a mortuary slab? There was a new concept. I glanced around to see how the others were taking such an idea. Everyone was concentrating on him, fascinated. Except Minnie. Minnie was looking at the wall: and the blue smudges under her eyes had shaded to purple.

"Now, I want to introduce you to the concept of inflammation, the body's universal response to injury."

He leant towards us. Though his angels were black, he was evangelical in his earnestness.

Classes in pharmacology were held at two pm, back on the university campus. Students scrambled back from the cross town hospitals, eating on the run.

Professor FL Robertson was as flowery as the rose he always wore: shirt cuffs shot two inches clear; Glenurquhart check suits that would not have shamed Jack Buchanan; gleaming, black hair; a thin intelligent face.

"The doctor's bottle, ladies and gentlemen, is the coin of medicine. In return for histories, in exchange for sores laid bare, in an earnest of trust for confidences revealed, this token is given. It marks your esteem of the complaint. It is a measure of your interest in your patient. And the way it is given is at least as important as the medicine itself. In every such transaction, you, the doctor, must give of yourself. You will hear the exciting changes the past few years have brought, and of the vast promise that pharmacological chemistry holds for the future. But –"

There was the same wary, almost weary, look I had seen on the faces of the Dean and Boss McKenzie: a resultant of disappointments, of failures, of bitter experience.

"– Don't throw out the old remedies with the bath water. Not all at once. I've seen panaceas arrive – and fail. I've seen new drugs have disastrous effects. Worse than the disease they were meant to cure. Think. Would I give this to my first born? To my mother? Remember always the great medical precept – *primum non nocere.*"

For once Wilson's Latin was of use.

"What's that mean?" I asked.

"Whatever you do, you mustn't make the patient worse."

There was a new notion. I had thought doctors always made people better. Here was I, bursting to get on with a career of success, but it seemed it could only be learnt on the back of a brisk trade in mistakes.

"Now, I want you to consider this general classification of drugs."

He turned to the blackboard, shot his cuffs even further and started to write. Pens came out, notebooks opened, and we set off on another lesson in how to write as badly as a doctor should.

Chapter 3

THE SIX OF US MADE A GOOD GROUP. Alexander and Abercrombie were now firm buddies; Wilson and I had this funny friendship with our mixed up dependencies; and Luke took a quaint shine to Minnie.

She asked him to share our communal macaroni cheese one night, then we had a big post-prandial session on the sarcomata, a nasty breed of cancers. Wilson had bought himself a microscope from his grand-patrimony, a real student luxury, and we spent a couple of hours arguing; hammering out understanding from the stained slides. Minnie asked us to her room for coffee later. Luke found the home baking and the quiet domesticity to his liking, while the unobtrusive bible appealed to his mission school beginnings. Having found his way, he came quite often. He seemed to sense there was more to her vulnerability than her slight build. He towered over her: protective; handing her on and off trams; making sure she got a seat in the crowded cafe. She was always school-marmish with Wilson and me, but the role was reversed with Luke. It was clear she liked being looked after.

But as the term wore on; as we walked behind Tommy Forrest and his staff, learning the art of the physician; as, later in the morning, we went to study Salmond Aitchison's black religion; as in the afternoons Flower Robertson showed us what might be done to alleviate symptoms, it became apparent that all too often there was nothing to be done; that all the doctor could do was watch the inexorable approach of death.

This was really brought home to me a few weeks later when, at an eight-thirty a.m. mortuary call, we hung over the little, tiled balcony to see Salmond Aitchison draw the liver and lights and lessons to be learned, from Mrs Boyd.

It was one thing to take refuge in the flowers and tears and ceremony; to close the box and scatter a handful of earth on it. But it was another to watch the humanity gutted; the humours that had carried the ineffable forces of life sluiced away, without a vestige of soul or hint of meaning.

The city I loved, with its noise and bustle, its sheer jump for joy life, was full of people on their way to death. Whatever childish notion I had ever had, that I would find help for my chair-bound, marvellous father, died the implacable death of pathological fact. And it was clear that any benefit my Granny Aitken had, from the digitalis tablets she took to keep her old heart from racketing about, would soon be spent. I now had enough knowledge to recognize what the mechanisms of her death would be.

It seemed the only job a doctor could do for certain, was to pronounce life extinct.

The faint, blue mists of depression wraithed about us, looking for victims. As I looked around the whole year assembled in the materia medica lecture room, I realized there was no longer a schoolboy or girl face left. The cold, inevitable obverse of life that was to be our daily dole; that we could never escape from, was frosting us all.

This was not to be borne. The student ragging took on a more frantic edge; the drinking became heavier, as we sought a sanity-saving, schizoid outlook, that would cushion life from these daily lessons.

My own salvation was helped by three things. First was the example of the marvellous nurses I worked beside in the wards. Their guts, their cheeriness, set a target that was difficult to match. These kids were as deep into the heavy end of things as anyone. Perhaps the sobs in my neck, as I explored the subterannean grottoes of the hospital with a relay of lace-caps, weren't always of rapture?

Second, my visits to the farm were, for still unfathomed reasons, the most soothing thing in my life. The chemical signals of my progress in medicine – the smells of iodoform, paraldehyde, ether, acetone – I gave up with relief, and let the ancient reeks of decaying dung, fresh turned lea, and newly crushed grass pour into my system. And at night, I absolutely luxuriated in the tick of Matt's clock, as it slowed my hectic life to a more reasonable pace.

Third, my Friday night sessions in Boss McKenzie's firm, where the immediacy of surgery; the feeling of doing something, was an active, addictive antidote. After the episode with the severed hand tendons, Minty gave this an added boost.

"Time you gave up the Gate on Fridays. Come over to the wards instead, and stand behind me."

So, on Friday nights, I tagged on at Minty's elbow as the acute cases admitted from the Gate were seen and discussed on the big ward rounds.

Boss's firm ran four wards: two male, two female; one hundred beds nominal. It was a pint and quart deal, however, as no patient referred from a GP was ever turned away until Boss had seen him in person. There could be beds up the middle of the wards; beds in the corridor; beds in the sludges; even a bed in the residents' sitting room on one occasion: but no candidate for admission was ever refused.

More, the sub-specialties were in their infancy. A severe complicated fracture might warrant transfer to the orthopaedic wards; or a gouged eye, hanging from its stalk might be sent to the Eye Infirmary for expert care. But, in general, prudence fought a losing battle with surgical conceit, and hell mend the patient.

The standard bearer of this surgical hubris was Boss McKenzie. He, or his people would take on any damn thing, or he'd know the reason why.

The end result was that on Friday nights the four wards were full of a mix of road traffic injuries, fractures, burns; a slew of stab-holes, knife-slashes, and kicked in faces; an assortment of twisted bowels, torted testicles, blocked bowels, busted appendices, stoned kidneys, split spleens: any damn thing in the surgical index.

But what a table of learning to feast from. I kept my mouth shut, and looked and listened hard. To begin with, Boss ignored me, but when Minty pushed me to the front of the big, white-coated entourage, he would crook his finger at me.

"C'mere, sonny. Palpate that abdomen – that rectum – that gall bladder. Don't take all bloody night about it. What d'you feel? Eh? Eh? Right."

Or more often wrong. He would smack my hand away in disgust.

"For God's sake, Minty. Take this ignoramus somewhere, and tell him about it. Don't let him near me again until he knows it backwards."

Minty would cough his Capstan chuckle, and steer me to a blackboard or, if the opportunity was right, the snug of the Maryhill Harrier, next door to Pacitti's, where he would draw me diagrams in carefully spilled beer, and fill my despairing soul with encouragement.

"You're getting on well with Boss. He likes people who can stand the heat."

"I've noticed."

The reward for riding those red rages was to be given lists of the more interesting cases. That suited Bobby Mair and Minty. They wanted to get their hands on as much as possible early in their surgical career.

Richards and McFarlane were more senior, and could expect wards of their own, in due course. They kept their faces shut, and got on with what they were given.

But Paul Baillie was different. By his seniority, he should have had his own firm long ago, and his persistent failure to attain this prize stained his life with spleen. He raged in a grin of pained silence when Boss was holding court; and when Boss wasn't there, he fulminated with impotent threats.

"Boss seems a bit sore on Baillie?" I asked Minty.

"Piddling Paul? He can't operate to save his life."

Minty's own cheery competence allowed such a comment.

"Boss knows it. Uncle Tom Cobley knows it. Worst of all, Paul himself knows it. Degrees by the barrowload. And hands that can hardly tie shoelaces. No aptitude for operative surgery. Physical? Psychological? Who knows? But when the blood is spurting, he gets into the most God-awful shambles. Can't trust him in a fix. You watch him and learn what not to do." He grinned in frank, black humour. "I'll watch you, and see if you'll ever be any good."

My apprenticeship was under strict surveillance.

Later on receiving nights, I wangled myself into the big double theatre, and stood gowned and masked to disguise my lack of knowledge. I absorbed the grinding work-load, the lack of sleep, as case after case was wheeled in. Most times I was left to hump stretchers and wheel trolleys, but there were times when Minty let me put on a pair of gloves, stand across the table from him, and showed me how to open an abdomen. I watched and watched; learned and learned.

I soon saw that Minty's dismissal of Paul's surgical technique was well earned. Even to my novice eye, the others ranged from sound ability to Boss's own, supreme surgical flair.

But Piddling Paul was in a pit of his own digging.

Always an untidy worker, he became worse under stress. He threw forceps on the floor, complained the scalpel blade was blunt, or this or that instrument wasn't out. He would start to do things one way, then change his mind. His soubriquet was self-endowed. He had one response to trouble – he piddled about.

Scrub nurses worked with him in hostile silence, which was the more noticeable for the giggles and camaraderie at the other table. Everyone around him became emotionally drained.

I noticed that Boss kept an eye on Baillie's results. And as promised, Minty kept an eye on me.

Near Christmas, Minty said, "Meet me in the Horseshoe bar. Monday. Pies 'n' pints on me while we talk. Cut a class if need be."

I wasn't sure what he had in mind, but it sounded good. The Horseshoe was one of the great Glasgow howffs, full of fag-loving, beer loving, sausage-and-mash-loving men, with never a woman to be seen. Minty was already at a table, with beer in place, when I got there.

"Gee, Minty. This is great."

"Right. Down to cases. From some things you've said and your general attitude, it seems you fancy taking up the knife in a serious way?"

"If that's not too pretentious at my stage."

"Quite the opposite. That's what I want to tell you. I think you have a good pair of hands and the right personality. Make a surgeon, if you work at it. Boss agrees."

I stared at him in disbelief. Boss agreed? I thought he barely noticed me.

"Point is, if you are serious, you should start planning your career now."

"Now!" I yelped. I was all for compliments: very massaging to the ego. But this was pushing lady luck too far, surely?

"Yup. I wasted a lot of time." His tone told of real regret. "Most people do. After they graduate, they take the foot off the pedal. Fart about. Ship's surgeon on a boat to Japan. A year's GP in Barra. Broaden the mind and all that. 'S load of shit. "You have to stamp surgeon all over you from now on. Go for the class prizes. Give papers at the Medico-Chirurgical Society, especially if any of the profs are to be there."

"Isn't that a bit brown nose?"

"Shit right up to the sinuses. But that's what it takes. And you should aim for more distinctions. Especially, you should go for the Macewen."

Named after one of Glasgow's sons who became a world authority, this was the top undergraduate prize in surgery.

"Then, you must get your fellowship in view from now on."

I couldn't take this all in. But Minty was dead serious. And, so far, he had been a marvellous tutor: runners at Lanark; which nurses would go; hospital gossip. But most of all, he knew surgery: the books, the practicalities, the politics.

"You aim for your primary six months after you qualify. The big problem is, once again, anatomy. Most guys let it go. By the time they qualify, they've forgotten the lot. Have to go back to the beginning. The trick is to keep it up."

My psychic accountant got out his cash ruled ledger.

"How long have you been qualified, Minty?"

"Seven years. Three more until I make consultant."

"Ten years," I said, as in eternity.

"But you can cut that by three, if you do what I tell you. Now, about the final fellowship exam. Most guys do it on the hoof. Work in the wards by day. Read at night. Tired as buggery. Can't take it in. If I had to do it all again, I'd start a piggy bank. When I'd done enough post-graduate work, say two, two'n'a half years, I'd take six months off. Sit on my arse. And read. Journals. Archives. Textbooks. Nine to five with half an hour for grub. Same as any office worker. Nights you swim. Walk. Go on the bones. Next morning, back to work, nice and fresh."

I was in a chariot of new ideas, and Minty was whipping the horses. But he was entering me in a race I could never run. As soon as I'd framed my scroll, I'd have to start paying back some of the debt I owed Maisie and Jock.

"Minty, I could never afford that."

"Wrong attitude. Starve. Let your bum out to the Royal Marines. Anything. This is a hard dug nugget of advice. One last thing. You can pass an undergraduate exam on reasonable knowledge and a little luck. Final fellowship's different. You're expected to talk to the examiners on their own level. Argue your corner. 'F you come up against a man whose ideas are different, you can be in trouble. You have to get papers and examiners to suit you. You must accept that even the best candidates can fail once, even twice, before it comes right."

That would make me twenty-six, and I still wouldn't have a penny in the bank. The guy with the cash ledger shoved his figures in front of me again. If I graduated at twenty-two, that would give me three years to set aside a war chest of, say, two hundred and fifty quid for six months digs, food and exam fees. Where could I ever get money like that?

"I had never thought of any of this, Minty."

"Most undergraduates don't. That's why I'm taking the trouble to tell you."

"I appreciate that. Another pint?"

"No. I'm operating at two. I'll pee all over the theatre."

"It's on the slate then."

"Bribery. Just what I like. Listen, you're late for your lecture anyhow. Whyn't you come and we'll see what's making this girl's tummy sore?"

Later, as I held retractors for Minty to ease an ovarian cyst the size of an orange out of the pelvis, the little man with the cash book came back with an idea.

When I was twenty-five, Connie would be twenty one.

Chapter 4

ONE EVENING, SOME WEEKS BEFORE MY TALK with Minty, I was sprawled on our decrepit couch reading about the effect of cold agglutinins in pneumococcal pneumonia, when Wilson said, "This December is Noelle's eighteenth birthday. I'd like to take her to the Christmas ball in the Union. Trouble is, I don't know where she'd stay. D'you suppose Minnie would put her up?"

"Yeah. I suppose she might."

"I could bring a camp bed from home," he persisted.

I knew him. There was more to this conversation than just a place to kip. I shut the book. The pneumococci were safe for another night.

"I'm sure Minnie would make a most acceptable chaperon, if that's the opinion you're looking for. I'm sure she would write to Noelle's mother, all very proper and correct."

"It would be even better if Connie came along. You wouldn't like to invite her?"

I laughed out loud. "You're a cool bugger, you are. No. I would not like to ask her. She can't dance anyhow."

"I know. But Noelle's been teaching her. And there's a hop in the village the week-end after next. Noel will be home, and he's taking Sheila Fullarton. We could go together, and you could coach Connie a bit more."

"You've been conniving at this, you sly bugger. Haven't you?"

He grinned with unashamed complicity.

"Well, I'll think about it," I said, seemingly thankless as a churl.

But, I danced a little ball in my scheming brain. After all, the kid never got out. As a gesture of disinterested courtliness, it couldn't be beaten. When the ball was over, I would bow modestly, and put any gratitude on hold. The fact that there was nothing to beat compound interest on unclaimed obligation as an emotional IOU, was a mere coincidence.

That Saturday, after tea, I went to the scullery window of the Armstrong house. It was thick barred against burglars, but behind them, morose and alone in the suds and steam, Connie was the one who couldn't get out. I scrabbled at the glass, and she slid the window up.

"Hi, kid. I hear you've been practising for a ball?"

"Noelle says I might –that you –"

She looked at me in sullen suspicion.

"No maybes about it. Come to the hop next week. We'll put in a bit of practice."

I did a twinkle toes in the gravel, holding an imaginary waist. She looked tempted, but was still suspicious.

"Why me?"

Why her indeed? I mustn't be patronizing, nor hurtful, nor above all, let any hint of my postulated duplicity show.

"We're pals, aren't we. Conspirators. Besides, we can't let the other four have all the fun."

A small dawn of hope rose in her face.

"You mean it?"

"Trust the older man in your life."

I had scored right on her unsuspecting heart. She beamed. I should have felt pleased with myself, but my self-congratulation had a sour taste.

The following Saturday, Wilson and I presented ourselves in the Armstrongs' hallway. The girls hadn't yet learned the joys of keeping a man waiting and were already standing buttoned into coats: hair under chiffon scarves.

"Daddy is going to run us down, but we'll have to walk home," explained Noelle. "They like to be in bed by ten."

A fruity contralto floated through from the sitting room.

"These girls must be home no later than eleven."

"Mummy," wheedled Noelle, "if we're walking home, that means we must leave by half-past ten."

"Oh, very well. But no later than eleven-thirty."

Whatever else, respectable girls had to be bolted and barred beyond temptation before the Sabbath chimed.

The dance was being run by the British Legion. The crowd was as varied in texture as a slice of salami: utility dresses and demob suits; bell-bottomed AB's from Port Edgar and blue serge WRAAF's from

Turnberry; farmers with big hands and their wives with hot tonged waves in their hair; slicked back spivs with their bottled gold dolls; guys on the make, wallflowers on the wilt.

The Masonic Hall venue had a pine-knot and splinter floor; an array of bent-wood chairs against the wall and a big eye painted on the wall, to see things didn't get out of hand. The three piece band was stomping at the Savoy, when the girls came out of the cloak-room.

Noelle and Sheila had been at this sort of thing before. They exuded a practised attraction that shone across the hall like bee purple.

But what of Connie, my date for the night; my wild card for a suitable future?

She had done her best with a gingham check dress in brown and white. It had a white, button down collar, but under this she had run a broad yellow ribbon, and tied it in a showy bow at the neck. She had complemented this with a similar bow in her hair. She set off the outfit with a pair of black, glace pumps, and a pair of her treasured nylons.

From the door of the cloakroom, she looked at me for approval. So far as she knew, I was a make-do partner for a couple of dance dates only. But I also knew I was her first date of any kind; the one man in her perspective right then. How I reacted would be life and death for her. It wasn't difficult. She rated an alpha plus for being herself; not taking a silly shot at sophistication.

"You look great," I said, and she actually blushed.

She had a good sense of rhythm, and after a couple of rounds of trampletoes, we slid into a partnership that blended well.

"Hey. Thought you couldn't dance. You're a natural."

She didn't quite flower in my arms, but she certainly came into bud, one I would have no difficulty picking, if I ever needed.

Odd times we boys swapped partners.

Sheila was a bright, no-nonsense, farmer miss, with a first-hand knowledge of bulls and what their balls were for. No amount of conniving would get her into the shrubbery, unless she was good and willing. But if Noel ever did get her under the laurels, I guessed he would find her enthusiastic and innovative. She danced well, and I liked her.

Bur partnering Noelle was like having chewing gum on my shoes. She was a regulation dancer: no imagination. I could sense her counting under her breath. She clung to my upper arm with a nail-sharp, pincers nip of her fingers.

"You and Scoular. You're great friends?"

I was being sounded out for loyalty? I laid my ears back.

"Yup. Good ole buddy buddys."

She searched my face for sarcasm, but bland dissimualtion was another of my talents.

"Yes. I can imagine. What, with sharing his flat and everything."

I had suspected her of steely qualities, but this nick with the stiletto took my breath away.

"You have asked her to the ball?"

Not Connie, I noted. Her. There was only one lady in the company, and she wanted the lower orders to know their places.

"Yaw. Should be a jolly night."

She missed a step.

"Sorry," I said, obsequious as a flunkey. "My fault."

She showed her little teeth at me, nodding in agreement; pleased with my attitude.

"It's a pity you couldn't take up with her. Regular, I mean. Mummy thinks our foursome outings are very nice. And it would be such a help to Scoular and me."

A bed in Wilson's attic was worth just so much. I was pondering the effect of lowering her pretty little knickers and skelping her arse for all to see, when the dance ended and a happier solution appeared. Someone tapped my shoulder.

It was young Watson, breathing whisky fumes like a pot-still on over-time. He was in full dancing regalia, a three piece suit of brightest blue. New before the war, it had Oxford bags that covered his shoes and a double-breasted waistcoat with tiny lapels.

The forty-nine shilling tailors had done him proud.

I had noticed him smoochy dancing: fondling bums, nuzzling necks. Now he was going to dance with the Major's daughter. Show her. Show every bugger in the hall.

"Dance?"

There was no title; no servility ; no request. This was a challenge.

As the daughter of the biggest landowner around, she had to be seen to be democratic, but from the look she gave him, I had the notion this was no condescension to the plebs.

I went back to Wilson. "Lost your girl, I'm afraid."

He looked over at them, surprised. Then he shrugged his shoulders. Position had its duties.

"Like to sit this one out?" I asked Connie.

"Oh, yes. I've not sat down all night."

I smiled at her innocence. It was a shame it always had to die.

In the propriety of dress-kilted gatherings, the eightsome reel is a lively affair, yet ordered; the figures of eight weaving in decorous correctness. At country hops, the footwear stamps the floor, the dust rises, and the intricate patterns are converted to arm locked swirls, the man using the girl as ballast to make her sail faster and faster. The 'hoochs' take on a quaver of danger.

Young Watson birled Noelle around faster, wilder, than anyone had ever seen. Her face took on that glittery look, and her eyes dared him more. There was not a hint of fear.

"Damn fool," muttered Wilson. "If they take a spill at that speed, she'll break something."

The only danger he could see was physical.

I shook my head at Connie.

"There's trouble brewing in the sheiling tonight, young missy. Don't say I didn't tell you."

She didn't understand what I was talking about, but she laughed anyway, happy to be there in the music and noise.

At the interval, we fetched the girls lemonade and ices. Seeing them settled in a clam of gossip and giggles, with Noel to dance attention, Wilson and I eased off to the gents. This white-washed loo, scented with chloride of lime, was the scene of a minor flood. Cigarette butts had choked the drain and the stallion, beery waters from a hundred lusty young men overflowed the fireclay channel, and made a plashing puddle on the wooden floor, before dribbling to earth through cracks in the floorboards.

Wilson made a little *moue* of distaste, and turned into one of the WC compartments. But I kept my place in the line of men: hell, my shoes were waterproof.

When I took my stand, I found myself beside young Watson. By that time, he was at the staggery stage. He had his forehead against the cool, tiled wall; his feet well splayed for balance and was spraying his peeping toecaps with studied concentration. He swivelled his eyes at me.

"S'you, then," he said, in vast good humour.

"Ah-huh," I fawned in agreement: anything to keep in his good books.

"Yuir big pal. He's wi' the Major's dochter again?"

He rolled his eyes to indicate Wilson somewhere out of earshot.

"Ah-huh."

Answer rhetorical questions all night, so I would, if it kept him happy. He dropped his voice to a stage whisper you could have heard in Falkirk.

"Ah've aye fancied a wee bit o' big hoose cunt, and yon's gaun tae be the fastest wee ride in the Lothians," he winked at me in sozzled solemnity. "There's been naebody there yet."

He affirmed this with the knowing certainty of the whoremaster.

Now, I had known exponents of the casual rodger all my days in Faifley: quick stand men who had barely time for a word of thanks afterwards, but young Watson was in a class of his own. A natural boaster, he was for ever cock-crowing on his midden. You couldn't believe half he said. But his sexual exploits were different. He retailed these with the studied understatement of the true connoisseur. With him in a haystack or under a hedge, any furry fanny would have the same chance as a rabbit with a stoat. This opinion was going to be interesting.

"Yuir big china? He isnae up tae it. Too bluiddy much the gentleman. But when she does go – oh, ho. By the Christ!" He waggled his head, suddenly incoherent at the fornication that would be let loose in the land.

Any further sharing of girlish confidences was cut short by Wilson. He had got his balls back in his cotton shorts and, no doubt remembering his previous fiasco with young Watson, his dander well up. I was zipping up my fly, ready to leave before my shoes floated off without me, when he splashed out of the privy, and thumped young Watson on the shoulder.

"If I ever hear you talk about my girl like that again, you'll answer to me for it."

Young Watson staggered, holding the wall. He weaved as he stood. Even in that state however, he recognized the corn. Wilson was being noble by his lights, but it came out like Victorian melodrama.

"By the Christ. Touch me, wid ye." His slurred tone was wondering. "Ya fancy, big, hooer's bastard. Wan o' they days I'll pey ye back for that. He stuck his face forward, his beaky nose predatory. "An' as for yer wee tart, ask him."

He nodded at me in boozy conspiracy, then his legs gave way and he sat down with a splash.

"By the Chris'," he shook his head in more wonder.

"For the love of God," I urged Wilson, "let's get the hell out of here."

Wilson glanced down at young Watson in his best, red-blooded, blue-blooded way. He had issued a challenge and been refused. His honour had been restored.

"Sure," he said, and paddled confidently to the door. He was in a great mood for the rest of the dance.

Walking home that night, we were in pairs, Wilson and Noelle trailing far behind. I said. "Now , young lady. I'd be honoured to take you to the Christmas ball."

"You're not just being kind?"

"What's wrong with kind?" The white knights of this world were invariably kind. "But, we're chums as well, aren't we. I'll teach you some more fancy steps. And what a girl shouldn't drink. We'll meet some people. Have a few laughs."

We had reached the house. The porch light had been left on. She looked at me then.

"I'd like that."

For a moment I wasn't sure what I had done. Then the awkward, shy uncertainty disappeared. She stepped forward and kissed me on the lips. This time, sexuality flared between us, like lightning in a Leyden jar. It would have been so easy to close the circuit; keep the electricity coursing. But that wasn't the game-plan. I let it earth into friendly neutrality by taking her latch key and letting us in.

We went to make cocoa. Connie seemed happy; hummed a snatch of 'Stardust'.

Me? I was beginning to realize that, in time, all good scatologists got used to the smell.

Chapter 5

MINNIE DID WRITE TO NOELLE'S MOTHER FOR US. Dignified the letter was, with promises of locks on the door, and propriety to make the Vestal virgins jealous.

Mama graciously allowed herself to be persuaded. I thought she would have made up to a bordello madame, if it would have furthered her petite darling's social future, and further cook Wilson's willing goose.

Wilson tricked out our flat in streamers, and shiny balls and red-berried holly all the way from the manse garden and helped Minnie turn her small bedroom into a squashed seraglio of camp beds. To complete his grand design, however, he wanted a present for Noelle: something special for that eighteenth birthday. After classes one day, he hauled me off to a jeweller's shop in Candleriggs.

"Come and see what you think?"

The owner was a little, old Jew: benevolent; black cuffs from wrist to elbow. He beamed at seeing Wilson again.

"My young man. You've come back. See, I saved it for you as I promised."

He kept his treasures in tiers of glass fronted cases. He rifled one of these, and brought a black, velvet covered tray to the counter. From it he lifted a pendant. It was of filligree gold, set with pale, sparkling aquamarines. It was Noelle to the life: sparkling, showy, lacking the quality of diamonds. I raised my hands, surrendering to his taste.

"That will suit her perfectly," I was able to say with complete conviction.

Wilson was pleased with me, and with the old man. But most of all he was pleased with himself. I could sense the sort of scene he was planning.

While he was waiting for the bauble to be wrapped, I poked about, peering in the cases. My eye was taken by a necklace. It was as different from Wilson's gift as you could get.

Scotch pebbles are all greens, browns and russets. Usually they are cut flat, polished to a gloss, and set in silver as ornaments to wear with tweeds or a kilt. These stones were rough-cut, chunky and strung to form a heavy necklet. It was unpretentious, yet strong and distinctive. It would set off Connie's gypsy skin, her vixen eyes, her peasant build.

Next afternoon, my mind wouldn't settle to the sedative properties of the barbiturates and later I sneaked back to the shop.

"I was here yesterday with a friend. I noticed something. I wondered if I could have a closer look at it?"

"Yes. I remember you. Show me where."

He brought the necklace out. It looked even better close up.

"It's nice, isn't it?" I said.

I liked to make my own decisions, but I was in strange territory. Even a profit-oriented opinion would be a help. But there was no mistaking the sincerity of the old man, as he fondled the stones.

"I've never seen its like before. Yes son, it's really fine."

"The other guy. The pendant was for a birthday. This is –"

What was it? Ground bait from a knight whose notions of honour were dubious? A hooked lure that could be reeled in later?

But the old man had a way out for my conscience.

"An unbirthday present?"

I laughed in sheer relief: absolution straight out of Lewis Carroll. I paid him several acres of singled turnips, he made a profit and I felt better than I might have: a bargain whichever way you looked at it.

The ball created great interest in the Greig household and Agnes in particular was curious.

"The wee one. You're eh – you're no' goin' oot wi' her?"

Walking out was serious stuff with Agnes.

"No. No," I laughed warily. Had my knight's move been rumbled?

"It's just that she doesn't seem to get much fun. We're just making up the party."

"She's awfu' young, you know. Much younger than yon other one."

"Agnes, you don't need to draw me pictures."

But she was merely boxing the women's corner. She nodded, satisfied. I could be trusted to do the decent thing. I wished I had the same trust in me.

On the day, Wilson and I and the girls were chauffeured to Dalmeny station in a style I was getting to like. Some illegal clothing coupons had yielded a blue dress for Noelle, with a cape and cowl to match: little blue riding hood. It was all very fetching, and didn't she know it. Aunt Winnie had released the purse strings for Connie as well, though the tweed suit was thoroughly sensible. It would do for church and special occasions, before settling to years of workaday use. The guardian ethic rode hard. Still, the tweed was in bold autumnal checks that enhanced her colouring.

"Nice," I complimented and she squeezed my arm.

I hadn't expected to enjoy the occasion too much. Wilson's conniving had made it lack spontaneity, but the girls' bubbling excitement was catching, and we piled out on to the platform in a fizz of laughter. There was a bit of a crush to get out, the others got a step or two in front of me, and I found myself walking beside the woman I had helped with the parcel. I had noticed her once or twice before, getting on or off the Fife train, but her reaction on the Richter scale of recognition had been the merest flicker: a quick glance, then away.

That afternoon she gave me the same minimal nod of acknowledgement, but suddenly it wasn't enough. I had to make some gesture that would reach through the sad mask; include her in our fun.

"They'll be talking about us if we go on meeting like this," I quipped. I would never write gags for Tommy Handley, but it was the best I could do at short notice.

For the second time in our railway-starred lives we looked full at one another.

At first she seemed startled, then she smiled. It wasn't much: a slight relaxing of the mouth from the thin, grim trap of self-containment behind which she hid her feelings. But it also flowed from the eyes. They crinkled into laugh lines that were there from long ago, and her tragedy took on a new dimension. I grinned back and hurried to catch the others.

Minnie met us at her door with all the presence of a professional duenna.

"Put the cases down, boys. We're going to have tea, and get to know one another. Come back at six o'clock," she ordered.

Wilson and I were shut out on a gale of giggles and *bonne femmerie*. No matter the stern face of the turnkey, behind closed doors, they were all girls together.

The twice-a-week option on a tanner-in-the-meter bath had been exercised by Minnie for the girls, so Wilson and I did what we could for our sweaty bits with a sponge and a big, enamel basin. Wilson donned a splendid, double-breasted tux which shouted black market, while I tried on the shiny dinner suit I had hired. We paraded in front of the mirror like bashful penguins.

Wilson made a thing of putting the leather pendant case into his inside pocket and patted it in satisfaction. I slipped the Scotch pebble necklet into my folded handkerchief and kept the fact to myself.

When we knocked at Minnie's door, it was opened by Luke, napkin over his arm.

"Good evening, gentlemen. This way please."

Our surprise grew to wonder at the sight of Minnie's living room. She had a table set for a pre-ball supper. Then the door to the bedroom opened. There was a glimpse of a riot of discarded clothes, and a fragrant fall-out of talcum powder, as Minnie shooed the girls before her.

It was my first experience of ladies in full ball regalia. The dresses were surprising enough, lending years and sophistication at first glance, but nothing had prepared me for the enhancement of every female attraction: the promise of half-contained breasts; the high-lit eyes; the parted, reddened lips; the fashionably dressed hair. Then I remembered women had been at this game since civilization began: what did I expect?

Devious white knights weren't the only pieces with moves on the board.

What the hell? I would enjoy tonight. I went to Connie.

"You look lovely," I said, once again with absolute sincerity. No doubt the dress was make do and mend, like everything else she had, but for once the image transcended the reality. Her eyes positively glowed at my compliment.

The supper was short on haunches of venison and boars' heads, but Minnie had worked wonders with her cooker on the landing. We had a cold supper which showed the Scottish Women's Rural Institute at its very best.

The girls were allowed a little wine, and a thimbleful of sweet liqueur. Minnie's regime for growing up was beautifully crafted. Then, the table cleared of all but glasses and coffee cups, Wilson simply couldn't resist the audience. He drew the jewel case from his pocket. "Happy birthday, darling."

Endearments come hard north of Carter Bar, and this one had a manufactured sound. But the scene was enough to draw a little murmur of approbation from the assembled company, and the annointed pair looked happy with themselves and each other.

I glanced at Connie. I wouldn't call it envy: more an acceptance. I touched the necklace in my pocket, but that was to be a transaction for two.

It was time to go then. I took both of Minnie's hands, turned them up and kissed the palms.

"Minnie. How can we thank you? Are you doing something nice, later?" I asked to include her in the ball spirit. " Going out somewhere?"

"I – uh – Luke – uh – we –" The plural pronoun hung in the air. "– There's all the tidying up to do."

Minnie was the best kind of presbyterian Christian, right up there with the twelve apostles. Equivocation was as foreign to her as anaphylactic protein. Her face went white with the reaction of being less than frank.

I rushed in with a babbleful of inanities to cover my gaffe.

"You mustn't mind if we rush off now. We want to get there early. You've been an absolute pet."

The irises of Minnie's eyes flared open in relief. Her taut little frame relaxed in the bliss of sharing her secret with someone she could trust.

I turned to Wilson, almost snarling. God keep his big foot out of his mouth.

I needn't have worried. He was head over heels in the misty romance he was creating for himself that night.

"Oh, yes. Thank you, Minnie. The supper was very nice. You must have – ah – gone to a lot of trouble."

The afterthought trailed after like a guard's van, with no emotional momentum of its own. I don't think it registered that Luke was still in the flat.

The ball was a genteel affair, with a lot of the professors on show; lads on their best behaviour; and a selection of girls you could take home to meet mummy.

I wondered if Maisie would like Connie. I thought she would.

"Hope you've been practising," I grumped, as we took to the sprung floor. "Keep off my toes this time."

"Huh," she said in frank disdain.

As we slid into the beat of an impeccable, eight piece, swing band, I had to admit her confidence was well founded. She improved by the step. I held her away from me, and nodded.

"Not bad. Not bad at all."

Gunned by a few teaspoons of alcohol and a pint of adrenalin, she laughed: deep, happy, full of herself.

"Told you so."

The place was full of medicals, and we didn't stick exclusively with Wilson and Noelle. They had gone off to chat to some other people, and Connie and I were sitting alone when I noticed Johnny Newton. He was the babe of the class, a fresh-faced, blond, effortless genius, whose one aim in life was to get it in. Since his freshman days, he had squired a stream of what he hoped were lay me down Lolas, but had been condemned by his babyish good looks to unremitting failure. That night his partner was a certified bang by the name of Norah Naysmith. A well cantered lady in the naughty stakes, she had become notorious over several annual intakes of medicals, and on a night like that she was as welcome as typhoid Mary in a pump room. All over the shop, red-faced guys gulped and turned their backs.

Forlorn, and looking for company, Johnny tried us.

"Hi, Neil. Can we sit here? This is Norah."

"Sure. Come and join us."

The girls took to one another in the attraction of opposites. They got their heads together, and tossed the tosh around like confetti in a breeze. Then Norah went to powder something and Johnny did his nice young man thing: asked Connie to dance. I watched them, and it was clear from their animated talk they had hit it off well. The clarinet tootled a final arabesque; the maestro said "That's all for now folks" and the band dissonated into a thirty minute interval. A happy-looking Johnny piloted Connie back to the table. He turned to her.

"I did enjoy that. Maybe later –"

I raised an eyebrow at him.

"Here's your date."

Norah arrived and took his arm. His pleased look sickened a fraction. "Coming to supper?"

"We'll be down in a minute."

"Keep a place for you, then."

"I think you've made a conquest," I jealoused, as Johnny went off.

"I think so too."

"Hussy. And you'll be hungry again, I suppose?"

"Yup."

There was no shame to this strapping miss.

"Before we go."

She was amazed. There was grub to be had, the hall was emptying fast and I was waxing with the words. I pulled out my handkerchief and slid it over to her.

"In my circle, we don't go much on birthdays. Unbirthdays are the thing. This is to celebrate yours."

She took the handkerchief with unaffected surprise: laughing. She expected – what? A kewpie doll for a keepsake? A trick snake on a spring to scare her? She undid the folds.

The laughter drained from her face, the smile held in place by force of will, until she assessed this new phenomenon. There was so much to growing up. At last she looked up at me.

"It's –" She stopped.

"Don't you like it?"

"Like it? Like doesn't begin to say. My colouring. And I know I'm no sylph. It matches everything about me. It's so – thoughtful. I've never had anything that matters so much since Daddy gave me this ring."

She wore a silver pinkie ring which had her initial as a signet. There were no tears, only a sad-happy smile of recollection.

"There you are, then. Present from me in his place. Memento of your first ball. Put it in your purse. Now come and feed your insatiable little face."

There was a back stair down to the buffet: dark; full of couples on the steps, necking, swapping yule-tide gropes.

"Watch you don't stand on something soft," I warned and went ahead, shifting bodies out of the way. Halfway down, still holding my hand, she stopped. She pulled me back beside her and pressed into me, head up, lips open: inexpert, but willing.

"Thank you. Oh, so thank you. I'll put it in my secret place. Keep it for special occasions."

The kiss was almost solemn, if you can imagine such a thing and it went on for a long time. There was nothing demanding on either side, but the gentle inter-mingling of saliva was as intimate as any other form of intercourse. We parted lips on a simple, yet deep, emotion I had never known before.

God Almighty. She did trust me, just as much as she said. My silver shield turned black with shame.

When we got to the buffet, Johnny and Norah were by the window. He stood up waving.

"Here."

Over the ice-cream I watched him. He was smitten all right and Connie ignored him with just the right amount of arch inattention.

Presents from older men, and now a stricken beau in her net. No wonder she was looking so terrific.

"Smashing girl you've got," he said later.

"Not really my girl, young John. She's Wilson's girl's cousin. I'm just being nice about things."

"No strings?" he sounded disbelieving. Well, he wouldn't understand about suitable partners, and two hundred and fifty quid, and trust. I know I didn't.

"No. But she's not the kind of bint you usually look for."

I bunched a fist, and shoved the knuckles under his nose.

"I warn you, I'm in *loco parentis*. Toughest papa you'll ever meet. Hands off. Prick pointing at the ground."

"Oh, no. Not that. I mean, she's really nice."

He wangled another dance later. Norah and I sat it out, watching them.

"Think we've got a case?" she asked.

I looked at her, uncertain. But she was speaking for both of us, neither bitter nor jealous: merely philosophical. We smiled at each other. It was barely *nostalgie de la boue*, but we both knew we had missed something in life.

I watched the romance budding in front of me quite happily. Other than his craze to lose his virginity, Johnny was a nice guy. When Connie came up to town next year, someone like him might be very nice for her. He would never be a problem to me if I did want to ride into the sunset with her on my saddle. In the meantime, it would save me becoming more involved in the dangerous emotion of that kiss. In the further meantime, I might even win a football pool.

BOOK FIVE

Chapter 1

HALFWAY THROUGH THE EASTER TERM, Wilson realized we were also halfway through the course.

"In two'n'a half years, we'll have qualified," he said. "If all goes well," he added reverently.

The Dean's augury had, once again, come true only the week before. Flower Robertson was expanding on the use of gold in rheumatoid arthritis. He had his back to the class, writing on the board, when a guy called Jackie Gillon shot to his feet, with a bang of his wooden seat. A little titter from the class anticipated some kind of student jape, though no one could imagine what, for Jackie was as sober a guy as you could meet on a week's retreat in a monastery.

Flower turned in surprise. He was an excellent, respected lecturer, and had little trouble with student classes.

"Yes?"

Jackie stretched his right arm above his head, and shook a forefinger of doom at heaven.

"God. God has spoken to me."

The buzz was stilled by a strange, strident quality in his tone.

"I have heard His voice."

I glanced at Flower, to see how he was taking this strange outburst. His face was a study of immediate comprehension and, of all unexpected things, pity.

"See."

The whole class craned this way and that, to miss nothing of this bizarre scene.

"See."

Jackie Gillon took a wallet from his inside pocket. He fumbled with the contents and pulled them out, one by one: a train season ticket, return journeys in the daily lessons of becoming a doctor; two pound notes, currency reserves against a run on the bank; a syllabus for the Medico-chirurgical Society, extra-curricular lectures with a bit of fun thrown in; a programme for the Cecilian Society, gentle music to soothe his soul.

But there was nothing there to soothe his mind. It crumpled as we watched. His experience of God was replaced by total incomprehension of the things in his wallet. He studied the documents in turn, then let them fall, scattering around him in imitation of his wits.

Flower was grave; concerned; kind. He raced up the steps, until he was level with Jackie Gillon's row.

"Mr – ah – what's his name? Gillon? Mr Gillon, do come along here and show me your wallet. I would like to see it more closely. Do come."

He stood, arms outstretched, welcoming; caring. Jackie stared at him. In a world suddenly become unintelligible, he found the sympathetic tone attractive.

"God is watching us all."

"Yes, Mr Gillon. Of course He is. Make room. Help him along."

Jackie was fed along the standing row of students until he reached Flower. They went down to the door slowly, the prof's arm around Jackie's shoulders, then out of the lecture room.

"What the hell was that all about?"

Psychiatry was an untaught subject, so far. A vague knowledge of Dali landscapes; the crescendo music at the movies, when all was understood at the parting of a curtain, were the only kind of experiences any of us had in that abstruse subject. But some intuitive instinct warned that this was madness, and feared contagion.

"Has he been all right. Have you noticed anything odd about him?"

Mickey Mulligan was Jackie's running mate. He fielded questions in suprised Liffey tones.

"He seemed fine, so. Maybe a bit quieter than usual, but nutting like dis. Nutting at all."

Flower came back in quarter of an hour. In other circumstances, the class would have disintegrated into a noisy rabble, but we were quiet that day. The delicate membrane encompassing our own normality had been demonstrated in all its flimsy vulnerability.

"Ladies and gentlemen. You will be aware, I am sure, that you have just witnessed one of life's great misfortunes. Your fellow has been afflicted by some form of acute mania. And you have had a graphic illustration of how suddenly these things can come on." Sane to psychotic in five seconds flat. "At a guess, I would say schizophrenia, though others more skilled than I in such matters, will pronounce more fully." I doubted if they would improve on FL Robertson's immediate grasp of the situation, or his empathy with the needs of a mind so suddenly blighted. "In the circumstances, you may feel it appropriate to abandon the lecture?" He paused to gauge our collective reaction. "If I may suggest? Your careers will be punctuated by many tragedies. Yet you will be expected to deal with your next patient as if nothing had happened. If it doesn't offend you, I think we should carry on."

He gazed at us, and there was a mutter of agreement. We were glad of a working plan. He nodded in grim satisfaction.

"This will be good practice, I'm sure."

Contemplating our good fortune that far, Wilson and I decided on a beano: a night of real student roystering. For once, I deserted the Northern General on a Friday. I broke the bank and we had supper at Guy's; took a box at the second house of the Pavilion; and trampled all over the silver slippers of the girls at the Piccadilly Club. Later, Wilson got a bit out of hand and I had to keep an eye on him. He was desperately sick as we weaved our way home and, as we turned up the hill at the corner of Gibson Street, his legs threatened to give out. A couple of night beat bobbies stopped and watched us with predatory interest.

"We're nearly home," I beseeched them. "Just up the hill. I'll see he makes it."

They eyed us impassively, but I was able to keep Wilson on his feet until we got out of their sight.

Next morning, he eyed me ruefully.

"Silly damn thing to do," he shook his head.

He was right. There was enough working in favour of the Dean's prediction without him being booked as drunk and incapable.

"Oh, well," I shrugged. "Part of life's rich learning curve."

And Wilson was growing up. He was no longer quite so soft.

We went to the farm together that morning, the escapade well put behind us. But Wilson's learning curve had another roller-coaster swoop to come.

He had taken a bashful fancy to Siobahn, Rab's girl. She came to visit as often as she could, and Rab and she were full of each other in every way. Big, bouncing fucks, you imagined. Rab mooned about her like Ferdinand the bull, and it wasn't flowers he'd been smelling.

Every time Siobahn saw Wilson, she ragged him about her girls.

"They still talk about you."

For ordinary, you might not have guessed she was Irish, but then she thickened her speech into a gently mocking brogue.

"Thon big, blond, gude lukin' fulla. Is he stull there?"

Wilson flushed, bashful yet pleased. "Nice girl that." He became her devoted, second-line beau.

It was a relief to hear from Matt that morning, that the couple were formally engaged. Wilson was enthusiastic.

"That's great. When's the wedding to be?"

"Soon," said Matt. "And thank God for that. Sooner they get a place to themselves the better."

Such ardent loving would benefit from a more regular timetable. They might even get some sleep into the bargain.

The three of us were walking through the yard of Preston's Neuk. I was due to help young Watson at the slurry pit: Matt and Wilson to bag some grain from the silo.

We kept an eye open for the girls, who had arranged to meet us there. Connie, who had lately started to raise pullets for pin money, had begged some of the grain gleanings for poultry feed while Noelle was coming along to look decorative and admire her young man. He had recovered from his hangover and was being shown to advantage that morning: chest bulging out of his shirt; blond down glistening on his arms; for once doing something that counted.

"The Greigs will be pleased," Matt went on. "She's right suited to the boy. Used to a farm."

The agricultural omens seemed good, but what about the ecumenicals?

"Will the families mind a mixed marriage?" I asked. Catholic-Protestant unions had the ignition characteristics of fire-damp in that part of the world.

"No. Both sides are sensible. Besides, the Greigs are really fond of the girl."

But acceptance was not to be universal. As we came up to the slurry pit, young Watson caught the drift of things. He already had the planks off the pit; the tractor backed up; the suction hose ready to spew slurry into the spreader tank.

"Wha's tae be wed, then?"

He had all the countryman's interest in his neighbours' doings; all the whore-master's curiosity about who might be bedding his leavings.

"Rab and his girl."

"Whit?"

He stood stock still, disbelieving. Then he ratchetted the engine down to idle, that he might the better hear this juicy tit-bit.

"He's never gaun' tae wed her? Naw?"

He appealed for sense. Even his arch rival could not contemplate such folly. But our silence awed him by its implications.

"By the Christ. Can ye imagine? Raise a pack o' fuckin' Fenian weans?"

He looked at Matt, daring him to differ. But Matt was the wrong quarry.

Me, now? He had tried me before, and found me wanting. Would a rowel work this time? He raked the flanks of my valour.

"Ah mean? Mairry a fuckin' pape?"

He almost pled with me. Would I react this time? Stand up for my friend?

I let out not a cheep.

Young Watson gazed at me for a long moment, but I stayed as immobile as a yogi in a trance. Then he closed one eye at me, knowing and amused. I was no conundrum. My balls weren't big enough.

He ignored Wilson and, since there was no more sport to be had, he gave his definitive opinion, as the girls came across the yard.

"Ah mean, fuck her stupit. Heid doon the brae. Right up tae the boot-laces. But wed?"

"You wouldn't say that if Rab were here."

It was Wilson, thinking of his previous triumph; eyes flashing in the Harry Wharton style. I groaned in disbelief.

Young Watson couldn't believe his luck. He turned on Wilson slowly, sizing up his options at leisure. The girls came up to us at that moment, and his eyes switched to Noelle. An unlovely joy dawned all over his thin, hard face.

"But Rab's no' here."

The simplest remark. A statement of the plutobvious, made politely.

Wilson had never been in a brawl in his life; didn't know what to do now. But he stood four-square and upright. I could just imagine him in the Daniel Mendoza posture of defence.

Young Watson read him like a line diagram for idiot instruction. He'd never met anyone so green. His eyes flicked at Noelle again, then back to Wilson. The smile became a chuckle, but this was no belly laugh burbling happily in the bowels. This was a thin, malign snicker.

I wanted to shout at Wilson: to warn him. But of what?

Young Watson was several feet away from him. Any attack, boot or fist, would be telegraphed. Besides laughter, no matter how miserable, was an unlikely cry of battle.

But I had forgotten the cachination of the joker.

Young Watson played the oldest trick in the book: the gowk's gambit; the dummy sold to the dumbest. He looked away from Wilson; looked at Noelle, the grin saying 'Watch me'. Wilson relaxed momentarily, his shoulders dropping. Still looking the other way, young Watson suddenly lunged at him with the fierce yell of the bayonet charge. But his weapon was no more than his cloth bunnet: snatched from his head; wielded by the skip; flailing at Wilson's face in soft and harmless menace.

Surprised, startled, Wilson fell back a step.

Slurry pits were new fangled at the time. Over the winter, a hundred cattle had been wintered in a shed with a concrete floor. Channels and drains led to a big pit, where their excretions had matured into a brew of quite appalling stink. It should have been covered by a layer of railway sleepers, to keep man and beast safe from its mephitic depths. But young Watson had removed these, ready to suck out the slurry, and hose down the walls of the chamber. Wilson stepped back on air, a substance not noted for its retroactive qualities.

Surprise, realization, and consternation chased over his face as he stepped into waist-deep, liquid shit. For a long moment only young Watson laughed. You couldn't blame him. It was the classic sucker ploy of all time.

Wilson tried to haul himself out of the pit, but the suck of the foetid glaur held him back. Matt held a bit of rope to him, and helped haul him out. Wilson stood, the glutinous crud running from his trouser legs; squelching in his boots.

Wilson looked around the faces for some comfort, but the scene was too rich to sustain our initial dismay for him. Smiles and sniggers endorsed young Watson's sly triumph. Even Noelle let him down.

She wasn't enjoying the experience at all: girl friend to the booboisie. Her look was of utter exasperation. I looked at her, wondering if she would come all the young Missy; the laird's daughter? Threaten young Watson with her daddy's wrath.

Not a bit of it.

As Wilson's stricken eyes dropped from her face, his humiliation complete, Noelle was staring at young Watson, daring him to try anything with her. Young Watson measured the dare, grinned, then turned his back on her. She bristled at the impertinence and turned to Wilson – too late. He was walking away towards the pump in the yard with the gait of a defeated, puddling, Michelin man.

"By the Christ, but this has been a funny mornin'," young Watson said out loud. Since no one disagreed, he started to whistle 'Lilliburlero', the soldier's hymn to a battle won.

Later Matt said to me. "Young Watson's a bad bugger. He'd have murdered your friend in a fight."

I nodded. I knew that all too well.

"He'd maim a man without a thought."

Maim? An odd word.

"Like a bluiddy animal. You'll need to watch him."

I would need to watch him? I looked at Matt, startled. His warning was not only presumptive, it was predictive.

I had a lot of respect for Matt, but that was one time he talked rubbish. The only place I'd watch young Watson was from the other side of a high, barbed wire fence.

Chapter 2

FOR THE REST OF THE SESSION, I burned a mountain of candles over Salmond Aitchison's notes; went over five years' past pathology papers; wrote specimen answers to every question, then memorized them until I was word perfect. And, at the degree exams, I bagged another pot, honours in pathology, along with a pass in materia medica.

"That's the fella," crowed Minty, pleased for me. "Now, what about all that crap about not being able to afford it?"

"I'm working on it," I reassured him with as much confidence as I could muster. Connie might be an answer I didn't want to use, but so far I had come up with nothing better.

"Good boy," he urged. "I'll bring in my copy of Last's anatomy for you. It's a post graduate bible on the subject. Page a day from now on."

"Thanks Minty. Page a day?"

"That's it. Keep the subject bright, clean, and lightly oiled."

I was due to go to the farm at the end of the week: another summer to save siller towards my winter expenses; another three months to slake my curious need for the farm; another twelve Fridays to add to my experience of surgery. The night before I was due to leave, however, my Granny Aitken turned ill.

I arrived at the same time as the doctor. He didn't even bother to take off his coat and did no more than place his stethoscope bell between the two top buttons of her nightie. Such a perfunctory examination would have had him slung out of any medical exam on his ear, but he gained top marks on my test card. For, then, he sat on the edge of the bed, held her hand, and took all the time in the world to listen to her blue-faced, crackly-chested complaints, with grave compassion. Then he gave an explanation to the family in which terms like ventricular output and pulmonary oedema were notably absent, and words like 'grave' and 'done' ranked high. I went with him to the door.

"Last time I saw you, you had measles. I hear you're a medic yourself, now?"

I nodded. It was nice to be recognized as a putative brother.

"Done your materia medica, have you? Good. Here's a scrip. for some Nepenthe. Give her the drops in brandy and sugar. Increase the dose as she needs."

He emphasized her primacy. I wasn't to bugger up the comfort of her last hours with any burgeoning medical conscience.

"It'll make things easier for everyone."

As an only child, I did well for aunties. I had aunties by blood, by marriage, by conviction, and just because I liked them . Come a wedding or a funeral, they descended in pinnied droves to see things were done right. Those lineal descendants of the Red Clydesiders were as conservative as a blue rosette when it came to the propriety of such matters.

When, at last, the opiate made the old lady sleep-fast and bier-bound, these aunties formed a rota that did the ladies of Scutari proud. She was bathed, powdered, dressed in clean linen; her skin rubbed with eau-de-Cologne; her body wastes removed, all with brisk expertise.

The man in me; the surgeon allegedly maturing, was humbled.

It was a struggle to get Jock in and out to see her: his chair bulky and awkward. He realized this, and gave up his visits.

"You've all got enough to do."

He hadn't seen his mother for a couple of days, when she died.

"I'll away and tell him myself," I said.

Maisie was busy with the laying out.

"Aye. He'll want to know, soon as may be."

I went to Faifley.

Jock had managed to push the sideboard away from the window and wheel his chair close, so he could see down into the street. The far side of the tenement canyon was vivid with afternoon sunlight: the pavement loud with skipping cries. The Nazis did that: a glimpse of freedom now and then to break the spirit.

I said nothing: stood inside the door, watching him. He didn't turn round.

"She's away, then?"

"Yes."

He nodded. His future stretched before him: the long years until he found the same release. This four by six prospect was the best he could hope for.

I hadn't cried for my Granny Aitken, but I snatched the key, strung on a bobbin, that hung on the back of the door.

"I'll be back in a minute."

The mid-stair cludge was chlorinated and scrubbed, until it was damn near as sterile as Boss's theatre. I sat down and massaged the tears away.

My plans were laid, long term. They'd pay off in time. I would bloody well make them. Head down; keep slugging at the books. And if the price of getting Jock and Maisie sunshine on their faces meant marrying some bloody orphan in the process, so be it.

I went back to Jock.

"The funeral arrangements? What do you want done?"

As the eldest son, the rest of the family would defer to him.

"Aye. We'll talk about that in a minute. But first, there's something between you and me. Or rather, between you and my mother. Sit down."

There was a pocket on his chair to hold letters or a magazine. He slipped his hand into this and pulled out a manilla envelope.

"Your gran wanted you to have this. She gave it to me months ago. I've no idea what's in it, nor do I want to. Put it away and look at it later. And never mention it to a soul. Not even my Maisie. I've seen more grief over an auld body's leavings than you would credit. Squabbles about wee bits o' things. That's no' to happen wi' my mother."

Her memory was to be spared any such miserable sacrilege.

Later, in the quiet of the flat, I took out the envelope, and opened it. Inside was a wad of tissue paper, folded in a bundle, and holding what? My granpa's watch chain? Not heavy enough. Perhaps his cuff-links?

I shook the bundle out and unwrapped the folds. There was nothing in it. But the thin white paper was printed on one side with black ink scroll-work. The Bank of England was promising to pay five pounds a go for each sheet. There were fifty such sheets.

There was no note. Of course not. That wasn't her way. I would know how best to use it. But the amount of scrimping and saving of bawbees and silver threepenny bits was unimaginable.

I had to sit down. I had joined the inheriting classes. I felt a gush of happiness, then of sheer bloody relief. Happy that I could now see my way to take Minty's hard learned advice; relief that I could bury forever the temptation about Connie's money.

The feeling lasted two, whole, wonderful days, until my Granny Aitken's funeral. Wilson attended it. He was soberly dressed and grave in manner, but there was no hiding he was in a good mood about something. It kept bubbling through the solemnity of the occasion. Later, in the flat, when we had laid aside the black ties and loosened the white collars, he said, "I've got some good news. At least – it is for my family."

From his look, I suspected there wasn't a lot of joy in it for me.

"You don't know this, but my old man is an expert on Aramaic. It started as a hobby. Unusual in a parish minister. He gave talks. Wrote papers. Did odd lectures in universities and theological colleges. He became known to all sorts of people in a quiet way. It's truly ecumenical, you see."

"Common origins, and all that?"

"Right you are. Anyhow, he became a recognized authority. A few months ago, some wealthy churchman put up the money to endow a chair in Aramaic studies at the university here. My father was encouraged to apply – and – well – he's got it."

"What marvellous news," I was really pleased for the minister. He had been so decent to me. "I am glad for him. For you all. Does that mean they'll be coming up to town to live?"

"Yes. Septemberish. They hope to get a town house in Kirklee." A thin, terraced house with three stories and a basement. "There'll be lots of space. I'll have a room of my own. Trouble is, I won't need the flat any more."

Until that moment, it hadn't dawned on me. I had lost my free digs.

"It didn't seem to matter too much as long as you had your grandmother's place to go back to. But now – well, my folks and I, we've talked it over. You could share my room."

I winced for the effort this right-doing gesture must have cost. But, though I had just been holed under the water, I wouldn't cry lifeboat if it killed me. I enthused my voice and leaned towards him in earnestness.

"You're not going to believe this coincidence, but my granny has left me a little money. It means I can be independent until I qualify."

The windfall would find me no more than a garret where I could make a drawerful of porridge every Sunday night, to last the week in cold slices. Ah, well, easy come, easy go. We moneyed people took such things in our stride.

Wilson's relief was almost palpable.

"Funny how things work out, isn't it. You must thank your mum and dad most kindly for their offer."

I would just have to get back to my studies in knight rottenry when I went back to the farm next day.

Chapter 3

RESIDENTS IN THE VOLUNTARY HOSPITALS were paid in coinage of a peculiar amalgam: experience, getting their faces to fit with a consultant and a dose of well-chastened self-knowledge, as the depths of their ignorance were exposed.

At a pound a week, with white jacket, food, and a bed thrown in, money didn't weigh in the equation. The hours were all that God sent, with more manufactured on an ad hoc basis. A signed contract was unthinkable; time off a hollow laugh; holidays never dreamt of. Newly qualified doctors queued up for this initiation.

With the National Health Service came a formal contract, a raise to two pounds ten, and a statutory holiday of one week in six months.

Boss ignored the latter.

"No one's going to tell me what to do in my own bloody wards."

And no one did – for a while.

At first Boss demanded – and got – the kind of residents he had always had, jumping to his word in scared obedience. But that July, one of his incumbents struck, a guy called Joss Shearer. He was laying off at Minty one Friday, when I arrived from the farm.

"I don't see why that old highland bugger should give me such a hard time. I'm due my week off. If I don't get it now, I'll lose it. I'm simply going to tell him I won't be in next week."

Minty lectured him like a hell-fire preacher.

"You can't. You simply cannot leave him flat. I don't give a damn what the contract says. At the least, you must allow time to find a locum. You'll never get a reference if you do this."

"I'm off to the army in August. He can't hurt me there."

"But you may want to come back eventually. And Boss has a memory for insults, real and fancied, like an elephant. It would be plain stupid to antagonize him like that."

Shearer stayed mulishly determined, and suddenly Minty looked at me.

"Wait a minute. This farm job you do, Neil. Could you get a week off?"

"I think so. The busiest time isn't until August."

"You might just save this clown from getting his balls in the mangle. Would you do a student residency? You've done plenty of clerking by now. And you've been on the receiving rounds often enough to know what goes on. You and Pringle might manage to fudge it between you."

"Minty. Could I? I'd love that."

Minty turned to Joss. "You will not be Boss's blue-eyed boy, I can tell you, but he might just buy it. He's going away for a few days next week, so it won't affect him too much. Neil, find out about time off. Then the pair of you turn up at his morning tea-party and keep your mouths shut. Leave the talking to me."

I phoned the farm and squared myself with Sandy.

"It's a great opportunity for me. I'll make it up to you any way I can."

"Aye, aye," he agreed. "You're no' one for skiving. But I'll haud you to extra time later."

"Great, Sandy. And thank you."

I wangled myself into a corner of Boss's room, half hidden by a filing cabinet, while Joss stood by, holding a list of cases for theatre. Minty waited until Boss took his ceremonial cup from sister and registered satisfaction with his first sip of tea, then he bent over and talked in Boss's ear.

Boss's nostrils pinched in. A red surge mottled his malar skin.

When Minty finished talking, Boss nodded minimally: fractional acquiescence. Minty turned; took his own cup from sister; rolled his eyes at heaven. Joss thought he should get in on the act then.

"About this theatre list, sir?"

"You're on holiday, I hear. Well, clear out. You."

"Me?" I squeaked.

"Yes, you. 'F you're my houseman, now, gimme the list."

Joss opened his mouth to protest his sea-lawyer rights.

"Where's the bloody list," Boss roared at me.

Joss fled. I snatched the paper, turned on my heel, and nearly fell over getting the paper to him.

Boss scanned the names. "You. Come and scrub for me."

"Yessir."

My daddy hadn't been a CSM for nothing.

"This old man with the acute obstruction. Know him?"

"Yessir."

"I'll do him first. Get him prepped. And tell Kennedy."

He barked his disposition of the rest of the list as I flew to get Ken Kennedy, Boss's favourite anaesthetist. He was a flabby, unflappable guy, who always wore suede brothel-creepers in memory of his days with the eighth army.

"Mr McKenzie wants to do this obstruction next, he's in a bit of a –"

I thought of several words.

"– hurry."

It seemed the most diplomatic. Ken Kennedy absorbed the pause resignedly.

"Another of those mornings, eh? You're a student, aren't you?"

"Aitken. Sudden promotion. Student resident as of twenty minutes ago."

"Tell me all, later. In the meantime, we should get on with the pre-med. What d'you suggest?"

"Atropine?" I tried. "He looks a bit blue. Miss out an opiate in case respiratory depression makes him more anoxic?"

"You've been reading the books," he accused, looking pleased. "How much atropine? And how fast?"

"A hundredth? Slowly into a vein?"

"What else is there to say?" he shrugged at me in satisfaction.

The old man was on a trolley in the theatre ante-room. I drew up the solution; checked it with Ken; injected it. Then I shaved the abdomen; helped the orderly get the patient on the table; changed; scrubbed; was waiting ready, when Boss appeared beside me, snapping his gloves tight.

Hadn't I done well? I had better do well and even bloody better than that, if I was going to work with him.

He swabbed the skin with iodine; towelled up the operation area, folding the sheets to give him a field, a narrow strip of the swollen abdomen; nipped in the towel clips.

I was excited to be working close up to him. Minty had shaken his head in admiration, when he tried to explain to me.

"He's fast, of course. Very fast. He learned his surgery in the days you had to get in and out in a hurry. But it's more. Watch when he gets in a jam. If you can learn that, young Aitken, there'll be lots of guineas in it for you."

But maybe I could have chosen a better day for my initiation?

"You," Boss growled. "Do what I tell you. And don't get in my bloody road."

The fuse was still smouldering.

"Knife."

He held out his right hand. The scrub sister smacked a big-bellied Bard-Parker into the middle of his gloved hand, and Boss went for a long, paramedian incision: a big, bad-tempered, six inch slash to one side of the umbilicus.

Normally it would have saved time. Normally it would have sliced skin and subcutaneous tissue only, taking him down to muscle in one stroke. Normally it would have demonstrated his mastery to the millimetre.

But the old man had been ill for months. He had become dispirited by recurrent abdominal pain and vomiting. He had become tired of doctors who couldn't find out what was wrong with him. He had become depressed; stopped eating. He had become debilitated; emaciated. The belly muscles, under-used and under-nourished, had thinned and thinned. They were paper thin, now, when his recurring partial obstruction had suddenly become complete.

Boss's knife went through five layers of skin, subcutaneous tissue, muscle, peritoneum, and bowel wall, like some clinical Samurai. He slashed the bowel open in what turned out to be three different places. A fountain of thin, wet, faecal residue blew out in a farting rain that spattered Boss and me and the scrub sister, in smelly indifference.

Everyone watching looked up or down or away: anywhere but at Boss. Looking at the fireball was known to melt your eyes into jelly.

Suppose I tried a leaf out of Minty's cheeky book? It might put a pin in that hydrogen balloon of temper: let it out slowly. If not, the explosion wouldn't be any worse.

"Looks like you struck oil, sir."

I'd never win the captions competition in *Punch*, but it sent the scrub sister into a snicker of overwrought relief.

For the first time I could remember, the intolerant blue eyes really took me in.

"Cheeky young bugger," he said mildly. "Get all this cleared up and change."

The orderly and I did what we could for the floor and table, with phenol-soaked swabs. Then we changed drapes, gowns, gloves, and Boss started to mend his mistakes. And I began to see what Minty had been talking about.

Boss was magnificent.

He was an old bully and a tyrant but by God, he could operate.

His hands had none of the fictional qualities: nothing long, or sensitive about them. Blunt mechanic's fingers, they were, scraped with rose thorns; the nails bruised blue-black with off-duty manual work.

But scrub them aseptic, case them in latex gloves, confront them with a shambles like this, and you could stand back and wonder. The fingers seemed to have brains of their own: working without his volition: fast, easy: gentle with the tissues, even tender. As I watched, I forgave him every mean, bullying, miserable fault, and settled at his feet to learn.

He repaired the perforations, then resected a polyp the size of a grapefruit. It had been growing slowly; obstructing the last few feet of large bowel intermittently. Now you feel the pain; now you don't: defying diagnosis. Finally, it had twisted on its stalk. Arterial blood pumped in, but the venous return failed. It blew up like a pregnant tennis ball, and blocked the bowel like a plug in a bath.

The growth turned out to be simple: no cancerous change; and the inevitable infection, result of Boss's intemperate slash, was minimal. The old man was quids in. He left the hospital twelve days later, with a small healing wound, an extra half stone on his frail bones and swearing by Boss, just like me.

Later, I found myself a minor hero for braving Boss. Minty encouraged me.

"That's the business. You're learning well. It's the only way to keep out of the shit with the old bugger, if you'll pardon the execrable pun."

But I hadn't finished with the brown stuff: not that week.

After lunch, Boss headed a fast visit to the wards, the rest of the staff trailing in his wake. The details of his three-strike knife stroke had been well raked over, but his contemptuous grin silenced any criticism. Not one amongst them could have retrieved the situation with such panache, and damn fine they knew it.

I scuttled at his elbow, noting investigations to be done; taking instructions for the afternoon list.

"That should keep you lot busy until I get back," he said derisively. "You, Aitken. You'll get me at Shaw's Howe, if I'm wanted."

He turned on his heel, swirled his coat tails at us, and strode out of the ward. Some rooster.

"What's he do at Shaw's Howe?" I asked Minty. That was an old fever hospital out on the road to Loch Lomond. I couldn't imagine what an ace surgeon did there.

"Nominally, he's the visiting surgeon. Quick sprint round the premises once a week. On tap for emergency advice."

"But in fact?" something about his tone made me ask.

Minty gave me a leery wink, and kissed his bunched finger tips.

"Aaah. That's where he keeps Easy Annie."

The lubricious soubriquet had all the wounding qualities of a spear; the thrusting, casual penetration of any passing centurion. I had to laugh at his glee, and joined in the vicarious crucifixion of some woman I had never seen.

"Who is she, then?"

"Never seen her, myself. Before my time. But I had the gen from Finnie McLaren. Up and coming gyn. man at the Royal Jericho these days. But he was a resident here in Annie's time."

"Here?"

"Yeah. She was Boss's scrub nurse. I can't get all the story out of Finnie."

He shook his head at his own failure. Minty was a past-master at digging out hospital dirt.

"Big mystery there. She was married to a medic who went off to the war. He was killed at Dunkirk and about the same time, Annie lost her uterus in a hurry. Boss did it himself in a private home."

He looked at me sagely. Private homes carried overtones of discretion.

"Rumour is that a foetus went in the bucket as well. More rumour that it would have looked like Boss if it had got to term. But this was in 1940."

He spread his hands in supplication. The threatened German invasion gave everyone more to worry about than an illegal abortion.

"Anyhow, there she was. A widow with built in contraception. The guys climbed all over one another to get at her. She took them on, six deep."

He mourned for not being among the standing armies she had vanquished.

"She was voracious."

"Was?"

"Yeah. Boss took her over as his exclusive property later. His wife's a nut. In a home, somewhere. So, he has bother getting regular hot dinners. He wangled this job for her at Shaw's Howe. Keeps her out there all to himself. Nobody sees or hears of her these days. But enough of Boss's extra-marital affairs. Let's get the rest of the week sorted out for you"

He and Pringle drafted out a list of duties that shouldn't cause me too much trouble: writing case notes, simple laboratory procedures, routine ward handcrafts.

"What about emergency calls?" I asked.

There was a night-long trek of lace-caps to the residents' quarters for advice, reassurance and come see what you think of the patient in bed ten, doctor.

"We've thought about that. You go first. See if you can deal with it. If you can't, wake Pringle."

Boss was back from Shaw's Howe in time for his afternoon tea, and to take his place in the evening operating teams. By two am he had seen everything ordered to his satisfaction.

"I'm going home, now," he announced. That was my cue to leap to his side, help him on with his overcoat and see him off the premises to sighs of relief from the staff left to finish things off. Outside his room, however, he paused.

"That old man. I'll just take a last look at him."

He threaded his way among the green shaded beds to stand beside his patient. The old guy was asleep, but Boss reached out and took one of his hands in his own. He stood for a moment, looking at the bone-proud, thin-jawed, toothless, white-bristled face of a life long lived.

It was the same sort of transaction the doctor had had with my Granny Aitken; a wordless communication of some deep import. This was something else I had to learn about.

Then Boss grunted. He seemed satisfied.

"See that drip goes on for at least twenty-four hours. Sister will keep you right if you aren't sure. And try to keep that bugger Baillie away from him. If you need advice, ask Minty."

I walked out with Boss to the tarmac car-park; opened the door of his Rolls Royce; caught the whiff of leather and polish.

"Lovely car, sir."

My envy was wholehearted.

He chuckled, satisfied. And why not?

He made ten thousand a year from his private practice. He had a docile, obsequious resident again, just like he wanted. And he had just got a patient out of the literal shit by his own undoubted expertise.

"I'm off to Gleneagles tomorrow. I'll be home next Thursday afternoon. G'night, Aitken."

I clunked the heavy, coach-built door into place, and watched the car out of the gate. Then I went to bed for a sleep of ups and downs to check sudden temperatures, and suspiciously bloody dressings. But in the morning Pringle was well rested and satisfied with his understudy.

Chapter 4

NEXT MORNING, I WENT WITH PRINGLE for a breakfast of Jimmy Logan sossidges and HP sauce. Then we made a report on the waiting list patients, who were also admitted on receiving day, for discussion on the morning ward round.

When Boss was due, there was always a little burbling in the bowel: a charging of the fight or flight systems. But that morning was as relaxed as a Sunday school gala. Piddling Paul gave everyone a treat; showed us all how it ought to be done.

He sat on Boss's chair. He joked with Boss's sister select. He sipped the first cup of Boss's special order tea. He was matey with the others. Later, on the ward round, he asked for opinions and advice. He made decisions based on reason and argument.

As it should be.

And yet, there was something flawed about it all, the final consensus lacking authority. We had been at half a dozen bedsides before I spotted what was wrong.

Consultation with Boss in charge was brusque and peremptory. But, once he had allowed such discussion as he saw fit, any decision carried his warranty. He would back his staff to the hilt and, if need be, carry the can himself.

Paul used the consensual approach to slide out of any such commitment. Every decision was made in the name of the collective, anonymous we. I knew his surgical technique carried little respect, but I now found his probity equally suspect. He was enjoying his romp in the unfamiliar fields of leadership before men who didn't trust him an inch. So, it was a supreme irony when he landed himself with the most difficult case of the round; a case I had written up myself and now, at Minty's insistence, had to present.

Danny Daly was a docker: a beer belly on legs: chancer in chief of the longshoremen's guild. An unlovely man: large on fags and booze, rich in the skiving arts and bar-room law. My toes curled every time I came near him. I started my presentation.

"Fifty year old man. Manual labourer. Long history of epigastric pain coming on two hours after meals. Relieved by antacids. Lately has had a lot of vomiting. Copious amounts of greenish fluid, with undigested food in it. There is also a strong family history of duodenal ulceration. Father. Two brothers. A recent barium meal shows – an active ulcer crater and considerable narrowing of the pylorus. Marked delay in gastric emptying."

I slicked the X-ray films out of their envelope and held them up to a viewer. Minty winked at me in satisfaction. I had just given a text-book description of recurrent duodenal ulceration with scarring, and resultant narrowing, of the valve leading from the stomach to the duodenum.

There was no argument about this but there was great argument about what should best be done to alleviate the problem. There were two main lines of surgical treatment.

First, partial gastrectomy: part of the acid-forming area of the stomach was removed along with the defective valve. The two ends were then joined, thus reforming a passageway free of obstruction, while the production of destructive acid was much reduced.

Second, gastro-enterostomy: the stomach was laid alongside the first part of the small bowel, and a window was opened between them. Thus, the narrowed valve was by-passed, and the excess acid allowed to drain into the intestine.

The arguments were fearful and learned: papers in journals, lectures in medical schools by adherents of the one, and disciples of the other. In his best judicious manner, Paul expounded on these at the end of Danny Daly's bed, holding his audience in rapt apathy. At the end, he posed his finger tips together, and asked, "Now, gentlemen. Which of these would be the best course of action here?"

Danny Daly's tobacco-stained fingers and his well-cultivated beer-gut foretold lots of surgical problems. Paul's inviting 'we' was, in fact, looking for a muggins: someone else to take on such a pig of a case. His colleagues looked ceilingwards without a word. At length Minty spoke up.

"Mr McKenzie seems to think the odds are in favour of gastrectomy."

Of all the things Minty could have said, that was the wrongest. All of Paul's dispassion, all of the reasoned demeanour went down the stiver. Plain, old fashioned jealousy took over.

Boss McKenzie thought that. Well, Paul Baillie was boss that morning. Pique overtook self-preservation.

"Quite so, Millar. But it seems to me the indications here are for gastro-enterostomy. Aitken, put him on my own list for Monday morning."

The others raised their eyebrows in a mixture of disbelief and *schadenfreude* and I wrote the docker up for lots and lots of trouble.

Paul did the operation as planned, and as not planned. I was dodging about the theatre, giving pre-meds, writing notes, helping to keep the second table in production. Now and then, I sidled up beside Pringle, who was assisting Paul, to see how things were going.

They weren't.

To start with, Danny the docker took to his anaesthetic like a donkey taking a staw at the world. His lifelong dalliance with Miss Ethyl Alcohol made him immune to the lesser charms of Dame Ether. A flow rate of anaesthetic that would have felled a mammoth simply irritated him into a heaving, cyanotic limbo. By the time the gas man got a tube down into his trachea, and the respiration into some kind of control, the operation was already half an hour late.

Then there was finding the maguffin.

The bowel is hung from the back of the abdominal wall in a kind of convoluted, membranous sling, known as the mesentery. All thirty feet of the intestine loop and twist within these thin, shiny folds.

Then, between the abdominal wall and the intestinal structures lies a safety curtain of similar tissue, called the omentum. This is sometimes called the policeman of the abdomen, because it can wrap itself round, and isolate any parts of the intestine which are inflamed.

But the mesentery and the omentum also double as fat stores. And Danny Daly's beer belly meant he carried as much blubber as a a small whale.

Paul's abdominal incision opened up a tunnel of fat, at the bottom of which the loops of intestine slithered and slopped in a universal coating of thick, yellow tallow. Identifying a particular part was like spotting a pet cobra in a snake pit full of grease. On top of this, the omentum had tried to wrap itself around the chronically irritated ulcer, quite altering the normal anatomy.

After an eternity of fishing about and tutting and muttering, Paul sighed with relief, laid together the surfaces to be joined and started the by-pass. Intestinal tissue is delicate, however and the stitches have to be fine. Paul was shown at his very worst. The finicky sutures took him an age. The operation, already late, went on and on. Theatre sister had to spell her scrub nurse.

"Better go and have some lunch before it's all finished."

She said it sniffily; loudly; adding to the tension.

Paul finished just on two o'clock. Everyone was tired, hungry and late for the afternoon's work. Danny Daly was wheeled back to the ward and put in a bed beside Boss McKenzie's old man. It was a bad choice. Over the next few days, the contrast between the men became striking. Boss's fiasco flourished; Danny the docker failed.

It was subtle at first.

At the Tuesday round, Paul was expansive. It had been, by any standards, a difficult operation, and Paul had some justification for feeling good.

"How are we this morning?"

"All right."

Danny Daly was grudging in his admission.

"You made life very difficult for us yesterday, but we managed."

The pronouns were royal in intention that morning, Paul claiming all the kudos.

"Sister? Any problems?"

He paid lip service to her position, her agreement taken for granted. But her reply lacked enthusiasm.

"He seems all right so far, sir."

I looked at her in surprise. Morag Fleming was the best of Boss's hand-picked team of ward sisters. She had a sixth sense for trouble, which Boss took absolutely as gospel. But Paul was oblivious to the nuances of her answer, and swept us all on.

Next day, however, Danny Daly was lying listlessly on his pillow. He simply nodded to show he existed. And this time Morag stood her ground.

"I'm not happy about this man, sir."

At the end of the bed, Paul's expression became just less than pained.

"Why?"

"It's difficult to say."

Boss would have paused; listened to his sister try to formulate her instinctive feelings. But Paul showed his impatience.

"Any positive findings, sister? Vomiting? Pain?"

"No."

"Temperature? Pulse?"

"All normal, sir."

"I always respect your opinion, sister," he said in a tone that did nothing of the kind. "Let me know if your worries come to anything."

The ramrod already up her back became even straighter.

"I certainly shall, sir."

The Thursday morning ward round was supposed to be a quick affair, the object of the exercise to free as many beds as possible before the next day's assault. But that morning, there was one silly hold up after another. By the time we came to the docker, Paul was perfunctory and even more impatient: and the antipathy between Morag and him sparked like a big charge of static.

Danny Daly looked smaller, his humanity diminished. His skin had the greasy look of a thin, cold sweat, and a kidney bowl beside him held a watery gruel of brownish vomit. The sister drew Paul's attention to this.

"It seems unusually foul, sir. I wonder if it could be faecal?"

Paul went up the wall. "Faecal? How could it be faecal? Don't talk rubbish. You mean faeculent. Quite understandable in the circumstances."

The words, from the same Latin stem, were utterly different in implication. Paul's meant that the patient was still digesting microscopic shreds of his own tissues and blood at the stitch lines. Add in a little infection by the normal coliform bacteria of the bowel and you had good reason for a foul stink. Paul explained these elementary facts to Morag as if she was soft in the head. She was stunned by his effrontery. He went over the vital signs again.

"Has he had any pain?"

"No, sir."

"Pulse? Temperature? Respiration?"

"All normal, sir."

Nature's black box was stating unequivocally that everything was on course. Paul looked around his white coated cohort, but nobody said squeak. He was left to shell his own peas. He swallowed visibly and his handsome face showed a tinge of petulance.

"Start him on oral fluids."

A slow drip of sterile water through a naso-gastric tube would test the fine stitch line, and help wash away the evil-smelling stomach contents.

By mid-day, there wasn't a white coat to be seen, and the wards had emptied of recently scarred patients, happy in loosely fitting clothes, as they walked, still twingeing, back into life. Pringle said, "I'm off to see the wife."

He had maried a nurse a week before starting a year of residences and all possible chances of reconsummation, no matter how brief, were taken eagerly. I was alarmed.

"You aren't leaving me on my own?"

"You'll be fine. Everything in the wards is quiet. Besides, I've spoken to the receiving resident. He'll come over if you have any panics. You can go to bed this afternoon."

I could have measured the amount of uninterrupted sleep I'd had in two turns of a very small hour glass. The thought of the sand flowing for hours on end had the attraction of the Fairy Godmother's spell.

I was deep in conversation with Nod, when I was shaken awake by an evening duty lace-cap, with a hand-fitting bosom and a worried look.

"Hi. Nice to see you. Coming in?"

I raised the covers invitingly, but this was no time for decubital dalliance.

"No. This is serious. I'm awful worried about that gastro-enterostomy man. He started to vomit more this afternoon, and he's suddenly gone downhill. Will you come and have a look at him?"

The 'you' had a purposive ring about it.

"Me?"

I pulled the covers tight. This whole affair was away above my speed.

"You've got to do something."

Her caring instinct was leaking all over her protocol, and damned my vacillation with impatience. I put on a dressing gown, and trailed behind her through the bright evening sunlight that slanted into the ward.

I didn't have to be qualified in anything to see the change in Danny Daly. He had a yellow, defeated look about him. He lay in a foetal huddle. In the kidney basin, the brownish vomit now had a glutinous thickness, and was stinking even more. The indices were now reading red alarm: the respiration shallower, faster; the temperature a degree above normal; the pulse tripping along at a trot.

But why?

"Let's have a look," I said, and helped nurse undo the many-tailed abdominal bandage.

She pulled the dressing clear. There was no sign of redness at the wound; no smear of pus to account for the signs. What the hell was wrong with this conundrum going bad under my eyes?

As I leaned over him, he suddenly belched in my face: a tiny burp of gas: a weak, helpless gesture, with little hope of relief. I jerked away in sudden, deathly suspicion. Though this exhalation was without the raspberry flutter of an anal sphincter, it had the unmistakable olfactory quality of a hundred school-boy whoopees; countless bare-arsed blow-offs in the gym.

Danny Daly had just farted through his mouth: miasma of some awful disorder.

I looked at the lace-cap. The urge to say something; to see how it sounded when formulated into speech, was strong. But for some reason, I thought this was one time Junior Aitken should keep his mouth shut. My mind buzzed with the impossible.

Faeculent or faecal?

The first, as Paul had said, was a recognized, acceptable aberration: a temporary, unusual result of the healing process. The second was a sign of a major surgical disaster; sign of a passage between the stomach and the large bowel.

Normally, this would be due to some advancing, destructive process, like cancer; or the result of major trauma. Either way, such a calamity would be obvious and dramatic in a short time, with the loaded bowel emptying itself into the stomach, and then through the mouth.

But in this case, a pre- and post-operative fast for five days would leave the bowel empty of all save the minimum of waste matter to be produced in a thin dribble of vomit: slow to develop: subtle, insidious sign of a major surgical cock-up. I needed wiser counsel.

"I'll phone the receiving resident," I said.

The nurse nodded aspersively: high bloody time.

"I can't come over this minute," he explained. "A double-decker bus went under a low bridge. Sliced the top off. We're stacked at the moment. I'll bring a consultant with me as soon as I can."

It was a fair offer. But a consultant from another firm pulling chestnuts out of Boss's fire?

"Listen," I stalled. "Leave it with me. I'll see if I can't get one of our own people from somewhere."

"Fine," he said, glad to be relieved of the chore. "Let me know."

I sighed, and phoned Paul Baillie. Almost to my relief, he was out.

Who could I try now? Minty? He might come if I shouted at him but it was clear that he, like the others, didn't want to be involved. I blew out a lungful of indecision and made up my mind.

Boss McKenzie was due home that afternoon. I rang him.

Chapter 5

WHEN I FIRST WENT TO THE GATE, Willie Roberts had wised me up about Boss.

"He takes it as a personal affront if a patient doesn't do well. Doesn't matter who operated. If it happens in his wards, he wants to know. On the other hand, if you've made a muck of something, as long as you're honest, and tell him at once, he'll support you against all comers. And if you're not sure about anything, you can phone him at any time."

Now I'd find out.

At the other end, the phone came off the hook. I waited for the usual growl, but this voice said, "Helloo."

A dove call inviting confidences: exuding comfort, availability and confidence.

Of course. He wasn't expecting me. This was the nesting call of private practice; the golden guinea voice for the GP with a patient in trouble. I would have to disappoint him.

"Sir. This is Aitken. From the wards."

Now for my head on a plate: John Aitken the Baptist. But no, this was a voice for all professional colleagues needing advice.

"Yes, Aitken. What's the trouble?"

"Sorry to trouble you so soon after your holiday, sir. It's kind of a long story, sir."

I realized I was rushing my words, and that all these sirs were too much lard by half. I had to be professional, and sycophancy wasn't on that menu.

"Staff nurse and I – "

That wouldn't do either. Any reasons for hiding behind a starched pinny had nothing to do with clinical surgery. Try again.

"– I – " that was better – "think a patient isn't doing well."

"Where's Pringle? What does he think?"

"Pringle is out. He isn't due back until midnight. He arranged for the receiving resident to cover."

"You'd better ask him, then."

No sarcasm, for once: a mild suggestion.

"I have."

"Well?"

"He did say he would come. Offered to bring his own consultant with him. I wasn't sure you'd want that."

There was a silence, seconds long, then he said, "I think you'd better tell me all about it, son."

So I told the story of Danny the docker: the lack of signs, the dearth of symptoms, the foul vomit. Then I nailed myself to the cross of my own certainty.

" I think the vomiting is faecal."

"What? You realize what you are saying, boy? Who operated?"

"Mr Baillie."

"Where is he?"

"Not at home."

"Now, Aitken. Take a moment. I want you to think about all of this. Then tell me. How certain are you?"

Fear of being wrong. Fear of being right. Pity for even the unlovely Danny Daly. Wondering what I had done to my undergraduate career. The sheer excitement of the grey cells in synch. Let's get at this patient. Let's find out what's really wrong with him. Whatever happened to cool clinical appraisal? Well, these were the ingredients I hoped to build a career around and Boss was making me fuse them together in the white hot crucible of decision.

"I'm sure."

"Right. I'll be with you shortly."

Boss lived in Symington, a pretty little village in Ayrshire, twenty miles away. I heard the double doors to the ward bat open in thirty minutes flat. There was only one guy in the world who came into the place like that. I was dressed by then, and was having some contraband tea and toast in the ward kitchen when he steamed past. The lace-cap and I had to run to keep up.

Danny Daly was at the head of the ward, next to the duty table. A screen curtained his misery from the few patients left. Boss went straight to him, took the unlovely paw in his hand and unashamedly patted it.

"Not feeling very well, eh?"

Danny Daly shook his head, a miniscule protest of despair.

"Tell me. Since your operation. How d'you feel now? Better? Worse? Just the same?"

Danny Daly was a compulsive liar; a cheat forever figuring out some angle to his advantage. But the grey lady of death was in the ward. Enough to frighten the truth out of anyone.

"I'm no gettin' on like I was. I was all right the first day, but noo – this shitey stuff is awfu'. The smell –"

This man, who had disgusted me, was disgusted with himself. We all have our dignities.

Boss took the kidney basin of vomit and sniffed at it.

"Right," he swivelled to the staff nurse. "Get on to your office. Get a theatre set up for me."

She whisked off with a sniff that said she knew it all along.

"Don't worry, Daly. I'll soon have you sorted."

The 'I' was as telling as the Singer clock at midnight. For the first time in three days the docker's face lost the hunted look. As we left the ward, Boss said, "Have you mentioned what you think to anyone else? That nurse?"

"No, sir. It seemed wiser not to."

The hard look glared me into further silence.

"Good. You keep on keeping your face shut. Not a word to anyone. Now, go and find me Ken Kennedy. Tell him I want him right now."

Fifty-five minutes later, I stood on the other side of the table from Boss, and peered back into the snake pit. Although Danny Daly had lost pounds of fat, identification was still difficult.

"God. I'd get lost in there," I said with sudden feeling for Paul Baillie.

"Better start finding your way, now, if this is how you hope to make a living. Now, pull on those retractors. Nurse, gimme some big saline packs."

This time, there was the added problem of shock. Danny Daly was losing his life force by a disastrous surgical entropy, and this further assault on his defence mechanisms would bring on shock like a train. The faster Boss could work, the gentler he was, the less pressure would that lethal engine build up: but even he would be hard pressed. He had the big, shadowless lamp tilted this way and that, but the best he could illuminate was a small saucer of light at the bottom of the fat-lined tunnel. He enlarged the incision to something short of a manhole and pushed folds of hot, moist gauze among the coils of bowel, isolating, identifying.

My arms began to cramp with the effort of holding the retractors; keeping the wall of fat from folding in. I stuck my head sideways to let the orderly towel my forehead dry of sweat.

Then, right over the hole as I was, I couldn't miss Boss's finger, as he found a suture line. It was joining the stomach to the first part of the ileum, as it should.

God. I had been wrong. Painfully, shamefully, too big for my boots-fully, wrong.

But Boss wasn't satisfied. He traced the ileum back to the duodenum; pointed to it diving deep, before bending back in a U-turn to meet the stomach at the pyloric valve, just as the books said it should. Except you couldn't actually see the meeting place. There were a couple of inches buried in fat where you had to take that on trust.

Boss trusted no-one except himself.

"Gimme another couple of packs, nurse."

Again Boss pushed the glistering coils out of the way, and followed the bowel back to the bend where vision was so difficult. Over the mask; under his cap, the skin around his eyes was crinkled into concentration. He was damned if he'd let it beat him, and I had a sudden shaft of shared insight with this crotchety old bugger. I knew just how he felt.

"Ah."

His grunt had almost the relief of orgasm: a profound satisfaction. He pointed wordlessly. The coil of ileum looped back. But it didn't join the stomach. It went under it. Boss's finger traced this wayward organ, and found that it disappeared into the paracolic gutter. It was not the stomach. It was the large bowel. Paul had anastomosed the wrong structures: plumbed the gas into the hot water system.

At the south end of the patient's chemical sleep, Ken Kennedy was all for getting this patient off the table before he did something untoward, like dying.

"Found the problem?"

Boss straightened up, rinsed his hands in hot saline.

"Did you think I wouldn't?" he crowed, at his jovial best. "There's a problem at the stoma."

Understatement of the decade.

"It seems to be folding in on itself. Kinking."

He glared at me over his mask, daring me to utter a word.

"You get back to your crossword, Kenny. Let me worry about what's in here."

Ken settled to three across; his dials and his rebreathing bags. He wasn't interested in surgical pathology; only in getting the patient off the table alive. The scrub nurse was busy with her trays of instruments. The only two people in the world who knew what was really wrong with Danny Daly were Boss and I, but he had already cloaked this awkward truth with a vague abstraction: a kink.

"I'll have to undo the stoma. Re-establish the normal anatomy. Nurse, gimme a bowel clamp."

Usually Boss was a good communicator: running commentaries; keep the whole team informed, but that night he talked only about golf.

"Ever been to Gleneagles?"

"No, sir." That was the haunt of the Pullman classes.

"Play golf?"

"No."

"Have to get you started. Can't be a good surgeon, if you don't play golf."

He gave me a hole by hole account of his recent holiday; talked away any suspicion of a surgical disaster; reduced this five alarm emergency to an unusual complication. Neither Ken nor the theatre nurse would give the incident a thought by next day.

Boss undid the fatally flawed juncture; resutured the bowel and the stomach.

"Aitken. I'll close now. You get off and see to the tea."

Ken begged off. He wanted to go home and eat what was left of his oven-dried dinner. I had a tray set for two and the tea infusing by the time Boss arrived. He was in an immense good mood: expansive, genial as I had never known him and curiously easy to talk to. He relaxed in his chair; lit a gold banded Corona from a leather case he carried; sipped at his tea.

Danny Daly was never mentioned, nor Paul Baillie. The conversation got around to little old me: my family, the Faifley tenement, the lack of space, the problem of digs. Such self-revelation was an indulgence for me. I liked to keep my cards close to my chest. But for once I found it easy to let it all out – I wasn't sure why – then I stopped short.

Had I been whining; sounded disloyal to my parents?

"They've been great to me. It's just – I don't want to hang around their necks any more."

Boss threw the end of his cigar in the fire.

"You don't sound disloyal, Aitken. Just harassed. Now, this man we've operated on."

We. I liked that.

"I'll see the family myself in the morning. And you tell them only that there has been a complication. No details. You leave that to me."

As I was showing him out, Pringle sauntered in, in a state of post coital satiation: relaxed: let the next twenty-four hours bring what it would. Even the sight of Boss produced only modified alarm.

"Don't bother to come out with me, lads. Goodnight."

Pringle looked after him, then at me in indignant disbelief.

"Lads?" he said. "Lads? I've been here six months working my hairy little arse off, with never so much as a kind word. You're here six days and it's lads. Just how did you manage that?"

I shrugged with a nonchalance I hoped would carry me through the next few days.

BOOK SIX

Chapter 1

THE DANNY DALY BUSINESS WAS WORTH a five minute gossip in the morning, when the surgical staff arrived. They were in high glee about Boss being brought in to sort out one of Paul's cases, and mildly curious about the problem.

"Kink?"

"That's very unusual."

"That should be written up in one of the journals."

"What did it look like?"

I played ignorant.

"You would need to ask Mr McKenzie. I couldn't see all that well." Pringle added confirmation.

"I remember. Terrible problems with exposure. He was so fat."

Only Minty gave me a funny look.

Then the Gate bell went, and Pringle sprinted off. Minutes later, he sent over a plumber who had poured half a pint of molten lead into one of his gumboots, fusing the rubber to the foot. He followed that in close order with a twelve year old lass who had been stotting a ball on her way to school. It had gone high onto an asbestos roof, and she had shinned up a roan pipe after it. She came down much faster, through the tiles, and impaled herself on a metal spike. It had gone in one side and out the other. On the way it had traversed the spleen and the transverse colon. She was conscious, tearful, and worried.

"Whaur's ma ba'. Haw, mister. The polis will they keep it 'cos Ah went up on the roof?"

The loss of her ball was a catastrophe she could comprehend. She fingered the sawn off end of the inconceivable.

"Will this come oot? Will ah hiv tae stey like this?"

"Don't worry, hen," I said as I cuddled her head. "That man there. He'll soon get this out."

"So I will," Minty assured her. "And I'll get you a nice new ball into the bargain."

Both of these patients went to theatre on the stat express and Danny Daly's problems receded fast into the realms of a funny thing happened while I was in theatre last night.

At nine-thirty, I slid off and went to get Danny Daly's family ready to meet Boss. Usually, neither he nor Paul came in until ten on those long receiving days, in deference to their seniority, but Boss had said he would be in early.

Our intensive care was the best in the hospital: a screen around the bed, some glucose saline into a vein, and a prayer from the hospital padre. The docker's wife sat behind the screen, alone by the bed. She had been summoned by night beat bobbies, and had had the long dawn to contemplate the result of complications, a basket word that was going to mean whatever Boss cared.

"You must be tired," I said. "Have you had any breakfast?"

"Aye. The nurses. They've been that kind," she gestured at a cup and plate on the bedside locker – cold tea dregs, and a wedge of toast and marmalade.

She was a shilpit wee creature: a bauchle: a nondescript. Unhappiness sat in every line of her face: set by years of disappointment over hopes that had never run high anyhow. Yet she had a grave dignity, sitting bolt upright, with her hands clasped patiently.

"Mr McKenzie would like to speak to you. He's the chief. If you're ready, I'll take you to him."

She looked at her man, who was in a hectic, sweating sleep, and shook her head, but the bad dream wouldn't go away.

"Aye. That wid be fine. Need tae get awa' hame, then. Let the weans ken. They're a' merrit an' oot the hoose, noo."

The woman always held the family together.

In Boss's room, I placed a chair for her. She sat down, clasped her hands again and looked up at him.

"You've been told there was a complication?"

"Aye."

The assent was qualified. No one had explained a damn thing to her.

"Well, I've sorted that out."

That I again. He stood in front of his fire: big as a church; big as a great bloody cathedral. He was so immense, she had to believe him – more, believe in him – without question or qualification.

"As far as last night's operation goes, everything is now absolutely as it should be. The trouble is his general condition. Very poor. He hasn't looked after himself over the years, has he?"

She nodded. No way could she deny that.

"More's the pity, for it's up to him now. I can do no more."

It was a rotten, calculated, bare-faced confidence trick: and absolutely brilliant. Paul's name was never mentioned. The whole affair was centred on Boss, this *deus ex chirurgica*: larger than life and twice as possible. If I did my part now; kept my mouth shut, Paul was off the hook. And I might have won myself a powerful patron. But if I spoke up; played the fink, surely there would be an action for negligence? Danny Daly might get great lorryloads of fivers? Or, much more important, if shock and infection carried him off, this poor loser in the three-legged race of marriage would find herself unhobbled, and with all the lovely boodle to herself.

There and then, I had the choice.

It didn't take me long. I'd get noble if and when I had my fellowship in the bag, my career on a high road of success, and a private practice of my own. In the meantime I showed Mrs Daly out, and wrote culpable operation notes to Boss's dictation.

"Get hold of Baillie when he comes in. Tell him to come straight to this room and keep everyone out of here until I've finished with him."

There was to be a drum-head court martial, with Boss the drummer boy, the judge and the firing squad. I hung around the lift door until Paul arrived, then posted myself guard on the door. After a few moments, though, I was summoned to take part in the proceedings.

"Aitken. Baillie here doesn't believe me. Tell him what we found."

The lack of a formal title in my presence flayed what was left of Baillie's self-respect. His eyes went wet with fear. He looked at me for some relief from his ordeal, but I had none. I recounted what I had seen in my best student phraseology, too obviously recalled from memory to be part of any destructive plot.

He went from grey to a putty colour. He reached for the back of a chair. His legs collapsed him on to the seat. He licked at lips gone sticky and flaky.

"Now, Baillie. If this gets out they'll sieve you down for fish bait. Malpractice. Newspapers. Damages. I don't have to tell you. But we might just get you off with it. Better go sick for a week or two. A month. You'll never be missed."

Boss was wielding obloquy like a butcher's cleaver.

"And when you do come back, you won't be doing any more major surgery. Not in my wards."

Of course. Why had I been so dense. Nothing must spoil the reputation of his beloved, bloody wards.

"Don't get in such a funk, man. You still have your appointment. You can do out-patient work. And you do insurance reports, don't you? You can work up that side of things."

It was the last resort of the failed surgeon: pen instead of scalpel.

Baillie left somehow, forcing his legs to work. I followed him after a decent interval and ran right into Minty.

"What the hell is the matter with Paul? He looks sea-sick. You're holding out on your uncle. Confession is what you need. You'll feel better. What's been going on?"

Curiously, he was right. I had to get Mrs Daly off my chest.

"Minty. It's more than my life is worth if this gets out."

"I knew it," he said in deep gratification. "I just knew it. It's this kink nonsense, isn't it?"

"Yes."

Later, in the Maryhill Harrier, I told him the story.

"An ileo-colic anastomosis?" He was awed. "Jesus to Murgatroyd. There's mistakes, and then there are God Almighty fuck-ups."

He paused to see if he could think of worse, but he couldn't. Then he addressed my moral problem.

"Well, suppose you had sung out? He may get something out of it, but there's no guarantee. By any standards, it was a difficult operation. And as Boss said, made worse by his own life-style. A good lawyer would make a meal of that. It will be different for his wife if he dies, of course."

He eyed me speculatively. It was too late to worry about that now.

"What about the old guy the Boss sliced open? Wasn't that just as bad?"

Minty made judicial mewings.

"I can't agree. Boss's case was an emergency. Red hot. Paul's case was cold turkey. Besides, Boss retrieved the situation, and the old boy's doing fine."

I let myself be convinced. It was easier than guilt.

"Besides which, you won't have done yourself any harm by phoning Boss as you did. Sticking your neck out. You wait and see."

I was all for being in Boss's good books, but I couldn't think of any practical good that might come of the affair.

See imagination? It never was my strong point.

Next day, Joss Shearer got back from a week in the rain at Tighnabruach, and I got back to the rolling, fertile acres beside the Forth. I was busy from the minute I arrived. Dave McDonald had put a graip tine through his foot and was laid up. That left Sandy short of a man and that meant work for me all hours. But Danny Daly wasn't easy to forget. In the end, I phoned the wards.

Danny Daly was dead. I would have to live with my denial.

The following Friday, I went back for more. That's what you have to do.

I was clerking cases in a corner, when Minty came up to me.

"He wants you to go to Shaw's Howe with him today."

"Me? What for?"

A sly grin slid over his face,

"I don't know, but you'll get to meet Easy Annie."

I winced at the repetition of the casual, male slander. She must have some other qualities? Raised carnations? Was kind to her old mother?

"And I want a blow by blow account of what goes on."

"Every last detail," I promised him.

After his morning tea, puffing cigar smoke, and trailing me behind him like a little red caboose, Boss steamed out of the door of the Northern General. I opened that lovely, solid door for him, scuttled round the other side, and climbed in a Rolls. As he drove us in state through the grey, stone gorges of Maryhill, he said, "Know anything about this place we're going to, Aitken?"

"Not a lot, sir. Except it's a fever hospital."

"Right. And most of it is still used for infectious diseases. But your interest lies in a block at the back of the hospital. At the start of the war, it was policy to clear all long term cases from the teaching hospitals. Make room for the air raid casualties expected. Every ward had its share of such patients. Pathological rarities no one knew what to do with. So, they squeezed the accomodation at Shaw's Howe. Emptied a pavilion, and filled it with such cases. Now, the newly qualified men needed all the experience of acute medicine they could get, before going to the war. As you can imagine, residents for such a place were in short supply."

I could see all that, but where my interest lay was quite obscure.

"Somebody suggested appointing a senior student. Someone with common sense, a good pair of hands, and the savvy to phone for help when needed. You can use a phone, can't you."

I had the feeling I'd been plugged into the electricity: a mild disbelieving buzz. And my voice came out at the squeaky end of the vocal register. "Yes."

"The scheme never got off the ground. There isn't much need for medical advice. It's mostly nursing and TLC. The sister in charge came to run things on a day to day basis. She gets help from staff physicians and visiting consulants, as needed. The block was supposed to be phased out at the end of the war. But that hasn't happened, so far. The people staying there have come to look on it as a kind of sanctuary. And, of course, there are always more of these disasters. So, there's still a thriving – if that's the word – case load. And the resident post was never formally cancelled."

The transformer in my head buzzed even louder.

"Now, the medical super out here is an old chum of mine. I've spoken to him. If it will help you, you can have the job."

Was this the price of Mrs Daly?

"What would it mean, in practical terms?"

"You'll get your bed, laundry and meals. No money. You won't appear on any payroll. That way, we can still wangle it under the new NHS."

Wangle? The Boss was putting on the old English for me?

"It will be understood that you are a student, with vacations and study leave. In effect, you will make yourself useful to sister any way you can, during term time."

This cruel old bugger was handing me no slender lifeline. This was a total support system. My conscience was sinking under the weight of the bribe, so I held it under till it was good and drowned.

"Sir, this would be the most tremendous help to me in all sorts of ways." My mind raced: preserve my independence, save my stake money, get on a happier footing with Connie again. "I don't know how to thank you."

He gave me a look. Abject servility would do for a start.

"There's only one proviso."

I didn't care what he came up with. I'd give Daniel Webster lessons in dealing with the devil to keep this berth.

"You must pass muster with Sister Urquhart."

Easy Annie.

The cast was light, the lure innocent: but I had the notion he was fishing. Had I nibbled at the tasty gossip of hospital corridors?

"She's a dragon then, sir?"

I was as innocent as any Cherubino: never heard tell of his infamous lay.

Boss laughed: this time without malice, or threat, or sneer. I was so right, it was funny.

"She'll have you toasted for tea, if you don't shape up, sonny."

Boss twirled the Rolls off the main road into a formal driveway lined with beech trees. A merchant's estate in the countryside south of Loch Lomond, it had been acquired by Glasgow Corporation before the first war, and turned into a hospital, with pavilions spread in the parkland. The offices and doctors' mess were in the old mansion house, and some Emergency Treatment Service huts from the more recent hostilities had been squashed amongst the original buildings.

Tarmacadam paths ran in a neat geography, but the neglect of wartime had allowed dockens to burst through the driveways; buttercups to stifle the flowerbeds; and the once white stucco of the pavilions to turn patchy grey with lichen. We stopped behind a pavilion built into a slope. I followed Boss, as he climbed the stairway to an open verandah that ran around three sides of the pavilion.

It was a pleasant day: warm and bright, with a few puff-ball clouds. I noticed a sister coming to the head of the steps. No doubt Easy Annie was taking the air; coming to give her flowers and chocolates surgeon the old come on.

Not wanting to stare, I looked where my feet were going. I schooled myself to wheedle, fawn, ingratiate myself: any damn thing it took to get my slippers under the resident's bed.

But I was curious too. What would she look like? Would she have the sly eyes of the coyly licentious, or the hard case stare of the harlot? Would she have a motherly, welcoming smile, or the tight, frightened face of a Messalina past her best?

As I came to the top of the steps, I took in narrow feet in flat, black regulation shoes; a thin, almost gaunt frame, made more so by the stark, dark blue dress. The Corporation didn't run to lace and bows and the white apron and headdress were absolutely plain. The whole impresssion was one of severity. It was well suited to a face that had once known how to smile, but which was now set forever in the sad lines of a heart broken beyond mending.

Chapter 2

FOR ONE INFINITESIMAL MOMENT I had an impression of consternation in her eyes. But my perception of such an unlikely reaction was immediately rubbished.

"Good Lord. Sir Galahad," she laughed.

My face burned. See if I would carry her bloody box again.

"You know him?" Boss said and he wasn't best pleased. I had assured him I had never heard of his mistress.

She defused his suspicions with genuine amusement.

"This is the boy who carried my box at the station. It was so heavy. I told you about it at the time. So gall*ant*."

She Frenchified the second syllable.

"Stiff-necked as a Castilian grandee when I came to offer him a bob. You must remember."

That must have been some recounting. So much for the private communion I thought we had shared. The wide, grey eyes looked at Boss: invited him to join my reduction to the ranks of the absurd.

He sissled his sibilant chuckle.

"Ss.Ss.Ss. So you were the buck. Well, you had better meet formally now. Sister Urquhart."

I shook the long, thin hand, cool as an Eau de Cologne compress.

"You made a good impression that day. Now see if you can keep it up."

Then they went through the door and off down a corridor, which made a fourth side to the verandah.

There had been no give-away glances; no smirks of satisfaction past, nor yet to come. Nor had there been the slightest body contact. Apart from discomfiting me, the meeting had been almost ceremonial. And now they were deep into matters allopathic: talking about the patients who lay ahead.

I skulked behind, mortified: whittled down to size three in baby boots: wondering what had set the sister off like that. My dealings with her had been momentary: the briefest exchanges of words; encounters of eyes. Yet I would have bet money she would never be casually hurtful.

She would, without doubt, live up to her saurian reputation with any resident who didn't shape up: destroy him at a gulp. But this ridicule?

The wards were spruce and orderly. Any sister worth the starch in her apron would see to parade ground neatness: covers even, pillows straight, patients seated to attention in bed, or in wheelchairs at the side.

Yet there was a difference from the barracks discipline and sparseness I was used to at the Northern General. Here, there were montages of photographs pinned to the wall behind each bed: box Brownie snaps of families, pets, homes; bigger portraits of weddings, christenings. The locker tops were crammed with the whims of daily life: the well dottled pipes, the Swan Vestas boxes, the silver hunters and watch chains of the men: the knitting bags, the brightly coloured Bertie Basset boxes, the lavender-water bottles of the women.

Then, too, the patients were dressed differently. No shorty gowns, or towelling robes, or sloppy mules, the uniform of the teaching hospitals. Here, there was a motley of mufti: tartan mohair dressing gowns and big, bumphly cardigans; grandma slippers with zip up fronts and sandshoes, brown, other ranks, for the use of.

Standing orders had been modified.

It took a few moments for the significance to sink in. Boss had been explicit about the case load, but until then, it had conveyed nothing to me in human terms.

Now I understood.

These people had had their contracts with life cancelled: a one-sided sacking with no union to intervene; no possibility of arbitration. These beds, these lockers, these chairs; a day room off the corridor; the verandah for sunny days; a suitcase in the store-room, were all they had left in the business of being someone. The rest had been forfeited to their diseases.

Classification was impossible. The place was a pathology index run wild; an exhibition of the implacable will of God. It would have been much more bearable to bury them dead. Since we couldn't, we would bury them alive.

At each bed, I had ample time to consider the cases: the lopped, asymmetrical uselessness of multiple dismemberment; the muscle blight of motor neurone disease, leaving only a few fingers to gesture: the voice weak and gargling through secretions that could not be coughed away, prelude to drowning in them; the black, slow suffocation of chronic chest disease with lung failure; the creeping, invincible gangrene of diabetes, frosting toes, then feet, then whole limbs into sugary decay; the drooling, skelly-eyed, imbecility of the sleepy sickness that had plagued the land for a few disastrous years.

Yet, whatever their complaint; their dolour, they sat up as best they could: important for a few moments every week, courtesy of the double act played by Boss and Sister Annie.

Boss's progress was, if possible, more regal than his rounds at the Northern General. He stopped at every bed. The bigger the human disaster, the more he listened and nodded; joked and encouraged. He countenanced their misfortune; stared them in the face of their bane; gave weighted attention to every small complaint.

Here was no ruthlessly cheerful but unseeing eye; no professional detachment further distanced by indifference: but someone who gave them a chance to vent spleen, distemper, depression, and sheer, manic, bloody outrage, at what fate had perpetrated on them.

When he left the bedsides, the difference was obvious. I could see that the patients sat straighter; were animated, often laughing, now their humanity had been vindicated for a few moments.

And at each stop, his nursing sister reinforced his attentiveness by small, calm movements: moving a pillow, soothing a brow, easing a dressing; but, mostly, by her all-encompassing, grey, grave gaze.

They left me to myself; left me to walk behind, to observe, to absorb, to try to take in the enormity of what was going on here.

I didn't find that easy, but as we came to the end of the round, I thought I had put not a bad face on things. And, at least, I had suffered no further ignominy. If all went according to Boss's usual habit, there would be a cup of tea in sister's room in five minutes: one I was suddenly looking forward to.

See expectations?

As we came to the last bed, Boss said.

"What about Rankine?"

Sister Annie's eyes were at their widest, greyest, bleakest: something else she had been looking at.

"I'm afraid there's more crusting at the eyes. It's painful when he blinks. The crusts should be removed again."

" We'll let him do it, shall we?"

Him was me. Boss's grin was a thin grimace of challenge.

What the hell? After all I had seen that morning, there was nothing left that could possibly faze me.

Sister Annie summoned a dressing trolley and screens for the last bed. Partitioned from the world, we ranged round a guy who'd been at the carnival; bought himself a clown's disguise: an all-in-one celluloid nose and black, horse-hair moustache, mounted on thick black frames which had no lenses.

"Well, soldier?" Boss was at his most jovial; his fiercest.

The head nodded and bounced in answer. Alert, pale blue eyes peered through the empty lens frames. Lamb noises emphasized how good he felt: a curious bleating tone, without resonance; without fricatives or plosives or labials.

Sister Annie leaned forward, and removed the thick rimmed glasses. With them came the nose and the moustache: the best the prosthetic department could do.

There was nothing left of the centre of the face. A triangular hole stretched from the root of the nose to the lower lip, and an edentulous lower gum. The cavern was lined by moist, pink mucous membrane, incongruously healthy and normal. Boss waved at the sight.

"He had an epithelioma. Right on the bridge of his nose. Ignored it for – how long was it?" he appealed to the hole in the head for verification. "Two years, was it?"

The head bounced and nodded and bleated in agreement.

The doctor cost money and at first, the sore wouldn't have seemed serious: slow growing and painless. First he would have tried Germolene and hot lint and herbal balsam.

"Then he had some X-rays. But they burnt off his whole damn nose. Trouble was, they didn't kill all of the growth. It started up again. But they couldn't risk any more treatment."

The malignancy was still feasting on the edges of each cheek: an isosceles of ruin brought about by the growth and radiation necrosis. The two eyes still, improbably, acting in conjunction, rolled and winked on either side of the apex: while ulceration nibbled at the sight of both, in sores that ran in thin pus; and which, here and there, had scabbed over in a vain attempt at healing. I had expected nothing like it. The ward floor heaved. My gorge rose. My mouth poured saliva.

Three things stopped me disgorging my breakfast over my boots.

The first was Boss. He must have noticed my face: green; the sheen of sweat. His grin grew, as he savoured my imminent ignominy.

The second was this rare show without a face. To signal our first meeting by splashing my stomach contents on the ward floor would be to underscore his monsterhood. What he needed; must at all costs have, was an affirmation of his right to be seen as just another man.

But most of all, I simply wouldn't show myself up again in front of this starched dame who had already mocked me.

Boss watched me for a long moment, the grin unchanging. Was he disappointed I had failed to tickle his bleak sense of humour ? Or could it be I had just passed some harsh test?

He turned back to the patient, as Sister Annie pointed to the problem.

"See here, Aitken. These crusts need to be removed. You get on with that, while I'm having my tea."

His bloody tea.

He sailed off with those coat tails flying. Sister Annie summoned a nurse. No lace caps here: little, plain bonnet like a Dutch doll.

"Nurse will help you. And you will be gentle?"

I said nothing.

"But there, I'm sure you will."

The grey eyes had seen something favourable after all.

When I had finished ministering to the wobbly eyes, I orienteered my way along the unfamiliar corridor. It ended in a door marked 'Resident'. Just before it, double glass doors led out to a glass-roofed atrium, mildly arboreal with potted palms and creepers. After the sights of the morning it seemed especially airy; light; cheerful. Doors opened on to the ward kitchen, a clinical laboratory, a staff toilet: and the lair of Sister Annie.

There had been precious little sign of femininity so far: and certainly no evidence of the voluptuary. Perhaps, now, there would be a hint of the petticoat? Touches of pink? A hint of perfume?

But no. The room was stark as any novitiate's cell: walls unadorned; desk laid with blotter, temperature charts; ward notes: all in minutely correct detail.

The one gesture of cheer was – naturally – a pot of tea stewing in the hearth and a tray with cups, milk, sugar, a plate each of sandwiches and cake. By that time, I knew, the tea must have been distilled into a brew, black and bitter enough to bring on instant tanninosis of the stomach. But I wanted nothing more than a big draught of it: retreat into a corner; hold the cup two-handed; close my eyes in the soothing steam.

But I had to pipe for my Orange Pekoe first.

"How long d'you give him, Aitken? That last patient?"

My mind balked at trying to put a time on a life like that. How long could a man live without a face, the mask we all hide behind? Smiles, frowns, amusements, loves, hates – or the counterfeits thereof – all rendered impossible by this pink, moist, pit of destruction. I fell back on a garble of conventional pathology, while I tried to encompass this new, unimagined, unimaginable morbidity.

"Ah– yes – well – depends on different factors. The histology of the tumour. The differentiation of the cells–"

Boss's face went bleak with disbelief. If I had passed some test in the ward, I was ploughing this one.

I floundered on, but he cut me short.

"Don't be such a damn fool."

My face went red for the second time that morning.

"Sister. How long?"

She had been sitting, hands clasped: prim and proper as a Philadelphia quaker. Now she enunciated the pragmatics of such a state: so obvious, they hadn't crossed my mind.

"His sight must become affected soon. I doubt if he'll be able to stand being blind as well. We'll find him somewhere. The bathrooms are popular. They can lock themselves in. It gives them a privacy of sorts at the end."

Finding suicides was another part of her job, it seemed. No wonder the grey eyes were uncompromising.

"Better get Mitchell, the eye man, to look at him anyhow, sister."

No matter this would be the most useless, futile gesture, Boss would see the man without a face had every attention.

"And what about this fellow?"

I had as much dignity left as a slave on an auction block. Perhaps she would look in my mouth; examine the teeth; prod the belly muscles.

But my trials by ridicule had served me better than I could have hoped.

"Yes. I think we can make something of him."

"Your lucky day, Aitken." Boss's tone was still as dry as an ounce of alum, after my exhibition. "I'll get away back to the Northern, now." Breeze in unexpected: put the fear of God in everyone. "Sister will show you the resident's quarters. Tell you what she expects of you. Maybe have a few jobs for you while you're here. You can find your own way back."

She nodded in brisk agreement. Sooner I knew my place, the better. She showed him out, and came back into the room.

"I shall go for lunch now. Then there are some dressings you can help with. I'll be half an hour. You can finish the sandwiches and cake, if you like."

I eyed those grey eyes again. The food didn't amount to a whole lot of lunch pail, but the gesture was thoughtful: even kind.

This lady was a funny mixture.

Chapter 3

BACK AT THE FARM NEXT DAY, I TOSSED THE NEWS AT WILSON.

"By the way, I've found somewhere to stay."

I told him the story: casual: never let him guess how hard he had hit me. He was glad enough, in a perfunctory way. He was well into the young squire mould, often walking about the fields with the Major, taking a proprietary view.

On my side of the green baize gates, however, the prospect was rosy too. All of my main worries had answers in view, and the coming year was a breeze as far as examinations went. The two degree subjects were minor: public health and medical jurisprudence; why water closets were good for your health and how to stay out of jail. Word was these could be passed on a week's hard cram.

The rest of the session would be filled with small specialty clinics. We would have to rush all over town to places like the Ophthalmic Institute, and the Ear Nose and Throat Hospital. Beyond those foothills, of course, the finals lay: the big subjects – surgery, medicine and now obstetrics. There would be a continual layering of texts and lectures; knowledge and know-how; techniques and practice, for the day we would be let loose on a trusting population.

Connie and I got on famously that summer, the more because I no longer felt I had to work so hard at my knightly charade and in September I snuck her off to Glasgow and got her signed on at the RSAMD; the royally wrong place to learn short-hand and book-keeping. It was easy.

"You'll be busy with your own arrangements?" I suggested to Noelle.

"Would you be so sweet? Look after her?"

She now sported the drawl of languid boredom that went with doing life classes: if one had seen one john, one had seen them all. Wilson had been a shade reserved about her drawing other men's cocks, but such was the price of artistic sophistication. Nor was Connie's auntie any more interested. She waved the pair of us away in lethargic dispassion.

Left to ourselves, I steered Connie up the steps of the academy; oversaw her double-crossing registration; bought her a couple of second-hand book-keeping texts, to help the deception along; and left her off with Johnny Newton for a couple of hours. Johnny had pestered me to act as courier, until he had arranged a date.

"He's sweet," she confided on the train back. "But I could never take him seriously."

Just as I figured. Wasn't I the clever sod.

"I wouldn't let on to Noelle about him," I warned.

"You don't like her, do you?" she said. "I wasn't going to anyhow."

Before term started, I gave myself a week off. I feted Jock and Maisie to the best I could afford: treats I would luxurify as soon as I could manage. Then, since the girls' courses had both already started, Wilson and I met them most lunchtimes for a Scotch pie and a cup of tea at one of James Craig's tea-rooms.

Connie was as high as a pressure-cooker on excitement, her secret threatening to burst out. But, in Noelle's company, she did manage to suggest a boring old diet of spacers and shift keys, compared to her cousin's artistic stardust. She gave away her real state of mind only when she winked at me and by wearing the pebble necklet.

"It's the new me," she confided, as I helped her off with her coat and scarf, which had hidden the bauble.

Noelle got her eye on it at once.

"Where did you get that?" she demanded, almost indignant.

"I saved up," answered Connie.

Her tone proclaimed the blatant lie and that Noelle would have to lump it. Noelle bared her little teeth in a smile that would have done credit to a tiger shark.

Wilson looked on in benign incomprehension, which I aped. No point in adding to Noelle's venom. I could understand the kid taking this kind of swipe at her, but I wasn't sure it was wise. Still, Connie seemed satisfied with one little nip of independence: no blood drawn. She settled to her usual laudatory role: admire all of Noelle's doings. By the time the bill came, I thought it had all been forgotten.

See presumptions?

Apart from these pleasant interludes, the original sextet sat around a coffee table in the Georgic tea-room, and, using Malcolm Ritchie's notes, tried to cook up a timetable that would allow us to stick together. But it was a mixture that wouldn't rise. We couldn't all be fitted into the small clinics. In the end it was agreed we would meet up for the main lectures on the campus, but for the rest, we would split up into the easy pairings that had already evolved: Alexander and Abercrombie, Minnie and Luke, Wilson and myself.

I found myself unexpectedly glad that Wilson still took our old chums act so much for granted. God alone knew the formula, but the chemistry went on working, despite the way our lives were diverging. I let him arrange things for us without argument. At the end of it all, he announced himself very satisfied, except for the gynaecology class.

"Best I could do was the Royal Jericho. Everywhere else was full. Clinic of some chap called Finlay McLaren. Don't know much about him, do you?"

Where had I heard the name? Of course, he was Minty's source of the dirt on Easy Annie. D Finlay McLaren to his menorrhagic patients: Finnie McLaren to his buddies.

Now, the chances of a clinic student winkling anything of a personal nature out of a consultant was as unlikely as me transcribing my medical notes into Linear B. But I badly needed to know more about this lady; to find out what made her tick: and a million to one chance was better than no dice game at all.

"I think you've done very well, young man. I'm pleased with you."

He grinned all over his chubby face, and I grinned back, our friendship suddenly stronger for a new acceptance of our differences.

"How're the new digs turning out?"

"Fine. Really good in fact. I have to get out there now. Meet you in the Union tomorrow at eleven?"

I ran for a northbound tram and this perplexing sister.

At the beginning of the week, I had thought it politic to go to Shaw's Howe earlier than officially required: show willing to Sister Annie; put my spare shirt in a drawer; see if I could pan a little gold from the stream of hospital gossip. I went to see the super first: Boss McKenzie's chum.

Dr Norman Ball was a thin man, with crinkly white hair and few words.

"So you're McKenzie's protegé, eh?"

I was a protegé? That was several shades better than the Judas I had been to Mrs Daly. I thought it better to agree.

"Yes, sir. He seemed to think Sister Urquhart would knock me into shape."

He inclined his head in agreement.

"Yes. A remarkable lady. How she has stood the emotional drain of that place all this time?"

He shook his head and had me fill out a couple of forms. Then I went to my digs, case in hand; feeling good. But Sister Annie soon fixed that when I knocked on her door.

"You've come, then?"

It should have been rhetorical, but once more I had this sense of undercurrent; of reserve. What had I ever done to her?

"Good. As soon as you are ready, there are some things you can get on with."

Not a word of welcome, nor of thanks for showing up early.

My little kingdom was literally *en suite*. A vestibule led to bathroom to bedroom to sitting room back to vestibule. At the far end, another door led on to the balcony as it finished its run around three sides of the pavilion, and a mirror image of the steps I had climbed the first day.

"Private entrance, should you wish," she had said that first day, in a tone that implied she didn't and I shouldn't. She wanted everyone to come past her door: get her beady eye on them. The bedroom was standard hospital issue: bone hard mattress, bedside rug the size of a prayer mat, light green distemper above white tiles. The sitting room was a surprise, though. The green distemper had been overlaid by a carnival of stencilled mannikins. They were flying kites, spinning tops, bowling hoops: the colours bold and bright.

"There was a diphtheria epidemic in one of the paediatric tuberculosis wards," she had explained. "We took four of them in here until quarantine was lifted."

Was there a softening of that unsmiling face at the recollection?

"I'll have it painted over."

"No. Please leave it. Cheers the place up."

She had taken me at my word and the mannikins welcomed me, even if she hadn't. I put on the starched white coat that had been left out for me and went to find what my duties were.

Sister Annie ran through the things to be done for the ward patients. They were all straightforward and within the competence of any student at my stage but there was plenty to keep me busy. As she went through the list, I noticed the name of the Good Soldier Rankine was no longer on it. I asked about him.

"Mercifully, he took a heart attack."

I found myself relieved she hadn't had to look for him in one of those grim bathrooms. She wasn't my engaging personality of the nursing establishment, but those bleak, grey eyes, and that bitter, hurt look seemed to have tholed so much.

"If you will see to the clincal tests in the morning, before you go? Then it would be a help if you will help lift some of the heavier patients for dressings. But that could be left until your afternoon classes are over."

Her thoughtfulness was showing again.

"That would suit me very well, sister."

I found if I dug myself out of my pit and scampered about a bit, I could get the side-room stuff done by eight: Esbachs, haemoglobins, stained films and the like, with the Bunsen burner roaring cheerily in the fast-darkening, temperature-dropping, winter-approaching mornings; bacteriology cultures and the more complex biochemistry packed in a sample box, ready to go to the main laboratory.

A fast breafast, and I was off to town: to a routine of looking at skins and in eyes and down throats and up fannies. I learned enough about the first three to get me by, if all else failed and I ended up a National Health Service GP in Townhead. But for me, the most interesting clinic was gynaecology.

I had, by then, enough experience of acute abdominal emergencies to know how sly, feminine conundrums could sneak up on an unwary surgeon: a hot Fallopian tube mimicking an appendicitis; an acute gall-bladder, with upper epigastric tenderness and referred shoulder pain, straight from the book, turning out to be an ectopic pregnancy. A general surgeon had better know the distaff side of things in case he found himself unwittingly operating in the powder room.

And Finnie was a good tutor.

Mondays and Wednesdays, he lectured Wilson and me on abortions, accidental and otherwise. Not much you could do about the first, and absolutely nothing you should do about the second.

"It will be surprising if you go through your professional careers without being asked at least once – and I mean begged, implored and entreated – by some distracted woman threatening suicide. Or the parents of some poor kid you know, who let it happen just the once. I have only one word for you. Don't. All you will get yourself is bread and water in the pokey for three years and your parchment in the bin."

He taught us about the bear trap of irregular menopausal bleeding: the benign sign of metropathia or fibroids; or the malign gore of cancer?

"Learn this catechism and never forget it. You assume every woman over forty, with irregular bleeding, has cancer, until you've made quite sure she hasn't."

He went through the whole textbook of problems that the men didn't have.

On Fridays, however, Wilson and I split up. Alternate weeks, one went with the registrar to the out-patient department and violated, in his turn, a series of stirrup-hung, looking-away-with-embarrassment, bear-it-all-in-silence ladies in gloved search of diagnosis; while the other went to stand behind Finnie in the main theatre, to learn how to mend the organ of desire; tighten the lax, man-devastated passage; stop the poor woman falling out of her own insides.

On one of these occasions, I was getting myself ready to stand behind him; hold forceps; cut stitches. I gowned myself, then snapped myself into a pair of latex gloves. There's a trick to it: enough talcum powder; dive the hand in fast; get the fingers right up first time, to avoid wrinkles. It takes practice before it looks easy.

"You've done that before."

I told him about my sessions in Boss's firm.

"That old bugger. Haven't heard of him for a while."

From his tone it was clear he had heard a whole lot at one time. I wondered if I could steer him onto the subject of Easy Annie, but before I could get around to her, he had hooked a stool under him with his foot, and was seated before an anonymous, draped passage of birth. Perhaps I could get back to it in the changing room?

"See this."

He plunged a speculum up to its hilt in the vagina, and racked it open. He clamped a pair of tisssue forceps onto the lower lip of the cervix, and pulled it down for me to see. The tip of the entrance to the womb was bloody; ulcerated; eaten away.

"This is an early case of carcinoma, with no obvious spread. All I shall do here is amputate the cervix. Keep radium up our sleeves. Now, watch how I do this."

Finnie began his attack. He was fast, almost aggressive, in contrast to Boss. I watched, fascinated; comparing techniques; figuring out my own style. I was on my way back to Shaw's Howe before I realized I had clean forgotten to pump him about Boss's paramour.

Chapter 4

THE TERM TURNED INTO A REAL FAIR-GROUND of new experience, and I was happy in the way that happens when there is worthwhile work to do. The only mild reservation I had about the whole fourth year set-up was Sister Annie.

At first I kept my mouth shut, and simply got on with what she told me to do. In time, however, I began to relax. Not that I became her Little Boy Blue, not by a long blow of the horn. But she began to countenance the fact that I did not need constant supervision; that I could be trusted to do what she expected. This, however, led to no change in her attitude. I was kept strictly at arm's length.

When I make up my mind, I can usually get on with people: old men, wee lassies, tram conductors, piano players; anybody. Nothing deep, you understand. No plunge into the murky pools of psyche. A mere canter on common pastures; a nibble at the short grass of common interest.

And the more so with ladies.

This isn't a big, macho, sexual thing. It's just that from three to ninety-three, I find them prettier than men. They attract me more. I like the way they dress and walk and smell nice. I love their curves, and the soft feel of them. I love the way their dresses swish and their eyes shine. They make the world feel good.

But not this dame.

No matter the overture I made – and I tried the lot, from hospital gossip, to the price of carrots, to where she liked to go on holiday – I got the same response: a large and icy mitt. I was treated with grave deference. Our relationship was confined to a professional propriety. And as for laughter – that strange bird I had caused to fly on my first day – that was kept in a cage.

The real Sister Urquhart – the sinning wife, the raging nympho, the paid-up mistress, the angel of mercy, whoever – could not be teased from behind this screen of punctilio.

I had to disappoint Minty in his prurience.

"She may have been la Grande Horizontale in her day, Minty, but somewhere along the line, she's been stood vertical, and had a bloody great poker rammed up her jaxi. I simply cannot imagine her getting lukewarm, never mind in heat."

A couple of further gleanings of chance information confused me even more.

In the last week of term, for instance, one of the nurses gave me a startling insight into her life. Nurses all worked long, long hours, to the order of a stern, matriarchal establishment. The precepts of personnel management were simple: poor pay, rigid discipline, and sackings with no right of appeal. The long shifts bristled with duties. Studies were crammed into off duty hours. Ward protocol was enforced to the letter. Yet it bred a spirit you wouldn't believe. These girls were magnificent.

Of course, time off was a joyous, hallowed release, and no one volunteered for extra duty. Yet, Sister Annie seemed to spend more time in the wards than could ever be encompassed by a duty roster, even one made out by a Victorian work-house Matron. When I asked this nurse about it, her reply was so simple as to seem naive at first.

"I don't think she has anywhere else to go."

"She must have some family?"

"Nope. She just lives in the sisters' home."

I smiled, the feeble grimace of eating my own words. Living in the multi-ocular society of a hundred women, Sister Annie's every move would have been as well charted as a Bartholomew's map. I was left to suck on a conclusion as bitter as a quassia draught.

Whatever she might have been in the past, at the present moment, Sister Annie must be lonely.

The next shaft of mystifying illumination came on the last Friday of term, when Wilson cut his gynae clinic.

"Noelle has a class demonstration. Pictures on the wall. I have to go along and admire."

"Your friend not here today?" asked Finnie later and I mumbled an excuse for Wilson. "Well, the list is very small. Couple of cases only. Both dilatation and curettage. You can have a try at them. I'll sit by you. Then we'll have some coffee. I have something for you."

He let me get the feel of the dilators as I broached the womb, the ultimate cavern of femininity; the right amount of pressure to put on the curette, as I scraped the sharp-edged spoon over the inner surface and ladled out the faulty lining in small, bloody, fleshy spoonfuls.

Later in his room, I poured coffee for us, while he fished in a filing cabinet for a big envelope and a brown paper parcel.

" Your friend is all right, but you try harder. These are a first class certificate and a book on gynaecological surgery. Class prize. Maybe help your ambitions."

I had let some of these show, as we worked together.

The certificate was official, and that was a pretty little feather for my collection, and Minty's approbation. But I also knew the book had come from his own pocket.

"That's very decent of you. Thank you. The book looks great."

I then told him about Minty's suggested timetable.

"You know Minty well?"

"Yes. He's been a great buddy to me."

He nodded in amiable recognition of a mutual chum. And then seemed a good time to go for the less obvious prize I had let slip when talking to him before.

I told him about Boss and the Shaw's Howe job. I didn't make a big thing of it, just chat over the coffee, but it was the perfect lead in.

"There's a ward sister there who's a bit fierce. Sister Urquhart."

I didn't put any question in my voice: simply dropped the name into his pool of memory; see if any memories rippled out.

"Urquhart? Anne Urquhart?"

The name stopped him dead. His cup was half way to his mouth, but he put it back on the saucer, untasted.

"Of course. I had forgotten. She's still there, then?" But this was no Easy Annie he was remembering. Nor a dragon. Nor a saint. This was Anne before the fall. An Anne who had all the lost innocence and romance of Avonlea. "What a creature. Lovely. Absolutely gorgeous."

My ears laid back at that, spooked as a jackass at a rattlesnake. Gorgeous?

"Terrible tragedy that." He wasn't talking to me. He was reiterating something he hadn't cared to mention for a long time. Then his timetable caught up with him. "Must fly." He swallowed his coffee and shook my hand for luck. "Give Minty my regards. And stick in at the books. I'm sure you'll do well."

When I got back to the pavilion at Shaw's Howe, I couldn't take my eyes off Sister Annie. Gorgeous, the man had said: but I simply couldn't imagine it. Whatever had caused it, the sadness had branded her permanently.

Later, I was changing a suprapubic catheter, when the lady herself came up to me.

"You still get the Fife train sometimes? Get off at Dalmeny?"

"Yes. Most weekends."

"Can I ask a favour, then?"

At least it wouldn't be to carry her box. She wouldn't dare: not after her effrontery.

But it was.

"I have such a heavy case." The grey eyes were steady and I sensed she was ready for a put-down. "If you would be kind enough to take it for me, and leave it at the ticket office, I could have it picked up from there."

I ran over a few richly deserved, smart answers in my mind.

"Sure. Glad to. I can take it with me now. I spend the night at the Northern General. Get the milk train. Will that suit?"

"That would be pefect. If I have it ready by six? At the sisters'home."

"Fine."

The constraints of the recent war had pushed four of the senior sisters into one of the EMS huts: a rectangular Ministry of Defence prefab with plaster-board walls and an asbestos tile roof. It had a small, central vestibule leading to a communal sittting room and two little wings, each with two bedrooms and a bathroom. When I arrived later, the IN–OUT indicator showed Sister Annie was one of two in for the evening. I rang the bell.

Sister Tutor Dorothy Lang opened the door: Nutty Dottie, allegedly as full of kernels as a Dundee cake.

"Good evening Sister Tutor."

Her full sail silhouette was recognizable from any quarter: powerful bosom cleaving the waves of life; cloak flying like colours nailed to the mast. She had a pair of rimless *pince-nez* fastened to her collar by a gold pin and a chain. She clipped them on her nose, low down and beamed at me in amiable expectation of a regulation medical student. What she saw, however, seemed to dismay her.

"Oh," she said. She seemed taken aback. Then she collected herself.

"This is very good of you. The case. It will be so heavy. Bed linen, you know."

"Happy to help," I said, on my best polite, trying to improve on the first impression I had made.

She pointed up one of the short corridors, and I went up it. I knocked and went in on Sister Annie's invitation. A suitcase lay open on the bed. It had been used to hold a clutter of souvenirs from years past: photographs, certificates, letters; the sort of rubbish we all keep to try to give significance to our years on earth. She had emptied the lot onto the only chair in the room and was filling the case with sheets and pillow-cases.

"Sorry about the mess. I'll only be a moment. Clear yourself a corner of that chair, and sit down. I have a friend in the QAs. She's out east. She has a cottage at South Queensferry. I go there sometimes –"

That explained the various sightings of her in the station.

"Look after it for her."

If this was going to be a long explanation, I thought I might as well be comfortable. I eased my backside further on to the seat, and looked down to make sure I didn't put my foot on something breakable. It was then I noticed the photograph, a studio portrait half-covered by a book, and I was struck by what I could see. It had been shot in a soft focus, which gave it a hint of imprecision; a suggestion of haze, which was oddly haunting. It was the head and shoulders of a girl: sixteen, maybe seventeen.

Curious to see more, I took a quick squint at Sister Annie, but she was still busy folding linen into the case. I edged the book away with my toe. Some ineffable quality about the portrait – the hair style? The cut of the simple, short-sleeved blouse? – dated it from the late thirties. There was a strong family resemblance to Sister Annie. A sister? A cousin? There was the same bone structure; the same wide spaced eyes. Although the portrait was in black and white, I knew they must be grey.

But there the likeness ended. Something inward shone through: a sense of happiness, of sheer, shimmering joy. On the threshold of womanhood, she was yet in a bloom she would never surpass.

This sweetest of sixteens was full of her first love: whole-hearted; without reservation, or doubt. For this girl it had been no cuddly adventure in calf love; no randy adolescent scramble. It had been the supreme attachment: the one and only time.

Every feature was highlighted by the emotion; imbued with its intensity. She was absolutely gorgeous.

Gorgeous?

This was no family likeness. This was Finnie McLaren's Anne.

I looked at the present reality, a few feet away and for the umpteenth time wondered just what had happened to her. It wasn't until I hefted the case onto the luggage rack next morning, that the final dimension of her tragedy really struck home. A recent luggage label showed her previous destination. The last time Sister Annie had packed her nightie in this case, she had been a passenger to Gleneagles.

Whatever rapture she had felt at sixteen, she was now a mere nineteenth hole for Boss on his golfing weekends.

BOOK SEVEN

Chapter 1

ALTHOUGH PARTIES WEREN'T MUCH IN MY LINE, that Christmas vacation brought two that I had to attend, one literally with bells on.

The first one was Wilson's birthday. He had mentioned it to me a week or so before.

"You're asked, of course. Will you bring the girls through from the farm? Connie can bunk in with Noelle."

Noelle was a regular visitor to the town house by then. But Connie had other plans.

"I'd love to come, Scoular. And it's very generous of your parents to offer me a bed. But they will have quite enough to do organizing the party, without worrying about an extra guest. I'll arrange something else."

This was all so reasonable as to defy argument: and was the more welcome to Noelle, since she liked sharing attention with no one. Later, Connie let me in on her scheming.

"As you know, I've been out with Johnnie a few afternoons. Gone to the flicks. Home on the tea-time train. Said I'd been with some of the girls."

As a liar, she was almost as good as me now.

"Aunt Winnie has swallowed it quite happily so far. But I'd like to stay over on a Saturday, sometimes. Go dancing with him."

The springs of youth were bubbling. I would have to make sure they were safely channelled

"I wondered if Minnie would put me up, now and then? I could start off with this party. Get Aunt Winnie used to the idea. You see Minnie every day. I wondered if you would ask her for me?"

Who better to supervise my long game? Make sure she got into bed on her own?

"Yeah. Sure. Next time I see her."

The fewer people who knew what Connie was up to, the better, and, since Wilson was around a lot during the day, I waited until one night after tea, and took a tram back to town. Bend Minnie's private ear. Going up to her door it was quite like old times: smells of cooking; rots, wet and dry; clothes airing in front of gas fires.

I knocked on the door: the confident rattle of someone sure of his welcome. Minnie opened the door as if she'd been waiting right behind it and with a big, radiant smile to match my own mood.

"Why, Neil. How lovely."

So lovely that I was invited to come right on in, and she would put on the kettle? Well, no. Not quite. The delay was as fractional as a light wave, but it felt like a one-hour time lock, as I teetered back on my heels.

"Oh. Of course. Do come in."

The table was set for supper for two.

"You shouldn't have bothered, Min. I've just eaten."

The smile was anxious. This was no time for ironic pleasantries.

Minnie's hair was very fine. Done up in its usual bun, it had never looked more than neat: but now, undone and cascading, it came to her waist at the back, burnished and gleaming.

She wasn't quite hopping from one foot to the other, but there was an agitato quality to her stance. I hurriedly told Connie's story.

"– so she wonders if she can stay here the night of the party? And maybe some Saturday nights next term? Not have to worry about trains? There's this boy."

One time, Minnie would have found this a weighty decision: responsibility for a kid Connie's age. But that night, all she said was, "Tell her she can come anytime."

And it wasn't just to get me the hell and gone out of there. She spoke with a new and deep conviction. As I left, Luke arrived at the door. He was in his slippers.

"Come far?" I enquired mildly.

One thing about being black, you can't flush up.

"Downstairs. A room came vacant."

I had never seen Minnie look so well, her usual little nictitations of tension stilled. I turned and kissed her on the mouth with great tenderness.

"I'm happy for you, Min. I'll tell Connie. G'night, Luke."

I was thoughtful as I ran downstairs. I liked Luke a lot: one very straight guy. And Minnie was pure spun gold. But Scottish preconceptions hadn't moved much with two world wars. Racism, in its nasty form, was never a big issue in such an innately republican society: just sheer, narrow, perverse, presbyterian, bloody ignorance. I hoped the pair of them were up to it.

Wilson's party was a douce affair with cider cup and charades. The big event of the evening was his parents' present to him. Round back, in the mews lane they had parked a 1937 Morris Eight, with a blue ribbon on the windscreen wiper. There were 'Ooh's of delight for him. He kissed his mum and shook his dad by the hand; opened the door for Noelle, and buzzed off around the block. I took Connie back to the ice-cream and jellies.

"You're a bit pensive," she said.

I laughed away my giveaway frown. Jealous was nearer the mark. Life was so bloody easy for him. Too easy for his own good? He needed some real problem in his life: one only he could sort out.

The next party involved Boss. He was a great guy to give staff treats: a picnic in the summer-time; a dance at New Year: no expense spared. That year he had booked a party into the Locarno: streamers and funny hats; dance the old year away and the new one in.

Minty was enthusiastic.

"Scope for a little dalliance there, lad."

I was all for joining him, at first. But then Boss took a hand in things.

"I like all my sisters to be there. You had better bring Sister Urquhart."

I didn't need the diplomatic skills of the Chinese ambassador to realize there was more to this than a courtesy escort. Why didn't he issue instructions to her as he did to everyone else?

"What's all this about?" I asked Minty plaintively.

"I can only guess. It would be just like the old bastard to want to parade her. But she never has shown up at any of these dos."

"Why ask me to ask her?"

"Then he can blame you if she doesn't come, old son. You should know by this time," said Minty pityingly, "he must be seen to be infallible."

And she wouldn't attend that year either.

"You must thank Mr McKenzie for me, but I can't manage," she said flatly.

"I can't persuade you?" I wheedled. I was clearly the meat in a sand-wich of wills and, as such, liable to get a dollop of mustard about my private parts.

"No. I don't care for dancing now."

The qualification slipped out unnoticed. Had she liked to dance once, then? When she was gorgeous?

"Besides, there is to be a party here that evening."

"A party? Here in the pavilion?"

"Yes. We shall need all the help we can get. I couldn't possibly not be here."

An unlikely emotion stirred in me. Suppose we both stuffed Boss. Oh, I owed him a lot, but he was such a cocksure old bugger.

"Could I help?" She was startled.

"That would be wonderful. But that's unfair. You'll want to be at the dance, surely?"

"Don't worry about that. I'll come to your party, if it will help."

The grey eyes looked at me gauging, weighing.

I reported back to Boss.

"You couldn't persuade her then, sonny?"

The reductive was savage. I thought I should get all the bad news out of the way at once.

I explained about the party, and added. "I offered to help. I was sure you would want me to do that."

The look he gave me explained why the messenger was severed from his head sometimes.

The party was a pathetic success.

I dressed myself up as the New Year: tackety boots, cotton-wool boobs with Noddy bells for nipples, a fairy tutu of surgical gauze, a kiltie hat, a red nose, a bow and arrow to kill off the Old Year.

The despoiled inmates seemed to want that. Get it over. Get on with the next one. Have another try. For a few hours they could pretend a fresh start; another future.

I played the house-doctor panto script for the past hundred years. I clog-danced, led the singing, guyed the Matron, handed out black bun and shortbread, spiked the orange juice with gin. I kissed everyone under the mistletoe twig I carried like a brand. I got the cheer of the night when I dared to buss Sister Annie under its protection.

She was in mufti that night: a dark blue dress, almost as severe as her uniform. But it showed that her figure, which had seemed gaunt, was only pared to the essentially feminine. Her face was as immobile as a Uffizi marble when she presented her graven face to my cheeky peck: but for the first time, the grey eyes looked in mine from close up.

I had a quite uncontrollable reaction to their nearness. Absurdly; preposterously, I felt my mouth become dry.

The moment I drew back; reviewed the spoiled looks, remembered the harlot's history, the emotion disappeared. For a while, though, the memory of it worried me, until I realized what it had been.

Pity.

That's what it was. That was what was running in my veins that night: pity for the whole, ruined, courageous population of the pavilion. It was only to be expected some should spill over for her.

I laughed in sheer relief.

After that evening, Sister Annie treated me with less formality.

Chapter 2

IN THE NEW TERM, WILSON CAME ACROSS the problem I thought would be good for his inner man – and it was all my fault. I had been at him for ages to spend some time in the casualty department.

"Interesting. And good for you. It will help your confidence no end."

Eventually, this got to him. He turned up one Friday night and I introduced him to Bobby Mair.

"Friend of mine. Same year. Keen to do some casualty work."

Bobby took Wilson at my word, and he had the same sleeves up initiation I had. I went over to the wards then, and returned about ten to see how he was getting on.

He was already in bad shape: holed: down by the head, and going willingly deeper by the moment. I could tell at a glance. And this girl was worth two glances from any man: his whole undivided attention, in fact.

Wilson was suturing a ragged, three inch laceration in the scalp of a six year old gangster: a bullet-headed bandit with the arse out of his breeks, and a breath sour with Woodbine fags. Tough as the cobble-stones in Castle Street, this little nut wouldn't cry if you twisted his arm off. But – though he would have been nailed to the wall rather than admit it – it was awful good to be held by someone, while the mending was going on; to be sat on a knee, and cuddled into comfort while the stitches were going in.

And he was cooried into a lap that made me wince with envy. An Indian girl: third year student nurse, from her uniform: pale hands to be loved, all the way from the Shalimar.

I knew as much about Indian lore as a small teaspoonful of curry sprinkled in my stew, but one look told of caste and privilege and family protectiveness. They were implicit in her air of breeding and reserve; her delicate features; her shyness, still strong after three years of frank, alien, male regard.

But she had not come across such ardour before. Wilson's admiration was almost wanton in its obviousness. I could see her respond, despite herself: a diffident, disbelieving wonder.

"Ah, Neil," he said as he noticed me. "This is Andy. Fell off a wash-house roof. And this is Shiraz. Neil Aitken. My buddy."

Andy eyed me contentedly from his cuddle.

"Hello," she said. The very vowels were restrained and gentle.

"Hiya," I said back.

It wasn't difficult to be warm in my tone. I liked her at once. She might be shy, but there was nothing secretive about her gaze. She was exactly what Wilson's big soul craved; exactly what he had read – mistakenly – into Noelle's mean little soul. The mysticism deep in this girl's eastern soul; the transcendence of her ages-old religion attracted the poet in him like a lodestone.

As they worked together at this close quartered task, I could see the very force lines form: bonding markers between irresistible poles of east and west. Neither of them had a hope in hell from the start.

Wilson's morality was right out of the cold baths and noble thoughts school of Dr Arnold. The girl would have been equally schooled in the ways of her people: obedience – subservience, even – to father, family, possibly to the choice of some future husband.

But neither of them was prepared for Krishna to step out of the magnesium flash and smoke. The great god had given her a sexuality that glowed like molten gold behind the demureness: quite different from Noelle's glittering, but ultimately selfish flame. It was as lethal as spur terminals on the national grid, and I watched in awe as Wilson, at his big, blond, good-looking best, grasped them willingly, to close the circuit.

Later, he tried to get it off his chest, but he had never tried to formulate emotion of that intensity before.

"That girl. That Indian girl. She's – she seems – she's a smasher, isn't she?"

The banality was half rhetorical; half looking for an answer.

"Old chum. That is a very attractive young lady. Guys in her home country would give lots of rupees to own that. Watch you don't drown in her. Or get her dad after you with a scimitar or whatever they use for ritual castration."

The enormity of what he was contemplating dried him up into silence. He grinned at me in sick helplessness. His visits to the farm; the cups of tea with Noelle after classes, became much fewer. He blamed pressure of studies, but he wasn't a good liar.

"Is there something worrying him?" Noelle asked me soon after. "This thing he does with you on Friday nights? Is it upsetting?"

"Oh, very," I assured her. "Lot of nasty sights. Takes everyone a while to get used to it."

Maybe Shiraz would go back to Kashmir before the damage was irreparable. Trouble was, in his present state, Wilson might prefer the Karakoram to Campsie Glen and go with her.

Come the end of January, however, Wilson's conscience caught up with him long enough to suggest some practical way of keeping Noelle sweet.

"It's charities day next week," he said one Sunday at the farm. "Let's all get dressed up. The four of us. Just what we all need. Chase the winter blues."

He took Noelle's hand ostentatiously, with a faint stain of guilt colouring his cheeks. She brightened. She had been missing being the centre of attention.

On that day the students descended on Glasgow in a riot of fancy dress and shook a handsome ransom of pennies out of its citizens. A week-long softening up process of concerts, stunts, and amusements culminated in a great raid on the city on the Saturday. Parties were organized to pirate the suburbs in the morning, and all hands were summoned to the sack of the city centre in the afternoon. The last cans of coppers were collected by six, then several thousand tired, but for once justified, young sinners went on the town.

It took some organizing, though. At that time of year there would be snow, maybe: more likely rain. Costumes had to be adaptable. The best idea was to have a rendezvous: a place for a change of clothes if the weather was soaking; a break at lunch time; some food and a beer; change back into civvies for the evening.

"If we can get onto the Bearsden team for the morning, you can all use my place," I said grandly.

I had one small problem: a nursing sister, who, in her uniform, gave the impression of being gaunt; who had once been gorgeous; and who was a stickler for the propriety of her pavilion.

"It won't be a party," I explained. "Not exactly. But there will be people coming and going. Leaving their gear. Changing their clothes. But I guarantee to have every one off the premises by seven at the very latest."

The grey eyes probed mine. Could I be trusted?

"If you're worried about noise, I'll make sure they use the steps at the side."

She still wasn't convinced. That way she couldn't keep tabs on who went in and out.

"I also thought we might go round the beds. The costumes will be weird and wonderful. Cheer the patients up?"

She nodded grudgingly. She hadn't thought of that.

"As long as there's no – " she actually paused, looking for a word – "nonsense."

I almost choked. Boozy mayhem; bawdy ditties; fornication. I could see the suspicion. For the first time since I met her, the eyes showed emotion: hot, wary. Primed by her own past experience? Well, poachers knew all the best tricks. Still, such double standards were too much to swallow.

"I promise, I'll lecture them all severely. Bunch of rascally medics. Can't trust them an inch. But you know, in a way, this is my home."

I said it gently. I didn't want to forfeit the better relationship we had had lately. I simply wanted to make a point. But the remark pinked her; drew a bead of blood.

She flushed. For once, the grey eyes dropped. I should have enjoyed my little victory, but I didn't. I wished I had kept my slack mouth shut.

I had my future before me: buy a mud hut, a semi-detached villa, a stone castle, depending on how all this scheme of Minty's turned out. At her time of life; in her situation – widow, mistress of the back tees, wanton – where would she end up?

Sister Annie and I agreed a truce in which the terms were undeclared, but implicitly put my neck on the chopping board.

Trouble was the party snowballed.

First Abercrombie wanted to come: make up another foursome with Alexander and their girls; then Luke and Minnie, and one or two others. Eventually I thought, what the hell. Make it an occasion. I got in some crates of beer, and a few eats. For once I would play mine host.

On the day, I found that Billy Anderson had tagged on. He was a prurient lecher and I wasn't keen on him. His chariot of desire for the occasion was a black ringleted, bubble-head from Dough School, but I could hardly turf him out for that. When they had all arrived, I climbed on a chair.

"Listen, you lot. I'll leave this side door open. Come and go by the steps as you please. But not in and out of the main door. The pavilion sister doesn't like noisy medical students and I don't want slung out on my ear. Whatever you do be – um – discreet."

That should allow elbow room for most things.

Then we went to threaten the hoi-polloi with unloaded collecting cans.

By the afternoon, I had become separated from everyone but Noelle and Wilson in the crowds of shoppers. Connie, in particular, had taken off early with a heavily disguised Johnnie, to win pennies in a happy duet. Noelle had been all right for the first hour, winsome in a Bo Peep costume. But you had to pound the pavements to get results. Her feet, her legs, got tired; her back was sore; she felt cold: and all in small, snipy doses of moan. By six, I had had enough. When we handed in the last cans, I declared the rest of the evening my own.

"I'm trysted to a large Scotch in Lauder's. Then I'm going back to Shaw's Howe to change. Shall I see the pair of you in the morning?"

There were forty acres to plough, and Sandy expecting me as early as I could manage.

Noelle looked at Wilson expectantly: run us all back to the Lothians in his flivver? But that stricken young man had no such notion.

"Yes – well – I can't manage to take you back myself. Sunday receiving, you see. I'm expected."

Each firm took Sundays in a six week rota, but this was an excuse of desperation. He wanted his arms around his lissom Indian princess: didn't matter how.

"Oh, Scoular."

There was no mistaking the disapproval. His face took on a harried look: a winded fox looking for any kind of cover. I've always been against blood sports. I turned her sharp little fox-hound nose on me.

"That's right. The Gate resident is ill. Mr Mair asked your young man if he would help out. You would take up with a medic. But you've got tonight to celebrate. Make the most of that. I'll collect Connie from Minnie's place and we'll meet you in the station. You'll have company in the train."

Noelle was mollified into a pouting acceptance and any debt I might have owed for the Hillhead flat had just been repaid with interest.

"Where is Connie, anyhow?"

She was looking for anyone's blood now.

Once again, I lied with bland assurance.

"She's with Minnie and Luke. We're meeting up later."

I waved them goodbye and trekked up Renfield Street to Lauder's bar, where I wiped off the funny face, put my foot on the brass rail, and was waylaid by the cousins McIntyre, two muckle highlanders I met in the Union sometimes. Alastair, the elder, said, "You'll have a dram with us, Neillie."

There was a lack of option in his tone.

"Well, maybe just one. I was thinking of going dancing. I'll need to change," I pleaded.

"Chust so. Chust so."

That was a terrible night.

I had heard vaguely of the Tartan Hand: the gaelic underworld, without which Glasgow would have ground to a halt. A third of the barmen, half the polis, and two thirds of the nurses came from north of the highland line.

The McIntyres trailed me around back shops, hotel kitchens and pub cellars. They were full of cousins, or someone who knew a cousin. And in every single rendezvous, there happened to be a bottle of malt whisky, fresh from some distillery in the heather. They had a brisk way with a cork, these teuchters – they threw it out of the window, and wouldn't rest content until the bottle ended neck down in a bin.

I got back to Shaw's Howe in a 1935 Ford fifteen that fired on three cylinders sometimes and had a Guinness label, carefully cut to make a circle, for a licence. In my quarters, I inspected the place as carefully as my drunken state would allow, but apart from a slight, general untidiness and the bed-cover slightly rumpled by people sitting on it, I could see nothing that might displease a martinet.

Bloody sister.

But as I threw the bed clothes back, there on the sheets, invariably left pristine by the maids, were the signs of love making: a little harvest of lovelocks; a few, short, springy, black hairs that could only have come from the mons *veneris*: a dried stain, the size of a beer mat.

Billy bloody Anderson. I might have known. Still, as long as he had kept his bang up the bloomers quiet and quick, there would be no harm done.

I fell on my face, and sleep banjaxed me.

Chapter 3

THE DEPILATORY SIDE EFFECT OF Anderson's squalid balling went right out of my head. It wasn't until a couple of months later that particular squab began to sputter on the spit.

I had volunteered to take the Greig weans off Agnes's hands: a sausage sizzle over a fire of sticks in the Littlehaugh wood. On the Saturday morning, I was busy packing a pan and various fryables into a satchel, with wee Sandy and Jean supervising my efforts, when Connie came in. I was concentrating on taking enough to eat: didn't pay much attention to her.

"Coming with us?" I asked.

"No."

"Stick, then."

She wandered about the bothy, poking at this and that, picking things up idly, tossing them down again.

"You going up to town today, Neil?"

"Nope."

"Just wondered if you would be company on the train? I'm going up later this morning."

The contents of my pocket lay on top of a dresser.: keys, coins, handkerchief. She picked up a penny and spun it idly.

"Honey. I love you dearly. But you couldn't get me on that train with a five pound bribe. Much more important things to do here." I winked at the children.

"Seeing Johnny?"

"Yes. Nothing special. I'll be back in the early evening."

"Will I come to meet you?"

Me and my caring ways.

"No. Yes."

Even through my busyness, the ambivalence struck home. The packing was done by then. I put the satchel aside and, for the first time, really paid attention to her. There was something different. The peasant attractiveness, lately very strong, was at a peak that day. The strong gypsy face, the high Mongol cheek bones, the blooming, tanned skin.

Quite superb.

What was I thinking of? How stupid could I be? All this and money in the bank?

She might be uncertain, but I had just made up my mind. I would meet her off the train that night. See off Johnny Newton for good and all. Hobble this goose so I'd be there when the golden eggs started to come.

"See you later, then? Which train?"

She seemed suddenly glad to have her mind made up for her. I smiled at her with the confident air of a man who knew what was good for both of us.

See counting your chookies?

When I got to the station, the spring day was darkening into an early, cloudless evening. Connie had had enough time to see a movie, have her hand held, share some kisses in the back row: all for the last time. When she graduated to my class, she'd soon forget all that.

174

The train came in with a huffing of smoke, and a hissing of steam. Before it stopped completely, some carriage doors slapped open. Confident young riders of the iron rails skipped out; ran for the barrier. No particular reason, just the hell of being first.

I expected Connie amongst the first three. By six, I was craning over the barrier to see where she was. I saw her almost fall out of her compartment.

"Connie," I shouted in alarm.

"There's something wrong." I fought past the ticket collector.

As I reached her, she slumped into my arms. This was no maidenish vapouring. This was a real collapse, with ten and a half stone of well-bottomed young woman to drag to the waiting room.

"For the love of God, lassie. What's the matter?"

The peasant face was greasy with sweat. Even in the poor light – half gas-mantle, half lingering day – I could see that the morning's bloom had turned to a sallow seediness. The vixen eyes looked sick and hurt.

"Nothing. Nothing. It's all right. Really."

She was distressed into a vehement incoherence.

"Just get me home."

"You look hellish. What's – ?"

"Just – get – me – home."

The station master arrived, alarmed by the commotion. Connie smiled at him in a ghastly effort to reassure him.

"I felt unwell on the train. Very sick. One of these sudden gastric 'flu's, I think. There has been some amongst my classmates."

'Flu, gastric or otherwise, was something I knew nothing about. That was GP territory. I supposed an hour in the clickety-clack, with an infection developing, and her stomach revolting at every iron revolution, could make her sickly-yellow and collapsed: want only to get to bed.

"We'll take a taxi."

In the back seat, my arm around her for comfort, I said, "I'll phone your doctor."

Again, there was a quite uncharacteristic, hysterical edge to her voice.

"Neil. I just want to get to bed. Be left alone. Can't you understand?"

"Well, I'll get Noelle to look in on you."

"No. Not her. Certainly not her."

She got out of the taxi by the back entrance; insisted I leave her. I watched as she walked by main effort through the gate in the hedge, and disappeared into the house. When, next day, I saw Noelle, I asked, "How's Connie? She seemed most under the weather last night."

"She's got 'flu or something."

Her disinterest was informed by a strong desire not to go anywhere near something she might catch.

"All she wanted was tea and some aspirin. Says she doesn't want visitors."

Her tone implied that was fine by her.

I accepted the quarantine as common sense. Noelle would be back at her classes in a couple of days, and I would see her then.

On the Monday morning, as I was leaving the bothy for my classes, Matt came in and handed me a brown envelope. It was sealed and had my name on it.

"I got it frae the wee body that works tae the big hoose, as I passed the back door"

Since Connie had gone to college, a daily woman helped with the chores.

"The wee one sent it."

I tore open the package; shook the contents into my hand.

My room key and a note.

"Neil, I am so sorry, Connie."

I tossed the key in my hand: remembered the elaborate charade with the spinning coin, so clever I hadn't realized anything was missing. Well, well. It wasn't only Billy Anderson who had been tempted by the side entrance and a vacant room. Then I remembered the funny illness. Was there some connection? Had Johnnie been at the rape end of a seduction? Had sudden, penetrative, painful sex been too much for Connie? Induced an emotional crisis?

Yet she had seemed physically affected: shocked. What the hell had been going on? Puzzling away in my own dunderhead, I sailed into disaster.

When I reached Shaw's Howe, I could tell she had been waiting for me: Sister Annie. As soon as I walked into the atrium, I knew. She was coming out of her room when she got her eye on me. The mouth, thin anyhow, flattened into a slit of hostility that had been biding its time.

"I want a word with you."

She almost whispered in her abomination of me.

My mind had been busy on how I could get the truth out of Johnny Newton, but Sister Annie's detestation cut across this satisfying daydream like a cuff over the ear. Her tone; the intensity of her dislike, put my back right up. It didn't take any great leap of imagination to guess her anger was something to do with the filched keys, but the worst I could imagine was that she had caught the pair of them in my bed. That might rate me a lecture, but this reaction was out of all proportion.

"Come into my office."

I don't take kindly to that tone of voice at the best of times, but the peremptoriness; the deliberate omission of the magic word blew any remaining chance of propitiation clear out of the water.

"Tell you what, sister," I said chattily, "I've just got off the train, and I'm hungry. I'm going to put my bag in my room. Hang up my coat. Have a wash. Then I'm going over to the doctors' mess to have a bite to eat. If it's all that important, whyn't you come and talk to me while I'm titivating myself up."

I knew I was putting my precious lodgings in hazard: but I also knew this was one confrontation I had to meet head on. As I walked away, she almost ran to get ahead of me.

"Yes. Yes. This will be even better."

In the little vestibule, she paused at the door of the bathroom, then hurled it open.

"A pretty sight. How do you explain this, sir."

The best I could manage was a weak and unoriginal imprecation: a plea for understanding.

"Jeeeesus Christ."

I dropped my bag, my coat, and my aggression in a heap. This was standing in the bath. This was a hospital mattress. This was the biscuit mattress off my bed. And this was thick with congealed blood.

"D'you think I don't know what went on here. What you must have connived at?"

"No. No." I tried.

It sounded feeble, even to me. But it wasn't a denial, only an attempt to get her to shut up long enough to let me think.

The clues had been all around me, but for some reason – thick-headedness, wilful blindness – I hadn't strung them together. Now, this final evidence marshalled them into an irrefutable answer.

Only a few things would cause bleeding like that: an acute haemorrhage that had cost someone a couple of pints of blood, pouring out in a few frightening moments: a bloody gangland stabbing; an oesophageal varix, blowing its top; a tuberculous infection rupturing an artery; or, in this place, empty and secret for a few hours, a botched and amateurish abortion.

It wasn't Billy Anderson who had mussed up my bed on charities night.

Sister Annie took my paltry negation as further sign of admission of iniquity.

"I should report this to the police."

I must have looked my consternation: not for myself, but for Connie and her procurer.

"Ah-hah," she cackled in triumph at the giveaway on my face. "That's just what you deserve. Of course, all the evidence is circumstantial."

They had had the sense to put the *foetus delecti* down the plughole.

"But I shall certainly let Mr McKenzie know. Tell him you can no longer stay here."

If she would only be quiet for a moment, and let my pity for Connie and the cold anger I felt Johnnie, reach some kind of equilibrium; give me some chance to explain that lack of imagination and sheer bloody fecklessness were my only crimes.

But, no. She would rave on, little flecks of spittle spraying out at me

"Oh, I just knew there would be goings on that night. But I trusted you."

Her voice broke on a broken promise.

"Now this."

This desperate, bloody act of destruction.

"You. You young cad!"

The word should have been ridiculous: a quaint notion of betrayed honour right out of a 'B' movie; out of date as anti-macassars and smoking caps.

But that word hurt most.

"You lied to me."

I turned on her, and she stepped back, stiff and suddenly frightened: found herself brought up short by the door jamb.

"Be quiet," I said slowly. "Not another word. Now you listen."

I prodded the bib of her starched pinny with a hard forefinger.

"I don't give a damn what you think. I know, or I can guess – like you – what went on here. But I had nothing to do with it."

"I don't believe you. You must have given over your key."

Of course, that was how it must seem to her. I was abruptly deflated. I sighed at the impossibility of arguing my case with this frothing female.

"Listen, Sister Annie –"

She gasped in affront at my further impertinence; the savage misuse of her name.

"– I'm not going to argue any more. You've got your mind made up. Well, you had better get on with it. Report me to the polis. Or the Dean of the faculty. Or the bloody Brigton Billy Boys."

She flinched away from my crude male anger, the lash of profanity, like a glove across her face.

"– But you can take it as gospel. I don't tell lies."

Even as I spoke, I realized I was stating a great and new truth. Of course I told lies – great blistering whoppers – all the time. It was a way of life for me.

But I would never lie to her. And, of all people, she should have known that.

The fuel of our anger ran out then: a tap shut off. But our relationship, which had at best been cool and lumpy, was now a frozen, twisted mess.

She looked at me, a long appraisal, with no abatement of bitterness. Then she turned and left. She was white, her face even more gaunt than usual. I went to the mess. I had been hungry, but I puddled my meal in my plate and pushed it away half-eaten. The realization of the hole I had dug for myself grew, as I scowled out of the window at Ben Lomond.

I got rid of the mattress later: a midnight visit to the hospital's coke furnace. At least she hadn't had it impounded as evidence. I got a fresh one from the store, and slept badly on it. Usually, I can sleep on a clothes line.

I cut the next day's classes and went back to the farm. Some smarming of Aunt Winnie and a bag of grapes got me into the sickroom.

"See if I can cheer the patient up," I said.

Some cheer.

I sat at the head of Connie's bed, and got the whole sobbing story over my shirt front.

"I'm so ashamed."

The loss of virginity might, at best, have been written off to romantic experience; at worst, repented at leisure and in the secrecy of her own mind. The pregnancy, however, had precipitated a calamity she could only ever remember with fear and shame. And it had broadcast its bloody outcome to a stranger; an angry nursing sister.

"I couldn't believe it. Johnnie said he had taken care of things. But I'm never late. And then I was squeamish in the mornings. I was terrified when I realized. The thought of telling Aunt Winnie. And you.

Johnny was distracted. If we had to get married, he thought his people might put him out. He would have to leave medical school –"

Another victim for the Dean.

"There seemed only one thing to do. He got some stuff. We thought your rooms would be so private. That you would never find out. Anyhow, he gave me an injection. I had the most awful cramps, but at first, there was no bleeding. Then he gave me another one. We waited ages, and still nothing but cramps. It was after they had worn off, and we were thinking of leaving. There was this great gush of blood and stuff. He didn't expect so much. I – we – were so frightened. Then the bleeding got less. Johnny said things would be all right, and I put on a couple of sanitary pads. We didn't know what to do with the mattress. Johnny stood it in the bath to save any more mess. We were just leaving by the side door, when this sister came in from the other door. She must have heard us. We just ran. Have you seen her?"

"Yes."

"And – ?"

" Don't you worry. She'll never find out who you are. I'll see to that."

I was at my reassuring best. Connie turned her face up to me and kissed my cheek. Then she snuggled into my arms.

"I always feel better when you're around. Safer."

Now Sister Annie had my medical career by the balls, there would never be a better time to clinch a suitable partner. All I need do was forgive her little peccadillo, and reassure her I'd be around for ever. But I told myself it was unfair to take advantage of her at such a time.

It was odd how the moment was never quite right.

"How's the bleeding now?"

"Almost stopped. I'll get up tonight. Be back at my classes in a day or so."

I nodded. The young, healthy brood mare would be replacing blood by the minute. I smuggled out a bag of bloody pads, and went back to town.

Chapter 4

FOR THE REST OF THE WEEK I kept as far away from Sister Annie as I could. In the ward, messages passed between us in terse, frigid sentences. There was nothing I could do about the fuse of her anger, as it burned inexorably towards Friday and Boss's visit: but at least the polis didn't arrive, nor a letter from the faculty office. And Boss, for all his imperiousness, would surely give me a hearing: more than she had.

I went on with my classes in case I survived this debacle, but for once my work in the pavilion was half-hearted. The emotional drain of these dependent people was too much to bear on top of my own troubles. And this came to a head when, the night before Boss's visit was due, the nurse on night duty came to waken me.

"Willie McPherson is crying. He seems awful upset, but he won't tell me what's wrong. Will you come and have a look at him?"

"All right," I sighed, without enthusiasm.

For once, it was difficult. Usually I was keen to get at the problem; enlarge my experience at every possible opportunity. Grudgingly, I went to see Willie.

He had been a corporal in the Gordon Highlanders in the First War. On a night raid, both legs had been shattered by machine gun fire. He had lain in front of his own lines from then to the next blessed, black night of a stretcher party. He survived the blood loss, the shock, the exposure by dour endurance, and the extra fluid in the water-bottle of a dead comrade. The surgeons had made him stumps – mid-thigh on the left: below knee on the right – that should have taken prostheses. But contamination with Flanders mud had left him with a bone infection that went chronic.

To begin with, the recurrences came weeks, months apart. There was time for the sinuses to heal; the wounds to dry up: get out the wooden legs again; give him some hope of hippity-hoppity independence. But it never lasted.

The periods between breakdown became shorter, as the balance between infection and immunity swayed away from him. Eventually, the sweet, stinking flow became unstoppable; his wounds required daily dressing; and all hope of independent survival died. As with so many others, the pavilion became home to Willie.

When I got to him, that night, Willie was still crying. He was sitting up in bed: rocking himself backwards and forwards obsessively, in a travel of no more than six inches. His mouth was open for the gasping expulsion of little, whimpering moans: "Aw haw. Aw haw."

"What's the matter, Willie?"

He shook his head. If he let that awful truth out, he would never get the consequences back in their cage. I copied Boss. I reached for Willie's hand. It seemed such a simple gesture.

But I had no right to start on that transaction. I was too full of my own troubles.

"Come on, Willie. If you don't tell me, I can't help."

There should have been a transference; the trust flowing from him.

"It's the pain in my leg."

"Let me see."

Nurse pulled down the bed-clothes. The stump of Willie's right leg was as white as a belly-up flounder; cold from the knee down. The big artery that feeds the lower leg had been plugged shut. No wonder Willie had pain: nerve ends screaming for oxygen that would never come now.

Yet there was more to Willie's cries than pain: an apprehension of some long dreaded event whose time had come. And well I knew what it was.

Willie had put up with all sorts of treatment: antiseptics to bathe and irrigate the wound; tonics to boost his resistance; several courses of sulphonamides. Boss had even wangled him some penicillin in its early, scarce days. They had, in the long run, made no difference, but Willie didn't object or complain.

One treatment, however, he simply would not contemplate. Willie was determined no more of him would be cut off; land in a surgeon's pail. Over the years, this resolve had transmuted itself into a conviction, that if that ever happened, it would be the end of Corporal McPherson.

Time and again, on his rounds, Boss had reviewed the pus-drooling stumps; given the same jovial assurance.

"I'll need to take some more of these off for you. It's your only hope."

"No, you'll no'. No' if Ah see you comin'," Willie defied, resolutely. He was defying not only Boss, but fate.

They had always laughed: straight man and comic. But, now, the clowns had gone home. Willie McPherson had been fed a line that had only one, unfunny answer. More of his leg would have to come off now.

But I couldn't tell him. I couldn't face meeting his eyes and pronouncing his battle lost: nor was there an alternative of honourable surrender.

"Listen, Willie –"

Willie looked at me then, expecting the truth, no matter how hard; expecting me to honour his courage. He squeezed my hand momently, trying to spark the bond he expected between us. I looked away from him and my voice sounded its treachery.

"– I'll away and get you something for the pain."

He let go my hand. The precious moment when his trust should have been rewarded, died between us. I fled from his bed-side, wretched and ashamed at failing him so badly; knowing the depths of my own inadequacy. I headed for the phone to contact the duty resident; arrange some morphia. The nurse was with me, ready to open the drug cupboard, and double check the dose.

"There's Sister Urquhart," she muttered.

The gaunt-looking, stern figure was coming into the ward.

"Why is she here so early?"

"We have orders always to phone her, if something like this comes up."

Was she really that dedicated? I found myself wishing the whole wretched thing between us had never happened.

Her gaze was level: cool rather than cold. We had another truce, it seemed, at least until this trouble was over. Willie was moaning again, worse than ever. She registered the sounds with dismay.

"D'you know what's the matter with him?"

"Yes. He has a popliteal artery block."

She was shocked.

"Oh, the poor, poor soul."

She knew, as well as I, Willie's hidden agenda.

"What shall we do?"

The we was faintly comforting.

"Mr McKenzie will want to deal with this himself. His firm is receiving today, so I'll phone his registrar. Get things teed up. Right now, I must organize half a grain of morphia for him."

She nodded and went towards Willie's bed. I arranged for the dope and then phoned Minty. He was already in the Northern General, having to deal with some early morning crisis.

"Leave it all to your uncle," he promised.

When I got back to Willie, Sister Annie was stroking his forehead with a long, cool hand.

"There, there. There, there."

His moaning; the obsessive rocking, had stopped. He was looking at her face with the trust I had lost.

I had her check the tablet, then dissolved it in a teaspoon of water, heated over a spirit lamp.

"IV," I said.

Sister Annie drew the pyjama sleeve above the elbow; tightened the material into a tourniquet. I swabbed the big blue vein that bulged up; slid in the needle; then slowly transported Willie to the Islands of the Blessed.

"What now?" she asked, but not of me. She was asking herself how Willie would stand the rest of his life.

"I'll go with him in the ambulance," I volunteered: a gesture to make me feel better.

The grey eyes watched me.

"I'll stay with him until it's all over, " I added desperately: anything to claw back some self respect.

Her look stayed level and emotionless.

Chapter 5

MINTY WAS ALREADY AT THE GATE WHEN WE ARRIVED. He had a look at the leg and confirmed the diagnosis. Willie was in a pin-pupil plane above his pain by then. Minty frowned at his florid, peaceful face.

"Any idea what his blood pressure is?"

"Last time I took it, three days ago, it was in the foothills of the Himalayas."

He pulled a face.

"That bad. I think we had better run an ECG."

Electrocardiographic monitors were fiddly, temperamental things out of the Heath Robinson notebooks. The scratchy readings often needed intuitive, even inspired, interpretation: cross your fingers and guess your best.

But there was no doubt about Willie's recording: inverted T waves from all over the front of his chest. His coronary arteries were well on the way to being stopped up as well. It would take nothing to shut one off completely and precipitate a full scale myocardial infarct: kill him on the spot.

Willie was a prime anaesthetic risk.

"Boss won't like this. Not one little bit. Ken Kennedy is on holiday. Better get the locum anaesthetist in here, fast."

Ken's experience in the techniques of knife-edged survival was unrivalled in the hospital and Boss's belief in him was sublime. The knowledge that his favourite gas-man was not on tap put Boss in one of his thrawn moods that morning. You said white? He'd say black, blue, or purple with polychromatic pink spots on it: any damn thing to be different.

Boss arrived soon after, and when he got to Willie's bedside, he humphed in derision.

"I said more of that damn leg would have to come off, didn't I?"

That put him in a better mood, which lasted until the morning tea ceremony.

"I suppose I had better do the amputation myself," he said, his voice comfortable with his own capability, and tinged with a callous satisfaction.

"If you think that would be best, sir," agreed Minty. "There may be a problem with the anaesthetic, though."

At that point, Ken Kennedy's stand in arrived. She was a registrar with a pony tail and an unfortunate hen-toed walk, who made up for lack of experience by a high-pitched yatter of textbook theory. It was her first appearance in Boss's wards and, from the look on his face, likely to be the last: which impression gained ground as the unfortunate initiation went on. Minty explained the case to her but when he got to the bit about the cardiac complications, her voice rose another half tone, in jerky, unfinished sentences.

"I had better check – that is, if you intend to go on with – if Mr Millar is right, though –"

There was a collective holding of breath: a silent prayer that the silly cow wouldn't set Boss off again.

"Well, get on with it," he snarled, giving her a glowering look.

She neighed in a nervous laugh, and went out of the room with the ankly, sideways prance of Lippizaner dressage, never taking her eyes off him. She cavorted back in a few minutes, even friskier with fright. Her voice was now in a squeaky soprano which registered the terrified certainty that whatever else she might do that morning, she was not going to lumber herself with Willie McPherson's death on the table.

"His general condition won't – I couldn't possibly – a general anaesthetic wouldn't –"

Boss had no interest in the niceties of anaesthesia. All he wanted was a patient who wouldn't run around the walls.

"Well, give him a spinal," he said, and dismissed her. At least, that was his intention.

But this lady was a trier.

"I'm afraid that even a spinal would be diffficult."

Boss gave her his attention then: the whole, black-browed preface to incineration, when she was saved by Piddling Paul.

"Sort of case they used to freeze in the twenties. Literally."

Over the months, Paul had crept back into the fringes of the surgical flock. The lists Boss gave him were shameful for a man of his seniority: hernias and varicose veins; lumps and bumps of the most superficial kind; haemorrhoids and ischio-rectal abscesses: the very arse-work of surgery. I don't know how he stood it. I suppose he thought that if he did this penance long enough, Boss might relent.

I caught the look Boss gave him as he was speaking, and I thought Paul should shut up before he got the blast intended for the girl. But he was beguiled by the thought of once again being in the body of the surgical kirk, and he ploughed on with his pointless piece of medical history.

"They packed the leg in ice and salt for several hours. Gave the patient a huge pre-med. Even a drink or two, if I remember –"

I don't know why he didn't see the change in Boss's expression.

"– then, of course, the faster the operation was done, the better."

He gestured at Boss in sycophantic deference to his speed with the knife.

The anaesthetist was forgotten. Boss was beaming now: a veritable sunshine of regard for Paul, who basked in the unexpected warmth.

But he hadn't allowed for solar flare-out.

Paul capped his tale with the old legend about the fastest amputation ever: the offending leg, the assistant's thumb, and the patient's penis - all in under two minutes. There was a definite chuckle at the punch line of that old surgical chestnut. The others had never known the whole story of Paul's disgrace, but they recognized a brave attempt at rehabilitation. No doubt Boss would send the anaesthetist packing: fleas in both ears: get someone more senior to do the job.

"I think that's a splendid idea, Baillie."

There was a collective wheeze of surgical dismay. He couldn't be serious? Not in this day and age?

He turned back to the anaesthetic registrar.

"You're definite? He isn't fit for either a general or a spinal?"

"Absoutely." One way or another, she wanted out of this.

He turned away, and I thought she would change her discipline: take up dermatology, or biochemistry; something non-combative.

"Right, Forsyth. You and young Aitken. You get away up to the library. Find any references and bring them here."

Forsyth, the most recent ward resident and I trailed to the big, book-lined room. There were indeed a few cases: heroic measures in the days of chloroform with its nasty, lethal side effects; and when spinal anaesthesia was in its infancy. We carted the four, big, bound volumes back to Boss's room. He barely glanced at them.

"How long in the ice?"

"Two hours minimum."

"Right. Aitken, you arrange for a supply. See what the kitchens can do. If they can't manage, Phone Tullio Equi, and tell him I need it for an emergency."

Tullio Equi was the biggest pokey hat man in town.

"After that, get a bottle of the best whisky."

He gave me a couple of pounds from his wallet.

A sop to his conscience? Or was there more to this affair than I could see?

Then he played his joker; his ace in the hole: the wildest card in the whole damn pack.

"You, Baillie."

Paul's initial satifaction had faded to uncertainty about what he had begun. He produced a bilious, uncertain grimace of a grin. What now?

"It's your idea, so you had better do it."

Baillie was in a bind of superb cunning. It was the most major operation he had been offered, since Boss's punishment. If he agreed to do it, Boss might be sweetened into lifting his embargo; but Baillie would also accept the cruelty at the value Boss was putting on it.

So Paul should refuse? Stand up and let Boss count his sole opposition – for no one else had said a word?

But I knew what else was in Paul's mind; in the minds of everyone there. Let one man say inhuman, unjustified and Boss would do it superbly and probably beat that bloody record while he was at it. And in two days time, he would range us all round the bed to hear Willie McPherson's unqualified blessing.

Paul managed an acquiescent mutter and Boss grinned, his morning made.

"Aitken. Is there anything I should see specially at Shaw's Howe today?"

"No sir."

Not in the medical sense.

"Good. Give Sister a ring and tell her I won't be out. I want to see this. You know McPherson well, by now. When he's awake enough, tell him what's going to happen."

I knew very well what Boss was doing. He was delegating me to take his place; trusting me to deal with Willie as he would himself.

But I had already lost Willie's trust and now I compounded that by keeping Boss's defection from him.

I did tell him what I hoped were kind lies about the surgery he must undergo; assured him he would feel nothing; minimized the amount of his leg he would lose. But I simply could not bring myself to tell him that his champion had quit the field; even less the manner of his dereliction: capricious, even malevolent.

I did what else I could for Willie. I stayed with him; talked to him; saw every wish attended to. I made sure the ice and salt was packed tight around his leg. I fed him whisky. I laced his last two drinks with tincture of opium, and by operation time he was maudlin' fu': wandering the mazy byways that lead to unconsciousness.

I helped struggle him on to a trolley, his limb white frozen; wrapped in a sopping mackintosh full of ice cubes: then on to the operating trolley.

The theatre was packed. Word had got around. Boss fronted the throng.

For a few minutes Willie lay crooning 'Comin' through the rye'; enjoying his notoriety. But the song came to an abrupt end. Just as theatre sister went to bandage his eyes against this further scission, he noticed Boss in the watching crowd. Even in his stuporose state, the implication shot home. He reared up on an elbow.

"Sur. Haw, sur. Are you no' daein' this yersel'?"

Boss waved away the remark with jovial reassurance.

"You'll be fine, McPherson. A good man is doing the job."

But before the bandage went in place, Willie looked at me one last time. I saw the fight go out of him and knew another burden I would have to live with.

Willie didn't scream once, but he groaned: great shuddering moans of martyrdom, barely bearable as the flesh was cut; insupportable as the stainless steel tenon saw grated its agony through the cold and into his mind.

It took Piddling Paul fifteen minutes to get the leg off, fashion muscle flaps and get the stump sewn up. Although he sweated like a prize fighter, the murmurs around endorsed it as a fair effort.

After it was all over, Paul was the centre of attention. Minty looked at me and said thoughtfully, "I wonder? I just wonder if Boss was at his tricks?"

We looked at Paul. He had done it. He looked years younger; jubilant; confident as I had never seen him.

After the operation, I didn't hang around. I went to the farm and on the Monday morning I gave Shaw's Howe a miss too and went straight to my classes. After that, I went to see Willie in the ward, but the body bin had secreted him away half an hour before. I asked Forsyth what had happened.

"There was no obvious cause. He just turned his face to the wall and died. I had him slated for a post-mortem tomorrow, but Boss wouldn't hear of it. Said I had to put myocardial insufficiency on the certificate."

He was obviously worried about telling whoppers to the procurator fiscal. This time, however, I had to agree with Boss. It saved Willie's mortal remains from further desecration and there was no doubt in my mind that the diagnosis was right. Willie McPherson's great heart had been able to take no more.

Then I took myself off to Shaw's Howe, perhaps this time to pack my bags? I met Sister Annie in the long corridor that serviced the wards. She stood straight and starched and almost gaunt, as I went up to her.

"Have you heard?" I asked.

"About the operation? Yes. And I telephoned again this morning. He seemed to be holding his own."

I wondered if she knew what had really been in Boss's mind? Was it the legitimized cruelty of whim? Or a calculated kick in the professional arse for Paul; part of a make or break rehabilitation after the death of Danny Daly? I would never know.

"You haven't heard, then? He died this afternoon."

"I see."

She didn't see at all, but I did: again and again. I couldn't get Willie's eyes out of my mind.

"I couldn't help him, you know."

The busy corridor, alive and rattling with tea-time trolleys was hardly the place for a confessional, but we never can pick the moments when remorse overwhelms us.

"I didn't know how to face him – how to tell him."

I felt my eyes begin to prick and burn. Oh, God. Not that. Not in front of her.

I blinked and blinked; saved any tell-tale dribble on my cheek. Maybe she hadn't noticed. Then I took a deep breath. Steady the Buffs.

"Well, that's all over. But I can no longer go on with this other thing hanging over my head."

I looked right at her. I may not have been able to face a dying man, but Dervish sisters, I'd face them as they charged.

"If you want me to clear out, I'll go. No need to involve him."

We both knew who I meant: the most powerful force in both of our lives.

"And, whatever you say, I am truly sorry I swore at you."

"Well –"

A grudging start.

"– I've been reconsidering – and – I'm going to give you the benefit of the doubt."

The damning verdict of a Scottish court: not proven.

BOOK EIGHT

Chapter 1

WILSON'S AFFAIR WITH SHIRAZ WENT on like a fire in a coal bing: smouldering away with hot, smoky glances of promise which burst into the hot blue flame of requital whenever they could manage.

A few weeks after Willie McPherson's death, Wilson again wanted to renege on a promised visit to the farm.

"You could make up a yarn," he pleaded. "You're much better at it."

"Abso-bloody-lutely not, old chum. If Noelle hasn't smelt a rat by now, one more fable, and she'll be after us both like a Jack Russell."

"We've been very careful. I'm sure no one suspects."

The tunnel vision of clandestine lovers.

"Suspect. The pair of you are the talk of the hospital. If you go on like this, someone's going to blow the whistle."

It wouldn't take much to make him glad if that happened: take the whole thing out of his hands.

"You know," I went on. "This affair of yours. It's only going to bring a whole lot of grief for everyone."

"I never dreamt it could be like this. You can't understand."

"It's obvious you're very taken," I allowed. "And I don't blame you. But apart from Noelle, and the difficulty in learning Urdu, what about your mum and dad?"

That was a dish of unpalatable pie to set before a lover. He looked miserable.

"And what about her parents?"

"She has great respect for them. It would upset them a lot."

"There you are, then. Listen. Come through to the farm this weekend at least. Don't do anything drastic. These grand passions often run a course, so I understand."

I nailed him to that promise while his resolve faltered.

That Friday night wasn't busy. Wilson was able to bid a satisfying au revoir to his Brahmaputra Belle, and the pair of us dossed most of the night on the battered easy chairs in the residents' lounge. In a fine spring morning he drove us to the farm, and we arrived there unusually well slept. There was no doubt Noelle was glad to see him. Her smile of welcome was something even she couldn't fake.

"See?" I nudged him.

"Yeah," he agreed, convinced against his will, and went off in the arms around the waist cuddle of the couple with an understanding.

Matt and I spent the morning harrowing the middle meadow, the big, spiked rakes bouncing and banging behind us. We put the big Olivers in high gear, and were finished in good time to join the queue for the Major's pay parade. I stuffed the poke in my hip pocket, and went back through the yard with Matt.

It was unusually busy. Rab was there: Siobahn to meet him, and walk with him; stiff backed in an effort to support her bulging, gravid belly. Wilson was there, with Noelle on his arm; Connie, too, forcing herself back into a normal life.

I walked through the crowd: chaffing, blethering; loving the spring sunshine; the Willie McPherson episode losing its sting.

The biggest crowd was around open doors of the barn, people crowding in.

"What's all the fuss?" I asked Matt.

"Young Davie Yuille's to be married next week. They're going to ride him into the village on a gate. Want to have a closer look at the fun?"

We threaded our way through a perimeter of onlookers, mostly women.

"Puir laddie. Hope they're no' too sore on him."

Inside the barn the menfolk were attending to Davie's rites: breeks off, shirt outside in; trussed like a roasting fowl. Already his face was whitewashed; his hair full of sawdust. There was a pause: looking for further ideas to celebrate his advancement to the married state.

"Boot-black," was the cry. "Polish his feet."

"Whit wey his feet?" one wag suggested. "Why no' his balls?"

There was a roar of laughter and approval. No real harm would be done, and if it didn't all come off before the night, so much the merrier.

But young Watson was in the front rank.

"Boot-black? That's for bluiddy bairns. What you want is tar. Tar and feather his bollocks and his prick."

There was a moment of uncertainty. Some of the older men shook their heads and moved away. Even the young bloods were awed.

"Oh-ho. Naw. We couldnae."

Couldn't? Young Watson didn't know the meaning. He jeered them into action.

"If you're a' that feart, Ah'll dae it. Somebody get the tar and a haundfu' o' feathers."

His goading; the fact that he would do the infamous, hilarious deed; the knowledge that they could hide behind his audacity spurred them on. They would be able to talk about it for years after.

"Juist think on him gettin' it aff."

Young Watson made a gross, masturbatory pantomime: knees bent, leaning back, aiming an imaginary cock the size of an Indian club at the roof. That was beyond missing. There was a howl of agreement. Davie's mischievous bunch of pals had become a ravening mob in the thrall of young Watson.

Davie had been accepting the proceedings with a resigned grin. He had done the same sort of thing to others too often to complain. But the prospect of this new pre-nuptial rite posted disbelief and dismay on his face.

"Haw. Naw. Haw, Christ. No' that."

But the affair now had a momentum that couldn't be stopped. Someone ran to Coalheugh, where bitumen was being used to patch a tarmac surface; someone else to Connie's chicken house for a handful of feathers.

I had already waved to Connie. She was standing on the outskirts of the crowd with Wilson and Noelle. Like the rest of the women, the girls had been looking on at Davie's conjugal initiation with a mixture of giggles and not-quite-shocked prudishness. But the thought of seeing his cock coaxed erect, then dressed in such black and white, epithalamial finery, was more than they could countenance.

The other women began to move away, shocked; tutting; shaking their heads: men and their awful ways.

Connie had a bucket in her hand. On her way for feed, she too had been caught up in the crowd; stopped to watch the show.

"Let me through, please. I need some meal for my chicks. Let me get it, then I'll be out of your way."

In the lull, attention switched from Davie to her. Her sturdy constitution had made up the blood loss, and restored her colour. The hormone storm of her recent pregnancy had not yet fully died away. The blast of humours that prepare women for motherhood was still charging her system. This new, deepened attractiveness was enhanced by an unusual leanness: residue of shock and emotion. She had an aura of vulnerable femininity quite different from her usual capable, look-after-myself air.

Young Watson noticed the change. As Connie wound her way through the crowd, his mutter was easily heard.

"By the Christ. Will ye look at the wee wan. Is that no' ready for the knife."

There was a snicker of randy appreciation from the bucks surrounding him.

The meal was at the back of the barn, kept in an old-fashioned, high-sided, wooden kist. Connie had to lean well over to get at the feed: pulled the khaki dungarees hard into the cleavage of her bum.

That far, it had all been bawdy, male appreciation, but this tightly drawn arse was too much for young Watson.

"Christ-oh," he slavered. "Oh ah'll need tae get a haundfu' o' that."

His disciples tittered. What would their wild messiah get up to now? Young Watson realized he had an audience hanging on his every move. He couldn't disappoint them. He walked over to Connie.

I felt Matt glance at me.

But, after all, what could happen? Young Watson wouldn't dare get up to his usual horny handed gropings with a girl from the big house, would he? A bit of a cuddle was all he had in mind, and Connie could stand that. There would be no need for heroics on my part.

See wishful thinking?

I reckoned without the pheromones that were scenting the breeze; the one in a trillion vapours that were inflaming young Watson like a hound-dog scenting a bitch in heat.

He walked up to the gluteal cheeks, taut and bulging with promise; straddled his crotch against them; reached around Connie's waist to take the bucket with his right hand.

"That's too heavy for a wee lass like you."

The realization that something else was up spread among the crowd. Women turned back. Onlookers, content to wait for Davie's appearance in the yard, now crowded in at the doors. The atmosphere of fun had changed.

Connie jerked erect, but his encircling arm stayed tight. The bucket dangled from one hand, earnest of his feeble excuse.

"There. Noo. A wee kiss for helping you."

She had turned around into him. Her left breast was held hard against him. His crotch now caressed her pelvic arch. The crowd went suddenly quiet. More people now looked at me.

I was her protector?

But what the hell. It was still only a cuddle. She would survive. I made no move.

Then I noticed her face. It was rigid with revulsion.

"Let me go. You smelly, filthy, disgusting pig."

I could imagine what she felt: the rank reek of tobacco on his breath; the sour smell of stale sweat: the unmistakable, rancid stinks of male power.

Young Watson was used to shrieks, gratified or coyly scolding. With Connie, I guessed he had expected indignation; anger even. Then he would have stolen his kiss, and walked away, laughing. But Connie's cry was of loathing; of out and out disgust.

That offended him; got at his pride. Worse, it showed him up in front of this big audience.

He would show the snotty bitch; show every bastard watching.

"The likes o' me no' good enough for you, eh? C'mere."

He dropped the bucket, put both hands around her buttocks, and began to writhe his hard snake hips in and out at her. Connie screamed then, and pounded at him.

"No. No. No."

He buried that great beak into her neck; took one hand from her backside, and reached for her breast. Connie's cries became hiccupy and hysterical as this mammary stimulus fired memories of her recent disastrous pregnancy; the botched despoiling of her first child.

He wasn't to know that, of course. Nor Matt. Nor any of the other, by now silent, voyeurs.

But I did.

Matt was looking at me in frank disbelief. I could sense him tauten, readying himself to do what he could about this, but I shook my head at him, a minute sign that this was my affair. I sighed, and walked over to the struggling couple.

"Let her go."

Young Watson took his nose out of where it had been nuzzling. He looked at me in amazement.

"You gaun' tae mak' me, then?"

The tone was conversational.

"If I have to."

He still couldn't believe it. He had tried me so often before: found me wanting. Then he canted his head at me. The magnitude of his opportunity dawned on him: almost everyone on the farm to see him centre stage, and victorious. He grinned at me, and kneaded Connie's breast with hard, hurtful fingers.

"Juist how ye' gaun tae manage that, then?"

Any attempt to wrestle them apart would increase his fondling of her: legitimize it in the name of good, clean catch-as-can. Then, again, sending him a message in the mail wouldn't help either.

There was another way.

I moved a step closer, very casual like: but it shifted my balance on to my left foot. I swivelled all my weight on to it, and skewered the longest, straightest, hardest left I had ever delivered. It shaved Connie's face, and hit him right on the point of that arrogant bloody beak. I felt a satisfying, scrunchy feeling all the way up my arm.

It was the last thing I enjoyed for a while.

Young Watson went over quite spectacularly: catching his heel on a discarded sack; arms up in the air; bunnet flying. He sat up; dabbed his hand to his nose and his lips; looked at the blood.

"Ya hooer's bastard."

He sounded quite chummy. At long last I had obliged him.

"By the Christ, but you'll tak' what's comin' tae ye noo."

Chapter 2

SANDY, FINISHED WITH THE MAJOR'S PAY PARADE, came into the yard just then. He came up to the crowd to see what was afoot. Taking the scene in, he pushed his way through the crowd, red-faced and excited. As the grieve, his first thought was to bring order; to stop this before it went further. But Rab held his shoulder and Matt muttered in his ear.

Young Watson stated the situation for all to hear.

"Listen tae me, grieve. He started this. No' me. If he wants tae fight, it's nane o'your bluiddy business. If you step in here, we'll a' ken yuir wee student mannie for whit he is. A fuckin' crapper."

Matt and Rab nodded soberly, and Sandy knew they were right. I'd never live it down if he stepped in for me. Still, as grieve, he couldn't sanction such lawlessness.

I solved the problem for him. I stepped back: gave young Watson time to get up; Connie to run for safety.

"Away and take a walk, Sandy. Matt will look out for me."

"Is that what ye want, lad?"

What I wanted was my mummy, but it was too late for that.

"Yes. Come back in a wee while."

Pick up the bits.

As he left, I slipped off my wind-proof working jacket, and gave it to Rab.

"Watch yourself, now. He's a bad bastard, that. Maim you if he gets the chance. I've seen him do it."

Maim? Funny adjective. I remembered Matt had given me the same warning. I turned to the matter in hand.

"Noo," crooned young Watson, his lips set in a bloody grin. Then he came for me.

Boxing was no game plan for the scrap I was in. All my years with the steamers had taught me to think in terms of three minute rounds; rules; punches. Young Watson would use whatever would do most damage: boots, elbows, head. There would be no breaks until it was all over; the only rule was to win.

He would want to close and maul but that was the last thing for me. I had no match for the strength of his arms and chest, born of hard slogging work since he was fourteen.

What I might have going for me was my wind and my footwork. Oh, and into the bargain I was a clever bugger: could read books with big words and everything.

He kept coming at me with little rushes; trying to grab me, so he could get us chest to chest. And he did land the odd Sunday punch. Taking these on the arms or chest was bad enough, but if he caught me about the head, my brain rattled about in its wee bone attic.

I had a longer reach with my left. It didn't do much real damage, but it made most of his big punches miss, and saved me from getting tangled in his gorilla grip. In the passing, I did manage to sink some seven pounders in his lower ribs and after a bit, his breathing took on a whistly wheeze. I began to think I might just hold my own.

But I reckoned without one thing. For the second time in ten minutes, his pride was outraged: first Connie's palpable revulsion; now, this rabbit's resistance. And all in front of an audience which would pass a judgement to last the rest of his days about the farm. His anger became manic. He came at me, running hard.

This time, he made no attempt to weave; duck; protect his face. I got in another jab on that nose, frothy with blood and hammered another hook in his gut. I heard him grunt with pain and effort but then he was through to me with a great looping punch, right out of the haymakers' convention. It caught me on the left temple: all four knuckles, full belt.

I had been there before in the train sheds: another, mazy world. But I had never seen the flash of light so bright, nor heard the music so clearly. I had this paralysing weakness; this need to lie down. Other times, though, there had been a referee to hold the other guy back; give me a count of eight, while I rested on one knee.

Young Watson gave no such respite. He had me by the shirt; rammed me against the barn wall; smashed his forehead down into my face. I felt my nose splinter, as the back of my head hit the stone wall with a sick-making crack.

My senses were almost gone. I could no longer hear the shouts of the crowd. My left eye was shut completely. The peripheral vision of the other was gone. All I could see was young Watson's snarling face at the end of a one-eyed tunnel. In that numb, silent world, a small pool of consciousness still registered in a detached way. I remember thinking: "Christ. I'm for it now."

With what was left of my vision, I saw the attacking edge of his rage fade. He had me now: take me at his leisure. But even as I hung by the shirt collar, tight in his hand, what was left of my awareness latched on to this fractional mistake. Even as I waited for my face to be broken, I wondered if I could make anything of this fleeting let up. I let my head loll more slackly. It was an easy act and enough to convince him I was out on my feet. Instead of smashing my face, he allowed himself another kind of gratification.

He went for my balls.

I felt the hard hand grope at my crotch and I remembered the warnings from Matt and Rab. But the worst thing he could imagine for me was the best thing he could have done. There's nothing will make a man react faster.

As his hand closed, to crush and bruise; to produce exquisite pain; to spey my manhood, every reflex in me reacted. For the briefest second – all the time my fire-alarm, jangling instincts needed – his Adam's apple stood out: sharp and angular and unprotected.

This cage of cartilage protects the common entrance to the gullet and air-pipe, just where they diverge. The gullet is a squashy tube, difficult to injure: but the air-pipe is another foot and a half of shafting altogether. Designed to admit air only, it is guarded by a quicksilver valve which shuts on the instant if anything else tries to enter. A spasm of damage control will cut off intake to the lungs for long seconds, until the foreign body is coughed out. Remember the last time something went down the wrong way?

Well, sometimes it will react in the same way to external injury. If I was lucky, I might just save getting my balls in a twist I couldn't unravel.

I brought my right elbow up in a forearm smash, and felt his larynx squash against the vertebrae of the neck. The valve shut tight in protest, and young Watson went surprisedly, mottlingly quiet.

With the fight, his respiration rate must have been twice the normal count: forty per minute: one stertorous, straining gasp every one and a half seconds.

And then there were none.

His hands flew to his throat, trying to comprehend by feel, what his mind would not take in. His grasp on my collar and my manhood gone, I slumped in reaction and relief. But I could afford no miscalculation now and mercy would be the biggest mistake of all time.

I drove the steel toe-plate of my working boot into his shin.

His face went puce: no relief from the carbon dioxide build-up in his blood; the larynx still in spasm. He jerked forwards, bent double in a reflex of agony. One hand went to guard the shin; the other was still at his throat. As his head came forward, I brought my knee up, and caught him right between the eyes. He went down like a bag of sand.

I went willingly down beside him on my hands and knees. My cerebral cortex was calling for urgent shut down: blackness; sleep; a chance for its delicate mechanisms to recover.

But it wasn't time for that, yet. Young Watson wasn't quite out and, as long as he was stirring at all, I would need to watch him. He, too, got groggily to his knees and we faced each other on all fours. He was all animal, then, programmed to continue the fight at any cost. He looked around. He got his eye on the handle of a broken graip: three feet of hard-wood club. He made for it on all fours.

I looked for some kind of answer.

The barn doors were old and huge. The blacksmith had been in a few days before to measure up for one that had rusted through. The iron replacement was lying ready for Matt and me to fit, in a spare half hour. Three inches long and three feet wide, it would even the odds.

I got to my feet, and weaved my way to pick it up. As I turned to face young Watson, Matt, Rab, and some of the other men were protesting.

"That's enough. One of you will be killt, next."

My sentiments entirely. But how to get young Watson to back down without loss of face.

Sandy, returning from his worried, unwonted walk, provided an answer. He came up to the crowd just then, and saw the new level of confrontation. At that, his grieve's authority would not be gainsaid.

"Watson. You boy. Put thae bluiddy things doon. Noo mark this. The first one tae tak' a step, an' Ah'll go for the polis. That man will get the jile. The pair o' ye if need be. Noo. Ah've tellt ye."

He was in earnest: custodian of the farm's reputation. A fist fight he had made himself swallow, but this was a draught too much.

I saw young Watson's shoulders come down in acceptance. Never in my life will I be so glad to see anything again. He tossed away the graip handle with a sneer. He was still unbeaten: stopped by a technicality.

"A' right, grieve. Dinny fash yoursel.'"

I dropped the hinge; stood unsteadily. Relief flooded Sandy's face. He hadn't been sure he could rein in young Watson. He tried for a conventional ending to the bout.

"C'mon. The pair o' ye. Shake haunds."

Young Watson looked at me: a long calculating glance. I was aware of a change. Respect would be too strong a word: more a grudging reappraisal. He nodded at me, the movement almost imperceptible: but that was as far as he would go.

"Naw, naw, grieve. That's for bluiddy weans. Him an' me. We're no' in a bluiddy Bible class."

He would climb down no further. He caught up his waist-coat, set his bunnet on three hairs and pushed his way out of the crowd. He shook off his father's attempt at support. He'd walk away by himself: unbeaten; defiant still, even if he was unsteady and limping. He went to the pump in the yard, and had his father douse his head.

Sandy looked at me, clucking and tutting.

"The mess you're in. Ah hope I did right by ye."

"Nothing else you could have done, Sandy. And you came back right on cue."

I had to sit down again, my back to a straw bale. Connie came to crouch by me, wiping away tears and snivels.

"Oh. You look terrible. And it's all my fault."

"No. That was nothing to do with you. That has been on the cards for a long time."

Matt and Wilson hunkered down to estimate the damage.

"Your nose is broken," Matt guessed. He had been around a few fights in his day. Wilson added his opinion.

"That gash in your nose. And the one in your lip. They'll need stitches. I had better run you back to the Northern General."

Even as he said it, I could sense his relief. I had leant on him to come east: now it was my fate to take him back again; turn my battered face to his good account.

"What a pal."

My sarcasm left him unmoved.

"I want to come with you in the car. Make sure you're all right," insisted Connie, and I couldn't dissuade her any way.

Wilson went for his car and I leant against the straw, feeling sick. Matt did what he could for my face with a handkerchief soaked in water from the pump, where young Watson was now towelling his head with his shirt. My wavering consciousness found some things out of focus; others paradoxically sharp and clear. I was gazing hazily at nothing in particular, when I noticed Noelle. Her expression was etched in unforgettable detail.

She had been pushed aside; marginalized; given no part to play in the drama. When Wilson offered to run me back to Glasgow with such obvious alacrity, he had made not the slightest reference to her. Alone now, she looked around the yard. Her gaze fixed on young Watson as he hirpled away. Even as I watched, her pouting disappointment gave way to a look of sulky, wilful defiance .

Wilson drove into the yard then. Matt and Rab helped me into the back seat with Connie. As we left the yard, I could hear Davie Yuille shouting in alarm.

"Ye canny leave me here. Wan o' you buggers come back an' cut me free."

Chapter 3

I SAT IN THE BACK OF WILSON'S CAR with Matt's hankie wadded to sop up the blood. Connie cuddled me into her shoulder, but I was aware of her only intermittently. I kept sliding into a daze of semi-consciousness. When we got to the Northern General, the registrar on the Gate was a guy called Donnie McMillan. We had potted a few frames of snooker in the residents' mess, and he winced when he saw my face.

"What hit you?"

"It felt like a tram-car."

He shrugged. What was a bent nose to a manly chap like me.

"Walk him along to the OP theatre, Wilson," said Donnie. "I'll be along in a minute."

Shiraz was there, doing her duty shift. She seemed shocked at the sight of my face.

"Oh. My goodness me. You had better, please, lie down."

At least she was attentive and sympathetic. Wilson was only pathetic, his face one great simper when he saw her.

"You've been a wonderful comfort," I said to Connie. "He'll get you some tea, now."

Wilson took her off for a Poonakandy cuppa; Donnie came along, and I had twenty numbed minutes of sharp needles, bright lights, and shiny instruments, as he pulled my lacerated face together and aspirated half a fluid ounce of bloody serum from each of the soft blue fruits that were the eyelids of my left eye: and twenty seconds of genuine, shouting-out, pain and tears, as he pushed my nose as straight as it would go, with an almighty squidge of his big, broad thumbs.

"'S always more difficult when it's been broken before," he justified himself, without a vestige of compunction.

After he had finished, I took a look at my face in the stainless steel side of the sterilizer. It was out of shape: lumpy with dusky, purple bruises; raw with multiple, small abrasions. Despite the aspiration, my left eye was still closed; the root of my nose was thickened and still off centre; three stitches in a horizontal gash above my nose, and two in a vertical split in my lower lip, stuck out in stiff, black, silken ends from a plasticized spray dressing. I felt my teeth gingerly, but none of them moved.

"Bums up," he said next, and shot a lance of pain all the way from my buttock to my heel, as he gave me some prophylactic penicillin.

"Your arm, next."

The anti-tetanus serum made me wince too. Oh, but you could have too much pain.

"You will fight in a farm-yard," said Donnie, with no sympathy. "I suppose I needn't tell you, but I will, anyhow. Although your face looks bad, it's your scone I'm bothered about. Those skelps must have had your brain banging about inside, like a ping-pong ball."

I nodded: the very phrase.

"There could be a reaction, and we don't want you going down in front of a bus with a post-traumatic fit. You should go to bed for a day or two."

I nodded. The advice was for my own good.

"Shall I take you back to your parents' home?" asked Wilson, who had left Connie for a moment; come in to see how things were.

"Unh unh. Not that. If my mother sees me like this, I'll get another hammering."

"Come home with me then."

He could irritate the hell out of me sometimes, this guy, but came through true blue when it was needed.

"Nice of you, old son. But no. My place at Shaw's Howe will be as quiet as anywhere. Always is at weekends. I'll sneak in. Rest up until

Monday. Be as right as rain then. I would be grateful if you will run me out there. Then you can take Connie back to the farm."

I tried to set his mind back on its earlier, sensible course, but the thought of Shiraz coming off duty soon had thrown him for an outside loop.

"Now I'm back, I think I'll stay here. But I'll see Connie on to a train."

I was trembling badly by the time I climbed back into Wilson's car, great bouts of ague-like shivering: part reaction to extreme physical effort and sheer, blue funk; part to the second, calculated dose of adrenalin incorporated in the local anaesthetic. This upset Connie all the more. She started to cry again: freely, helplessly. No one had warned her about this.

"Oh, Neil. What's the matter? Scoular. What's gone wrong?"

I felt so weak, I didn't think I could manage the outer stair to the side door. But, at that time on a Saturday, the pavilion should be quiet: no visitors; the nursing staff busy serving tea. Even Sister Annie took Saturday afternoons off. With luck and a little reconnaissance by Wilson, I should be able to sneak through the atrium to my rooms.

Wilson took a gander to the manner overdone: gum-shoed in and out like a Keystone Cop.

"Like you said. All busy with tea. No one about. Come on."

What a trio: Wilson pussy-footing like an overdone Lemmy Caution; Connie looking like she'd been at a wake; me with a face that felt it had been in a concrete mixer.

Right in the middle of the atrium she caught us: centre stage, with the arc lights full on. Gaunt, severe, Sister Annie opened the door of where she should never have been.

"What —" she started.

I took one disgusted look at her: but it was an effort too much. I keeled over at her feet.

I was vaguely aware of commotion; of Connie crying even more; of lifting hands; of cool sheets. I came to only a couple of times in the next eighteen hours, when I needed a piddle. I managed, by hanging on to bed and walls and cistern, to compensate for the dizziness that still came over me in waves. Otherwise I slept in a big, black pit, disturbed only vaguely by this stiff, starched woman who came in to see me whiles.

She bathed my face, and fed me codeine tablets, and gave me sips of water. She had cool hands: the most marvellous, comforting touch.

On the Monday, I woke quite suddenly and I knew the worst was over. My head was working properly again. After a look in the mirror, I knew that all I needed was a few more days to let the bruising settle; until I could show my face anywhere outside a Mary Shelley sequel.

I found I was ravenous. I was contemplating getting up; risking the reaction in the dining room, when my bedroom door opened. Sister Annie stood there. She carried a tray set with food.

"Ah. Awake. I wondered. You haven't eaten since you arrived. I thought you might like something in here. Private."

The thoughtful lady was at home again.

"I'm starving, as you guessed. And I would have felt self conscious in the dining room. Thank you."

She put down the tray; plumped and patted the pillows at my back; helped me sit up in bed. She brought the tray over; settled it in my lap; then went to stand at the foot of my bed.

The food had been chosen with the state of my mushed lips in mind: scrambled eggs; jelly; iced tea with a straw.

"This is really nice."

I was playing for time; wondering how to explain my latest lapse into crime: street-fighter as well as abortionist. Then I realized she was not her usual brisk self. She made one or two remarks of, for her, quite supreme inanity, her eyes fixed on my hairy chest.

I realized I had no pyjamas on; remembered the anonymous, helping hands. Perhaps the sight of my hairy bits had struck her inarticulate with wonder? But among the battalions that had soldiered in her trench, I couldn't be that special?

"I – I – ah – find –" she started uncertainly. Then she decided to get it over with. She kept her eye on the delicate line of my left clavicle and plunged on.

"I find I owe you an apology. The young girl who was with you –"

"Connie?"

"Yes. She was very upset. I sent your friend away and took her to my room to get her calmed. She told me the whole story. About that night. About her boyfriend. About how you have been so kind to her. Looked after her. And then the awful fight you got into. When no one else would stand up for her."

I felt stained with guilt. She didn't know about the false knight; the money.

"No. No. It wasn't like that. That would have happened anyway. Sooner or later."

She raised her eyes to mine, then: the big, grave, grey eyes, and hushed me with a little move of her hand. She must finish her expiation.

"I should have known." She sounded as if she had been having an argument with herself. "A real Sir Galahad." I almost groaned, ashamed that the truth was so different. " I want you to know that I am truly sorry."

She paused. Was there a little expectancy? Was she hoping that her apology would be gracefully received? Could we try for the start of something better?

But she had read all the wrong reasons into my Donnybrook with young Watson: a barn-yard brawl in which gallantry had struck no blows. I waved her quiet in my turn: brusque with embarrassment; awkward at this fresh perception of my own dishonour.

"Yes. Well. It's all over now."

No courtly acceptance: cut short by a boorish bruiser in sore need of a shave. She swallowed my put down visibly.

"I just wanted you to know."

She turned abruptly and left me to a meal which was no longer so appetizing. My food was still brought to me over the next day or two, but it was delivered by one of the ward maids. Sister Annie did not visit me again. The incident bothered me. It was the second time I had been rude to her within a few weeks, although this time unintentionally.

I had a few visitors: Wilson, Minnie and Luke. Even Minty came to wonder at the state of me. I had Wilson post me sick at the various classes; Minnie arranged for me to copy her lecture notes; and Minty brought me the gossip from Boss's wards. He was disappointed in Sister Annie.

"I see what you mean. She doesn't exactly cause a rush of blood to the corpus cavernosus."

Connie was different. She was bowled over by her. She came to see me one day after her classes, and rattled on about her.

"She was so kind to me that night. At first I thought she was going to be awful. When I started to tell her about the baby, she froze up. Seemed really angry. But when I told her about Johnny and how scared we were and how we didn't know what to do and how I was ashamed to tell you and how you always stuck up for me and then that awful man Watson and how I felt and how you made him let me go, and everything –"

She stopped, embarrassed: the memories not yet buried.

"Seen Johnnie?" I asked.

"Yes. Once. I told him I didn't want to see him again. Not for a while anyhow. He seemed miserable about the whole thing."

"So he should."

She was quiet for a moment.

"It takes two."

She kissed one of my bruises and left: a much grown up young lady.

After she left, I shrugged myself into a polo necked pullover; put on a pair of light shoes. The recollection of Sister Annie eating dirt still bothered me. Her apology had taken some swallowing of pride, and I hadn't made it any easier. I thought I would take a stroll; stop in at the sisters' home; see if I could make amends.

I sauntered along the gravel path that wound around the perimeter of the old estate, until I came to the main driveway. I turned into that, to meet Nutty Dotty, twinkling along on her paradoxically slim ankles.

"Good evening, Sister Tutor. You're in a hurry."

"Yes. Going out tonight. Bus to catch. Oh, your face. I heard about you. Are you feeling better?"

The state of my battered mug had been the subject of sisterly gossip.

"Yes, thanks. Do you know if Sister Urquhart is in her quarters this evening?"

"Yes. She's in alone tonight. Poor dear."

The remark made me curious.

"She was kind to me," I said, gesturing at my battered, still unshaven face. "I thought I might call on her. Thank her properly."

"Oh."

She looked as if she wanted to let me in on a big secret.

"There's my bus. I must fly."

She ran off, moving her bulk with absurd ease.

I went to the Sisters' home, and tried the sitting room first. I crossed to the door, and raised my hand to knock. But then I paused; cocked an ear. There was an odd sound I couldn't place at first. I stepped closer and listened at the thin panel.

A woman was sobbing: Sister Annie.

I poked at the door with one finger. The latch had not caught properly, and the door swung open a noiseless inch. I put my left eye to the slit and peered in.

The room was east facing: dull at the best of times. That evening, its sole cheer came from a single element of a three bar fire: one miserly kilowatt for a miserable lady. Easy Annie was sitting on the floor in front of it: knees tucked under her; head cradled on the seat of a chair. This was no paroxysm of grief over a sudden tragedy. These were the intermittent shoulder-shaking snuffles of some long felt ache in the soul.

"Ahem."

A stage cough straight from the pen of Terence Ratigan.

"Oh."

I knew how to capture the attention of an audience. She gave a gaspy yelp of surprise and consternation. I had caught Sister Annie with her starch all wet.

"What do you want?"

She was smearing tears all over those sad features and her tone said me of all people.

"I'm sorry. Can I come in?"

"Don't you dare."

Any woman would be distraught: face all over the place.

"Can I help?"

"Yes. Go away."

I stood at the door.

"If that's what you want. It was just – I wanted to thank you. For looking after me. And I'm glad you know I was telling the truth. You got under my skin that day."

I might as well make a job of the amends while I was at it.

"Yes. Well. It was nice of you to take the trouble. Goodbye now."

For the second time in our acquaintanceship, this was not enough. I pushed the door open, slipped in, and sat on a seat a discreet distance from her.

"You always seem to put people – or me, anyhow – off. I'd like to do something to help. Perhaps if you told me what was wrong?"

"It's my birthday."

Now, I had heard that the passage of time weighed on the minds of ladies, but this reaction seemed excessive.

"Is that so bad?"

She turned on me: sneered at my flightless, youthful, male imagination.

"Bad? What do you know about it? How can you possibly guess?"

She enumerated the whys and wherefores of her misery in scathing detail.

"I'm spending it alone."

Belatedly; sheepishly, I noticed a measly few birthday cards on the mantel. There was no bouquet of roses from her surgeon lover: not one anniversary bloom from any of the legions she had obliged. Once again, her aloneness took on a more bleak dimension.

"I'm a year older. A year further on to nowhere."

I had suspected there was pain behind the severe starched manner, but nothing like this.

"I'm a widow."

According to Minty's history of events, the marriage must have been in the knackers' yard before her RAMC husband bought it at Dunkirk; nor did the timetable of her hectic liaisons suggest any period of mourning. Yet, now, ten years later, contemplation of her relictitude still brought desolation?

"And I'm lonely"

I had guessed that: but not this profound, dejected reality.

"I suppose all this must sound so self-pitying to a boy like you."

"A man like you," she amended at the scowl I gave her. "Not very brave, am I?"

The poor old bag. I couldn't leave anyone in such a state. Somehow, I had to turn the evening into an occasion for this broken martinet.

Chapter 4

"A BIRTHDAY? ON YOUR OWN? NEVER HEARD OF SUCH A THING."

She looked at me startled, as I surveyed the room desperately for possibilities; flogged ideas from the earthbound imagination she had scorned.

A couch and a couple of easy chairs were grouped around the fire; a standard lamp in a corner; a drop leaf table against a wall, with a spar-backed dining chair on either side; a glass-fronted sideboard, with cups and plates, for suppers of buttered toast; a record player, with an untidy jumble of seventy-eights under it. Hardly the setting for a Mardi Gras.

I remembered a chance remark she had made: she had liked dancing once.

"Can you dance to any of these?"

"Yes, but – "

"Great."

I got up and crossed to her: caught her hands.

"Trust me?"

"Oh. Well – "

It seemed she would try once more.

"That's the girl."

From her face, it had been a long time since she had been anyone's girl, but this once she would go along with such a mad rejuvenative idea.

"I'll be back in an hour. You put on something nice. That blue dress you wore."

I ran to my rooms, my bruises complaining. I shaved around the lumps; broke out a clean shirt; found my paypacket, still unopened, in my dungarees. Then I phoned the duty porter.

"Archie. This is Neil Aitken."

Apart from collecting the patients' bets, he was the general handyman, and ferried pharmaceuticals from the dispensary to the wards, on an errand bike.

"I need to borrow your bike for half an hour. A couple of drams in it for you."

Archie could transmogrify anything in the hospital into fluid measures from a spirits gantry.

"Aye. Right. You're on."

The Black Bull in Milngavie was a ten minute clip away: a solid establishment that had sold food and drink and lodgings for a hundred years. I got hold of the manageress and told her the story of the forgotten birthday with a mixture of wheedling and soft soap and brow-beating and further plain, corrupt bribery.

In fifteen minutes flat, she had ready for me a bottle of wine and a cold picnic for two, packed in little wax cartons. On my way back through the hospital grounds, I stopped at one of the dilapidated flower beds and picked some tulip blooms.

When I got to the sisters' quarters, Sister Annie had mended her face, and put on the blue dress: the one which made her look slim rather than gaunt.

"Nice," I said in genuine approval. "It makes you look less – "

I was going to say severe, but thought better of it.

" – More party like."

She looked at me. As always, the big, grey eyes were difficult to read but I thought she was pleased.

We moved the heavy furniture back; opened out the little table and set it in front of the fire. We fetched an extra couple of table lamps from the bedrooms. With the overhead light off and an extra bar of the fire on, the room was warm and cheery in the early summer night. It contrasted happily with the gloom of an hour before.

We spread the load from the basket into a modest feast.

"Where did you get all this?" she asked, impressed, as she counted the spoils off on her fingers.

"Chicken, ham, potato salad, green salad, fruit, biscuits, cheese, wine – " she paused " – flowers. You actually brought flowers."

The handful of filched blooms was somewhere short of a bouquet but, once again, she seemed pleased.

I opened the bottle. It was no champagne: *vin trés ordinaire*, with never a bubble to bless it. But the cork came out with a pop that at least sounded like a celebration.

I treated her like one of my favourite aunties: I knew all about that. I was cheery; fatuous; garrulous. I made terrible jokes, and awful spoonerisms, and even worse puns. I wove yarns of unbelievable nonsense; embroidered ridiculous fables: anything to lighten the load of misery that had been defeating her.

By the time we had gnawed the last chicken bone and seen off the wine, the summer dusk was falling.

"Now, we'll clear all of this away," I decreed. "Roll up the carpet. Have a ball, all to our own wee selves. You did say you liked dancing?"

"Yes. But it has been a long time."

I sorted through the pile of records; put the needle into the first groove of 'Begin the Beguine'. Then I offered myself up for a first, duty dance: a martyr in the cause of cheering up this unhappy lady. Because she had once liked to dance didn't mean she would be good at it. With that reserved, starchy, standoffish attitude, she was bound to be hard work: stilted; unyielding. I'd have to push her about the floor a bit; manipulate her through the turns.

"Would you care to dance?" I said, in my best ballroom polite.

The stiff, gaunt woman with the cool hands and the sad eyes that had once known laughter and who had once been gorgeous, stepped into my arms. Tony Martin was reliving a night of tropical splendour. And the tongue stuck to the roof of my mouth in disbelieving shock.

Glasgow was the ballroom capital of the kingdom. The city was mega-rich in glass-smooth, swung floors, and first rate bands.

"Ye dancin'?" was the intoduction to a corps de palais of invariable expertise; first rate partners. I enjoyed the arms around, full frontal, intimate formality with someone I had never met before; the challenge of blending disparate minds and bodies into a smoothly moving unit, within a few bars. In general, these girls were solid partners, whose rhythm came unmistakeably from the hips; a bottom that bounced a fraction of a second behind the beat: mark of the best jazz singers.

But once in a long while; every precious now and then, I met a different breed. Long girls, always, I was aware of them to somewhere about the bosoms: after which they disappeared from the earthly senses all the way down to the feet, which could anticipate any trick or twirl I might think up, of their own free will. It was like dancing with a chiffon breeze.

Sister Annie was the classiest example of that rare sorority I had ever had my arm around.

"I'm out of practice," she said.

For a couple of shellac sides, she was indeed a litttle rusty. I was terrified of trampling on these disembodied toes. Our linoleum square and stockinged feet took a some getting used to. But after that, I had never danced like it.

I looked at her reproachfully.

"I didn't know you could dance like this?"

All that fighting and feuding, when we could have been on a proper floor with a real band.

She laughed then: a lovely laugh, with not a hint of derision this time; a throw back to the time she had been the girl in the picture. It set the seal on an hour of real, uncomplicated enjoyment. We sprinkled stars all over Alabama with Tommy Dorsey; chopped wood with Woody Herman; danced in the dark with Artie Shaw. The atmosphere was as light as a fairy's wand. I was feeling really good about chasing the lady's black dogs; at putting those stupid misunderstandings behind us: looking forward to things being more pleasant in the ward.

At first the change was ineffable: the sensation just short of a headache when, before a cloud shows in the sky, you can tell a hot summer's day is turning to thunder.

First, I became aware of her body. As I fitted into her dancing style, her incorporeality became less alarming. I worried less about standing on her nylon-covered feet. The rest of that long spare body; those long, lean flanks, fleshed into consciousness under my hand; against my chest. From somewhere far outside any learning or experience I had ever had; from some deep well of male instinct, I knew I had never had my arms around a woman like this.

My mouth went slowly dry. The atmosphere in the room became thick; almost oppressive. By a common, unspoken lack of intent, our intricate steps became more simple; in time slowed to a mere balance from one foot to another. I pulled my head back a fraction to look in those grey, honest eyes. They would tell me fast enough if I was imagining things.

There was nothing imaginary about the jolt that rocked me. It was quite physical in its intensity, with all the attributes of a mild electric shock. There wasn't any way the logical part of my mind could grasp what was happening, so I let myself go mad.

Connie Boswell was weaving the spell of that old black magic around us as our steps stopped. It was the schmaltz; the flapdoodle. Fatuous rhymes for romantic fantasy: and I knew all of that. Yet, suddenly, they were the most perceptive lyrics ever written. Only those lips would put out the fire.

Right up to the last second, I was in a cloud of quite ridiculous desire. I wanted to kiss the cool, quenching lips of the gorgeous girl in the photograph; to know I was loved like that.

I should be so thirsty.

This was Lilith in my arms: no idealistic, hazy schoolgirl from years before. As our lips did meet; as that long gash of a mouth closed on mine, my last naive hope went up in a whoosh: a roman candle with a lit match for a present.

A bolt of sexuality surged through me. All the good advice I had ever read in the books with plain covers, was shown for arrant rubbish. Any schedule of seduction: the gentling, the stroking, the exploration of the erogenous zones according to the diagrams on page 36, was shown for the puerile prurience it was.

My hand went up her knickers like I was catching a mamba on the strike. Already she was a wet scalding smear. Foreplay was a strangled yelp; and consummation was an on the spot, momentary, frictionless immersion in a bain-marie of womanly secretions that felt hot enough to cook frankfurters.

Lovely Anne had gone for good. The starchy stand-offish sister was away on leave. The mistress of the golfing weekend had torn up her card.

Easy Annie was on the rampage again.

I picked her up from our linoleum couch in a snatch and lift that burst a couple of buttons off my shirt and carried her into the bedroom. I undressed her slowly: pausing at each fresh revelation of that much used, maid-of-all-men's body.

No wonder she was notorious.

There was nothing of the conventional venus about her: no voluptuous curves; no coy, secret places; no peeping pink nipples.

The whole impression was of length and leanness, with a broad bony pelvis, that looked almost uncomfortable; flat breasts that should have filled out and paid their way in the world feeding bairns.

I had never imagined anything so erotic. I now knew why the lads had queued six deep. Well, I might be last in line, but I would do my damndest to make me memorable.

I had all the help she could give me and we set about each other with a destructive rapaciousness that split the wound in my lip wide open again and revealed to me for the first time how pleasure could register on the pain threshold; and starred our lives with disaster.

BOOK NINE

Chapter 1

I CAME TO NEXT MORNING IN A HAZE OF SATIATION. I knew a few moments of blissful content, before the strangeness of my surroundings dawned, and the memory of the night snapped into focus. Every warning button in my system glowed bright, volcano red.

What had I done?

Sister Annie didn't make me feel any easier. As I looked around, I saw she was perched on an elbow, watching me in the pearly light of a good day to come.

"It's four o'clock. The place will start to stir. You'd better go now."

There was no invitation to further favours before the sun rose: just a brisk command to get the hell out of her bed.

The laughter had all gone and the fun and the ardour. All that was left was a hard look.

She sat up in bed. There were bits of caked blood all over her breasts, her belly, her thighs: tribute from my lips, the bottom one gaping again, and throbbing like hell. A small, detached part of my mind – the professional in training – noticed the broad, white, puckered scar in the lower abdomen. Something hadn't healed well.

Was that when Boss had relieved her of her unwanted babe: slipped it in a bucket bound for the incinerator?

I had never spent all night with a lady before, and I wasn't too sure of the proper etiquette. Despite her brusque dismissal, I surely could not leave without a gesture?

Offer to make us a cup of tea? Or perhaps a good morning kiss? Nothing succulent: the merest peck of salutation.

But Sister Annie was entirely businesslike.

"This will be a hobby of yours, I suppose? Like all young men?"

She had been considering the events of the night and intended no tribute to the thrills and skills of my lovemaking. This was a statement of fact she found bitter. Any attempt to formulate my chaotic emotions dried up in face of the arid conclusion she had come to.

I shrugged away all previous experience. Anything I might have been proud of had been shown for nothing more than a wee boy's cocksureness. Yet, though I couldn't define the reason, it wasn't only to salve my self-respect I found myself unwilling to expand on my previous exploits.

"Good. It's better that we understand each other for what we are."

It seemed she knew herself for something sour and unlovely.

"There must be no emotional nonsense. No rubbish about love."

She had tried that and found it wanting.

I looked out of the window. Meeting the girl in the picture had never been an option. I knew that. Yet, the image still tantalized me.

"Of course not."

I should grumble about losing a dream for such a reality? Most men would draw their back teeth with pliers to get this kind of offer.

"What will we do about him?"

My worry surfaced like an overblown diver from a hundred fathoms. There was only one him that big.

"You know about that, then?"

I spared her the dirt Minty had passed on to me.

"I found out by accident. Guessed, anyhow. There was a recent label on your case from Gleneagles. I knew he was there. It seemed too much of a coincidence."

When Boss looked over the counterpane after a hard night at the number one iron, did he too find her grim-faced and bitter, the features unsoftened by any memory of the night just past?

"He mustn't find out about this."

Not so much a warning: more a statement of principle.

"If he did?" I asked.

"He would be hurt."

"Hurt?" I was incredulous. "You couldn't hurt that iron-willed old bugger."

It was out before I thought.

"He's not like that. Not all the time. He can be very kind. I know he does things that seem awful. And he'll never back down. But it isn't that simple."

This was no justification of a cynical relationship, like the one we had just plotted. This was a plea for understanding from someone who cared.

"He was all through the First War. Almost four years."

The mud and the carnage; the ordained cruelty.

"Then medicine. Men who learned their surgery in the twenties had to develop a shell. Operating was surrounded by death. On the table. After. No matter what he did. How much he tried."

I had a sudden perception of him, as he told weeping wives and broken families he had failed. I understood, now, why failure had been expunged from his vocabulary.

"But there are other reasons. He had a son. Did you know?"

Had? Minty's gossipings implied the son was still alive, though no one knew much about him.

"He was a bad lot. Never out of trouble. Things that had to be hushed up."

"Did you know him?"

"No. We never met."

Just as well, from the venom in her voice.

"His last mess was the worst of all. He got a girl in trouble. Wouldn't marry her. She tried to hang herself. She was black in the face when they cut her down. Saved her life but by that time she had irreversible brain damage."

Black in the frontal lobes as well.

"He was sent off to Australia for a fresh start. But he never wrote. Not once. His mother doted on him. She went –" searched for a euphemism " – funny . She became reclusive. Withdrawn."

Withdrawn to a place with bars on the windows.

Boss's cruelty, his hardness took on a pathetic quality. They had been necessary for him to survive; to function; to keep on giving so much of himself to his patients, his craft, those bloody wards he loved so much.

I was suddenly, quaintly, embarrassed. This knowledge, this intimate detail, had come from pillow talk. Secrets; feelings passed on in the course of a tried and trusted and mutually dependent affair. So, what the hell was I doing here? How had I become caught up in this?

"He was hurt just as badly as his wife. But he would never admit it. Never show it."

That was Boss all right: the guy I knew.

"Or at least, only rarely."

That was the man she knew: when the reaches of the night invited terrible confidences.

"You must go now."

I pulled on my clothes and shoes.

"When shall I see you again?"

"I'll let you know."

She was in charge of things.

I had never had a secret paramour before. I had no idea how it would blaze from the forehead in letters of flame, as I sneaked out to join the lives of the deceitful. For life was full of these.

Wilson's eastern liaison was almost flushed out in the open by Mama Armstrong. After the fight, she had jaloused that her pretty babe was not pleased by Wilson's behaviour. At a meeting in the gloomy, green sitting room, she apparently delivered herself of a speech that would have put Katisha to shame.

" As good as told me, she expected us to be engaged as soon as I qualify," ranted Wilson, quite uncharacteristically.

I knew, and he knew, that had been the only idea in his mind, until he met Shiraz. But now – Mama had put the delicate balance of his affections in danger through the workings of Newton's third law: to every action there is an equal and opposite reaction: shove Wilson right into the arms of his Lotus love.

He fumed about the incident for days, but he was saved – or lost, I've never been sure which – by the customs of a civilization much older than ours. He came to me a few days later, stricken.

"Shiraz. She's going home."

I held my breath. He had booked a passage with the P & O as well? But, no. Fate had spared him the east of Suez experience.

"She's to be married. One of those arranged things. She has known all along, but couldn't bring herself to tell me."

The movies had turned to real.

I took him drinking that night: let him cry in his whisky.

"Probably never was for me, anyhow. I would never have had the guts. Just like you said. My parents. My background. That kind of thing." He laughed, a small, bitter chuckle of further self-understanding. Oh, he was learning all right.

Perhaps he deserved a consolation prize?

"When does she leave?"

"A few weeks."

"Would it help if you had my room key now and then?"

"What about the dragon?"

"Don't worry. I can fix her."

I was fixing her well and truly, whenever I could find the time and a place, but he wasn't to know that.

"Could you really manage that?"

I waved him quiet.

Of the other deceivers, one was totally unexpected: Minnie: such a gentle deception.

Minnie was as plain as rice pudding in her dress: few falderals or ornaments. The one thing she had always worn was the fine gold chain which held her mother's wedding ring. She kept it close to the heart: inside her blouse or dress. Only when she twiddled it, in times of agitation or abstraction, was it visible.

One day, in the ward side-room, she was trying to understand the complexities of the nephrotic syndrome. The intense concentration brought on a craving to fidget with her worry charm.

I was watching absently, when I realized there were now two rings. The second, in contrast to the old-fashioned, thick, gold band of her mother, was a slender gold hoop, on the raised shoulders of which winked a very small diamond which was at least as big as the Ritz.

Something else to keep my mouth shut about.

The third deceiver, of course, was Connie, but what with fighting and fornicating, I hadn't kept up with her progress as much as I might. One weekend, after my face had healed, I caught up with her in her chicken house.

"Hi, kid. Need a handy-man? Sandy sent me to help you."

She eyed me reflectively: pleased about something.

"How's drama school getting on?"

"I didn't want to say anything until I was sure. But now I can tell you. My drama coach thinks I might get into R.A.D.A. in London. There's an exhibition I can try for. There are auditions at the end of term."

She kept on surprising me. She would be a suitable partner for any lucky man, even if she wasn't going to inherit a bean.

"Good for you. Could you manage that?"

"The exhibition would pay my fees and some expenses, but it wouldn't be enough to live on. I've been saving, thanks to you and the chickens. But I still won't have quite enough money."

"Surely your auntie won't still object if you're successful?"

"Wouldn't she just. She's got herself convinced I'll be back in the house next year. Helping Uncle William with his books and typing, as well as all the other chores. I might have got him to stake me until I was twenty-one. But if she finds out I'm going to blow the coop – woweee."

I was suddenly alarmed for her – our – capital.

"She can't touch your money, can she?"

"No. But she'll make life as difficult as she can."

I nodded. Aunt Winnie could give the Wicked Queen in Snow White lessons in malevolence, when she put her mind to it.

"Don't worry," she reached up and kissed me on the forehead. "I'm making plans, old man. Just like you told me."

Some orphan. Soon as I was a little clearer in the head about Sister Annie, I'd get right back on my white steed and show this child if I was old or not.

The last deceiver was amongst us even then: but we didn't know.

Looking back, Noelle had been scattering vapour trails like a proton in a cloud chamber: odd times when she couldn't be found; bursts of excitement; intensification of that funny, glittery look – but retrospect is a great place to learn wisdom.

One incident, however, set her perfidy up for future revelation.

Connie came to me one day, near the end of term, her face a study of tears and chagrin.

"That bloody girl. D'you know. She's lost it. Lost my necklace. The one you gave me."

Wilson had been in the scullery, polishing his shoes. He came in behind us on stockinged feet.

"She pestered me until I lent it to her. Said it was for a special date with Scoular. When she came back, it was gone. Said the clasp must have been faulty. Faulty be damned. I could tell from the look on her face she was lying ."

She didn't realize Wilson was there.

"She's been jealous ever since I got it. I wouldn't put it past her to have hidden it away for herself. Something very funny, anyhow."

She gave a little yelp as she noticed Wilson.

"Oh, Lord!"

"Don't worry. I won't tell her what you said. I don't think – I'm sure she wouldn't – "

It was quite clear that he was anything but certain.

"When was this?"

"Last Friday."

"Ah, yes," said Wilson, remembering.

I remembered too. Wilson had been panting farewell in the loins of his other love that night. He looked at me; said only: "I'm sorry about the necklet. I hope it turns up."

Chapter 2

UNTIL THE SUMMER VACATION, MY AFFAIR with this Salome of the starched cuffs was a stop and start business: mostly stop. It was simply too dangerous. Meetings in or about the hospital were spiked with the chance of discovery and alternative *loci libidini* were difficult to come by.

Twice, at my suggestion, I cut classes, and we risked an assignation by the bonnie bonnie banks of history and song. She might not be my true love, but I thought the romantic connotations might lend verisimilitude to our affair.

See poetic licence?

We took the country bus that goes to Balmaha, getting on at studiedly different stops. But when we got into the bracken on the slopes of Ben Lomond, we found alfresco legover in the heather had drawbacks never mentioned by the poet.

Ever had midges at your private parts? It adds an exquisite dimension to orgasm.

The first time, Sister Annie bore it for the sake of satisfaction, but the second was an itch too much.

"It was a nice thought," she conceded. "But – ugh."

High road or low road, I wouldn't get her in the bracken again. That cut our options down to frustration level and I became obsessed with the idea of spending an uninterrupted night with her. Next morning, we would lie long, and read the papers and get toast crumbs in the bed.

But where and how?

"This farm you go to?" she asked one day. "How near is it to South Queensferry?"

"Twenty minutes. My bike does that run on its own."

"I've been thinking. Perhaps we could use my friend's place over the summer? When you're at the farm?"

"My libido's gone all funny at the thought."

"I could go there for the occasional weekend. If we stuck to that, it shouldn't raise suspicion."

She didn't have to say whose suspicion. Nor did she like to hear her own deception spoken out loud. Her face took on that hard look again.

"Has he – ? Does he know where it is?"

Her face could have been set in stone.

"No. No one has been there. I use it as a kind of retreat."

When the world of men got too much for her? Why, then, was I so privileged? Whatever the reason, it meant Boss couldn't sneak up on us; catch us in randy flagrante. What more could such a pair of carnal intriguers desire?

The rest of my fourth year passed with the front of my brain in a muddle of guilt and fear and worry. But nothing had the slightest effect on the atavistic bit where the sex drive lay. I lusted after Sister Annie, come hell or common sense. I sat my degree examinations and didn't even wait for the results. I went off to the farm the very night I finished with them, and read the results in the *Glasgow Herald* a couple of days later. Although the subjects were small and the exams a bit of a laugh, I saw my own name with relief – my papers had been welters of mediocrity. I glanced cursorily through the list and saw that all of the gang had also managed passes: all except Minnie.

I winced for her in real dismay. Minnie's total of resits was impressive and, although she had always passed at the second attempt, the implicit struggle, intellectual and psychological, was horrendous.

But I had my own, more pleasurable problems to worry me.

On my illicit weekends, I would have to steal away from the farm after work and be back early in the morning: leave no one a whit the wiser. But people who live on a farm have a nose for that kind of thing.

Still, I was known for being as odd as any student by then: running around the fields by moonlight, my feet shirring through the frost stiff stubble; setting off on my bike to see the see the sun come up on the Bass rock. I might get off with it.

In fact I did. Only two people came to know and both, in their different ways, I knew I could trust to keep their mouths shut.

Matt, of course, I had to tell.

"I'll be away on my bike after tea, now and then. Won't be back until the morning. I'd like to keep it to myself."

He pulled the thin shanked, steel glasses down his nose and looked at me.

"Aye. Whit aboot him?" He nodded at Wilson's bed.

"He won't be here."

Noelle was back to visiting Wilson's home regularly. A little quiet speiring at his plans would let me arrange things.

Our first week-end was all it should have been and left our secret intact. The second time, however, I thought for a moment the story would be all over the farm.

I was cycling back to Preston's Mains, in the marvellous light of a July morning at five o'clock, when I came on young Watson. He was walking and in the early stillness, heard me coming. Country-wise, he stopped and turned, as I came up to him: shoot the breeze for a moment with anyone who happened by.

Since the fight, we hadn't spoken: yet we had worked together, communicating in looks and nods and the grunted assumption that the other knew what had to be done. I couldn't call it friendly, but the frank hostility had gone. It would be an unforgiveable solecism to pass him by. I braked to a stop beside him.

"Fine morning."

"Aye, it's a' that. Eh – ye juist gettin' hame, then?"

"Uh-huh."

"Been oot a' nicht?"

"Yes."

A slow, understanding smile spread all over his face.

"Ye've – eh. Ye've somebody up the road, there. Gettin' a wee bit, like?"

For a moment I thought of lying, but then I saw there was only one thing to do: honour his own concupiscence: tell it in his own words.

"Head first. Right up to the bootlaces."

It was the first time I'd ever heard him laugh without an overtone of spite.

"Me too. Been at it since last nicht. Oh-ho. By the Christ. It's bluiddy rare, i'n't it. Nothin' like a wee bit o' cunt tae set ye up for yuir breakfast."

As we stood in an aura of post-coital satiation, the sun growing warm on our faces, I couldn't help but join his laughter. He was so right.

"Absolutely nothing. But I'm late. Need to go before I'm spotted."

"Aye."

He understood full well, and I suddenly knew my secret would be safe in this unlikely alliance of the flaccid lance. This made what happened all the worse.

A few weeks later, we were working together in the barn of Preston's Neuk. It was a hosepipe, Saturday morning: great splatters and sprays of rain driven by a gusting wind. But we had drawn a soft number: load a trailerful of straw bales under cover. They had been built roof high, and I was level with the rafters, chucking them down to young Watson, when he said:

"Ah winna gang further back in that raw. Come doon, an' start frae the front again."

"Och, no. I'll just finish this tier," I disagreed amiably. I couldn't see it made any difference.

Young Watson stood below me: legs straddled, hands on hips, grinning at me broadly. He was master of all he surveyed: and also of some secret that amused him.

The edifice of bales was a favourite place for the farm children to play. They climbed and burrowed and made houses out of the building-blocks of straw. As I yanked the next bale out, I found I had uncovered a room with an old blanket for floor covering.

"Some of the weans have been playing mummies and daddies up here," I said and glanced at him.

His grin was bigger than ever.

"It was you?"

Again he made me laugh. The nerve of him. Sneaking right into the middle of the farm to have it off with some biddy.

"Some mummy," he winked at me. And I suddenly understood.

"God Almighty," I said. We had stopped to stare at one another – he in amusement, I in awe – when Sandy came in, the rest of the men trailing behind him.

For once he was in a black mood: not to be crossed. He had loused the men early in disgust, little useful work being done in the rain. He was as wet as anyone and here were young Watson and I: dry, warm, standing gawping at one another.

"You, boy. You mucked oot Connie's chicken hoose yet?"

"You said after dinner, Sandy."

"H'm." He'd find something to stay cross about. "You, Watson. You no' got that bluiddy trailer away yet."

"Right the noo, grieve."

There were still ten minutes to go until twelve. Young Watson would show Sandy how it should be done; the whole lot of us. He snatched his oilskin, leapt into the tractor driving seat and gunned out of the barn.

On the far side of the yard, an underground cundy ran. After a hundred years of use, this main drain of mason dressed stone had silted up with dung and straw. Some fifteen feet of the flagstone covers had been lifted and the muck shovelled out, before the downpour brought the work to a halt. Young Watson went towards this in high throttle; twirled his steering wheel to run him alongside the mound of dirt. But a front wheel skid on the greasy cobbles landed the off-side wheel of the tractor in the open drain.

Sandy went up like a keg of black powder.

"You'll get that bluiddy thing oot o' there afore you louse, if it taks you a' bluiddy day. I'll juist see the Major's ready tae pey this lot, an' I'll be back."

He fumed off.

Young Watson's mood had changed on the spot. Made a fool of himself; told off by the grieve, all in front of a crowd.

"Ah'll get the bluiddy thing shifted," he gritted. "On ma lane, too.

Don't you lot worry."

He glared away any offer of help.

By a freak, the trailer had stayed upright, its load of bales intact. The thing was to get the shackle pin out; uncouple the trailer; haul out the smaller machine with one of the big Olivers.

But the coupling was twisted; the pin, normally eased out with a tap, wedged fast. What young Watson needed was a three-pound hammer with a flat end to knock the pin out. But there was no such tool to hand. He cast around for something and, in frustration, grabbed a fragment of broken flagstone. He smashed at the shackle in useless, increasing anger. At the fourth impact, the cast-iron coupling, already under stress from the skew force on the draw-bar, sheared across.

Sandy arrived back just in time to see the careless, wrecking blows. He had been angry before, but this was too much.

"Aye, Watson. But you're the bad bugger o' hell. Since you've come to this fairm, you've been up to the airse in shite. Weel, Ah'll keep you oot o' mair bother. Gin Monday, you can tak a bluiddy knife. Gang tae the laigh meadow, an' cut bluiddy thistles."

The insult was staggering. That was work for bairns, or a half-wit: never work for a skilled man.

"Cut thistles. Me. Ye must be fuckin' doitit, grieve, if ye think Ah'll dae a job like that."

"You'll dae what I tell you, or you'll gang doon the road," Sandy said, in a voice gone suddenly quiet and the more menacing for it.

The thing had gone too far to be saved; for either man to back down.

"Richt, then, grieve. You keep yuir bluiddy job. Ah don't need you. Ah can get work ony bluiddy place."

He looked around for anyone to challenge him, but the men hung their heads: not in fear, but as a mark of the gravity of the event.

The houses were still tied to the job: indispensible part of the bargain. Although the Watson father was not directly involved, it was inconceivable that he could stay on either. The family would lose their home. This bitter knowledge was clear in young Watson's face as he faced the grieve and the rest of the silent audience.

"Mind, Ah'm fuckin' tellin' ye, grieve. Ye havena' heard the last o' this. By the Christ but ye havena.'"

And he stalked out of the yard.

Chapter 3

THE WAY OF THE WATSONS' GOING WAS THE MOST depressing thing I had ever seen.

Of course I could see Sandy's point. Of course young Watson was a hash-bash merchant of the first order. Of course the incident had been insupportable; the latest in a long line of daring authority; daring everyone, to take him on.

But such a punishment?

They borrowed an open lorry. Young Watson drove, his mother and father crushed in the two-seater cab beside him. The younger weans huddled in the back, sheltering from a smirring rain under a tarpaulin. A table, a rickle of chair legs, some bed irons, and a couple of mattresses showed how little they had to cushion their lives.

"Have they got a place?" I asked Matt.

"Aye. It's no' far away. But it's no' much. A puir hoose and a nipscart farmer. They'll ken a difference."

The Watsons drove off without a wave or a gesture to anyone, their quitting made the more ignominious by a cantankerous, back-firing engine. The whole sorry episode affected me. It even coloured my performance in the borrowed bedchamber.

On that week-end's assignation, the last of the summer, one particularly explosive climax left me limp with obvious dissatisfaction.

"What's the matter?" she asked me sharply, warily.

"It's nothing to do with you," I fretted.

Then I told her the whole Watson story; how I felt for their ignominy and shame. As it poured out, her attitude changed. She relaxed, lay back and stroked my cheek with one long forefinger. At the end we lay silent for long minutes and I knew a great peace. I suddenly realized this must be how Boss felt.

"And this was the man you had the fight with?"

"Yes."

"You're a funny boy," she said, as if she still argued with herself about that.

Next morning, though, I felt as if my mind had been washed clean of unhappiness and hung out to dry on a sunny, windy day. When I took her an early morning cup of tea, I said decisively, "D'you know what I want. I want to dance with you. Properly. Good band. Good floor."

Glasgow was as parochial as a back-court drying green: meet your neighbour any old time or place. Since we both knew that well, any question of taking her dancing had been ruled as far too dangerous. But that morning it became a minor obsession with me. I harked and craked on about it until she gave in.

"All right. All right. The first night you come back to Shaw's Howe, if it will stop you going on so. But we'll have to be so careful."

"Listen. I know a place. Way out on the south side. No one there we could possibly know."

So, in best double agent style, we left the hospital separately; met up in Central Station; took the steam train to darkest suburbia. The Edwardian was an inspiration of its time: the thirties. Cinema below, ballroom on top, it was set to pay its backers a dividend for a hundred years and give its patrons the strict tempo of big band sounds, the smoothest of hardwood floors.

Sister Annie was at her best that night. The rampant sexuality that flared between us was transmuted into the most satisfying coupling of a different kind. She hummed in my ear, scented my nostrils with her hair, laid those long, cool fingers along the back of my neck. These were all the danceaday experiences of a hundred hops: but never had they been like this.

"Happy?" I ventured.

"Almost," she whispered. "Almost," and kissed my ear like a blessing.

It was a long trek back to Shaw's Howe. Train and tram would take an hour, so we left before the end: happened to join the cinema exodus; mingled with the one and nines as they went home, knowing Gary Cooper had made the west safe for wimmen and chillun again.

"Sorry about the long journey back. Hope you think it's been worth it?"

When I said that, she stopped; turned me to her; kissed me full and gently on the lips.

"Oh, yes. It was a lovely evening."

The cinema crowd eddied around us, amused, encouraging.

"Ye no' wait till ye get hame, son?"

Over her shoulder I saw Minty the second before he saw me. She couldn't see him, nor did I make her any the wiser. It wouldn't have helped.

Minty was a western buff. Sixguns, a back seat in the balcony, and a brunette in his arms for the no fighting bits, were agencies enough to make Minty travel miles to any flea-pit in the city.

His first glance registered recognition and approbation. That was how he liked to see his pupil in action. His look slid to my girl in curiosity, then away. Of course, he barely knew Sister Annie: had only seen her briefly on his visit to view my bashed face. He put his arm around his own date and walked all of six paces to the exit before it dawned. He stopped in his tracks and swivelled around in a disbelieving double-take that would have won him a contract with Mack Sennet.

I gave him a sheepish shrug. The knave of hearts had been caught with a whole year's supply of tarts up his jukes.

In the final, intensive year, the mornings were devoted exclusively to clinical work: one term each to obstetrics, medicine, and surgery. That term, the six of us had elected to stick with Boss McKenzie's firm for surgery. On the Monday morning, we had gathered in the side room, waiting for the teaching round to start, when Minty poked his head round the door. He beckoned me outside, then hauled me into the residents' sitting room. I was bigger than him by a fair bit, but he caught me by the lapels and banged me against the wall.

"Are you clean off your nut? Have you any notion – ? Any idea – ?" Imagination failed him. "How long has this been going on?"

"Six months."

"Six – ?"

The human mind wasn't built to take in such folly.

"How long d'you suppose you can keep this under wraps?"

My very lecture to Wilson.

"We've been very careful."

My own words again: I knew they must sound so feeble, but I wanted to believe them.

"Careful? In this town? Jesus Christ, Neil. How soft in the head can you get? What about last night? Suppose it hadn't been me? Someone else?"

I took his hands from my crumpled lapels: put my own hands on his shoulders: looked at him ruefully.

"Minty. I know you're right. But the dance was a one off occasion. It won't happen again. Promise."

Minty shook his head. He wasn't sure he could trust me. That made two of us.

"It better hadn't," he said ominously. "I've got news for you."

"What?"

"Boss is more and more taken by the notion of you going for the Macewen. Feather in his cap and a knobbly thumb up the bum of the professorial clinics. So you're in for some personal attention."

"Is that good?" I asked weakly.

"Best coaching you can imagine – if you can stand the pace. And if you can keep him from finding out you're shagging his *innamorata*."

Boss's coaching was indeed unique. Never slow to ridicule or sarcasm, he treated me to a course of considered roasting over a constant flame of jeers at my least mistake. At every bedside, any ignorance or uncertainty was spread out on the white counterpane for all to see, and the hide of any surgical *amour propre* I might have been growing had another strip torn off it.

Wilson, in his turn, wasn't spared, but he got nothing like the stick I did.

"He seems to have it in for you this term," he said one day.

I felt I had to tell him then. The articulation of such an aim might smack of big-headedness, to say nothing of what the fates might call down. But our years of friendship called for such honesty.

"I'm going for the Macewen prize. This is his way of helping me."

Wilson's eyes widened in real surprise. He had never dreamed of this. Lately, he had developed a hard, sarcastic turn of phrase. It forked out at me then.

"My, quite the little surgeon, aren't we."

The thought of Shiraz still hurt him, I guessed. And God alone knew what suspicions of Noelle he had for his comfort now. I bit on an angry retort.

"Naaah," he shook his head, as if to relieve it of some clinging irritation. "I didn't mean that. You work for all you get."

That was right enough. I felt buried in the stuff. Nights at Shaw's Howe, I worked till one or two in the morning; weekends at the farm, I pored over my tomes on the other side of the table from Matt, as he played patience and the range fire drew up the winter wind in moan of heat. Stolen nights with Sister Annie were relegated once more to the limits that desperation would stand.

We were all in the same boat: Wilson; Drew and Fraser; Luke and Minnie. Every Jack and Jill in the year began to show signs of strain as the finals loomed ever nearer. But of us all, Minnie fared worst.

Since her inconceivable flunk in June, all of Minnie's nervous habits had returned with a vengeance. Her happiness disappeared. Her dependence on Luke took on a desperate, clinging quality. And when, that very week, he broke the news that he had to go to London, she became quietly distraught.

"There's a problem with my grant. It's administered in best, impenetrable, civil service style through the High Commissioner's office.

I've sent letters and letters. But there's still no money. It will be quicker if I go down and see to it in person. I'll only be a couple of days."

Despite this reassurance, she was obviously upset and later Luke took me aside.

"You know her so well, Neil. Will you keep an eye on her for me?"

"Sure, Luke. Glad to. I'll see she comes to no harm."

See empty promises?

Next day, after classes, I saw Minnie back to her flat but I refused an offer of tea.

"Sorry, Min. Got to get my chores done at Shaw's Howe."

She didn't seem too disappointed, and I set about my crafty scheme. I intended to belt through my work at the pavilion, have a fast supper, and be back with Minnie in the early evening: keep her unexpected company over her books as we used to. But lust got in the way.

"Come to me," said Sister Annie, over the hospital phone. "I'll be the only one in the home for a couple of hours. Come round the back. To my bedroom window. I'll put the lights out."

She was breaking every solemn rule we had drawn up? The hell with rules.

Next morning, I thought to make it up to Minnie. I'd call on her early. Have that cup of tea. Squire her to our surgical clinic.

I let myself in the main door, ran upstairs and knocked a couple of times to no reply. Still asleep after a long night at the books, no doubt. It was happening to me more and more. From my days as her neighbour, I knew where she hid a spare key. I let myself in gently, so as not to waken her suddenly.

But no one was ever going to waken Minnie again.

"Aw, Minnie," I groaned, leaning against the door jamb. I had never dreamed the Dean's warning would encompass such tragedy.

I didn't need to feel her carotid pulse, nor put a mirror to her lips. I was four-fifths of a professional by then: knew all about the pallor; the post mortem staining at the back of the neck; the filmy glaze over the half open eyes.

I knew all about what to do, also. Touch nothing. Send for the polis.

She had taken the pills while sitting in her armchair at the fire: washed them down with the tea I should have shared with her. The cup was sitting in the hearth. The pill bottle had fallen to the floor. I took out my pen and turned it, so I could read the label.

Sodium amytal: three grains in each pale blue capsule. She'd had the whole fifty, I guessed. That would do it every time.

She had slumped off the chair: lay in a position she couldn't have learned in five years at the yoga: legs and arms like a raggedy doll; head slewed round, so that she stared at the wall. Some vomit had spilled out of her mouth, and dribbled down her blouse. Choking on her own bile would have helped the cause along.

The two rings had fallen clear of her blouse, and lay dangling. Had she held them fast to give her courage?

She had left two envelopes. That was a bonus. The polis liked at least one note: nice and tidy and according to the book. I used my pen again. One was addressed to Luke, the other to me. The envelopes were unsealed. I should leave them severely alone.

I read Luke's first. It was simple and sincere. She loved him and he must forgive her.

Mine gave the game away.

> Dear Neil,
> I'm so afraid of more failure. Failing the Church. Failing myself.
> But more, of failing Luke later on. He's such a fine man.
> Please help him all you can.
> M.

I don't suppose Minnie was thinking all that clearly when she wrote those notes. I thought she assumed the privacy of the contents would be respected.

I didn't think that at all. I thought the polis would be all over them. I thought Luke would be spared no detail of the contents of both notes. I thought he would be left with an awful bitterness. Minnie had been happy to wear his ring in secrecy, but the thought of different skins in holy matrimony, for all to see – ? That was a failure she couldn't forgive herself.

I put Luke's letter back on the table: pocketed the one to me: went downstairs to have the landlord phone the polis.

They were there in minutes with no sirens or shrieking tyres: but there was no mistaking the businesslike clump of boots hammering up the stair.

The reality was very different from the Sherlock Holmes movies, or the dry judiciousness of the forensic medicine lectures. These were big guys: tough, suspicious, hostile.

"Who're you?"

"You touched anything?"

"Anyone else been in here?"

"How well d'you know her?"

"Did you spend the night with her?"

There wasn't a 'sir' to be heard.

"I called for her. We're in the same year. Medical students."

"Oh, students."

They relaxed. We had been relegated to a sub-class of the race.

"Her boyfriend is in London. I was passing. Thought I could chum her to our clinic."

"What's his name."

"Luke Kinseboya."

"Kin – how d'you spell that?"

As I spelled the letters, I could see disbelief on his face.

"He's black?"

It wasn't forbidden, or indecent, or unusual, or illegal: just inconceivable. Anyone south of Clarkston was alien.

They gave the room a fast, expert examination: read Minnie's last words dismissively. I was glad I had put her letter to me on the landlord's fire while he was phoning.

The obvious evidence; the absence of struggle; my patently unrehearsed story, all seemed to convince them.

"We'll need a statement for the fiscal. C'mon down to the station."

I suffered guilt for an hour in the smell of Jeyes Fluid and floor polish, wishing I had gone for that cup of tea. I didn't tell them about that, either. Recording my shortcomings on a police file wasn't going to help my conscience.

The following morning, I met the Night Scot. Over a cup of British Rail coffee, I told Luke that the final examinations had been too final for Minnie. It was a foregone conclusion that the fiscal would accept the obvious.

Luke's grief was untinged by any other kind of hurt and for that, I forgave myself that bloody cup of tea.

A memorial service was held for Minnie on a dark December day: black storm clouds piling in from the west. The University chapel was packed with mourners: most of the medical year, the Dean and some of the lecturers, a smattering of distant family. I wondered what they made of the second ring and hoped they had the decency to bury it with her.

Chapter 4

BY THE LAST DAY OF TERM I FELT I HAD HAD ENOUGH of Boss and surgery for a while and Minty agreed.

"You've had a lot of surgical experience now. Far more than the usual undergraduate. You ought to concentrate on medicine and obstetrics now. The examiners have this funny quirk of wanting candidates to pass in all three subjects. Boss will be the first to agree."

Since I had been such a studious chap, I thought I was due a bit of r and r. What better than a roll and rumble with Sister Annie. I sought one of our weekend trysts.

"I can't," she said flatly. "I'm going to Portpatrick over Christmas."

An old harbour town in the south-west, washed by the tail-end of the Gulf stream, it was well known to the plus-four platoons for frost free greens in the winter.

"I see."

No cause to chew the carpet. I agreed the terms of engagement when I volunteered for service.

"His wife is worse. She's been having ECT without much effect. It's been miserable for him."

"You don't sound too happy, either?"

"It's all this damned deception!" she burst out. "You've no idea how I hate it."

There were depths to this emotion which were beyond my sounding. I stood in front of her feeling young and stupid.

"I'll see you when I can," was all the benediction she could give me.

I went to the farm next day, and sought consolation in Connie's company.

"Fancy the pictures?" I asked her.

Dead leery she had been since her disaster. Her physical recuperation was complete, but she was still nursing her psyche along on a regime of home at tea-time and working hard for this RADA thing.

"I'd like nothing better, Neil."

I took her to the local cinema, bought her a choc-ice, and later stood her a fish tea at the local Tally's. Over the haddock and chips she told me about her audition arrangements.

"When do you go?"

"Next weekend. I've laid my plans. I was going to ask poor Minnie again. But I've bribed one of the girls in instead. She'll say I'm staying with her, if Aunt Winnie gets nosy."

"What about your money problem?"

"Coming on. I've got enough to live on for the first year, now." Even in London a fiver a week would keep her in reasonable comfort. "I'd have liked all of the money put by, but I can get a job if need be."

I nodded. Then she, too, could follow Minty's advice: concentrate on her career; no distractions.

"Good girl. I'll keep my fingers crossed."

But my first loyalty was to myself. I would do much better than cross my fingers. I had the opening for a perfect black knight's gambit: a move that would deliver this unsuspecting damsel bound hand and foot with gratefulness. It was high time I put my spare time, starched lay out of my mind and, once and for all, made certain of Connie and a suitable future.

When we got back to the farm, I took her to the back door and kissed her gently.

"Good luck for next weekend. You worry only about that. I'll fix everything else."

The second Monday in January, the five of the group remaining started intensive medicine with Andy Graham at the Victoria Infirmary, for whose wards Malcolm Ritchie had given a strong recommendation. He was a Wishaw man with a seventh generation Lanarkshire accent that would have bent iron bars. Twenty years of a wife from Edinburgh, a villa in Pollokshields and three daughters at the Park School for young ladies had not polished a syllable.

He drove home the common-place because it was the most common, and he had four excellent subs, who took the same down to earth approach.

The firm's take was on a Wednesday and the biggest excitement of the first night was a cabinful of seamen who had mistaken a case of methyl alcohol for the ethyl variety. The addition of an 'm' to their hooch filled the admission room with men crazed out of their minds by the poison and liable to go blind or die in the cause of a good bevvy.

Our main job was to hold them down long enough to let a registrar get some sodium bicarbonate into a vein. With luck, it might undo some of the worst effects. This was all very dramatic for an hour or two but then life settled to the calmer routine of internal medicine. By half past eleven we were told to go home. I found I missed the continuous bustle and biz of surgery.

At Shaw's Howe, all was quiet too. Sister Annie had hardly spoken to me since her return from Portpatrick. Was this how such affairs ended? Buried under a burden of guilt? Withered away by lack of opportunity?

By the weekend I was glad to get away. I fled to the farm in a mood of high escape. As usual I cycled from Dalmeny. I must have been all of two miles from the farm when I noticed the smell.

The air was tinged with smoke.

It grew steadily stronger and soon I spotted the source: a plume of dirty, yellow smoke somewhere near Dykeliston. It wasn't until I crested the last hill and saw it for myself, that I could believe it came from the Armstrong steadings.

As I got nearer I could see the only building affected was the Preston's Neuk barn. The crow-stepped gable ends stood blackened. The high, slated roof had fallen in. When I got to the road junction, it was unpleasant to breathe. Although the fire was out, hot, black-speckled smoke spumed up into the air, then settled for miles around in a fall-out of greasy soot motes.

The big house was all right; the farm-houses intact; the cottages all standing. The damage had been contained. The yard was a shambles of filth and water; criss-crossed by coiling hoses; covered in puddles and lakes and seas of oily water. The ground was littered with damaged straw bales, hauled clear in an attempt at salvage. Charred straw lay everywhere in a tarry waste.

Two fire engines were there, any childish notions of bells and bravura wiped away by the reality of the weary, blackfaced firemen, still spraying the hot ashes. The paintwork on the facing buildings was blistered, and the roofs close by, still dreeped and splashed from their protective sousing.

Salvage officers picked cautiously at the edges of the barn, but the embers still flushed red and white, then flared into flame in the swirls of the morning wind. It would be next day before it was cool enough for proper inspection.

The farm people stood in serious-talking huddles.

The Major and his lady; Noel, home on leave; Noelle and Sandy, stood in one group. Matt came round the corner, carrying a dixie of tea. Agnes came at his back, with a trayful of scones and cheese for the firemen. I joined Matt.

"Aye, lad. A sorry business."

"Any idea how it started?"

"A bluiddy good notion, but nae proof. Young Watson was back in the village last night. In the pub. It's funny though. Whynie Deuchars swears there's whiles been somebody in the barn at nights. Mebbe a coortin' couple?"

He shot me a questioning look.

My laugh reassured him. The midges had put paid to thoughts of any kind of rustic rumpy-tump.

"Was anyone hurt?"

"No."

I stared at the scene. Young Watson had promised revenge. In an odd way I felt little anger for him. Instead I felt debased by that in all men which can cause such wanton devastation. The destruction of the straw bales was not only vicious, it was depraved. A whole year's growth had been lost; the benefaction of one whole cycle turned to sopping, tarry waste. Yet this was only a fraction of the damage man perpetrated on the planet every day.

"I'll away and change," I said to Matt. "There'll be plenty do."

Wilson arrived later in his flivver, ready to take Noelle for a spin and continue the slow repairing of their relationship. Give him his due, he too changed and got stuck into clearing up the mess.

Next day the salvage men arrived as I fried eggs for breakfast. By the time we got to the yard, they had already started the job of sifting through the ashes with expert, unhurried speed. The three of us took stiff-bristled brushes and shovels, and continued the job of clearing up. We hadn't been at it long, when the Major and his family arrived to see if the investigation had thrown up any information. Wilson downed his brush and went to pay his morning respects. The Major's missus wanted someone's head on a spear for this. It didn't much matter whose.

"Have you found nothing yet?"

Her husband was a rate payer and she wanted value for his money: but quick.

The officer was about to eat humble ashes, when he was saved such burnt fare. One of his guys yelled. "Over here, sir."

The officer stepped high over the fallen, charred rafters until he got to the spot. He and the fireman squatted to poke and peer at the ground. Eventually they lifted up some objects and put them into two little tie bags with labels. He wrote on the labels, then took the finds over to the Armstrong group.

Sandy was there by then and Matt and I joined them. This was something not to miss.

The guy in charge opened one of the tie bags to display the contents: the jagged base and shards of a green ribbed bottle. He held the bag out to us. Through the reek of smoke and char, the faint tang of turpentine was unmistakable.

"This and a slow match," he explained. "They can be miles away before the thing goes up."

The wiles of arsonists were no secret to him.

"But this is interesting, too."

He shook the contents of the other bag into his palm. At first they looked like little, soot-covered stones, until he cleaned one on his sleeve.

It was a rough cut, unusually chunky, Scotch pebble.

"Part of a bracelet, maybe? Or a necklet. See the holes for stringing it." He was pleased with his deduction. "Anyone know anything about this? Seen it before? I understand someone thought the barn might have been used for – ah – assignations?"

The Major was uncertain at first.

"I've seen that, surely. Someone wearing it? Doesn't it belong to Connie?"

"Any idea how it came to be there?" asked Sherlock Firehose.

From the red choker of guilt around Noelle's neck, I thought she had more than an idea.

"Probably coincidence," said the salvage man. "Probably been lost in the barn sometime before."

He was only thinking out loud, but Aunt Winnie jumped to the wrong conclusions like she was a filly in the horse of the year show.

"We must get hold of the girl. Find out about this."

"But it can't have anything to do with Constance. Remember she left to stay with a friend on Thursday."

The Major couldn't believe that his little, subservient Connie had been up to some slap and tickle among the bales, with a hot straw encore to follow the hot pants. But his wife could.

"Does anyone know this friend's address?"

Connie had covered her stage trip to London in vague obscurity, but she had left her conspiring friend's telephone number. Mama Armstrong hadn't understudied an SS Gruppenfuhrer for nothing.

"She will have to be brought home. This matter must be explained."

If she could place Connie within fifty miles of the fire, she'd have her guilty of arson.

The whole situation was now wildly out of hand for want of a word from Noelle or me. But I was honour bound to keep her visit to London secret; and Noelle was guilt bound to keep her indiscretions to herself.

"William. You must go for her now. Bring her back here to account for this."

She sailed off, Noel and his old man trailing in glum attendance. Matt and Sandy moved away, muttering in astonishment. The firemen turned to see if they could find evidence of a less circumstantial kind.

That left me and Noelle and Wilson: and there was nothing in the least circumstantial about what she and I knew of the little eyrie of love at the top of the bales.

I looked at Wilson, then. He only knew for certain about the necklace and who had lost it. He could only guess the circumstances. And such a guess was now weighted by his little darling's telling silence.

"Like the fireman said, there's probably some simple explanation. You'd better get off after your parents. There's a lot still to do here. I'll catch up with you later."

When I had met Wilson first, he had been as soft as meadow cloverheads; a shade slow on the uptake. Over the years I had watched him mature; become more street-wise.

Had he grown enough to give his girl the latitude he had allowed himself with Shiraz? Write it all off to experience, and the cost of suitability? After all, the pure bride in the wedding bed had been all his own idea. The Dean hadn't said a word about love but neither had he mentioned virginity.

Chapter 5

CONNIE'S DECEPTION CAME OUT. The flustered friend had to admit her complicity. She had no idea where Connie was, except it was somewhere in London. And, no, neither of them had ever been anywhere near Commercial College. She didn't even know where it was.

I was sorry for the Major. He seemed shrunken and disheartened by the duplicity of his ward, imagining the worst. His wife, on the other hand, swelled into a pop-eyed indignation at the nerve of this niece by marriage. This would never have happened if Connie had been in her blood line.

"When is the wretched girl due back?"

"Tuesday. Her friend told me Tuesday."

"We'll see what she has to say for herself then."

It was clear Connie was damned before she could get a word in.

Wilson ran me back to Glasgow that weekend. He was very quiet, and I let him brood. When he let me off for a northbound tram, I said, "I'll be late at the clinic for the next couple of days. Sign me in, will you?"

"Something on?"

"Nothing important, but it will take a little time. Thanks for the lift."

Monday morning, first thing, I went to the GPO in George Square: transacted my business.

Tuesday morning, for the second time in a few weeks, I met the Night Scot with bad news. From away up the platform Connie was waving and laughing and running. Success suited her. I caught her up and whirled her round.

"You got it. I just knew you would. Come and have some breakfast."

"M'm. I'm starving."

The poles might melt, but this girl would want her food. I bought her umpteeen rolls with sausages inside them. She laced them with tomato sauce: wolfed them down. I let her prattle on with her mouth full, all about the audition; who had said what. After a bit, she said, "You're very quiet. Is something up?"

"As up as it can get, kid. You've been rumbled."

She was dismayed for a moment: but nothing could keep her down; not that morning.

"That's too bad. But it was all going to have to come out anyhow. What happened?"

I told her about the fire and the necklace.

"But that was lost ages ago. And it wasn't me who lost it. How could I be to blame? Didn't Noelle tell them?"

"Well, she has this little thing she doesn't want to come out."

I told her about the love nest in the straw and young Watson. Connie was astounded at first and then the implications sank in.

"And I think I've got troubles? What about him? Scoular?"

"He must know. But as long as it doesn't become public knowledge, I think he doesn't want to know. If you see what I mean?"

"Ah. So if I blow the gaff?"

"Your cousin is in big trouble."

Connie contemplated that happy circumstance.

"If I say nothing, will they go on suspecting I had something to do with the fire?"

"Of course not. You were in London. You just tell the truth. That it was lost ages ago. If you're feeling charitable, you can keep her name out of it."

"There will be all hell to pay," she said calmly; even confidently.

I thought Aunt Winnie would be disappointed. She would have liked to see her victim quivering; pleading. I carried Connie's case over to Queen Street, and left her to the 9.40 and her fate.

There was a message for me on the pavilion pad that night. Could I meet Connie next day at the Charing Cross Skinner's? That was a place we sometimes met to have lunch.

I was late arriving: had to pick up a poste restante letter at the GPO. It took written authority to withdraw more than three quid from a PO savings account. I opened the letter; took the authorization to the desk; withdrew all of my Granny Aitken's legacy. I put the money in an inside pocket.

Connie had already bagged us a table.

"Well?"

"Oh. It was awful," she giggled. "Aunt Winnie went on by the lump. After all they had done for me. Etcetera. Etcetera. My acting career was dismissed out of hand. My RADA exhibition pooh-poohed as luck. Besides. Go to London? Live on my own? I asked Uncle William if I could have some of my money. There's a clause in the will about special reasons, if the executors approve. But she wouldn't hear of it. He – I – neither of us could get a word in. I certainly won't be trusted with a penny until I'm twenty-one. Indeed she threatened to see if they couldn't get the term extended."

I was alarmed: bugger up all my plans, that would.

"Can they do that?"

"No. It was just a threat to scare me."

She hadn't been scared off her food anyhow.

"What happened then?"

"I was told that if I put on a sack-cloth pinny, went back into the kitchen, and expiated my sins for a couple of years, I might just be forgiven."

"And?"

"I told her to go straight to hell."

That was my girl.

"So, here I am. Alone in the world. All my goods and chattels in two cases at the YWCA. I can stay there, until I go to London. I'll get a job for the summer. You can get Sandy to sell my chickens, too. That will always help."

Take on the world she would.

"You won't need a job," I said. "I guessed something like this would happen. So, I got something for you."

I slid the wad of notes to her: two hundred and fifty smackers to put her in my debt for ever.

"That's enough to keep you for your second year."

She took the notes; riffed through them; saw how much it was. She was quite bemused.

"I couldn't possibly take this."

"Of course you could."

"But why?"

Time for the big speech, now: the one that would pay a handsome dividend in a few years' time.

"I think you know. I love you."

She put her elbows on the table, and leaned towards me, searching all over my face for deceit.

I had been practising the scene in the mirror for months. All she would find was truth.

"I believe you do."

There. This eminently suitable partner was mine: and not before time.

"But not enough?" I sighed. So much for my golden failsafe. "Kid sister, huh?"

"Something like that."

"Pity. I used to wonder if some day – but it was never more than that. You've always been very honest."

Me? Honest?

"I feel – honoured – if that's not a stupid word," she went on. "I'm going to take the money. Do the best I can with it. For you."

"Fine. Great. We'll keep in close touch. Letters every week. Programmes with your name on."

"I'll pay you back when I get my money."

"I should bloody well think so."

"Listen. I want you to do something. I want you to leave me now. I'll thank you properly another time."

"If that's what you want."

I got up to go; stooped over to kiss her, but she turned her face away.

"I always cry at goodbyes. Let me do it in private."

BOOK TEN

Chapter 1

I HAD TO SPRINT TO CATCH THE AFTERNOON CLASS and squashed in beside Wilson as the lecturer came in.

"I hear Connie's in hot water?" he asked.

He sounded tentative. Maybe he was worried about how much Connie had let out of the bag? How much more a guy would have to swallow for the sake of suitability?

"Yup. She's been banished from the ancestral home."

As we turned our minds to the treatment of liver failure, he had a look of sickly relief. I thought it was time we all had a bit of relief from such cataclysmic events. They didn't half take a chap's mind off his work.

But cataclysms were the in thing that season.

The next one – the humdinger of the lot – started innocuously enough. Minty left a message for me to meet him in the Maryhill Harrier at opening time, one night in February. He had something for me.

"There y'are," he said, handing me a package. "That's the old surgical papers I promised you."

Seven years of collected surgical conundrums for an aspiring Macewen candidate to crack.

"Oh, Minty. I don't know what I'd do without you. Let me buy you a drink."

"Thought you'd never ask."

We swilled beer, and Minty brought me up to date with the gossip at the firm.

"There is one other thing," he said, and paused to make sure he had my attention. "Boss didn't arrange a Christmas outing this year. He wants to support his local operatic society instead. 'S at the King's in a couple of weeks. He's looking for you to be there."

Boss and his diktats. Oh, well. One night at the make believes wouldn't break the student mould.

"Thing is," he went on, "he wants you to ask Annie again."

"She won't come. He knows that."

"Ah-huh. I know that's the usual tale. And it's none of my business –" he paused uncertainly.

"C'mon, Minty. Spit it out."

"Well. You know I'm unhappy about this affair you've got going. You tell me you're being careful, but these things develop vibes.

People get to suspect. Don't ask me how. Despite all of your precautions, I think some insurance wouldn't come amiss."

This was just how I had lectured Wilson. Insurance sounded a good idea.

"How could I do that?"

"Persuade her to go. Then put on a public display of indifference. An act. Try to put him off any scent."

The cuckolder's *vade mecum*: chapter two.

"Y'know, you might be right."

So, next afternoon I caught Sister Annie at the top of the ward. With the po-faced expression I hoped I fooled the world with, I urged my *sotto voce* deceit.

"He wants you to go to this show."

"You should know by now, I won't go."

"Um. You don't think it might be wiser?"

"No. The opposite, if anything. He would wonder how you had managed."

"Suppose I laid it on a bit. About how difficult it was. You know how he likes to win. The fact that you had given in would please him no end."

"But what would be the point in it?"

"We could put on a bit of an act. Sit miles apart. Ignore one another. You know the sort of thing. A kind of insurance," I ended weakly.

The plan had sounded so reasonable when Minty proposed it. Now, it had this crafty, furtive ring.

"Is that what you want me to do?"

Her muttered tone couldn't hide the hint of anguish. Her face had taken on that hard look again: the features more bitter than I had ever seen them.

"Is that what you really want? More deception?"

In turn, I became exasperated. After all, she had suggested the game should go on. She umpired the scores, and made up the rules as she went along. Not that I was an unwilling player, but she did owe me a little something – like help keep me out of the shit.

"Well – I think it might be a good idea."

"Men. You're always after something, aren't you. Suit yourselves. First. Foremost. Every damn time. All right. We'll cheat yet again."

The venom in her tone out-classed a bite from a Black Widow spider.

The city boasted amateur operatic societies by the stageful. Long standing institutions, where enthusiasm overcame any lack of talent, they were part of the civic fabric. After the winter pantomimes, theatre managers were glad to let out their boards to these companies: make a bob or two in the dog days of February. The members sang their wee woolly socks off in draughty Scout halls and dingy school gyms for fifty-one weeks in the year, so they could flower like professionals for the fifty-second.

The Ayrshire Orpheans came from down Boss's way and he was the current Honorary President. As such, he had done his usual bit to make sure the showboat was shoved out with a splash. He had taken a block of tickets for the grand circle, and bestowed them lavishly – skivvies washing ward floors, sisters in the wards, fellow consultants at the lunch table – he nailed them all with impartial bonhomie.

"It's a good show. You'll enjoy it."

"Crafty old bugger," said Minty. "Who could refuse to go?"

I knew someone who could. Would have, indeed, if I hadn't got at her with my poltroon's scheme.

On the night, I went to the theatre on my own. Sister Annie was to meet me there with pre-arranged, pointed indifference. I arrived early, went into the bar, and sprayed some gins around the nurses from the Northern General, who had worked so hard beside me. Everyone had on a happy face. Chat flowed easily; jokes; laughter.

Boss's wife was still under psychiatric wraps, but he arrived with an entourage of Ayrshire racehorse owners and their wives. He was breathing cigar smoke and brandy fumes and conviviality. There was a chorus of 'Good evening, sir,' which pleased him all the more.

He looked around to see all was as he wished, and summoned me from Minty's side by a jerk of his head.

"I hear you persuaded Sister Urquhart to come this time. How'd you manage that?"

Was there a hint of suspicion in his voice? But, no. My terrified conscience was reading a threat into benign interest.

"Quite a few of the Shaw's Howe nurses are coming. She felt she should keep an eye on them. Besides, I told her how good you said the show would be."

He nodded expansively. He had said that, he had.

"She's not here yet?"

I had wondered about that too.

"Keep an eye open for her."

Oh, I would. I would. Wide open, and very, very wary, now he was on the scene.

I rejoined Minty and was levering the second drink of the evening into place, when he looked over my shoulder. His eyes went wide in alarm.

"Oh, my God," he breathed.

There couldn't be anything that terrifying in such a douce, mannerly crowd?

But there was.

I turned to see the contingent of Shaw's Howe nurses arrive. In their van, Sister Annie made an entrance that stopped the show before it began.

She was drunk: quietly, sullenly, plastered.

They had been on a pre-theatre warm-up, but the chaperonage had gone turnabout. The nurses had tried to control their dragon sister, but that night, she wasn't for curbing.

She had grown her hair longer, to my desire. I liked to have her sit with her back between my knees, so I could brush it: a honey gold curtain, falling to her shoulders. That night, it had been piled high into a would-be, sophisticated top-knot, skewered with a big diamante pin. But by then, wisps and skeins of fair hair had escaped into a corona of disarray.

But what stopped the bar buzz dead in its chatter, was her dress.

The post-war world of ladies fashions was agog with the 'new look'. This was the old look: old as Eve: straight from the catalogue of loose living ladies. It was as red as blood: a reminder that sin is an uniquely human concept. It was cut with an eye to economy: essentials only covered, and those only just. It was cut so low at the front as to show the early dawn of an areola; while at the back, I could have played knick-knack, paddy-wack on her spinal knobbles all the way down to the first lumbar vertebra.

It wasn't so much a dress as a notice for sale.

She flaunted herself down a column of men who parted before her with sighs of regret for the constraints of middle class decorum. She measured each man with a wet-mouthed, louche come-on: the easiest ride since the whore of Babylon. Every man in the place, that is, except me.

Well, that was what I wanted.

When she got to the bar, men crowded round her. A lady couldn't be expected to buy her own drinks on such an occasion: especially one like this.

"Watch your bum," muttered Minty. "You're about to get a large, jaggy projectile right up it."

Boss was at my ear, hissing.

"What d'you know about this?"

Me? She was his mistress. I was only the pinch hitter, when he was too busy playing golf.

"Nothing, sir."

My plea would have convinced a hanging judge.

And yet, was that true? Had I – he – we, between us, pushed her over some edge?

"See if you can get rid of her quietly."

Boss wanted her the hell out of there, before she started spilling the adultery in front of all his horsey friends.

I knew the feeling well.

I went gingerly towards her, and said, "Good evening, Sister."

She looked me down once, then turned back to the guy beside her.

I had wanted to allay suspicion? This public put down was a humiliation she could never have acted.

Short of calling a couple of commissionaires to frog-march her to the exit, this show was scheduled to run and run. I looked around at Boss and grinned in weak helplessness.

The overture was called then. Sister Annie sashayed her way into the auditorium and found a seat amongst her chicks. What a tale they would have to tell in the morning. The audience settled down to watch the confection: the Merry Widow.

Dear old Franz, he had never dreamt of such irony.

Sister Annie was sitting a few seats to the right of an aisle. My seat was to the left and a row behind. With the curve of the circle, I was able to keep an eye on her by a fractional turn of the head; the merest flick of an apprehensive eye.

Would she talk drunken profundities to her neighbour? Or stand up to conduct the orchestra? Lead the choruses?

She was restless to begin with, attention anywhere but on the stage. After a while, though, she settled back for a bleary-eyed look at the proceedings. To my surprise and despite my worries, they began to make an impression on me, too. I had never seen the show before, though I knew some of the tunes. Didn't everyone? I watched the story unfold. Tosh, of course. Romantic drivel. I scoffed at first. And yet? A hundred thousand times it must have been performed: on stages all over the world, a couple of film versions; an audience of millions. Like me, had they gone to mock? Yet stayed to be enchanted? To wonder if such a ridiculous emotion might, just, after all, be possible? Mein Herr Lehar had indeed been a master of his craft.

At the first interval I came back to reality; shadowed Sister Annie like an Eric Ambler hero. I had to keep her away from more booze at all costs. But I didn't have to worry. She went to the loo and spent a long time there. Then she returned to her seat and fell asleep before the next curtain went up. I sighed with relief, and settled to my unexpected enjoyment. There should be no more liquorous troubles that night.

See bottles? They bring troubles you'd never believe.

At the second interval Sister Annie woke up. She didn't leave her seat, but pulled a compact from her bag, and surveyed her face in the mirror. Discreetly, head bowed, she removed the courtesan's mask she had painted on earlier. That left an older, unbearably sadder woman.

How would the severe, starched lady of the wards come to terms with herself next morning? How would I? Where did our affair go from here?

But once again the curtain went up, and I willingly went back to make believe. By the time Danilo and the Widow came to reprise that lilting waltz, I was thoroughly hooked. I listened to the lady's last, surrendering lines.

"You cannot choose but know · "

My eyes, still on automatic watch, flicked at Sister Annie. One final glance of reassurance and the night's fiasco would be over. But I stayed to stare.

The way our seats were placed, a quarter turn of our heads brought us face on. From the other side of the aisle, she was looking full at me. The after effects of her monumental binge had left that sad face pathetic and raddled. But in the ruins I saw something that passed all understanding.

Even as I watched, she gave up some awful, internal struggle. Before my eyes I saw her resign herself to the inescapable. The long mouth lost its grimness. And those eyes that could be depended on above all else for truth, no matter how bleak, were the eyes that had looked out from the photograph taken all those years ago: the eyes of that gorgeous girl.

She loved me. She loved me the way she had loved before those bitter years had destroyed her. And the final words echoed it for her.

"I love you so."

I rose to my feet. Slowly, disbelievingly, she rose too.

There were tuts of annoyance; mutters of irritation, as we stumbled over feet to the aisle and reached out hands to one another. I put my arm around her and cradled her head on my shoulder, as I might have supported the survivor of some ordeal. Slowly we climbed the steps.

We passed Wilson, who looked amazed. We passed Minty, who stared at his feet, unable to watch such folly. We passed Boss, who kept his eyes fixed on the stage. But there was a wooden, unseeing set to his face.

Chapter 2

I WISH I COULD SAY IT WAS AN IDYLL; that the gorgous girl from the photograph filled my life with so much love, nothing else mattered.

But it wouldn't be true.

It is true that our first night was a wonder of whispered, quaintly chaste love, as the mother and father of a hangover made her pay dues of nausea and headache. But in between the Abdine powders and the cold compresses, the wide mouth had at last lost the voracious, driven lust. The lips were now, indeed, cool, slaking any and all desire I had ever known.

But in the morning, the alarming realities of our situation came home.

"You realize what you – we – have done?"

"Yeah."

I thought my devil-may-care grin must lack conviction.

"We'll need to go. At once."

Her tone hinted that Boss might send large men to break my legs any minute.

Before we fled, Anne – how marvellous to get my tongue around, my heart into, that mellifluous, untainted name – had a hurried pow-wow with Nutty Dotty. I could hear her friend's voice as it rose and fell in tones of horror, disbelief, and, finally, benediction. Wrapped in a blue, candle-wick dressing gown, she came to the door with Anne.

"I knew. The first time I saw you, I knew."

I remembered well: her odd reaction. What was it about me? But we hadn't time for that.

She pulled Anne's head down: showered a rain of little, petting kisses on her cheek; stroked her hair, like comforting a hurt child.

I got a kiss, too: a friendly cheeper, wet with tears.

"Be good to her. You don't know –"

Such a lot I didn't know. It hadn't mattered when our relationship had been purely contractual. But now? Surely I had a right to know now?

But Anne huried me away before I could find out.

"We can go to the house at Queensferry. Stay until you pass your finals. Could you manage your classes from there?"

My visits to the farm had imprinted a Murray's diary on my mind. From all over the north-east trains fed across the bridge and stopped at Dalmeny Junction.

"No trouble. Umpteen trains a day."

We fled precipitately and didn't stop until we locked the door behind us. Then we made up for our celibate night of the pink elephants. Next morning, however, came the practicalities of stolen love.

We laid our bank books together.

Hers had a slender balance only. A lieutenant in the RAMC hadn't left her with a large widow's portion; nor was the state generous to ladies thus bereaved by war. And, whatever her relationship with Boss had been, it hadn't included diamond bracelets or bundles of fivers under the pillow. For some reason I was glad about that.

My own bank book, emptied of my Granny Aitken's money for Connie, had a superfluous look about it. All it held could be hidden in the toe of a very small shoe.

"Don't worry," she said comfortingly. " We'll manage. But I shall have to get a job."

I was dismayed. A true love was entitled to a better deal, surely. Baubles; clothes; perfumes? We would have barely enough for baked beans and saut herring. She didn't seem to mind, but yet again I found myself dependent on a woman's generosity.

We did, however, have one bit of luck. Anne thought she would have to go to Edinburgh to find work, but it turned out that the regular district nurse was ill and unlikely to be fit again for some time. Since Anne's qualifications were suitable, she was accepted as a long term temp. I was all for taking on extra work at the farm, as well, but she gave me a brisk telling off for that idea.

"Think how many people are depending on you now. Your only task must be to pass your finals on time."

Chastened, I settled to our new, domestic routine. The wanton behaviour of our previous visits was proscribed. We were to be in bed at a respectable hour. In the evenings, I was to be banished to a box-room, where my books would be permanently laid out. I hadn't to come near her until my stint of work was done for the night.

On my first weekend at the farm, I took a deep breath and came clean about my new circumstances.

"I'll not be staying at the bothy any more. I'll be living at Queensferry until my finals are over."

I was sitting with Matt and Sandy at the kitchen table and Agnes was giving us tea and fresh pancakes.

"Ah," Matt said. He guessed what was coming.

"Eh. With someone. Her name's Anne."

Sandy looked taken aback. A bit of dirrydan kept the joints supple and induced a good night's sleep. But live with a woman unwed? Even after two world wars, such licence took a bit of doing.

"Will you still manage your weekend work?"

"More than ever, Sandy. We need the money."

I glanced at Agnes to see how she was taking it, but she had her back to me, busy dropping more pancake batter on to her girdle. When I had finished licking my fingers free of butter, I stood up looking at her unresponsive back.

"Thank you, Agnes. Your baking was lovely, as always."

She had folded a clean tea-towel around half a dozen of the pancakes.

"I'll leave them to cool. You can pick them up for your lass, afore ye go home for your tea. Sandy. Sandy. Mak' him put me doon."

Back at my classes, the guys were great. There must have been interest, curiosity, dire forebodings, when I wasn't there, but all I was aware of was a studied indifference, flavoured by an extra sense of welcome.

The last people to know were Jock and Maisie.

"Will you come with me to meet them?"

"Not yet. Tell them if you must. But I don't feel ready for that yet. I need to let things settle in my head. I never, ever meant for this to happen."

"Are you glad or sorry?"

"Oh, my dear. I'll never be able to tell you."

Her dear. I was her dear. I found the simple word more affecting than any more exotic term of affection.

And when I went to see my folks; to tell them, I had to take a new way home.

Jock and Maisie had been given a new house in a great housing estate being built on the periphery of the city: the good Clydesiders' reward in the socialist millenium; post-war pay-off for the patient proletariat. They had been delighted at the prospect: more room for

Jock to move around; a specially built ramp for his chair; even a spare bed for me, should I want.

When I got there, I thought it was hardly Greek Thomson, but I was glad they would have more space and light and air. It would do until I could get them moved to something better.

"This is nice," I said, as I looked around, but social chit-chat soon dried up.

It was the first time I had ever felt awkward about speaking to them about anything. They sensed my unease, however and, in the way of good parents, said nothing but waited patiently.

When I got it out, they still said little. I had the curious sensation of seeing myself across the room, as they must. I was a big lad now. Nothing they could do about it. I was grateful for their neutral stance. It would give their first meeting with Anne, when it came, an even chance.

I didn't wait long and when I left, I kissed Maisie, an unusual gesture between us. Then, on an impulse, I crossed over to Jock and kissed him too, a thing I hadn't done since I was eight. There was always going to be a lot of room for them in my emotions, no matter what other kind of relationship I got myself into.

To my surprise, our new domestic arrangements soon took on a long settled flavour.

Queensferry is named after Marjorie, a Scottish queen of centuries ago. But the Romans used it a thousand years before her. And no doubt coracles had skirled across the river, catching salmon, for millenia before that. An old, old place then, rich in history.

Our house lay halfway up the steep brae into which the town coories. To the east lay the grey, German sea; north and west, the great bens signposted the road to the isles; in front of us, on the firth, war service commanders had a last fling with their destroyers before handing them over to the breakers at Rosyth.

We took our place in this long running scheme of things. The good people of the town began to find their way to the house when a baby was due, or a child had whooping cough, or an old lady needed a bed bath; and I got to know the regulars on the train.

In this beneficent atmosphere, the lack of money, the worry over my increased responsibilities and the extra work I gave myself for the Macewen prize, became much more bearable. I even began to lose my fear of Boss.

To begin with I had cold sweats, worrying about what he might do. However, as the weeks passed; as the intensive medicine term drew to a close; as the finals loomed ever closer, and nothing disastrous happened, I became more confident. After all, what could he do?

So he wouldn't give me a reference, save for the shortest road to hell? Someone else would: Minty or Bobby Mair. So I would never work in the Northern General again? I would go south, then. South of the river to the Southern General. Or south of the border, down Mexico way. Any old place. The world was big, and I no longer needed him. Unless I actually went looking for him, I would never see him in my life again.

The only person I needed in this world was my gorgeous girl. And as those lovely days, those precious weeks went by, the awful lines of unhappiness smoothed and softened. Although the girl in the photograph had gone forever, the wide grey eyes stayed frank and honest in the same message of love. And that hum-drum old port on the Forth became a magic place. By the end of the term, I felt I never wanted to leave it.

Chapter 3

TO QUALIFY IN MEDICINE, EVERY STUDENT had to carry out certain practical procedures under supervision. One of these was to attend twenty births at the lying-in rooms of an accredited hospital.

There were various places this could be done: Rotten Row, in Glasgow; Bellshill, amongst the coal bings of Lanarkshire; across the Irish sea in Dublin, where the guys got to wet every baby's head in a vat of Guinness stout.

One of the lesser known places turned out to be a blessed answer for our domestic arrangements: the Fife Free Maternity hospital. Founded in answer to the tight-fisted ways of the coal owners, it usually served to train students from St Andrews University, but there was no bar to a mere Glasgow man. It lay three train stops away from us, across the Forth bridge. A return ticket would cost me eleven pence.

"When you see my train, you can put the kettle on."

"Very domestic," Anne said and kissed me absentmindedly – at first.

Although I had had formal lectures in obstetrics and had attended out-patient clinics, I had no real conception of what went on at the business end of a birth. Nothing in inert print; none of the line diagrams had prepared me for the casual intimacy of the delivery room, nor the variety of effort it took to push a baby down the birth canal.

"Push."

Pain-filled eyes with rarely a tear in them. The pop-eyed straining.

"P–u–u–sh."

Head rolling agony. The embarrassment as little farts and spurts of urine squirted out.

"P–u–u–u–u–sh."

Animal grunts. The tissues stretching to bursting point.

The first time I saw this affair from the bulging end, exhortation was not enough. The mother was tiring fast. The babe's heartbeat became irregular: a sign of distress. Time to get this affair over with.

I watched the inches long needle, as the registrar showed me how to freeze the nerve plexus which supplies the pelvis; the snicker-snack scissors as he demonstrated where to cut, to make the passage wider; the clankle-steel tongs, as he described how to clamp them on the baby's head: then the sweat-breaking – yet informed, and in a para-doxical way, gentle – hauling and pulling, with the girl-mother hang-ing around Sister's neck for dear life.

Only a male God could have ordained this. I felt ashamed of my manhood, that we should ask our women-folk to bear this for us.

Yet, in the end, there, in a skitter of water and blood and grease, lay a mannikin: future of the race. He lay on his back in this guddle and began to kick and punch; to squall; to hoist a parabola of crystalline piddle in the air, just to show who was boss.

I clamped and cut the cord; wrapped him in a towel; handed him to his mother. Then I saw the contentment, the utter happiness that suffused her face. And I knew that women had the last laugh. Manhood could never confer such satisfaction.

Those few days gave me a whole new insight. By the time I had helped twenty infants into the world, the melancholy that had threat-ened to swamp me from time to time, as I contemplated man's fid-dling attempts to influence life and death, had final notice to quit. The huge lesson of the farm, which I had found so difficult to encompass, had been rewritten for me in human terms.

Life was the business. This splendid event of living, with all that death, disease and destruction could throw at it, was the only cele-bration.

Of course there were failures. Sad women took home children who would be a burden for life, no matter how they were loved: or saw a little white coffin into a grave. For the most, however, they were events with a degree of happiness I had never dreamed of.

I managed my run of twenty cases in just eight days, thanks to the lusty ways of Fife miners. Then I went back to Anne on the run, stopping off in Dunfermline Toun on the way. I bought flowers – proper ones this time, with cellophane wrapping and ribbons. And there she was at the station.

"'S me. The working man. I'm home."

The clasp of arms. The burying of her face in my neck.

I whipped the flowers from behind my back.

"Flowers. You brought flowers again. You know we can't afford that."

There is no more poignant moment in life than the wordless sharing of love in a look.

I was so full of my experiences, that I poured them out to her on the walk home; over the meal she had ready; even as she tucked me in, ready to make up the sleep I hadn't had for days.

"Coming in?"

She shook her head and smiled.

"Not now."

I was vaguely aware of her coming to bed much later.

"Watcha been doing?" I murmured, with the perfunctory indifference of the half awake.

"I was out at a maternity case. All over now. Go back to sleep."

I cuddled into her back; slid my hand under her nightdress; cradled her breast: our usual sleeping arrangement. She was still smelling of Dettol from the confinement.

And suddenly all sleep left me. What an ass I had been. What a blind, selfish clown.

I had never given a thought to how she must feel in her barrenness: to know she could never share this wonderful experience of her sisters, except as hand-maiden; to know that conception had been cut from her in some fearsome act of surgery; to know that, no matter how desperate the act of coition, she could never produce the squashed, squalling, wriggling, pink fruit of love.

This was a pain I had not imagined before. But, that night, with my recent experiences fresh in my mind; this antiseptic smell redolent in my nose, I began to have some idea. I knew I could not let her face this alone any more. Some earnest of commitment was called for; one that might assuage at least some of that bitter knowledge.

She wriggled comfortably into me, and said "M'm," in sleepy content, as comfort flowed between us.

"Anne? When I get finished with all of this in June, will you marry me?"

She went suddenly still and I could sense she was bolt awake. She put a hand on mine: squeezed it into her breast. For a long moment she said nothing.

"That's a big subject. You get your finals out of the way, then we'll talk about it. But it was lovely to be asked."

The regular district nurse came back to her duties two weeks before my final examinations. Anne was out of a job.

She counted our pennies.

"We shan't starve until August. I'm not going to look for anything else just yet. I'll do some spring cleaning. Catch up on some sleep."

She had had a run of night calls over the past month.

For those last two weeks, she absolutely babied me: met my train, made me rice pudding, rubbed my weary neck and shoulders at night.

Truth to tell, I needed every last part of her indulgence, for I found myself jaded to the point of rejecting the whole mass of work. I found the effort to keep going harder and harder. I would put off going to my box room, until she insisted. When I got there, I found that the meanings of familiar words escaped me. The urge to stare at the wall in an unfocused gaze, to cover my writing pad in doodles, became almost insuperable.

But with her help, I stuck at it until midnight on the Friday. At the first stroke of twelve, I snapped my pencil in two, threw the bits in the air and went to find my gorgeous girl, who had gone to bed.

She had been waiting, through her sleep. She turned to me.

"Is that it?"

"Every last word."

"Nervous?"

"Terrified."

She drew my head down. Her nightdress always smelt of recent laundering: fresh; wholesome.

"Oh, my dear. You try so hard."

Enough to make a chap go big in the head, that sort of thing. But I became big in another department instead, and we got the night-gown off in a combined operation of eagerness.

Next day, she banished me.

"You say your parents have room for you. You must go home to them. I don't want to see you again until your name is on that pass list."

"I've seen you every day for months and it hasn't done me anything but good."

"Neil. You know what I mean. I want you to have nothing else on your mind. I have a superstition about us meeting during these examinations. I would never forgive myself if anything went wrong."

See plausibility? It sounds so damn reasonable.

"I want you to give me an exact copy of your exam timetable, so I can think of you every moment. But you must promise."

"All right. I know you mean it for the best."

And I meant to keep my promise.

"You swear? As you love me?"

"I swear. I'll send my folks a wire. What will you do when I'm not here?"

"I shall walk on the shore, and pick flowers and get *War and Peace* out of the library and have long hot baths all to myself – oh, you have no idea."

She was so disarming. So was Delilah.

I packed a bag, and we walked to Dalmeny station hand in hand.

Did we look like callow youth and older woman? I thought of us as glowing and entranced.

I hung out of the window, and we wrapped our arms around one another until the engine dragged us apart with its great, chuffing, triple expansion power. I watched and waved until a bend took her out of sight.

Chapter 4

I MEANT TO PUT ANNE OUT OF MY MIND for the whole time. That's really what I intended. And at the beginning it was easy.

I hadn't stayed with Jock and Maisie for years. They were glad to see me; proud to be able to give me a bed. We yarned about the Faifley days, suddenly transformed into that magical land of remembered childhood. I helped Maisie with her chores. On the Sunday, we got Jock in his chair, and went for a walk, a triumphal stroll to celebrate our survival as a family.

Then, on the Monday, I phoned Wilson to see if we could meet at the Union, but he had a better idea.

"Fancy going to Largs for a run?"

A breezy, bracing resort on the Clyde estuary: just the place to blow away exam fatigue.

"Y'know, young Wilson, you improve on knowing. I'd love that."

He took the Paisley road, and second-geared it down the Hailey

Brae to the sea. He parked the car, and we walked along the shingly shore playing ducks and drakes. We went as far as the memorial to the Viking battle, and by the time we got back, we were salt-whipped by the breeze; tired by our trudge through the pebbles; ravenous.

"Lunch?" He waved a fiver at me. "Dad is standing us this for luck."

His reverend dad yet again. I owed this family a lot.

"What about the terrace of that cafe?"

Nardini's was fronted by the sea: chairs and tables in the open. We ordered tea and sandwiches.

The promenade was dotted with sun seekers. The occasional paddle boat chunked past, to stop at the pier. We spoke little, but there was no sense of constraint, only of relaxation. I lay back in my chair.

"I had forgotten life could be like this. If we pass, we must do more of this kind of thing."

"I sometimes wonder if it has all been worth while. All the bloody effort," he burst out.

I was quite taken aback by the outburst. He wasn't bitter, exactly, but something was festering under the surface. Better let it out.

"Course it has. Even if only to say sucks to the old Dean and his predictions."

He managed a rather bleak grin.

"I suppose there's always that."

A year ago, he would have been full of plans; eager to marry his girl. But he had hardly mentioned her all day. I suddenly twigged. The poor sod. I hadn't realized how much of an effort it had been for him to swallow the business of the necklace. Trouble was, it had stuck halfway. Maybe a spoonful of sugar would help it down: sixty grains of sucrose from Ole Wiseacres Aitken.

"Ever hear from Shiraz?"

He looked surprised.

"No. We agreed to cut cleanly."

"M'm. Can I say something to you about that?"

"When did you ever give a damn what I allowed. I know you've helped me a lot over the years, but to tell you the truth, I haven't always liked you for it."

"Cain and Abel had their off moments too."

He thought about that for a moment, then gave me a hard, antagonistic look.

"Carry on, brother mine."

"I don't think you gave Noelle enough credit for the time you became involved with Shiraz. I'm sure your girl knew something was up. I think you put her through it."

"I never thought of it that way." He looked crestfallen. "I suppose I must."

"The Lord knows what went on inside her. What kind of reaction it produced."

He looked at me sharply, startled.

"I think she cared for you enough to hold on grimly. Say nothing. Deal with her own emotions the best way she could. Hope the whole mess would work out in the end."

Wilson's face was a study in slowly growing comprehension.

"And it has, hasn't it?"

More or less happy ever after was fair compromise for anyone in this world: especially if you threw in suitability.

He looked over at the Great Cumbrae for a long, long time, then he knuckled his eyes hard, as if to clear them of a deep weariness.

"How'd you like to go out in an oarie boat?"

Wilson sculled. I lay back and let him catch crabs to the best of his unskilful ability. Then he ran us back to town. Before I got out, I turned to him.

"Thanks, Scoular. That was great. The whole thing has been great. I have appreciated all of it. Everything."

He nodded and swallowed.

"Your parents? Are they settling into their new home?"

"Yeah. They like it."

"That's good. You will give them my regards?"

I suddenly realized we were both unwilling for the conversation to end. We would never have another day like this. Our salad days, with all their funny mixed emotions, were at an end.

I punched his shoulder and got out of the car. I didn't look back.

The main thing to take my mind off Anne was, of course, the final examinations. One hundred and something candidates. Three hour written papers on three successive days. Three clinical examinations of forty minutes. Three vivas of twenty minutes. Over twelve hundred hours of aggregated exam time. Every ward in the city had been combed for suitable cases; examiners booked; rooms set aside; timetables arranged for students in alphabetical groups. Wilson and I found we were to be nowhere near one another for much of the time.

"Won't see much of you."

"So it seems."

"Still, we can sit beside each other for the written papers."

"Yeah. Wouldn't know what to do without your ugly mug for inspiration. It's been around me for so long."

As we got to the door of the Hunter Hall we shook hands. All around, guys were doing the same: the women kissing cheeks and hugging each other.

"Good luck."

Inside the huge, vaulted hall, we sat at our tables. The papers were already in place, face down in front of us. When the great bell above tolled the first stroke of ten, we turned them over and were off in a controlled release of knowledge: a huge clockspring of effort, five years in the winding.

No turning the hands back now.

The days passed in small bursts of effort, then long hours, days even, of hiatus: maybe a clinical and a viva, morning and afternoon, then a couple of days with nothing.

At those times, like most of the guys, I gravitated to the Union; listened to the buzz; heard who the examiners were, what the questions were like. But one particular day, between my obstetrics viva and my surgical viva – my very last exam, and the clincher for the Macewen – I had nothing on. And, quite suddenly, I missed Anne. I missed the great, booming, driving sensation when I was with her: every sheet of emotional canvas up and bellying before this trade wind of love.

Twenty-four hours to twiddle my thumbs. And for what? A daft superstition.

What harm could it possibly do?

Much more to the point, look at the good it would do: a few hours of marvellous, inspiriting contact: one last, ardent encouragement.

I bought myself a day return to Dalmeny. I wouldn't push fate so far as to stay the night.

I walked down the hill, surprised at the number of people who smiled at me, until I caught sight of my own silly grin in the window of the dairy at the corner of our street.

Our street, indeed. No wonder I smirked. I let myself into the house with my latch key.

At once I sensed the house was empty but I called "Coo-ee," anyhow. She had no doubt gone for fish or eggs or one of her walks along the shore. The house smelled of polish. The windows glittered with recent cleaning. The furniture shone with fresh waxing. The spring cleaning had been a major operation.

I walked about for a moment or two, appreciating her housewifely talents, before a chill began: an enveloping, icy feeling that drove out all sensation of the bright summer day. This place, which had been our home, was empty of every last vestige of our stay. It had been returned to the neutral anonymity of her friend's house.

I felt a lurch in my chest, as my heart rate stuttered up twenty beats in the shock of realization. I ran from room to room; raced up the stairs. Everywhere told the same story. In the last room I came to, the bedroom we had used, I came on the final confirmation. My own case stood in the middle of the floor. I hefted it. It was full, ready to be taken away.

I went downstairs slowly, and sat on the second step, my head buzzing like a transformer. Slowly, through the jumble of static, one message came through. Although there was no note, no explanation, this thorough cleaning must have taken many days and been long planned.

Anne must have known for some time she was leaving me.

Although I had had nothing since breakfast, I certainly wasn't hungry. But I had a sudden need for a cup of tea. There was some left in the kitchen caddy, I had a shilling for the gas meter, and there was still a spark in the flint lighter. I had a mugful of the hot, strong brew as I walked about, looking for some clue.

There was nothing but this damned, impersonal cleanliness.

I was about to put the tea leaves down the kitchen sink, when my Granny Aitken's training brought me up short. Spoil the spotless porcelain? Never. For all Anne had left me, I could still admire the effort; the thoroughness; the gesture to her absent friend. I took the teapot out of the back door to empty it into the bin. It had not yet been cleared and was crammed with rubbish.

I had bought a *Daily Express* to read on the train: keep up with Rupert in the happier times of that morning. I spread it out on the ground and tipped the contents of the bin onto it.

Most were unimportant, even pathetic, but right at the bottom there was something significant: the torn remains of several attempts at a letter; different essays in giving me my notice to quit. I pieced them together.

I had been, variously, "Dear Neil", "Dearest Neil", "My very dear Neil". No matter the exact, sardonic title, however, they all made the same points.

She had indulged herself most unfairly –

I had never been an indulgence before: even an unfair one.

She blamed herself –

I might look foolish but I was clean as the driven snow: all her fault. She had to go to him. It had been in her stars for years –

And I thought astrology was rubbish.

I must believe she had loved me –

'Had' gave the whole thing a definitive feel.

She signed it A only: Anne or Annie, as I pleased, now.

I cleared up the mess; shut the door behind me; put the key through the letter box; trudged up the hill to the station, my case feeling unbelievably heavy and awkward. When I got back to the new house with the extra room, I shut myself in it.

"I've got a bit of a headache. I think I'll just get off to bed early. I want to be fresh for tomorrow."

Tomorrow? Wilson had had it right after all. The most pointless effort of my life.

I lay for hours. Eyes shut or open, it made no difference. I couldn't sleep, nor could I formulate cohesive thought. I lay, my head fuzzing and buzzing like a robot whose works have been got at. It was getting light when I did at last fall into a fitful, miserable sleep.

But I woke up feeling angry: smash something, anything just for the hell of it.

Maisie had gone by then. I got up and fed Jock; toileted and dressed him; sat him in his wheelchair: but for once I did it without thought or compassion. Then I shaved and dressed mechanically for the viva, the automatic pilot of habit carrying me through a haze of chaotic thought and increasing fury.

I wanted; I was entitled to; I was bloody well going to have some kind of explanation. Most of all I was going to find out why me? Why pick on Neillie Aitken for a sucker. I would go to Shaw's Howe that very afternoon; find the Sister Tutor who was such a pal to Sister Annie. I had long thought Nutty Dotty was just as daft as she wanted to be, and this was not a day I had any taste for fruitcake.

My viva was at the Victoria, a well travelled route, but that day I even took a wrong tram. For all I was an arch examination disciple of playing the odds, turning up in good time, getting myself composed, for once I arrived just on the bell. The registrar in charge raised his eyebrows at me.

"Runing it fine, old chap. Ready?"

I straightened my tie; smoothed my hair.

"That's it. You're lovely. By the way," he had his hand on the door, "the local examiner was taken ill this morning."

By convention, the examining teams were made up of a Glasgow man, and an external examiner from some other medical school.

"I don't know the new guy, but he seems all right."

He winked at me reassuringly, and threw open the door.

"The next candidate, gentlemen."

I walked in the door to a now familiar scene: some bottles with pickled specimens on a desk; a viewing box with an X-ray plate in place; two senior medical men chatting, laughing: quite human: put a candidate at his ease. They were against the bright morning light from the window, and for a moment I could not make them out clearly. But there was no mistaking one of the voices.

"Well, well, sonny. Come and sit down. We'll see what you know about surgery."

Sneering at me, having the last laugh, in which there was no vestige of humour, was Boss McKenzie.

The other examiner gave him an uncertain glance. It was an unusual opening gambit to him. But I knew it well: all too well. And I also knew damn fine what would follow. My anger blew then: an unstoppable geyser of hurt and jealousy. I did not sit down. I walked to the table, leaned my fists on it and said, slowly and distinctly, "I'll see you in hell before I let you examine me. Fat chance I'd have with you, anyway. And as for your bloody mistress, I wish you joy of each other."

It wasn't a very good speech: petulant rather than incisive. And I almost fell over the candidate's chair as I turned on my heel to march out.

The other examiner was on his feet, outraged.

"Come back here, sir."

I didn't pause. I wasn't going back in there to face further humiliation. Then, all of a sudden, I realized I was no longer going anywhere.

Chapter 5

I WENT HOME THEN: THIS NEW HOME which meant nothing to me. Jock looked at me with concern.

"Ye're awfu' white, son. Is something wrong?"

I looked at his stricken, paralyzed frame. I could hardly speak for the shame of having failed him; of having loused up the best chance I would ever have of helping him. All that sacrifice for nothing. And neither the easiest lay ever known to man, nor the love of my life, whichever she had been, was worth that.

"I'm so sorry. I can't tell you about it. Not yet."

"It's no' serious? No' the polis?"

If only it were that simple. That way I could serve a sentence and get it over. This sentence would last for the rest of my life.

"No. Not that kind of trouble. All in my own head." Once I would have said heart, but I knew better by then. "And all, all, all of it my own bloody fault. But you should know that I didn't pass."

I couldn't bear to tell him I never would now.

He shook his head, uncomprehending. How should he? I certainly didn't.

"Oh, there's a letter for you."

I handled the envelope for a moment. I knew her writing. This must be the fair copy; the final result of all her attempts; the seamless text in which she finally expressed the terms of our disengagement.

She had judged it to a nicety. There were always two posts: morning and mid-day. And delivering the mail on time was one of our national prides. Knowing my examination schedule to the minute, she had posted it to be sure it wasn't delivered until the last of my exams was over. That way she could dismiss me with a clear conscience. Failure on my part would be all my own work: nothing to do with any turmoil she might have created.

She wasn't to guess I would break my promise to her.

I knew the contents, so I stuffed the letter in my pocket. I squeezed his shoulder.

"Thanks for everything, paw. I wish I had been worth it."

He sighed uselessly. What could a man in his broken state do to help me; anyone. Then I went to see Nutty Dotty.

On the tram to Shaw's Howe, I took out the letter and debated if I should just tear it up. I wasn't sure I could bear to rub the lemon of reappraisal into the wound.

Of course I read it: anything that might bring her back into some kind of touch. But the contents were not what I expected.

Dear Neil,

I have written half a dozen letters to tell you I was going back to him. Now I know that I cannot, so I am leaving you both.

I want you to know that I love you more than life, which is why I must go. The difference in our ages, the things I have been, would never sit with your career, nor with my love. If you don't believe me now, you will in time.

You will be a fine doctor, of that I am certain.

I looked out of the swaying tramcar. I was never going to be any kind of a doctor now.

When, in my arms, you talked of your dreams and hopes, you worried in case you did not have some special quality that even your Dean could not define. I want you to know you have that rare gift in abundance.

You know all too well by now, that all patients cannot be cured. Some are difficult to help, even. But all of them, no matter how deep and bitter their anger and pain, can be comforted.

And, oh my dear, that is what you do so superbly well. You care about people and it shines from you like a beacon.

Of course, it isn't always easy. I know it can't have been easy, caring for me. But, eventually, I know you did. You cannot believe what that meant to me.

Do that for your patients always, and it will make this letter worth all the pain it has taken to write,

With all my love,
Anne.

P.S. Dorothy has something for you at Shaw's Howe. Please take it with my blessing.

I sat, slumped in my seat, unable to think. At the Bearsden terminus the conductor came up to me.

"'S as far as we go, mister."

I nodded. I went down the stairs, stiff as the Tin Man before he found the oil can. What a bloody mess.

I walked up to the hospital and found that the Sister Tutor was lecturing to second year nurses; would be cleaning off her blackboard in twenty minutes. There was a bench outside the teaching block and I sat on it to wait. The pupil nurses spilled out: cheery and chattering. The Sister Tutor stopped before me.

"Oh, you poor, poor things."

"Where is she? Just tell me."

In all the mess, that was the first thing; the most important to get sorted out.

"I can't. I don't know. She must have been planning this for ages. I see that now. You had better come with me. She left something for you."

"I would rather have some answers."

"Yes. Yes. I can see that."

We went to the sisters' annexe. I was left in the plaster-board sitting room where it all started. Perhaps the flimsy, impermanent structure had been an omen.

Sister Dorothy came back from her room. In one hand she carried a bag. Cradled in the other arm were two big studio portraits. She sat opposite me.

"I have a story to tell you. About Anne. There are only a few people in the world who know all of this. She was a lovely, lovely girl, when she came to us at first."

"Us?"

"Yes. I was a ward sister with Mr McKenzie at that time."

She turned one of the portraits towards me -the one that had done all the damage; the gorgeous girl.

"Beautiful, wasn't she? It's how she wanted you to remember her."

I grunted. My throat ached with the miseries of the past two days.

"You can see how much she loved him?"

I raged with jealousy at this stupid, dead hero.

"The husband? Yes. Written all over her."

"They were boy and girl sweethearts. Right from schooldays. He was the only one – until you."

God, how I wanted to believe that.

"She worshipped him. When he went into medicine, she decided to become a nurse. To be near him. You may know they worked together for a while in Mr McKenzie's wards? On the surface, he seemed all she thought he was. But, working with him, it came out gradually. He was" – she chose the word with care – "flawed. He could never entirely be trusted. Money. Promises. To do his work properly."

The gorgeous girl from all those years ago smiled out at us. Her trust had been absolute.

"There were tales from other nurses. He couldn't keep his hands to himself. Worse, he was sly about it. Devious. Weak."

Nutty Dotty might have stood an honest bull, but this guy had been a one for fly feels; quick belts up willing fannies: in the linen cupboards, against a wall. And all the time the gorgeous girl had been loving him; trusting.

"When he went to war, she was so proud. She was carrying his child. She looked exalted." Dorothy's memory was still vivid. "He came home on leave before he went overseas. She was so happy."

The Sister Tutor shook her head for an emotion so misplaced.

"He was killed only weeks later. She was devastated, but so brave. Even if the country fell, she would still bear his child."

Dorothy's voice changed then. She began to talk with clinical detachment.

"It blew up quite suddenly. She had noticed a discharge since his last leave. It seemed trivial. But overnight she developed an acute pelvic inflammation. It turned out to be gonorrhoea. A massive infection. Anyhow, I asked Mr. McKenzie to see her. He guessed at once. But such a thing would have been all over the hospital next day. Her husband's duplicity. The shame. The degradation. They would have killed her."

This was the over-reaction of a sympathetic friend. People don't die of shame. They live with it. But it had killed off every vestige of loveliness.

"Mr McKenzie had her removed to a nursing home. Did the operation himself. It was a close run thing."

I could imagine. The whole pelvis dusky red. Ovaries, tubes, uterus bathed in pus.

"But with his skills and the help of a very good young registrar –"

Finnie McLaren, of course. Between them, Boss and he had gutted Anne of her whole reproductive tract, along with the babe. Saved her life but condemned her to eternal bitterness.

"– and sulpha drugs. And prayer."

"And the help of a good nursing friend?" I hazarded.

Dorothy shrugged deprecatingly. "Well, she had no one else to turn to. Her body recovered. But she went quietly out of her head. A combination of things. The loss of her child. Anger. Despair. Disgust. Revenge, even, on that worthless, dead man. God knows. Anyhow, for a time she became"– again she sought for a word – "promiscuous."

And so Easy Annie had been born.

"She developed a loathing of all men. But, in a perverse way, these sexual encounters seemed to assuage the hate. She enjoyed men lusting after her. Their tongues out. Panting. And when they came inside her, she laughed at them. Reduced their supposed conquests to ridicule and derision."

closed my eyes; put my head in my hands.

"Then, one day, just as suddenly as it started, she came to her senses. Realized what she had done. What she had become."

We held a moment's silence for that awful moment. That sudden self-perception would have settled the bitterness even deeper into her face.

"She became withdrawn. Depressed. Wanted to leave the hospital. This life, even, I used to fear. Mr McKenzie was kind to her. A sort of father figure. I was coming out here as Sister Tutor at that time. He used his influence to get her a post here, where I could keep an eye on her."

I knew the rest. The broken girl had turned to them in different ways.

"I'm glad I know about this. It explains a lot. But one thing I cannot understand. Where did I come in? Why me?"

"Ah," she said. There was a world of understanding in her voice.

She turned the other photograph towards me. It was of a celebratory twosome: Anne and a young man. He wore an academic gown and carried a scroll: the regalia of a new graduate, a uniform I had hoped to wear. I looked at the photograph: then, shrugging, back at the Sister Tutor.

"I don't see –"

"Think. Think with her mind. With her heart."

I went over the details again. He was about my height. His hair, too, was cropped short like a boxer's. There was even a cleft in his chin, though not so deep as mine.

"Jesus Christ."

It was suddenly, limpidly clear. Of course it wasn't me. Nothing like. But there were enough features common to us both, that a broken heart ever aching for a cure; another chance, might have imagined a likeness. Dorothy nodded.

"At your first meeting the similarity was fleeting. She might have forgotten. But you were so kind. So – what was the word?"

"Gallant?" I suggested with sudden prescience. "As in the French way."

"That's right. How did you know? Anyhow, you made an impression she couldn't forget. Then she noticed you now and again. On the train. She laughed about it. Uncanny, she said. Not the looks, altogether. A way of walking. Mannerisms." Dorothy shrugged. "What could I say? I thought she was romancing. But then you turned up." On the coat tails of Boss McKenzie. "She had already heard him speak of this boy he had noticed in his wards."

What was it the Dean had said all those years ago? "The accidents of life. Fate, if you will."

"Gradually, she found you had all the qualities that rotten man of hers never had. Oh, you were a rough diamond. Jagged. Uncompromising. But you were dead straight. Honest."

I hung my head for the lies and deviousness that went on inside my head.

"So different. And, miracle of miracles, you came to love her."

Sister Dorothy turned to the bag then. She caught it up, and held it out to me.

"Anne bought this for her husband."

It was a handsome, unused, black Gladstone bag: the quintessential medical carry all. From its imposing outward appearance, anyone could tell it was stuffed with miracles and cures.

"She put it aside for after the war. But he didn't come back."

I took it in both hands.

"She never did have his initials put on it."

I stroked the fine-grained leather; fingered my own initials on it : gold-blocked and fresh. I couldn't bear to explain I would never use it now.

Chapter 6

TWO DAYS LATER, THERE WAS ANOTHER LETTER FOR ME: curt and to the point. I was required to present myself before Professor Sir John Thompson, Dean of the Faculty of Medicine at ten o'clock the following Tuesday. That the graduation ceremony for my classmates would be at eleven on the same morning was an irony that did not escape me.

I had been raised on a diet of war films. I knew all about being cashiered. I had my hair cut; the trousers of my suit pressed; the knot of my tie tight. I would accept my punishment with as much pride as I could muster.

Jock nodded in approval.

"Going to see your friends graduate? That's the boy. Show you're not down in the mouth. After all, in six months, you can try again."

I still hadn't had the heart to tell them how much more serious my situation was.

Jakey Thompson was already in his dress uniform for the ceremony. He sat in his gold braided gown, at his desk. I stood before him, rigid.

"I have here a letter from the external examiner at your surgical viva, alleging some quite extraordinary behaviour on your part. Is this true?"

"Yes, sir."

"Have you any explanation?"

None he would understand.

"No, sir."

"Do you know what you have done? And in front of Professor Stevenson. From Edinburgh University."

The antipathy beteween the two cities was legendary. I had not only shamed myself, him and his University, I had perpetrated this affront in front of his arch rival.

"I am sorry about that too, sir."

"Sorry. What use is that to me? Or you? Do you realize the enormity of what you have done? To impute that an examiner would not treat you with strict impartiality?"

"Yes, sir."

I didn't want a handkerchief tied over my eyes, but I wished he would get the sentence over.

The Dean's attitude changed then. He had been angry and affronted in his official capacity. Now the bleak face I remembered so well from that first lecture reflected a personal feeling: contempt.

"But in my eyes, your greatest offence was to lose control of yourself in such a situation. The gravest disappointment, to me, is that after five years of medical training, you have not learned to keep hold of your emotions under stress. Suppose this had not been an examination, but a patient you were dealing with? Allowing such a reaction must affect your judgment grossly. That is inexcusable."

"Yes, sir."

He shook his head in disgust.

"In such circumstances, I am sure the Senate can only rule one punishment fitting for such conduct. To send you down."

Although I had expected nothing else, when he pronounced the sentence I felt light headed and my lips stuck together.

"However–"

There was a however?

"– for reasons I cannot possibly guess at, Mr McKenzie has interceded on your behalf. He has asked that I deal with the matter inside the faculty."

I felt myself gape as in stupid.

"Further, your record up until now has been good. I see from the results you did obtain, that you would have been well in the running for the Macewen prize." He shook his head at such an unlikely tale. "In view of all this, I have decided not to refer this matter to the University authorities, if you will accept my punishment. You will rusticate yourself for six months."

He wanted me the hell out of his sight and hearing for a while, but this would not carry the stigma of an official punishment. I had been reprieved.

I felt myself sway and stood myself slightly at ease, before I went down like a guardsman on parade.

"There is one condition, however. I must have it confirmed from Mr McKenzie that you have apologized to him. Adequately. And in person."

A bitter, final humiliation.

"For God's sake boy, learn a lesson from all this."

To say "thank you" would have been the superfluity of all time. I simply muttered "Sir," and turned on my heel.

I went through the cloister; sat on one of the seats overlooking the Art Gallery. My relief was so great; my reaction to the last few days so intense, that I had to knuckle tears from my eyes.

In time, I was calm enough to go back into the quadrangle. The ceremony was due to start, and a crowd of graduands, parents, admirers spilled onto the usually sacrosanct grass. I mingled with them with the biggest smile I could manage: shook hands in congratulation: took celebratory photographs for others. It was a relief to realize how few people had registered my own failure, far too busy with their own success. Even the ones who did were dismissive.

"Hard luck. But there's always December."

How easily I had given that same advice.

Wilson was there with his parents and Noelle. He was the only one who knew how far things had gone wrong: from Macewen hopeful to dismal failure in one easy fall.

"What on earth happened to you? Of all people."

There wasn't a hint of self-satisfaction this time: only concern and wonder. But the reasons were now buried in the medical faculty office and better left so. I grinned stiffly.

"Not my day."

He repeated the litany. "Never mind. You're bound to do it next time."

I even laughed then, at yet another changeover in our roles.

"Is that a ring I see on this young lady's finger?"

I kissed Noelle's cheek, and bade very happy to his parents.

Later, as I stood at the back of the balcony and watched the ceremony below, I didn't feel any jealousy: only a slow coming to life again. Two hours before, I didn't think I had a future of any kind. Now one was reappearing. It would be six months late; a bit battered and bent: but a future for all that. All I had to do was swallow the final ignominy of apologizing to Boss; of accepting his magnanimity.

I went to the Northern General the very next day and got hold of Minty.

"Dear God, Neil. What are you doing here? I daren't mention your name. And your finals? What went wrong?"

"Minty," I said. "Oh, Minty."

"Bad as that?"

"Tell you all about it one day. Not now, though. Thing is I have to speak to him."

Jakey Thompson had known what he was doing. None of the comfortable anonymity of a letter of apology.

"I don't think you'll get within yards of him."

"He will see me about this. Tell him the Dean sent me."

"The Dean." Minty's voice went up two registers. "How'd the Dean get involved. You must have made a proper arse of things."

"Shit all over the carpet, Minty. Will you tell him I'm here, please."

"I'll try."

I hung about outside Boss's door, while Minty went to plead for an audience. I remembered the first time: the awful waiting. This was worse. Humble pie was giving me dreadful indigestion. Minty came out at last.

"All yours, chum."

From his tone, all didn't amount to one hell of a lot.

I went in to a scatter of teacups and chairs every where: the usual mess. Not so long ago, it would have been my job to clear this up. I stood awkwardly now. No position of any kind.

Boss didn't look at me.

"Well."

I started my ritual self abasement.

"I have to apologize to you, Mr McKenzie - "

Boss wreathed cigar smoke in the air and stared at the wall: anything but look at me.

"Professor Thompson said –"

But suddenly what Professor Sir John Thompson had said didn't matter one damn. Suddenly my intended penitence, formal to the point of insincerity, would not do. Looking at the hard-set face, the eyes seeing nothing in unfocussed anger, I remembered what Anne had told me about him.

This was the anger of hurt – double hurt. First, there was my treachery. But he, too, must have had a letter from her. Any hope that she might come back to him, must now have gone for good.

I changed my tune; shifted to another tack. "I am sorry. Really sorry. I never meant – never dreamt – "

The jaw in profile clamped the harder at my whingeing.

" - Perhaps if I had never seen the photograph."

He turned his head at that. "Photograph? What photograph? What are you talking about?"

"You must have seen it. She would be about seventeen at the time." At once his face showed that he knew it: the gorgeous girl. Maybe had a copy for himself, to sit and grieve over. "I couldn't get it out of my head."

He looked at me then, in bitter, unwilling understanding.

"But I didn't fully realize what had been going on, until I saw the other picture."

"What other picture?"

"The one of him. Her husband."

"Urquhart? She was well rid of him."

Dunkirk had given a hero's end to a bum.

I stood before him.

"Look at me. Look at me hard. And think."

The fierce, angry blue eyes searched my face in minute detail; recorded my faithless looks for ever. Then I used Nutty Dotty's prompt.

"Think as she would."

Slowly I could see comprehension dawn. It was unwilling at first. If he gave up anger as a protection, what would be left to shield his hurt? Then, for the only time I could remember, Boss dropped his gaze.

"All right. You've said your piece. I'll write to the Dean. Acknowledge your apology."

I was dismissed.

He rose to his feet, caught up his light top-coat from the stand, and marched past me to the door. But it wouldn't do to leave it like that. I was one of the few people in the world who knew this tyrannous old bully was not always what he seemed, and I wanted him to know that. I trotted at his heels, as I had so often done. At the Rolls he paused.

"Well? What now?"

Halfway between annoyance and vexation.

I opened the door for him. "I'm sorry, too, that I won't be able to start here with you next month as your houseman. I did want to do that."

There. My apology was as full, as sincere, as heartfelt as I could possibly make it. He climbed into the car; rolled down the window to look out; guide himself backwards.

"Well, if you don't make such a bloody cock-up of things next time you sit your finals, you'd better come to me in February instead. See and shut that door gently."

I closed the door with quiet precision. That was Boss: never a soft word where a hard one would do.

"She would want that. She would know I was the only one she could trust to lick you into proper shape."

That I again. Her life; mine: we would never be free of it. But there were worse things.

He looked full at me for a second, then purred himself out of the yard.

I walked slowly into the hospital; looked around for somewhere I could be alone for a while. I went into his empty room; shut the door on the world. Then I sat in his big chair and put my head back.

I knew the real pain had yet to come: the knowledge of having lost Anne, of having helped make a bigger mess of her already sad life. That would come slowly, exquisitely, like an injury to a frost-numbed finger.

I would go to the farm for six months; use my rustication literally. I had found answers there before, answers that didn't exist in logic.

Oddly certain that the same would happen again, I closed my eyes and slept.